Praise for Elizabeth Strout

'A beautifully measured first novel…which depicts the powerful emotions of adolescence – and, indeed, of later life –
with humour and sympathy' *Times*

'One of those rare and invigorating books that take an
apparently familiar world and peer at it with ruthless
intimacy, revealing a strange and startling place'
New York Times

'Bracing compassion with unsentimental humour, [Strout]
carefully wears down the isolation of her characters, aligning
individual hurt and small-town American heart with a fine
sense of proportion' *Elle*

'This beautifully nuanced novel steers a course somewhere
between the whimsy of Alice Hoffman and the compassion-
ate insight of Anne Tyler and Sue Miller, and is sure to
delight fans of all three' *Publishers Weekly*

'While *Amy & Isabelle* is a moving rites-of-passage novel, its
great strength is the avoidance of sentimentality. Another
strength is the cast of characters surrounding Amy and
Isabelle, each member of which is drawn with unshowy per-
fection…Alice Munro fans should lap up this atmospheric
and tender novel' *Image*

Amy & Isabelle

A Novel

Elizabeth Strout

Scribner

First published in Great Britain by Simon & Schuster UK Ltd, 1999
This edition first published by Scribner, 1999
An imprint of Simon & Schuster UK Ltd
A Viacom Company

Scribner and design are trademarks of Macmillan Library Reference USA,
Inc., used under license by Simon & Schuster, the publisher of this work.

3 5 7 9 10 8 6 4 2

Simon & Schuster UK Ltd
Africa House
64 -78 Kingsway
London WC2B 6AH

Simon & Schuster Australia
Sydney

A CIP catalogue record for this book is available from the British Library

ISBN 0-684-86159-3

Printed and bound in Great Britain by
The Bath Press, Bath

For Zarina

Acknowledgments

*I would like to thank Marty Feinman,
Daniel Menaker, and Kathy Chamberlain.
Their support has been immeasurable*

Amy & Isabelle

Chapter

1

It was terribly hot that summer Mr. Robertson left town, and for a long while the river seemed dead. Just a dead brown snake of a thing lying flat through the center of town, dirty yellow foam collecting at its edge. Strangers driving by on the turnpike rolled up their windows at the gagging, sulfurous smell and wondered how anyone could live with that kind of stench coming from the river and the mill. But the people who lived in Shirley Falls were used to it, and even in the awful heat it was only noticeable when you first woke up; no, they didn't particularly mind the smell.

What people minded that summer was how the sky was never blue, how it seemed instead that a dirty gauze bandage had been wrapped over the town, squeezing out whatever bright sunlight might have filtered down, blocking out whatever it was that gave things their color, and leaving a vague flat quality to hang in the air—this is what got to people that summer, made them uneasy after a while. And there were other things too: Further up the river crops weren't right—pole beans were small, shriveled on the vine, carrots stopped growing when they were no bigger than the fingers of a child; and two UFOs had apparently been sighted in the north of the state. Rumor had it the government had even sent people to investigate.

In the office room of the mill, where a handful of women spent their days separating invoices, filing copies, pressing stamps onto envelopes with a thump of the fist, there was uneasy talk for a while. Some thought the world might be coming to an end, and even those women not inclined to go that far had to admit it might not have been a good idea sending men into space, that we had no business, really, walking around up there on the moon. But the heat was relentless and the fans rattling in the windows seemed to be doing nothing at all, and eventually the women ran out of steam, sitting at their big wooden desks with their legs slightly apart, lifting the hair from the back of their necks. "Can you *believe* this" was, after a while, about all that got said.

One day the boss, Avery Clark, had sent them home early, but hotter days followed with no further mention of any early dismissal, so apparently this wasn't to happen again. Apparently they were supposed to sit there and suffer, and they did—the room held on to the heat. It was a big room, with a high ceiling and a wooden floor that creaked. The desks were set in pairs facing each other, two by two, down the length of the room. Metal filing cabinets lined the walls; on top of one sat a philodendron plant, its vines gathered and coiled like a child's clay pot, although some vines escaped and fell almost to the floor. It was the only green thing in the room. A few begonia plants and a wandering Jew left over by the windows had all turned brown. Occasionally the hot air stirred by a fan swept a dead leaf to the floor.

In this scene of lassitude was a woman who stood apart from the rest. To be more accurate, she sat apart from the rest. Her name was Isabelle Goodrow, and because she was the secretary to Avery Clark, her desk did not face anyone. It faced instead the glassed-in office of Avery Clark himself, his office being an oddly constructed arrangement of wood paneling and large panes of glass (ostensibly to allow him to keep an eye on his workers, though he seldom looked up from his desk), and it was commonly referred to as "the fishbowl." Being the boss's secretary gave Isabelle Goodrow a status different from the other women in the room, but she was different anyway. For example, she was impeccably dressed; even in this heat she wore pantyhose. At a glance she might seem pretty, but if you looked closer you saw that in fact it didn't really get that far, her looks stopped off at plain. Her hair was certainly plain—thin and dark brown, pulled back in a bun or a twist. This hairstyle made her look older than she was, as well as a little school-marmish, and her dark, small eyes held an expression of constant surprise.

While the other women tended to sigh a great deal, or make trips back and forth to the soda machine, complaining of backaches and swollen feet, warning each other against slipping off shoes because you'd never in a hundred years get them back on, Isabelle Goodrow kept fairly still. Isabelle Goodrow simply sat at her desk with her knees together, her shoulders back, and typed away at a steady pace. Her neck was a little peculiar. For a short woman it seemed excessively long, and it rose up from her collar like the neck of the swan seen that summer on the dead-looking river, floating perfectly still by the foamy-edged banks.

Or, at any rate, Isabelle's neck appeared this way to her daughter, Amy, a girl of sixteen that summer, who had taken a recent dislike to the sight of her mother's neck (to the sight of her mother, period), and who anyway had never cared one bit for the swan. In a number of ways Amy did not resemble her mother. If her mother's hair was dull and thin, Amy's hair was a thick, streaky blond. Even cut short the way it was now, haphazardly below her ears, it was noticeably healthy and strong. And Amy was tall. Her hands were large, her feet were long. But her eyes, bigger than her mother's, often held the same expression of tentative surprise, and this startled look could produce some uneasiness in the person on whom her eyes were fixed. Although Amy was shy, and seldom fixed her eyes on anyone for long. She was more apt to glance at people quickly before turning her head. In any event, she didn't know really what kind of impression, if any, she made, even though she had privately in the past studied herself a great deal in any available mirror.

But that summer Amy wasn't looking into any mirrors. She was avoiding them, in fact. She would have liked to avoid her mother as well, but that was impossible—they were working in the office room together. This summer arrangement had been arrived at months before, by her mother and Avery Clark, and while Amy was told to be grateful for the job, she was not. The job was very dull. She was required to add on an adding machine the last column of numbers of each orange invoice that lay on a stack on her desk, and the only good thing was that sometimes it seemed like her mind went to sleep.

The real problem, of course, was that she and her mother were together all day. To Amy it seemed as though a black line connected them, nothing bigger than something drawn with a pencil, perhaps, but a line that was always there. Even if one of them left the room, went to the ladies' room or to the water fountain out in the hall, let's say, it didn't matter to the black line; it simply cut through the wall and connected them still. They did the best they could. At least their desks were far apart and didn't face each other.

Amy sat in a far corner at a desk that faced Fat Bev. This was where Dottie Brown usually sat, but Dottie Brown was home getting over a hysterectomy that summer. Every morning Amy watched as Fat Bev measured out psyllium fiber and shook it vigorously into a pint-sized carton of orange juice. "Lucky you," Fat Bev said. "Young and healthy and all the rest. I bet you never even think about your bowels." Amy, embarrassed, would turn her head.

Fat Bev always lit a cigarette as soon as her orange juice was done. Years later a law would be passed preventing her from doing this in the workplace—at which point she would gain another ten pounds and retire—but right now she was still free to suck in hard and exhale slowly, until she stubbed the cigarette out in the glass ashtray and said to Amy, "That did the trick, got the engine started." She gave Amy a wink as she heaved herself up and hauled her large self off to the bathroom.

It was interesting, really. Amy had not known that cigarettes could make you go to the bathroom. This was not the case when she and Stacy Burrows smoked them in the woods behind the school. And she didn't know that a grown-up woman would talk about her bowels so comfortably. This, in particular, made Amy realize how differently from other people she and her mother lived.

Fat Bev came back from the bathroom, sighing as she sat down, plucking pieces of tiny lint from the front of her huge sleeveless blouse. "So," she said, reaching for the telephone, a half-moon of dampness showing on the pale blue cloth beneath her armpit, "guess I'll give old Dottie a call." Fat Bev called Dottie Brown every morning. She dialed the telephone now with the end of a pencil and cradled the receiver between her shoulder and neck.

"Still bleeding?" she asked, tapping her pink nails against the desk, pink disks almost embedded in flesh. They were Watermelon Pink—she had shown Amy the bottle of polish. "Setting a record or something? Never mind, don't hurry back. No one misses you a bit." Fat Bev picked up an Avon magazine and fanned herself, her chair creaking as she leaned back. "I mean that, Dot. Much nicer to look at Amy Goodrow's sweet face than hear you go on about your cramps." She gave Amy a wink.

Amy looked away, pushing a number on the adding machine. It was a nice thing for Fat Bev to say, but of course it wasn't true. Fat Bev missed Dottie a lot. And why wouldn't she? They had been friends forever, sitting in this room for longer than Amy had been alive, although it boggled Amy's mind to think that. Besides, another thing to consider was how much Fat Bev loved to talk. She said so herself. "I can't shut up for five minutes," she said, and Amy, keeping an eye on the clock one day, had found this to be true. "I *need* to talk," Fat Bev explained. "It's a kind of physical thing." It seemed she had a point. It seemed her need to talk was as persistent as her need to consume Life Savers and cigarettes, and Amy, who loved Fat Bev, was sorry her own reticence must provide a disappointment. Without forming the thought completely, she blamed her mother for this. Her mother was not a particularly talkative person, either. Look how she just sat there all day typing, never stopping by anyone's desk to ask how they were doing, to complain about the heat. She must know she was considered a snob. Being her daughter, Amy would have to be considered one too.

But Fat Bev didn't seem the least bit disappointed about sharing her corner with Amy. She hung up the telephone and leaned forward, telling Amy in a soft, confiding voice that Dottie Brown's mother-in-law was the most selfish woman in town. Dottie had a hankering for potato salad, which of course was a very good sign, and when she mentioned this to her mother-in-law, who everyone knew happened to make the best potato salad around, Bea Brown suggested that Dottie get up out of bed and go peel some potatoes herself.

"That's awful," Amy offered sincerely.

"I guess it is." Fat Bev sat back and yawned, patting her fleshy throat while her eyes watered. "Honey," she said, nodding, "you marry a man whose mother is dead."

THE LUNCHROOM IN the factory was a messy, worn-out-looking place. Vending machines lined one wall, a cracked mirror ran the length of another; tables with linoleum chipping from their tops were haphazardly pushed together or apart as the women arranged themselves, spreading out their lunch bags, their soda cans and ashtrays, unwrapping sandwiches from wax paper. Amy positioned herself, as she did every day, away from the cracked mirror.

Isabelle sat at the same table, shaking her head as the story was told of Bea Brown's egregious remark to Dottie. Arlene Tucker said it was probably due to hormones, that if you looked carefully at Bea Brown's chin you'd see she had whiskers, and it was Arlene's belief that women like that were apt to have nasty dispositions. Rosie Tanguay said the trouble with Bea Brown was that she had never worked a day in her life, and the conversations broke into little groups after that, desultory voices overlapping. Quick barks of laughter punctuated one tale, serious tooth-sucking accompanied another.

Amy enjoyed this. Everything talked about was interesting to her, even the story of a refrigerator gone on the blink: a half gallon of chocolate ice cream melted in the sink, soured, and smelled to high hell by morning. The voices were comfortable and comforting; Amy, in her silence, looked from face to face. She was not excluded from any of this, but the women had the decency, or lack of desire, not to try to engage her in their conversations either. It took Amy's mind off things. She would have enjoyed it more, of course, if her mother hadn't been there, but the gentle commotion of the place gave them a certain respite from each other, even with the black line between them continuing to hover.

Fat Bev hit a button on the soda machine and a can of Tab rocked noisily into place. She bent her huge body to retrieve it. "Three more weeks and Dottie can have sex," she said. The black line tightened between Amy and Isabelle. "She wishes it was three more months," and here the soda can was popped open. "But I take it Wally's getting irritable. Chomping at the bit."

Amy swallowed the crust of her sandwich.

"Tell him to take care of it himself," someone said, and there was laughter. Amy's heartbeat quickened, sweat broke out above her lip.

"You get dry after a hysterectomy, you know." Arlene Tucker offered this with a meaningful nod of her head.

"I didn't."

"Because you didn't have your ovaries out." Arlene nodded again—

she was a woman who believed what she said. "They yanked the whole business with Dot."

"Oh, my mother went crazy with the hot flashes," somebody said, and thankfully—Amy could feel her heart slow down, her face get cooler in the heat—irritable Wally was left behind; hot flashes and crying jags were talked of instead.

Isabelle wrapped up the remains of her sandwich and returned it to her lunch bag. "It's really too warm to eat," she murmured to Fat Bev, and it was the first time Amy had heard her mother mention the heat.

"Oh, Jesus, that would be nice." Bev chuckled, her big chest rising. "Never too hot for me to eat."

Isabelle smiled and took a lipstick from her purse.

Amy yawned. She was suddenly exhausted; she could have put her head on the table right there and fallen asleep.

"Honey, I'm curious," Fat Bev was saying. She had just lit a cigarette and was gazing through the smoke at Amy. She picked a piece of tobacco from her lip, glancing at it before she flicked it to the floor. "What was it made you decide to cut your hair?"

The black line vibrated and hummed. Without wanting to, Amy looked at her mother. Isabelle was applying lipstick in a hand mirror with her head tilted slightly back; her hand with the lipstick stopped.

"It's cute," Bev added. "Cute as could be. I was just curious, is all. With a head full of hair like yours."

Amy turned her face toward the window, touching the tip of her ear. Women tossed their lunch bags into the trash, brushing crumbs from their fronts, yawning with fists to their mouths as they stood up.

"Probably cooler that way," Fat Bev said.

"It is. Much cooler." Amy looked at Bev and then away.

Fat Bev sighed loudly. "Okay, Isabelle," she said. "Come on. It's back to the salt mines we go."

Isabelle was pressing her lips together, snapping her pocketbook shut. "That's right," she said, not looking at Amy. "There's no rest for the weary, you know."

BUT ISABELLE HAD her story. And years before when she had first shown up in town, renting the old Crane house out on Route 22, installing her few possessions and infant daughter (a serious-looking child with a head of pale, curly hair), there had been some curiosity among the members of the Congregational church, and among the women she joined in the office room at the mill as well.

But the young Isabelle Goodrow had not been forthcoming. She answered simply that her husband was dead, as well as her parents, and that she had moved down the river to Shirley Falls to have a better chance at earning a living. Really, nobody knew much more. Although a few people noticed that when she had first arrived in town she wore her wedding ring, and that after a while she didn't wear it anymore.

She did not seem to make friends. She did not make enemies either, although she was a conscientious worker and as a result went through a series of promotions. Each time there was some grumbling in the office room, this last time in particular, when she had risen well above the others by becoming the personal secretary to Avery Clark, but no one wished her any ill. There were jokes, remarks, made behind her back at times, about how she needed a good roll in the hay to loosen her up, but that kind of thing lessened as the years went by. At this point she was an old-timer. Amy's fear that her mother was seen as a snob was not particularly warranted. It was true the women gossiped about one another, but Amy was too young to understand that the kind of familial acceptance they had for each other extended to her mother as well.

Still, no one would claim to know Isabelle. And certainly no one guessed the poor woman right now was going through hell. If she seemed thinner than usual, a little more pale, well, it was dreadfully hot. So hot that even now, at the end of the day, the heat rose up from the tar as Amy and Isabelle walked across the parking lot.

"Have a good evening, you two," Fat Bev called out, as she hoisted herself into her car.

THE GERANIUMS ON the windowsill over the sink had bright red heads of bloom the size of softballs, but two more leaves had turned yellow. Isabelle, dropping her keys on the table, noticed this immediately and went to pluck them off. If she had known the summer was going to be this horrible she would not have bothered to buy any geraniums at all. She would not have filled the front window boxes with lavender petunias, or planted tomatoes and marigolds and Patient Lucys out back. At their slightest drooping now she felt a sense of doom. She pressed her fingers into the potted soil, checking for dampness and finding it too damp, actually, because geraniums needed bright sun, and not this soggy heat. She dropped the leaves into the garbage beneath the sink, stepping back to let Amy get by.

It was Amy who made their dinner these nights. In the olden days (which was the phrase that Isabelle used in her mind to refer to their lives before this summer) they used to take turns, but now it was all up to Amy. A tacit understanding: this was the least Amy could do—open a can of beets and fry some hamburgers in a pan. She stood now opening cupboards slowly, poking an idle finger into the hamburger meat. "Wash your hands," Isabelle said, and moved past her toward the stairs.

But the telephone, tucked neatly into the corner of the counter, began to ring, and both Isabelle and Amy felt a quickening of alarm. As well as startled hopefulness: sometimes it went for days without making a sound.

"Hello?" Amy said, and Isabelle stopped with her foot on the stair.

"Oh, hi," Amy said. Putting her hand over the phone and not looking at her mother, she said, "It's for me."

Isabelle walked slowly up the stairs. "Yeah," she heard Amy say. And then in a moment Amy said more quietly, "How's your dog these days?"

Isabelle walked softly to her bedroom. Who did Amy know that owned a dog? Her bedroom, tucked under the eaves, was stifling at this time of day, but Isabelle closed the door, and did it noisily, so Amy would hear: *See how I give you privacy.*

And Amy, twirling the telephone cord around her arm, heard the door close and understood, but knew her mother only wanted to look good for a moment, score an easy point or two. "I can't," Amy said into the phone, pressing her palm over the hamburger meat. And then, in a moment, "No, I haven't told her yet."

Isabelle, leaning against her bedroom door, did not think of herself as eavesdropping. It was more that she was too agitated to go about the business of washing her face or changing her clothes while Amy was still on the phone. But Amy didn't appear to be saying much, and in a few moments Isabelle heard her hang up. Then there was the clanking sound of pots and pans, and Isabelle went into the bathroom to shower. After that she would say her prayers, and then go down for dinner.

Although really, Isabelle was getting discouraged with this prayer business. She was aware of the fact that by the time Christ was her age he had already gone bravely to the cross and hung there patiently with vinegar pressed to his lips, having gathered his courage previously while he wandered through the olive groves. But she, living here in Shirley Falls (although she had suffered her own betrayal by her Judas-like daughter, she thought, shaking baby powder over her breasts), had no olive trees to walk through, and no courage to speak of either. Perhaps even no faith. She had doubts these days if God cared about her plight at all. He was an elusive fellow, no matter what anyone said.

What the *Reader's Digest* said was that if you kept on praying, your ability to pray would improve, but Isabelle wondered if the *Reader's Digest* might not have a tendency to make things a bit simple. She had enjoyed those articles "I Am Joe's Brain" or "I Am Joe's Liver," but the "Praying: Practice Makes Perfect" was really, when you thought about it, a little mundane.

After all, she had tried. She had tried for years to pray, and she would try again right now, lying down on her white bedspread, her skin moist from the shower, closing her eyes against the low white ceiling above her, to pray for His love. Ask and you shall receive. This was tricky business. You didn't want to ask for the wrong thing, go barking up the wrong tree. You didn't want God to think you were selfish by asking for *things,* the way the Catholics did. Arlene Tucker's husband had gone to Mass specifically to pray for a new car, and to Isabelle this was appalling. If Isabelle was going to get specific she wouldn't be so vulgar as to ask for a car—she would pray for a husband, or a better daughter. Except she wouldn't, of course. (*Please* God, send me a husband, or at least a daughter I can stand.) No, instead she would lie there on her bedspread and pray only for God's love and guidance, and try to let Him know she was available for these things if He cared to give her a sign. But she felt nothing, only the drops of sweat arriving once more above her lip and beneath her arms in the heat of this small bedroom. She was tired. God was probably tired as well. She sat up and slipped on her bathrobe and went down to the kitchen to eat with her daughter.

It was difficult.

For the most part they avoided each other's eyes, and Amy did not seem to find it necessary to take on the responsibility of a conversation. *This stranger, my daughter.* It could be a title for something in the *Reader's Digest,* if it hadn't already been done, and maybe it had, because it sounded familiar to Isabelle. Well, she wasn't going to think anymore, couldn't *stand* to think anymore. She fingered the Belleek china creamer sitting on the table in front of her, the delicate, shell-like, shimmering creamer that had belonged to her mother. Amy had filled it for Isabelle's tea; Isabelle liked tea with her meals when the weather was hot.

Isabelle, unable to contain her curiosity and telling herself that all things considered she had every right to know, said finally, "Who were you talking to on the telephone?"

"Stacy Burrows." This was said flatly, right before hamburger meat was pushed into Amy's mouth.

Isabelle sliced one of the canned beets on her plate, trying to place this Stacy girl's face.

"Blue eyes?"

"What?"

"Is she the girl with the big blue eyes and red hair?"

"I guess so." Amy frowned slightly. She was annoyed at the way her mother's face was tilted on the end of her long neck, like some kind of garter snake. And she hated the smell of baby powder.

"You guess so?"

"I mean, yeah, that's her."

There was the faint sound of silverware touching the plates; they both chewed so quietly their mouths barely moved.

"What is it her father does for a living?" Isabelle eventually asked. "Is he connected to the college somehow?" She knew he was certainly not connected to the mill.

Amy shrugged with food in her mouth. "Mmm-know."

"Well you must have some idea what the man does for a living."

Amy took a swallow of milk and wiped her mouth with her hand.

"Please." Isabelle dropped her eyelids with disgust, and Amy wiped with a napkin this time.

"He teaches there, I guess," Amy acknowledged.

"Teaches what."

"Psychology. I think."

There was nothing to say to that. If it was true, then to Isabelle it meant simply that the man was crazy. She did not know why Amy needed to choose the daughter of a crazy man to be friends with. She pictured him with a beard, and then remembered that the Mr. Robertson horror had had a beard as well, and her heart began to beat so fast she became almost breathless. The scent of baby powder rose from her chest.

"What," said Amy, looking up, although her head was still bent forward over her plate, a piece of toast, the inner edge soggy and bloodied with meat, about to go into her mouth.

Isabelle shook her head and gazed past her at the white curtain that billowed slightly in the window. It was like a car accident, she thought. How afterward you kept saying to yourself, If only the truck had already gone through the intersection by the time I got there. If only Mr. Robertson had passed through town before Amy got to high school. But you get into your car, your mind on other things, and all the while the truck is rumbling off the exit ramp, pulling into town, and you are pulling into town. And then it's over and your life will never be the same.

Isabelle rubbed crumbs from her fingertips. Already it seemed hard to remember what their lives had been like before this summer. There had been anxieties—Isabelle could certainly remember that. There was never enough money, and it seemed she always had a run in her stocking (Isabelle never wore stockings that had a run, except when she lied about it and said it had just happened), and Amy had school projects due, some foolish relief map requiring clay and foam rubber, a sewing project in home ec class—those things cost money too. But now, eating her hamburger and toast across from her daughter (this stranger) while the hazy early evening sunlight fell against the stove and across the floor, Isabelle was filled with longing for those days, for the privilege of worrying about ordinary things.

She said, because the silence of their eating was oppressive, and because she did not dare, somehow, return to the subject of Stacy, "That Bev. She really smokes too much. And she eats too much too."

"I know," Amy answered.

"Use your napkin, please." She couldn't help it: the sight of Amy licking ketchup from her fingers made her almost insane. Just like that, anger reared its ready head and filled Isabelle's voice with coldness. Only there might have been more than coldness, to be honest. To be really honest, you might say there had been the edge of hatred in her voice. And now Isabelle hated herself as well. She would take the remark back if she could, except it was too late, and poking at a sliced beet with her fork, she saw how Amy rolled her paper napkin beneath her palm, then put it on her plate.

"She's nice, though," Amy said. "I think Fat Bev is nice."

"No one said she wasn't nice."

The evening stretched before them interminably; the hazy, muted sunlight had barely moved across the floor. Amy sat with her hands in her lap, her neck thrust forward like one of those foolish toy dogs you could sometimes see in the back of a car, whose head wagged back and forth at stop signs. "Oh, sit up *straight*," Isabelle wanted to say, but instead she said wearily, "You may be excused. I'll do the dishes tonight."

Amy seemed to hesitate.

In the olden days one would not leave the table until the other one was through. This practice, this courtesy, dated back to when Amy was a toddler, a slow eater always, perched on top of two Sears catalogues placed on her chair, her skinny legs dangling down. "Mommy," she would say anxiously, seeing that Isabelle was done with her meal, "will you still sit with me?" And Isabelle always sat. Many nights Isabelle was tired and restless, and frankly, she would have preferred to spend the time flipping through a magazine to relax, or at least to get up and get started on the dishes. And yet she would not tell the child to hurry, she did not want to upset that small digestive tract. It was their time together. She sat.

Those days Amy had stayed at Esther Hatch's house while Isabelle was at work. An awful place, that Hatch house was—a run-down farmhouse on the outskirts of town, filled with babies and cats and the smell of cat urine. But it was the only arrangement Isabelle could afford. What was she supposed to do? She hated leaving Amy there, though, hated how Amy never said good-bye, how she would go immediately to the front window instead, climbing up on the couch to watch her mother drive away. Sometimes Isabelle would wave without looking as she backed down the driveway, because she couldn't bear to look. It was like something had been pushed down her throat to see Amy at the window like that, with her pale, unsmiling face. Esther Hatch said she never cried.

But there was one period of time when Amy would do nothing except sit in a chair, and Esther Hatch complained that it gave her the willies, that if Amy couldn't get up and run around like a normal child she wasn't sure she could keep taking her in. This made Isabelle panic. She bought Amy a doll at Woolworth's, a plastic thing with springy, coarse platinum hair. The head fell off right away, but Amy seemed to love it. Not the doll so much as the *head* of the doll. She carried the head everywhere she went, and colored the plastic lips red. And apparently she stopped confining herself to a chair at Esther Hatch's house, because the woman did not complain to Isabelle again.

But it was clear, then, why Isabelle would sit with the girl each night at their table in the kitchen. "Sing Itty Bitty Spider?" Amy might ask sweetly, squeezing a lima bean between her small fingers. And Isabelle— it was horrible—would say no. She would say no, she was too tired. But Amy was such a sweet little thing—she was so happy to have her mother right there, a mere arm's length across the table. Her legs would swing with happiness, her small wet mouth open in a smile, tiny teeth like white pebbles set in her pink gums.

Isabelle closed her eyes, a familiar ache beginning in the center of her breastbone. But she had sat there, hadn't she? She had done that.

"Please," she said now, opening her eyes. "You may be excused." Amy got up and left the room.

THE CURTAIN MOVED again. This was a good sign, if Isabelle had been able to think about it that way, the evening air moving enough to move the curtain, a breeze strong enough to ripple the curtain lightly, holding itself out from the sill for a moment as though it were the dress of a pregnant woman, and then, just as quickly, silently falling back in its place, a few of its folds touching the screen. But Isabelle did not think that at least there was a breeze. She thought instead that the curtains needed to be washed, that they had not been washed in quite some time.

Casting her eye about the kitchen, she was glad to see that at least the faucets shone, and the counters did not seem streaky, as they sometimes did, with the dried remains of cleanser. And there was the Belleek china creamer that had belonged to her mother, the delicate, shell-like, shimmering thing. Amy was the one who had brought it down from the cupboard a few months before and suggested they use it each night. "It was your mother's," Amy said, "and you like it so much." Isabelle had said all right. But now, suddenly, it seemed dangerous; a thing so easily to be swept by a sleeve, a bare arm, and smashed to bits on the floor.

Isabelle rose and wrapped the leftover part of her hamburger in wax paper and put it in the refrigerator. She washed the plates, red-stained water from the beets swirling into the white sink. Only when the dishes were done and put away did she wash the Belleek china creamer. She washed it carefully, and dried it carefully, then put it far back in the cupboard, where it couldn't be seen.

She heard Amy come out of her bedroom and move to the top of the stairs. Just as Isabelle was about to say that she didn't want the Belleek creamer used anymore, that it was too special a thing and too apt to get broken, Amy called down the stairs, "Mom, Stacy's pregnant. I just wanted you to know."

Chapter

2

THE RIVER DIVIDED the town in two. On the east side Main
Street was pleasant and wide, curving past the post office and town hall
until it came to a place where the river was only a quarter mile wide.
There the street became a bridge that had a spacious sidewalk along
each side. If you drove or walked west over the bridge and looked up the
river, you could see the back end of the mill and part of its dark under-
belly as well, built out over the granite slabs of foam-sprayed rocks.
When you came off the bridge there was a small park at the river's edge,
and it was here the sun could set so stridently in wintertime, slicing
pinkish golds along the horizon, with the bare elms at the edge of the
bank seeming austere and dark, emboldened. But hardly anyone went
into the park for long. The park itself was nothing much to look at, having little more than a broken swing set and a few scattered benches,
many of them missing a slat from their seats. Mostly it was teenagers
that you'd find there, perching themselves tensely on the edge of the
benches, hunching their shoulders against the cold, cupping bare hands
around cigarettes; sometimes in the dusk you could find a small group
passing a joint to each other, inhaling, throwing surreptitious glances
up toward Mill Road.

Mill Road was what Main Street became once it crossed over the bridge, and while Mill Road did lead eventually to the mill, it first wound itself through a section of stores that included an old A&P with sawdust on its floors, a furniture outlet with faded couches in the windows, a few clothing stores and coffee shops, a pharmacy that for years had had the same display of a dusty plastic African violet sitting in the middle of a bedpan.

The mill was just beyond. Even though the river there was at its ugliest—churning and yellow and sudsy—the mill itself, built in red brick a century before, had a certain complacent elegance to the way it sat, as though it had long ago accepted itself as the center of this town. For the workers whose families had come down from Canada a generation before, the mill was in fact the center of the town; it was the center of their lives, and their houses were not far away, scattered in neighborhoods on narrow roads where small grocery stores advertised beer in the windows with blinking blue lights.

This part of town was known as the Basin, though no one seemed to remember why anymore, and the houses here were often loose-looking and large, with three stories, one apartment to each floor, and usually a tilting front porch. But there were some single-family homes as well, shingled and small, with garage doors left always open, showing a confluence of tires, bicycles, fishing rods. A number of these houses were painted turquoise or lavender or even pink, and there might be a statue of the Virgin Mary in a front yard, or a bathtub filled with petunias and dirt, becoming in winter a serene mound of snow. In winter, some people put plastic reindeer or angels in the snow and decorated them with blinking lights. A dog, chained outside in the cold, sometimes barked at the reindeer all night, but no one thought to call the owner or the police, as they would certainly have done across the river, where people expected, or demanded, a good night's sleep.

This other side of the river, known as Oyster Point, was where the few doctors and dentists and lawyers of Shirley Falls lived. The public school was here, and the community college, built fifteen years earlier out toward Larkindale's field, and the Congregational church was here as well. A simple white church with a simple white steeple, very different from the huge Catholic church with its stained-glass windows, in the Basin up on a hill. It was on this Protestant, Oyster Point side of the river that Isabelle Goodrow had very deliberately chosen to live. Had she been forced, for whatever reason, to consider moving into the top-floor apartment of some lavender house with the Virgin Mary standing blank-eyed out front, Isabelle would have refused. She would simply have gone back up the river to the town she had left. But luck (she had sometimes at first thought God) had seen to it that the carriage house of the old Crane estate had been available to rent, and so it was there, on the outskirts of Oyster Point, beneath the woody hills and fields out on Route 22, that she had brought her small daughter to live.

The house, small and poorly insulated, turned out to be hot in the summer and cold in the winter, but otherwise it suited their needs. Built originally at the turn of the century as a small barn for a few horses, it had later been converted into a caretaker's cottage, and then the fire happened—the main house of the Crane estate had burned to the ground. It was never determined exactly what had caused the fire. Probably faulty wiring. But there were stories told of the Honorable Judge Crane's having had a mistress who set fire to his house one night. Another variation had the judge setting the fire himself, killing his wife first, then driving up the turnpike with her body propped up next to him, a hat on her head.

Or something like that, anyway. It was long ago and people were bored with it by now. At any rate, a great-nephew (now old himself) had eventually inherited the property—the poplar saplings growing new—as well as the cottage itself. He had rented the place to any number of people over the years—a professor from Boston spent a summer there writing a book, and a librarian with short hair had shared the house for a while with a kindergarten teacher (though old Mr. Crane never felt easy about them and was glad when they moved on). A few Canadians making their way down the river had lived there briefly while working at the mill, but Mr. Crane really preferred not to rent to mill workers, and at times the house stood empty.

It was empty when Isabelle Goodrow made her first cautious trip to Shirley Falls, scouting out the possibilities of raising her daughter there—and finding a husband, which was really what she hoped to do. The little white house struck her immediately as a perfect "temporary dwelling place." Those were the exact words she had used to Mr. Crane that day as he stood in the living room with his hands in his pockets, nodding his balding, age-spotted head. He had offered to paint the walls for her and allowed her to pick the color. She chose a pale, glowing beige, drawn by the name in the hardware store: Heavenly Gates. She sewed the curtains that still hung in the windows, planted a garden in the yard out back, filled window boxes with purple petunias and pink geraniums, and old Mr. Crane was pleased. A number of times he had offered to sell her the place at a very good price, but Isabelle, though she had a small nest egg left from her mother, always refused. It was a temporary dwelling place.

Except apparently it was not; they had lived here now for fourteen years. This thought could sometimes make Isabelle feel physically sick, as though she had gulped in stagnant water from a pond. Her life was moving forward the way that lives did, and yet she was no more grounded than a bird perched on a fence. And she might one day find herself without even the fence, for presumably at some point Mr. Crane would die. She hadn't thought of a polite way to ask what would happen to their rental agreement in case of this event. But she could not bear to buy the house, could not bear to stop thinking her real life would happen somewhere else.

Meanwhile, lacking an attic or basement, the house was insufferably hot in the summer, and this summer was the worst of all. There was no escaping the heat or each other. Even the two bedrooms tucked under the eaves hardly supplied much privacy, divided as they were by only a thin plaster wall. Isabelle, frightened of electrical fires, would not allow the fans to run while they slept, and so the hot nights were silent and still; through the thin wall they could hear each other turn over in bed.

Tonight Amy, lying in a T-shirt and underpants, a bare leg draped over the edge of her bed, heard her mother fart—a short, dry sound, as though some attempt had been made at being polite. Amy ran a hand over her face and rolled her eyes in the dark. Retreating to her bedroom after dinner, she had taken a small diary from her desk drawer, a gift from her mother the Christmas before, and written the words *Another heavenly day is done.* Her mother would read it, of course. She had been reading it all along. Opening the gift on Christmas day, Amy had known immediately that this would be the case. "I thought you were at the age where you might like something like that," her mother had said, and in the slight momentary evasion of each other's eyes the truth was understood. "I love it," Amy said. "Thank you very much."

So she had always been careful. She would write: *I had a fun lunch with Stacy today,* meaning they had smoked two cigarettes each in the woods behind the school. But this summer she had taken to writing the same line each night, gripping the pen with a vengeance: *Another heavenly day is done.* The same line now thirteen times, written carefully beneath the date. That done, she put the diary on the floor by her bed and lay back; but hearing down below the final cupboard door swing shut, knowing how her mother would move into the living room and flip through the *Reader's Digest* while she bobbed her foot, feeling how that black line between them was still (and always) there, how it ran from her bed straight down to her mother below, Amy had suddenly risen and called down the stairs, "Mom, Stacy's pregnant. I just wanted you to know."

So. She had done that.

And now it was dark and her mother had farted, and there was nowhere for either of them to go. Except to sleep, and in this heat that wouldn't be happening soon. Amy stared at the ceiling. The porch light that got left on at night came in through the window, and Amy could just make out the blurred stain that was there above her, the size of a dinner plate. It was nothing more than the result of heavy snows melting on the roof the winter before (although what a catastrophe that had been. "Oh, *hell,*" Isabelle said, standing in the doorway of Amy's room that night. "Oh, hell, hell and *hell,*" as though the sight were going to do her in).

But for Amy the stain was a reminder, a kind of painful friend, because in Amy's memory it had appeared last winter, in January, the night before she met Mr. Robertson.

SHE HAD NOT liked going to school: trying to position herself in the free-floating plankton of bodies around her. But she was not, she knew, one of those jerky queer people who actually stuck out, although a few years back, when puberty had the audacity to strike her earlier than the rest, she had thought this would be true. Instead it was like she was benignly passed over, except for the surprising friendship of Stacy Burrows, who belonged to the group of popular girls but who had nevertheless introduced Amy one fall day to her first cigarette and remained committed, it seemed, to their lunchtime forays, often the only bright spot in Amy's day. Her face, as she moved through the halls, was frequently hidden by the volume of long and curly yellow hair that seemed her one prize; even the popular girls would sometimes say breezily in the bathroom, "Oh, God, Amy, I'm so jealous of that hair." But her life was a quiet one, and there was often a vague and puzzling feeling of shame.

So on that particular day in January, while old Mr. Crane's handyman shoveled snow off the carriage-house roof, Amy had walked into math class expecting, of course, that nothing of interest would happen. She hated math, and she hated the teacher, Miss Dayble. Everybody did. Miss Dayble was old and she lived with her brother, who was also old, and for years the students had been making jokes about Doughy Dayble having sex with her brother. Which was a splendidly gruesome thought. The woman had terrible dandruff, and you could see her pink scalp exposed in places, bright as the color of some wound. She wore sleeveless blouses, even in winter, so every time she raised her arm to write on the chalkboard you could see a twisted little mess of gray-white hair, balls of caked deodorant clinging to it.

But Miss Dayble wasn't there. On that particular day in January a man stood in front of the blackboard instead. The man was short, with curly hair the color of molasses, and he had a full beard the same color, covering his mouth completely. He stood watching through his brown-framed glasses, tugging slightly on his beard, as the students filed in. The sight of him, the surprise of him, made Amy for a moment feel a part of the group around her; she exchanged glances with the popular Karen Keane. The students were uncharacteristically subdued as they took their seats. Already the place seemed different without the presence of Miss Dayble, the chalkboard a wide expanse of serious green, the big clock above the door showing the precise time of ten twenty-two. A collective air of expectancy hung in the room. Elsie Baxter tripped on her chair and giggled foolishly, but one would expect that of her, and the man's expression did not change. He waited a number of moments before he said, "My name is Thomas Robertson."

No one had seen him before.

Leaning forward slightly, holding his hands behind his back, he added in a kindly tone, "I'll be with you for the rest of the year."

In the dimmest part of her mind Amy sensed a huge, silent change taking place in her life; and she wondered how old the man was. You couldn't call him young, but he wasn't *old*-old either. So around forty, perhaps.

"Now listen, before we get started," Mr. Robertson said, in a low, grave voice (it was really a wonderful voice he had, different tones vibrating together), walking back and forth in front of the room, glancing at the floor, hands still behind his back, "I would like"—and here he stopped to look searchingly at the class—"I would like to hear from you." The pinkness of his mouth could be seen through the brown curly hair of his beard, and, smiling, he briefly showed thick yellow teeth, while wrinkles sprang to the corners of his eyes. "This is what I would like. To hear from you." He dropped his eyelids, as though to punctuate this particular point.

"Hear what." Elsie Baxter did not bother to raise her hand.

"Who you are, how you see yourselves." Mr. Robertson walked to an empty desk and sat down on top of it, putting his feet on the seat of its chair. "Before we get down to the business of numbers" (and he pronounced this "num-bahs" in the Massachusetts way), "I'd like to know how you picture yourself in ten years." He raised his eyebrows pleasantly and looked over the class, crossing his arms and rubbing his hands on the sleeves of his jacket. "So think about it. How do you see yourself in ten years?"

No teacher had asked them such a thing before, and some of the students moved in their seats with nervous pleasure, while others sat motionless, considering this. Outside, the winter sky was far away, remote. The room seemed an important place to be, the oiled wooden floors giving support to something substantial, the smell of chalk and perspiring bodies holding the hint of excitement, of promise.

"What happened to Miss Dayble?" Elsie Baxter suddenly asked, again without raising her hand.

Mr. Robertson nodded. "Oh, of course," he said. "You'd want to know that." Amy, who had not moved since taking her seat, now put her hands in her lap and wondered if the old woman had died; she didn't feel sorry if this was the case.

It was not the case. Miss Dayble had fallen down her cellar stairs and apparently cracked her skull. She was in the hospital in stable condition, but it would take the fracture a long time to heal. "If anyone wants to send her a card, I'm sure she'd be happy to receive it," Mr. Robertson said. Nobody did. But there was something in the concerned way Mr. Robertson's eyebrows rose and came together as he said this that made the class subdued, and those students who might otherwise have made a snide remark about what they'd like to send Miss Dayble refrained.

Mr. Robertson was silent a moment longer, staring at the floor, as though the reminder of Miss Dayble's condition required a pause of respect, and then, looking up at the class, he said quietly, "I would still like to know about you."

Flip Rawley, popular and handsome, with his good-natured face, tentatively raised his hand. He cleared his throat and said, "I'd like to play pro basketball."

"Beautiful." Mr. Robertson clapped once. "A beautiful game. Almost like ballet, I think—like some wonderful dance."

Amy glanced at Flip to see how he would take to the idea of ballet, but Flip was nodding his head. Mr. Robertson hopped down from his desk, light-footed, inspired. At the blackboard he said, "Look at this," and he drew the diagram of a particular basketball play. "Isn't that something—beautiful game," he concluded, dropping the chalk back into the chalk tray. "When it's well done, anyway." He dusted his hands on his corduroy pants and nodded at Flip. "Best of luck pursuing your quest."

After that all sorts of hands shot up. Maryanne Barmble wanted to be a nurse. She wanted to "help people," she said, but Mr. Robertson only tugged at his beard and nodded. Disappointment showed on Maryanne's face; she had thought he would like that, talk about the beauty of *her* quest.

"Who's next?" Mr. Robertson said.

Amy, peeking out from behind her hair, watched the man intently. He was short, it was true, but there was a sturdy thickness to him, a fullness to his chest and shoulders that gave the impression of some vigorous strength, in spite of the fact that he wore a pink shirt. His hair was longer than what she expected in a middle-aged man; had he been younger, he could have passed for a hippie over at the college. But he wore a maroon tie with his pink shirt, and a brown sports coat the same color as his corduroy pants. He was unmistakably a grown-up, invested with authority. His voice alone could tell you that.

"Let me say"—Mr. Robertson held his hand up—"that you people are at a critical point in your lives. You are not kids anymore." He walked up an aisle between a row of desks; heads turned to follow him. "You should be questioning everything," he said, clenching a fist with the intensity of this. Those students who had raised their hands now brought them slowly back down to their desks, unsure of what he was doing.

"You are young adults now," he continued. "There isn't anyone in this room"—and here he paused, standing over by the windows, raising his shoulders while his hands jingled change in his corduroy pocket— "who needs to think of himself as a child again."

The class was not entirely won over, in spite of the man's wonderful voice. They had not been thinking of themselves as children for quite some time, and they wondered if they were being patronized—though this was not the word that went through their minds.

"You've arrived at a point in your lives," he went on, "where you need to be questioning everything."

Amy wondered if the man might be a communist. With his beard and long hair, he might be leading up to the topic of marijuana, about to argue they should make it legal.

"Question everything," he repeated, moving an empty chair aside. His hands were large, as though nature had intended him to be a taller, bigger man, and there was something exquisitely gentle in the way he moved the chair. "Just for the mere exercise of the mind. That's all. Just to keep your mind on its toes."

He might not be a communist.

"Was it really Cheerios you wanted for breakfast this morning?" he asked, looking around at the class.

He might just be weird.

"Or did you eat those Cheerios simply from habit? Because your mother told you to."

Elsie Baxter, seated behind Amy, whispered loudly that she didn't have Cheerios that morning, but Amy ignored her, and Flip Rawley scowled and rolled his eyes to let Elsie know she should shut up, and in this way votes were cast for Mr. Robertson.

"Now," said Mr. Robertson, in a different tone, convivial, friendly again, rubbing his hands together. "Where were we? I was hearing from you. I *want* to hear from you."

Kevin Tompkins thought he might be a lawyer. Stuttering, he said more than anyone could remember him saying before: His cousin had been raped when she was just a little girl and the guy had gotten off scot-free. So he wanted to be a lawyer. Mr. Robertson asked a lot of questions and listened attentively to Kevin, who answered, stuttering and licking his lips. "Isn't life interesting," Mr. Robertson finally said. The black hand of the clock on the wall made a tiny click and moved to the next number.

He pointed his finger at Amy.

"Me?"

"Yes, you. What would you like to be?"

She was almost dizzy. "I'd like to be a teacher," she answered, but her voice was tight and might actually have quavered; horrible to hear her distress revealed in front of everyone. In front of him.

Mr. Robertson looked at her for a long time. She blushed, glancing down at her desk, but when she looked up through her hair he was still gazing at her impassively. "Really?" he finally said.

A wave of heat washed along her scalp. She saw how he ran his fingers slowly over his beard, a spot that was almost reddish in color, right below his lip. "But now, you see," he said, holding her gaze thoughtfully, "I would have said an actress."

From the corner of her eye Amy felt Flip Rawley watching her with a curious interest. It could be the whole class was watching her that way. Mr. Robertson leaned back against the windowsill, as though he had all the time in the world to consider this. "Or a poet, perhaps."

It made her heart beat fast. How did he know about the poetry in the shoebox under her bed? How could he know that she had memorized the poems of Edna St. Vincent Millay years ago, that she had walked to school on fall mornings filled with hope—*O world, I cannot hold thee close enough!*—and then walked home tired, discouraged, her feet scuffing to the words *Sorrow like a ceaseless rain beats upon my heart.* How could this man know that? And yet he did, for he had not assumed Maryanne Barmble was going to be a poet, had he? Nor Kevin Tompkins, with his stutter.

"Tell me your name."

"Amy."

The man cupped his hand behind his ear, raising his eyebrows.

"Amy," she repeated, clearing her throat.

"Amy. Amy what?"

"Goodrow."

"Amy Goodrow." He turned and walked to the front of the room again, leaning once more against the blackboard, a foot lifted casually behind him touching the wall. She assumed he was through with her now, his eyes were glancing over the classroom. But he suddenly said, "Amy, do you *really* want to be a teacher?" And she might have confessed that she would rather be a poet, if he hadn't blundered then, if he hadn't cocked his head and said, "Or is being a teacher just something your mother thinks is nice?"

The truth of this offended her. It was, in fact, Isabelle's idea that Amy be a teacher. Isabelle had wanted to be a teacher herself. There was nothing wrong with being a teacher, though. Amy had pictured herself doing this for most of her life.

"I want to be a teacher," she said quietly, and she could feel how he dismissed her then, with his casual "All right."

Sarah Jennings wanted to join the circus and become a clown. Mr. Robertson tilted his head in a friendly way and declared such yearnings noble.

SHE BEGAN TO hate him. She hated how he would sit on his desk, one foot placed on his chair, rolling his shirtsleeves up. After that first day he never wore his jacket. Instead he loosened his tie and rolled up his sleeves and tilted his head in what seemed a cocky way. She hated how he would run his chalk-dusted hand over the top of his curly hair, how he would hop down from his desk and walk quickly to the blackboard, writing numbers, drawing triangles, tapping the chalk so hard against the blackboard as he made his point that it would sometimes break in half, a piece flying to the floor, and sometimes he left it there, as though what he had to say was too important, too exciting, to bother with a silly piece of broken chalk.

And she hated how her classmates liked him, how excited they got when he would suddenly ask a stupid, personal question. (Leaning over his desk, he stared at Elsie Baxter one day and said, "Do you sometimes get *depressed*?") She hated how they fell for all of this. "Mr. Robertson," she heard them say, "—yeah, he's all right. He's cool." She thought he was probably a hypocrite.

"He thinks he's something special," she complained to Stacy Burrows, as they lit their cigarettes at lunchtime out behind the school. Stacy was indifferent. She didn't have Mr. Robertson—she was in the "dumb class," with Mrs. Weatherby—but Stacy might have been indifferent anyway.

"All men are rat-fucks," she answered, blowing smoke through her nose.

Amy told her mother that the substitute for Miss Dayble was a strange man with a beard.

"Short?" her mother asked, washing out pantyhose in the bathroom sink.

"You've seen him?" The thought was disconcerting.

"No." Her mother shook her head, draping the pantyhose over the shower nozzle to dry. "But short men often wear beards. It makes them feel more manly." Amy liked how her mother could be smart about things. "Just do your work," Isabelle advised. "That's all that counts."

And she did, bending her head over her desk in the stuffy classroom, the radiators clanking in the corner, Flip Rawley next to her, no longer looking at her as though she might be some future actress, but instead rolling his large eyes sideways trying to copy her paper, and she tried to ignore it all, writing her equations neatly, her long, wavy hair managing to cover most of her face as she sat at her desk and worked.

Until Mr. Robertson said one day, "Amy. Why do you hide behind your hair?"

A pinprick of heat stabbed her armpit.

He was leaning against the wall in a familiar pose: his arms crossed, one leg bent behind him with his foot pressed to the wall so that his barrel-like chest was thrust forward. The radiator in the corner made a knocking sound. Someone dropped a pencil.

"You have a perfectly glorious head of hair," Mr. Robertson said. "It's the first thing anyone notices about you. But you hide behind it. We hardly ever get to see your face. Are you aware of that?"

Of course she was aware of it.

"You're like a turtle, Amy." He was moving away from the wall. "Only instead of a shell, you have this carapace of hair." The class laughed lightly at this, as though he had said something obscene (although none of them, including Amy, knew what the word "carapace" meant).

"I saw a cartoon in a magazine recently," Mr. Robertson continued, walking down the aisle toward his desk. "I saw this cartoon, Amy, and I thought of you."

A dull, nauseating ache filled her head.

"Two turtles. One turtle has his neck out in a friendly way, the other turtle is all tucked up in his shell. And the friendly turtle is saying, Oh, come on out, everyone's been asking about you."

The class laughed again. Mr. Robertson rapped his knuckles on his desk. "So come on out, Amy Goodrow. Everyone's been asking about you."

The hatred she felt for him was so pure it was almost a relief, as though she might have been hating someone like that for years. She stared at her desk, tracing the numbers written on her paper and picturing her mother's long neck, and she wanted to cry to think she was the offspring of a turtlelike creature, she wanted to cry that the same man who had seen the poet (the actress) in her had now compared her to a turtle.

The bell rang, rattling through the room and ringing through the corridor, and the sound of classroom doors opening could be heard, banging against the walls. Chairs scraped, books dropped. He stopped her going out the door. "Amy," he said, beckoning with his head, "I'd like to speak with you a minute." She stopped obediently, her books held tightly to her chest. Students moved past her, some glancing briefly from her to Mr. Robertson.

Mr. Robertson waited until the classroom was empty, and then he said quietly, so seriously that he might have been telling her a grave secret, "I'm afraid I offended you. It was not my intention and I extend apologies. I'm very sorry."

She looked past him, her head tilted. They were almost the same height. She rocked on the side of her foot so as to not seem so tall, but she was tall, she was as tall as he was short, and so there they were, their faces inches apart.

"Friends?" he said, tilting his own head a bit as though to match the angle of hers.

If only she were someone else. Karen Keane, let's say. If she were Karen Keane she could make a playful face and say, "Oh, sure we're friends," and he would like her then; they could make a joke. But Amy said nothing. Even her expression didn't change. She could feel how her face just hung there without moving, half hidden by her hair.

"Okay," he said, "we're not friends, I see." She heard the smallest glint of something hard, chrome-edged, in his voice. He turned and walked away.

In the girls' room she wrote an obscenity on the wall. She had never written anything on a wall before, and as the pen made gritty, wobbly lines, she felt an affinity for whoever it was that had vandalized the gym the year before, as though she were capable of breaking windows now herself, this one right here in the bathroom with wet snow sticking to its pane.

The second bell rang. She was late for home ec class, and she had never been late to class before. But she wrote one more thing on the bathroom wall, because when you thought about it, the home ec teacher was an asshole too.

H<small>E LEFT HER</small> alone after that, but math class made her anxious. For one thing, she began to understand math in a way she never had, and sometimes during those bleak January days, when the sky outside the classroom was an unrelenting gray, the twiggy black branches of the frozen lilac tree tapping on the window, it would occur to Amy to raise her hand to answer some question Mr. Robertson asked, although she never did. But it made her anxious, particularly when those students who raised their hands would get the answer wrong, and Mr. Robertson, waiting by the blackboard, a nub of chalk in his hand, would say, "Anyone else care to give it a try?" His eye might catch hers briefly, and at those times she longed to raise her hand, but she was afraid she would be wrong.

She would not have been wrong. Mr. Robertson, turning back to the chalkboard, would go through the problem another time, or many times if he needed to, until he finally elicited from someone the answer that Amy would have given had she only dared.

And he could be strict when he felt like it. Poor Alan Stewart, a pimply-faced, sullen boy who sat in the back, was kept after school one day simply for clicking his pen. Elsie Baxter, big and boisterous, with grease by her nose, was threatened with detention as well, after blowing huge bubbles of purple gum and having them pop all over her face. But she apologized and threw the gum away, and Mr. Robertson, becoming kind, made a gentle joke. Anyone could see from the color rising in her face that she had a crush on him. ("Elsie doesn't come from much," Amy's mother said.)

No one wanted to anger him. He was popular because he was different, and if his energy was somewhat capricious, it was worth the air of uncertainty just to sit in a classroom and not feel dead. Even Amy, who continued to hate him, had a hard time not feeling that. One day, explaining a certain theorem near the end of class, Mr. Robertson banged the blackboard with his fist. "Can't you see the beauty of this?" he demanded of Alan Stewart who was yawning in the back row. "I'm telling you people, if you had any sensitivity, you would look at this and weep."

A few students laughed, but it was a mistake because Mr. Robertson scowled and said, "I'm serious, for God's sake. You have three lines here. Three *mere lines.*" He retraced them with his chalk. "And yet look at the beauty they hold." He seemed suddenly deflated then, and those students who had laughed now shifted in their seats.

But Amy, gazing at what he had drawn on the board, had a thought slip into her head, a line of poetry she had once read: *Euclid alone has looked on beauty bare.*

Mr. Robertson, glancing over the class, rested his eyes for a moment on her. "What?" he said, tilting his chin in her direction—but he was tired, and the word was spoken sternly. Amy looked down and shook her head. "All right, then," he sighed. "Class dismissed."

Amy's head would be aching when she had her lunchtime cigarettes. The cigarettes made her dizzy, and she leaned against the fallen log watching as Stacy rummaged through her pockets for a match. "You okay?" Stacy squinted as she lit their second one.

"I hate school."

Stacy nodded. "I hate school too. I puked this morning and I wanted to stay home, but my mother sent me anyway."

"You *puked*?"

Stacy nodded again. "My mom didn't give a shit. She hit me on the arm with a hairbrush."

"Are you kidding?"

Stacy shrugged and pushed up the sleeve of her navy-blue pea coat. "My mother's a fucking lunatic." She spoke with the cigarette in her mouth, squinting carefully at the reddish bruise on her wrist before she let the sleeve slip back down.

"Boy, Stacy." Amy tapped an ash from her cigarette onto the snow and stepped on it with her boot.

Stacy breathed out smoke. "These days I feel like puking all the time."

A headache was better than that, even if it lasted all day, the way Amy's headaches were starting to do, so that she still had it when she got home from school, sitting at the kitchen table, doing her homework in the chilly house. She got into the habit of doing her math homework first, and then before her mother got home she would go to her room and stare at herself in the mirror. She could not figure out what she looked like. Sitting on the vanity stool (it was an old barrel, actually— Isabelle had sewn a pink ruffled drape around it and put a cushion on top), Amy could not get her looks figured out.

Her eyes were far apart and her forehead was high, and Isabelle said these were both signs of intelligence, but that didn't matter to Amy. She wanted to look pretty, and she thought it would help to be short and have small feet. And even if it was good that her eyes were far apart, there was nothing special about them; they weren't a vibrant blue, or mysterious brown; they were just a murky green, and her skin was pale, especially in winter, when the skin beneath her eyes seemed transparent, almost blue.

Her hair, at least, was good. She knew this partly because people had told her so all her life. "Where did she get that hair?" strangers would say to her mother in the grocery store when Amy was still small enough to be riding in the wire seat of the shopping cart. "Look at that *hair*," they would say, sometimes reaching for it, running their finger over a curl, giving it a tug.

But Amy had known, the way children know things (know everything, Mr. Robertson would later argue), that her mother didn't care for strangers touching her daughter, commenting on her daughter's hair. It might have been Amy's earliest memory of guilt, because she had loved it when someone reached for her; she would turn her face in the direction of the hand, ducking her head to feel the cupped fingers of the stranger linger as the kind voice said, "Pretty girl, where did you get that hair?"

Not from Isabelle. Even the strangers could guess that. One glance at Isabelle's thin dark hair pulled back into a twist told them that. This was her father's hair. And here was the reason for Isabelle's tight-lipped disapproval—Amy had figured that out long ago. She could only guess that it stemmed from the fact that her father had died so soon after her birth; he'd had a heart attack on a golf course in California. "What was he doing in California?" Amy had asked, but the answer was always "Business," and Amy never learned a whole lot more. But she had inherited his hair, whoever he was, and she was grateful for that as she brushed it those winter afternoons in front of her mirror, different shades of yellow falling past her shoulders.

And then one day, leaving the lunchroom early (Stacy had not come to school), Amy bumped into Mr. Robertson as he was coming out of the teachers' room. "Hi," Amy said, only the sound did not come out, just her dry lips parting before she ducked her head.

"Amy Goodrow," Mr. Robertson said, continuing past her down the hall. But she heard his footsteps stop, and looking over her shoulder she saw that he had turned and was watching her. He shook his head slowly before he said, "Only God, my dear, could love you for yourself alone and not your yellow hair."

Isabelle, going through the diary months later with hands that were actually shaking, determined, as she sat on the edge of her bed, to find out when this all began, could find nothing more than the innocuous entry for January tenth: *Old Dayble fell down the stairs and luckily broke her head.*

Chapter

3

THE FANS WHIRRED in the windows of the office room. It was early, the day had just begun. This was always a quiet time, when the women still carried with them the scent of their morning soaps, when, greeting each other, there was still the whiff of toothpaste on their breath; and now they sat at their desks, working more steadily than they would at any other point during the day. Occasionally a metal filing cabinet was heard to click shut, a wastebasket scraped briefly over the floor. Avery Clark rolled up his sleeves and stood in the doorway of his office. "Isabelle," he said, "may I see you for a few minutes, please?"

And then poor Isabelle, because if she had known that Avery Clark was going to have her take dictation today she would have worn her linen dress. The dress was not pure linen, but it had some linen in it, and it was periwinkle blue. ("Fun to say, fun to wear," the cheerful sales clerk said.) Isabelle tried not to wear the dress too often. If she looked attractive too often, people might expect it and then notice all the more that, really, she was not.

And certainly she was not today, with her eyes puffy and scratchy from a bad night's sleep. (She had hesitated at Amy's door. "But what is Stacy going to do with the baby?" she asked. And Amy said blithely, rolling over on her bed, "Oh, give it away, I guess.") No, Isabelle had not slept well at all, and in her mind now, as she searched for her short-hand pad, was the thought that she would have to walk past Avery in this dumpy plaid skirt; it was too long and did nothing for her hips.

She couldn't find the shorthand pad. Papers and manila folders, benign and pale, lay on her desk. But she couldn't find her shorthand pad, and this was stupid, awful luck; she was an organized person. "Just one second, please," she said, "I just seem to have misplaced—" She was perspiring, but Avery only nodded indifferently, gazing out over the roomful of women, the backs of his hands placed on his hips. "Silly me," Isabelle said, slapping her hand down on her shorthand pad, which was there, had been there all along, on top of her desk. "Mrs. Silly," she said, but Avery seemed not to notice. He stepped back idly to let her by.

The two outer walls of his office were made almost entirely of glass, and this always gave Isabelle an added sense of exposure when she was in his office with him. All that glass was pointless anyway: it was there, supposedly, for him to keep an eye on the women he supervised, but the fact is that Avery Clark did not run a very tight ship. On those rare occasions when he was forced to speak to some recalcitrant employee about the poor quality of her work (there had been a dreadful incident years before when a woman's body odor was so offensive that the other women plagued him ceaselessly to call her in—an unpleasantness, he had confided to Isabelle, he would never forget), the meeting would be viewed with interest by the other women seated at their desk. "What's going on in the fishbowl?" they would murmur to each other.

But Isabelle was his secretary, and her presence in his office did not attract attention. No one, she told herself now, was witnessing her discomfort except Avery himself. And he did not seem interested. Shuffling through the papers on his desk, he said simply, without looking up, "Okay, then, shall we start?"

"All set."

There were many nights over the past years when Isabelle, having trouble falling asleep, would picture herself lying in a hospital bed while Avery Clark sat next to her, a look of worry on his aging face. Sometimes she was hospitalized for mere exhaustion, other times a car had knocked her down as she crossed a street, occasionally she ended up missing a limb. Last night she had been shot in a robbery, the bullet narrowly missing her heart, and Avery's face was pale with distress as the monitor she was hooked up to made a steady beep.

She was embarrassed to think of this now, almost stunned with shame as she sat across from his desk with the shorthand pad on the lap of her plaid skirt. His face, in the white light of the office, was preoccupied, vague—a slight dot of red on his chin left from his morning shave—separating her from the vast land of detail that made up his life. (She didn't even know his favorite food. Or if he had a piano in his house. And what was the color, she wondered right now, of the toilet paper that he had blotted his bleeding chin with earlier this morning?)

"All right," he said dryly. "To the Heathwell Lentex Corporation. Three copies. Dear Sir. Not sir. Look it up in the file and see who this goes to exactly."

"Yes, of course," she said, scratching this on her pad and then tapping the pen on her knee. "That will be easy enough."

She had tried over time to imagine it all, the jumbled compilation of details that made up this man. She had even imagined what he looked like as a child. (That moved her heart tremendously because he must have been tall and awkward.) She had imagined him on his wedding day, formal and stiff in his suit, his hair combed down. (He must have had his secret fears, all men secretly did.) And what was his life like now? She had pictured his closet, the shirts hanging in a row, his bureau, with a drawer for his pajamas . . .

"The contract stated explicitly that assumption of the risk would be with the buyer. See Clause Four, third line." Here Avery Clark paused, peering closely at a paper on his desk.

Isabelle pressed her lips together. Her lipstick felt gummy.

"Read that back to me, please, Isabelle."

She read it back.

"Hold on while I check this out."

She sat while he glanced through different papers. But she was terribly hurt, because it used to be that she would take her coffee breaks with him. It used to be that she would sit right there and tell him how the snow had sent water down under the eaves, or how the refrigerator sometimes made ice form in the milk, and almost always he would say, whatever the problem had been, "Well, I think you handled that well, Isabelle."

Now he said, "New paragraph," and only glanced at her. "Please note that in the last week of June of this year . . ."

Dear God.

The last week in June, not even a full month ago, was when her life had fallen apart. Disintegrated. As though her hands, her feet, her legs in their careful pantyhose all these years, had been nothing more than sand. And Avery Clark had witnessed it, which was the most unspeakable part of all. When she had gone into his office the very next morning blushing so hard her eyes watered, and said to him directly, "Please tell me, Avery. Should Amy still start here on Monday?" he had replied without looking up, "Of course." Because what else, Isabelle supposed, could he possibly do?

But they had not shared a coffee break since then. They had not shared a conversation since then, except for the most meaningless aspects of business.

His chair creaked now as he sat forward. ". . . three weeks to notify of undelivered goods."

But if only he would say something to her. A simple, "Isabelle, how are you?"

"Standard disclaimer attached. Please sign."

She closed her shorthand pad, thinking of a day last fall when she had told him how Barbara Rawley, the deacon's wife, had hurt her feelings *so much* by saying that to decorate the altar with bittersweet and autumn leaves was not appropriate, after Isabelle, being in charge of flowers for the month of October, had done so.

"But the leaves were beautiful," Avery had assured her. "Both Emma and I remarked that to each other."

That was all it took, that nod of his head. (Although she'd just as soon not hear about Emma—unfriendly Emma Clark, who stood around after church in her expensive clothes looking like she had a bad smell up her nose.)

"If you would get that out this morning then," Avery said.

"Yes, of course." Isabelle stood up.

He had spread his fingers across his cheek and was leaning back in his chair gazing through the glass at the desultory comings and goings of the women in his office room. Isabelle rose and moved quickly to the door so that her shapeless backside in this awful plaid skirt would not be exposed to him for long.

"Isabelle." The word was spoken quietly. She was almost out the door. She might have missed it altogether, that quiet incantation of her name.

"Yes," she said softly, matching her tone to his, turning. But he was glancing through the top drawer, his head bent slightly, showing the thin top of his gray hair.

"Did I say three copies?" He pulled the drawer out further. "You'd better make it four."

F AT BEV, TOSSING her empty orange-juice carton into the metal wastebasket, where it landed with a dull clunk in the quiet room, wiped the back of her hand against her mouth and glanced across the desk at Amy Goodrow. She felt sorry for the girl. Bev had raised three girls herself, and she thought Amy was strange—there was some lack of *commotion* in her face. Not that it wasn't dull as a doorknob working in a hot room with a bunch of middle-aged women. (She fanned herself with the magazine Rosie Tanguay had dropped on her desk that morning, saying lightly, "An article in here, Bev, on multiple addictions." Jackass Rosie, who ate carrots for lunch.) But there was something about this Amy, Bev thought, gazing discreetly while she fanned herself, that wasn't quite right, went further than just a dull job in a hot room.

For example, she didn't chew gum. Bev's girls had chewed gum constantly, moving great wads through their mouths, snapping it, popping it, driving everyone nuts. Roxanne, the youngest, now twenty-one, still did. Bev never saw her without gum in her mouth when she came over on Saturdays to use the washing machine, her eye makeup smudged and bleary from some party the night before.

That was something else, come to think of it. Amy Goodrow didn't wear makeup. She should. She might turn some heads if she put a little shadow on, darkened her lashes some. She wouldn't want to turn heads though, Bev mused, looking for her cigarettes; the girl was awful shy, ducking her head down all the time like a dog about to get whacked on the nose. It was too bad. But she didn't even seem interested in nail polish or perfume, and what teenage girl wasn't interested in those things? She never flipped through a magazine at her desk, never talked about clothes, never once used the phone to call up a friend. "Call somebody up," Fat Bev had said to her one particularly hot day when she could tell the girl was bored, but Amy shook her head. "It's okay," she said.

Well, it wasn't natural.

And what was the story with her *hair*? Who in their right mind would cut off a head of such lovely, wavy hair? Oh, girls went through their stages, Bev knew that. Her oldest daughter had dyed her hair red and looked like a fool for a while, and Roxanne was forever getting some terrible perm, moaning about it for weeks. But to cut off that hair. And it looked like hell, not even shaped around her face. Honestly, it made Bev shudder sometimes to look at that spiky hair—like someone who had had chemotherapy or radiation or whatever. Clara Swan's hair looked like that after she went up to Hanover for those treatments. Well, not really. Amy didn't have clumps missing from her head. It was just a bad haircut. A terrible case of bad judgment.

Bev lit a cigarette, the thought of cancer making her nervous. Clara Swan was only forty-three; but hers was a brain tumor, not lung cancer. A brain tumor could happen to anyone, you just took your chances. If Bev was headed for a brain tumor, she'd just as soon have enjoyed herself first. She exhaled, waving her fat hand through the smoke. Rosie Tanguay had said in the lunchroom, "I can't understand why anyone would smoke, with all the studies that have been done."

Studies. Rosie Tanguay could take the studies and shove them right up her skinny behind. Bev knew why she smoked. She smoked for the same reason she ate: it gave her something to look forward to. It was as simple as that. Life could get dull, and you had to look forward to something. When she was first married she had looked forward to going to bed with her husband, Bill, every night in that hot little apartment on Gangover Street. Boy, they used to have a good time. It made up for everything, all their squabbles over money, dirty socks, drops of pee in front of the toilet—all those little things you had to get used to when you married someone; none of it mattered when you got into bed.

Funny how it could wear off, something that good. But it did. Bev had kind of lost interest after the first baby was born. She began to re-sent Bill, how night after night he'd still want to do it, that rigid thing always there. It was because she was exhausted and the baby cried so much. Her breasts were different too after that tiny angry baby had sucked them till the nipples cracked; and she had never lost the weight. Her body seemed to stay swollen, and by God, she was pregnant again. So at a time when her house, her life, was filling up, she had experienced an irrepressible feeling of loss. Oh, maybe it didn't matter anymore. They still did it once in a while, silently, and always in the dark. (When they were first married they sometimes spent whole weekends in bed, the sun slanting through the window shade.)

She stubbed her cigarette out. She wasn't going to complain, she wasn't a kid anymore. But an ache stayed inside her. And a faint rever-berating hum of something close to joy lived on the outer edges of her memory, some kind of longing that had been answered once and was simply not answered anymore. She didn't understand this. She was mar-ried to a good man, and so many women weren't; she'd had the babies she wanted and they were healthy and alive. So what was this ache? A deep red hole she threw Life Savers into and potatoes and hamburgers and chocolate cakes, and anything else. Did people think she *liked* being fat? Jolly Bev. Fat Bev. She didn't like being fat. But that dark red ache was there, like a swirling vacuum, a terrible hole.

Amy Goodrow sneezed.

"Well, bless you," Bev said, glad to be able to speak. If you stayed quiet too long you got morbid. She was always telling her girls: Go find someone to talk to when you feel blue.

"Thank you," Amy said, with a tentative smile.

"You getting a cold? This crazy weather, who knows what bugs are hanging around."

The poor girl was too shy to answer that.

Well (Bev yawned and looked at the clock), living with Isabelle couldn't be a lot of fun. The apple never falls far from the tree, Dottie always said that, and Bev agreed. Isabelle Goodrow was odd. A typical Virgo is what she was. Not unpleasant, but pretty uptight. Something there to be pitied, Fat Bev thought, moving the telephone to see if her Life Savers had rolled that way, but, then, no one had ever figured

Isabelle out. Fat Bev felt the familiar tightening of her abdomen, and rose from her chair with a feeling of almost sensual anticipation, because God knows that one of life's pleasures was successfully moving your bowels.

AMY, GLANCING UP from her stack of orange invoices, had seen her mother in Avery Clark's office; the slight motion of her mother's arm, her downcast eyes, meant she was taking dictation. Nothing friendly was going on in there. Amy touched the numbers on the adding machine and felt in the deep part of her stomach a nauseating sensation she barely dared name: her mother was *attracted* to that man.

"You're lucky your mother's not married," Stacy had said to her one day out in the woods when the weather had first turned cold. "You don't have to picture her doing it."

"Oh, please." Amy said, choking briefly on her cigarette.

Stacy rolled her eyes, eyeliner curving on her heavy, pale lids as they half closed for a moment. "I ever tell you I saw my parents naked once?"

"No," Amy said. "Gross."

"It was gross. One Saturday I walk by their bedroom and the door's partly open and they're asleep on the bed, both naked." Stacy put her cigarette out on the bark of the tree. "My father has this white, fleshy, stupid-looking ass."

"God," Amy said.

"Yeah, so be glad you don't have a father. You don't have to imagine him doing it."

To be truthful, at that point in her life, Amy could not really imagine anyone doing it. She lacked a clear sense of what "it" actually was. Living with the watchful Isabelle, she had never been able to sneak into an X-rated movie the way some of her peers had. (Stacy, for example, had done that, reporting back to Amy a scene where a white man and a Negro woman did it in a bathtub.) And lacking an older sibling or two who might have kept dirty magazines under the bed, Amy knew very little at all.

She knew about her period, of course. She knew it was normal to have one, but she wasn't completely sure of the intricacies involved; Isabelle, a few years before, had talked briefly about eggs and a great deal about odor. ("Stay away from dogs," she advised. "They can always tell.") And she'd given her a pink booklet with a diagram. Amy thought she understood.

And then scrawled on the wall of the girls' room one day, in thick black Magic Marker, were the words *A man's dick inside a woman's hole for five minutes makes her pregnant,* and to Amy this made sense. But the gym teacher told the girls gathered in the locker room that information had been written on the bathroom wall which was incorrect, and the school had decided, as a result, to begin a sex education program that would take place in home ec class. Amy couldn't figure out what part of the bathroom-wall business was incorrect, and home ec class had proved to be no help.

The home ec teacher was a nervous woman, who lasted only a year, and whose long feet and knees that bumped out like two oranges had been a source of some hilarity among the class. "All right, girls," she said, "I thought we'd begin our sex education with a session on good grooming." She rummaged through her pocketbook. "The quality of your hairbrush," she said, "is connected to the quality of your hair." This had gone on for weeks. The teacher described different methods of filing one's nails, how to clean the toes, and then one day wrote a recipe on the board for underarm deodorant. "In case of some emergency, girls, and you find that you're out." They copied the recipe down: a mixture of talcum powder and baking soda and a little salted water. Later she gave them a recipe for toothpaste that was almost the same (minus the talcum powder) and lectured them on the use of the word "perspiration" as opposed to the coarser term "sweat." The girls scratched their ankles and looked at the clock, and Elsie Baxter was sent to the principal's office for saying out loud that it was all boring shit.

Anyway, that seemed a long time ago. Amy did not feel like the same person she had been back then, and now she could not suppress the knowledge that while her mother certainly hadn't been "doing it," she was, had been, *attracted* to her boss, that dreadful, dried-up man. It was the way his name used to come up at home, back in the days when Amy and Isabelle were talking. "Avery says I should trade the car; he knows a dealer he'll talk to for me." It was the way her mother would apply lipstick in the morning, rolling her lips together and saying, "Poor Avery is so overworked these days."

But Avery Clark was old and homely, and how could anyone possibly have a thing for someone like that? He and his wife looked like two dead sticks sitting in the church pew every Sunday. *They* hadn't done it in the last hundred years, you could be sure of that.

Amy sneezed ("Bless you," said Fat Bev) and glanced at the fishbowl again. Her mother was standing up, one hand holding her shorthand pad, the other smoothing the back of her skirt. Avery Clark was nodding his head, his stupid bald head that he combed his few greasy hairs over like nobody would know. Amy pushed a button on the adding machine, picturing the long, sloppy mouth of Avery Clark, his stained teeth, the dry breath she had smelled when he passed the collection plate in church. And those stupid old-man shoes he wore with the decorative little holes. He made Amy sick.

He might have spoken her mother's name, because Isabelle stopped in his door; Amy, glancing up again, saw the submissive hopefulness that lit her mother's pale face, and then saw it disappear. A hole opened in Amy's stomach: it was terrible what she had just seen, the *nakedness* of her mother's face. She loved her. On the black line connecting them a furious ball of love flashed across to her mother, but her mother had returned to her desk now, was rolling a sheet of paper into the typewriter. And immediately Amy felt that loathing at her mother's awkward, long neck, the wisps of moist hair stuck to it. But this loathing also seemed to increase some desperate love, and the black line trembled with the weight of it.

"So now, listen," Fat Bev said, popping a red Life Saver into her mouth. "What're your friends up to this summer? Didn't I see Karen Keane behind the register at Mac's?"

Amy nodded.

"Isn't she a friend of yours?"

Amy nodded again and pushed the Total button on the adding machine. Behind her eyes swirled the gray tears of some inexplicable anxiety and sadness. Once more she glanced at her mother, who was typing now, the begonia plant she had rescued from the windowsill jiggling on her desk. Amy saw a pale blossom drop into its leaves.

"Kids should have summer jobs," Fat Bev was saying, the Life Saver clicking against her teeth. "My kids all had jobs starting when they were about twelve, I think."

Amy nodded vaguely. She wanted Fat Bev to keep talking because she liked the sound of her voice, but she didn't want to answer any questions. She especially didn't want to answer any questions about Karen Keane. The thought of Karen Keane quickened the anxiety behind her eyes. They had been friends back when they were small. They had played hopscotch on the playground and run from the yellow jackets that swarmed around the garbage bin. One time Amy had slept over at Karen's house, a big white house on Valentine Drive with maple trees out front. The house was bright and sunny and full of noise; boys played out back, and Karen's sister talked on the telephone as she dried her hair with a towel. But Amy had been homesick, she had gone into the bathroom and cried during dinner because of the thought of her mother eating her own dinner in the kitchen alone. There had been good times too, though. Like when Karen came to her house and Isabelle let them make cookies. The girls had sat on the back steps eating them while Isabelle weeded her garden; Amy could still remember that.

"Everything changes when you get to junior high school," Amy suddenly said to Fat Bev, but the Life Savers had rolled off her desk and Fat Bev was leaning down to retrieve them.

"What's that, hon?" Bev asked, her face red from the effort, but her telephone started to ring, and, holding up a finger in Amy's direction, she said into the phone, "What'd your awful mother-in-law do now?"

But what would Amy have said, anyway? She wasn't *really* going to tell Fat Bev how junior high had changed things, how her breasts had grown so much earlier than the other girls', how she had slept on her stomach to try and keep it from happening but it happened anyway, and how her mother, pretending to be casual about this, had wrapped a tape measure around her chest and ordered a bra from Sears. And when the bra came it made her breasts look bigger, stupidly grown-up. There had been some kind of game at school where the boys would sneeze when they walked by her. "Anyone have a Kleenex?" they'd say.

"Oh, forget them," her mother said. "Just forget them, who cares."

But she cared.

And then the frightening morning she had woken to find a dark stain the size of a quarter on her underpants. She took the underpants to her mother in the kitchen. *"Amy,"* her mother said. "Oh, Amy. Honey, my word."

"What?"

"Oh, Amy," her mother said sadly. "This is a very exciting day."

She felt loathsome and frightened as she walked to school, her abdomen heavy, odd pains in her thighs, and an extra sanitary napkin packed in a brown lunch bag. (None of the girls had started bringing pocketbooks to school yet.) And she had been asked to stand in front of the classroom to diagram a sentence on the blackboard. She thought she would faint standing there, pass out from shame, as if the whole class could see through her corduroy skirt to the bulky monstrous thing pressed between her legs.

At the suggestion of her mother she had recorded the event in a notebook; Isabelle felt it was a good idea to keep track of dates so that your period wouldn't take you by surprise (but Amy's period had a mind of its own and was even now always taking her by surprise). And when Karen Keane came over one Saturday, Amy, just returning from the bathroom, had walked into her room to find Karen Keane sitting on her bed, closing the notebook quickly. "Sorry," Karen said, twisting a piece of hair around her finger. "I won't tell anyone. Honest."

But she had. She had told. And there were whispers and notes passed, and Elsie Baxter had even said, "So Amy, what's in your lunch bag today?" It was like she was a freak. And even later, when one by one the other girls grew their breasts and started their periods too, it was still hard for Amy not to think of herself as some freak, some queerish kind of ghoul.

"I asked my sister-in-law," Fat Bev was saying matter-of-factly into the telephone, "and she bled for six full weeks. Not gushing or anything, you know. Just a dribble, dribble, drip." She caught Amy's eye and held out the roll of Life Savers.

Amy smiled and shook her head. It could be there was nobody she had ever loved the way she loved Fat Bev right now. Big old Fat Bev, who could talk about bowels and menstrual blood without batting an eye, as if they were the most ordinary things in the world. And Bev, listening to Dottie Brown go on, was surprised to see a flicker of motion passing over the girl's thin face, some momentary tremor of longing.

. . .

Bᴜᴛ Mʀ. Rᴏʙᴇʀᴛsᴏɴ had taught her some things about pride, about dignity, about graciousness. He really, really had. He said to her one day (it was February by then, and the light was changing, holding some extra fullness of yellow, some hint of promise), walking down an aisle of desks, "That's a pretty dress."

Amy, bent over her desk with her hair falling past her face, hadn't even known at first that he was talking to her.

"Amy," he said. "That's a pretty dress."

She looked up.

"Very nice," he said, walking up the aisle toward her, nodding his head, raising his gingery eyebrows in a gesture of approval.

"She made it," said Elsie Baxter, eager to have a part in this. "Amy made the whole thing by herself."

And this was true; it had been a project for home ec class. Amy had gone to the fabric store with Isabelle, the two of them flipping through the Simplicity catalogue until they found the tent dress pattern. "Put the zipper in by hand," Isabelle cautioned. "Always put a zipper in by hand, it never looks messy that way."

But the home ec teacher with the bumpy knees said Amy must sew the zipper in using the machine, and seated at a sewing machine by the window, Amy struggled severely. The cloth puckered, the zipper slipped. Other girls, seated at their own sewing machines, laughed and talked and whispered swearwords at the mistakes they made, but Amy worked silently, her face pink with effort, her fingers sweaty as she took the crooked line of stitching out again and again. But she got it finally. And when the dress was done it was completely wearable. Some of the girls' dresses were not.

"You made it?" Mr. Robertson asked. He had reached her desk; she could see the brown corduroy of his slacks from the corner of her eye. Quietly, in his deep voice: "It's really very nice."

Amy bent over her desk, hair falling to conceal her face. She didn't know if he meant what he said or not. It could be that in some indistinguishable, adult way, he was making fun of her. Or maybe he was being nice. She really didn't know. And so she kept her face down.

Mr. Robertson finally said, "All right, class. Get started on the second problem, and then someone can put it on the board." But he didn't walk away. She heard him sit down at the empty desk next to her, and she pulled her hair back cautiously. He was watching her, leaning back in the chair with his arms crossed. His face was serious and kind; she saw he wasn't making fun. He spoke softly, his head bent forward with concern. "A woman should learn to take a compliment gracefully," he said.

A LOUD BUZZER sounded in the office room. It rang throughout the mill eight times a day, and now it was morning break; in fifteen minutes the buzzer would blast again, signaling the women to return to their desks, but for now they could roam the hallway, go to the ladies', or go into the lunchroom if they cared to, to buy crackers or cookies from the vending machine and flip open cans of soda or iced tea. Rosie Tanguay would eat carrot sticks from a wax-paper bag, and Arlene Tucker had brought half a chocolate cake from home whose frosting in this heat had slipped down over its sides and was mostly stuck into the moist crevices of its plastic wrap, where it would be removed by fingerfuls as Fat Bev filled Arlene in on Dottie Brown's continuous bleeding.

Amy stayed where she was, at her desk, gazing vacantly at the fans whirring in the windows, thinking of Mr. Robertson. Isabelle, almost nauseous from her lack of sleep, stood in the ladies' room, pressing a wet paper towel to her face, and was unable to think of anything except for the words her daughter had spoken last night when Isabelle asked what Stacy would do with the baby: *Oh, give it away, I guess.*

Chapter

4

BUT SOMETHING ELSE had happened that year. Back in February, a twelve-year-old girl had been kidnapped from her home. It happened in Hennecock, two towns away, and Amy and Isabelle were so intrigued by this that for three days they had eaten their dinner off TV trays. *"Ssshhh,"* they said to each other as soon as the news came on.

"The search continues for Debby Kay Dorne." The newscaster's face was solemn; he might have had children of his own. "Police report no new findings in the case of the twelve-year-old girl who disappeared from her home sometime between two o'clock and five o'clock on Tuesday afternoon." Amy and Isabelle leaned forward on the couch.

"Sweet," Isabelle murmured, as a picture of the girl came on the television. The same picture had been shown the night before and in the newspaper that morning: the girl's broad face, curly hair tucked behind her ears, her eyes squinting, as though the camera had caught her on the verge of a giggle. "Very sweet," Isabelle said, and then more slowly, "very, very sweet," and Amy moved closer to her mother on the couch. "Sssshh," Isabelle said, "I want to hear what he has to say."

Only what they had heard before. Debby Kay Dorne had started for school on the morning of February tenth, when she slipped on some ice in her driveway. The fall was not especially serious but she had stayed home anyway, and because both parents worked, she had stayed alone. At two o'clock the mother called and spoke with her, but when the mother arrived home at five o'clock the girl was gone. Her jacket was gone, and the house was locked. Nothing was missing and the family dog appeared calm. These were the facts that led the police to believe that whoever had taken Debby Dorne from her home was someone that she knew.

"Oh, boy," said Isabelle, sighing as she got up to turn the TV off. "When it's like that, there's nothing you can do." But for a number of nights she put a chair against the door.

And Amy could not stop thinking about it. Lying in bed, waiting for sleep, moonlight touching the frost on her window, she pictured the scene again and again: the girl in a green winter jacket falling on her driveway, notebook and lunch bag sent flying, skidding across the ice; the mother coming out of the house quickly. "Honey, are you all right?" The mother would be tired-looking, but pretty, Amy thought, and she would help the girl inside, help her take off the green winter jacket, hang it on a hook by the door. Amy pictured Debby lying down on the couch while her mother brought in the quilt from her bed, kissing the girl's broad forehead, brushing back the curly hair. Perhaps she said, "Don't answer the door."

The dog Amy pictured as something small, the kind that got excited when strangers came to the house, racing back and forth, scattering rugs, maybe knocking over a plant or two, but a dog that lay around quietly when he knew everything was fine. And maybe that morning he had been lying on the couch with Debby while she scratched his head and watched a game show on TV. But she must have gotten hungry, Amy thought—it wasn't like she had stayed home *sick*—and so she saw Debby getting off the couch, going into the kitchen and rummaging through cupboards, finding graham crackers and potato chips, returning to eat them on the couch while the winter morning sun fell through the window, making the TV screen light.

By now she was probably dead.

Arlene Tucker had a brother-in-law who used to work for the state police, and according to Arlene, most kidnappers killed their victims within the first twenty-four hours. Isabelle had reported this to Amy as soon as she got home from the mill.

So Debby Kay Dorne was probably dead. Amy couldn't get over this. She didn't know the girl, or know anyone who did know the girl, but she could not get over the fact that the girl might be dead. That she had dressed for school that morning, had walked out of the house hugging a notebook to her chest (probably covered with penciled doodlings of flowers and hearts and telephone numbers, Amy imagined, turning over once more in bed), thinking it was one more boring old Tuesday in winter, and having no idea at all—of course—that she was going to be kidnapped that day. Ordinary girls in small towns with curly hair and potato chips in their lunch bags didn't get kidnapped from home while they watched TV with their dog. Except they did, because this is what had just happened in Hennecock, two towns away.

"They formed a search party," Amy told Stacy in the woods the next day. It was terribly cold and their breath danced in front of them as they stood hunch-shouldered in their coats, fists jammed deep in their pockets. "They formed a search party of volunteers. My mother said it could even be that the kidnapper is in the search party. Isn't that kind of weird?"

But Stacy wasn't interested in Debby Dorne. Her full lips trembled with the cold as she gazed at the pine trees, whose needles were stiff with frozen snow. "I wish someone would kidnap me," she mused.

"But she might be dead," Amy said.

"Maybe she got sick of everything and ran off." Stacy kicked lightly at the base of a tree.

"They don't think so," Amy answered seriously. "Twelve-year-olds don't usually run away."

"Yeah, they do. She could hitch a ride to Boston."

"What would she do in Boston?" Amy had been to Boston on a class trip in seventh grade. She had seen, staring out the window of the bus, men sprawled on the steps of buildings, sleeping on benches in the park, filthy men with caked hair, newspapers tied around their feet. When she got home that night Isabelle had said, "Am I glad to see you! I was afraid you might be shot."

"She could prostitute. Sleep in the bus station, I don't know. Whatever runaways do." Stacy seated herself carefully on the edge of the snow-covered log, tossing her straight red hair away from her face.

"Myself, I'd just keep running." She looked at Amy and frowned. "I can't tell if I'm hungry, or not."

Amy took the package of crackers out of her pocket. It was their lunch; salted crackers with peanut butter and pink jam. Her fingers unwrapping them hurt from the cold.

Stacy dropped her cigarette and stepped on it, then ate a cracker in tiny bites, the way she always did, her full dry lips touching together lightly.

"Well, anyway," Amy continued, unable to stop thinking about Debby Dorne, "they checked with all her relatives and people like that—people you check with—and they say they're pretty sure it's not a runaway. The police said it right out. They suspect foul play. That she got kidnapped. She didn't have problems at school or anything, she was a happy kid."

"Bullshit." Stacy held the collar of her navy-blue pea coat tightly around her throat as she ate the cracker with her other hand. "No twelve-year-old is happy."

Amy considered this, eating one of the crackers herself, sweet with the pungent taste of jelly; the first cracker always made her ravenous. After she had another cigarette she wouldn't be hungry anymore.

"I sure wasn't. Were you?" Stacy cocked her head upward as a crow darted from a spruce tree whose branches were weighted down with frozen snow.

"No."

Stacy suddenly pushed Amy's arm. "Car. Duck."

The girls crouched to the ground. The sound of the car passing over the gravelly frozen road increased as it got nearer. Amy stared at the flattened cigarette butt in the snow and waited. Now that there were only the frozen branches of pines and spruce trees for cover, they were not as hidden from the road as they used to be. A person driving by could see them if the person happened to look. In the fall, when the girls first discovered the place, the autumn leaves were thick and breeze-lifted and private; the fallen log, waist-high and dry, a perfect place to sit.

The car was blue. "Shit, that might be Puddy," said Stacy, peeking sideways and referring to the school's principal. "It's okay, he didn't look."

They stood up again, leaning against the fallen log. "*Was* it Puddy?"

Amy asked. If they were caught smoking they would be suspended from school; it was inconceivable to think of Isabelle getting such a phone call while she sat at her typewriter in the office room at the mill.

Stacy shook her head. "Couldn't really see. Anyway, he's not going to recognize you. No one would suspect Amy Goodrow of shit. Still, put your hood up," Stacy advised, squinting at Amy critically. "You've got all that fucking hair." But she did it herself before Amy had a chance, tugging the hood over Amy's head while she held the cracker in her teeth. Her cold fingertips briefly touched Amy's cheek.

"I bet Karen Keane was happy when she was twelve," Amy said, remembering the white house on Valentine Drive.

Stacy took a cigarette from the plastic Tampax holder she always hid their cigarettes in. "Karen Keane would fuck a rock if there was a snake underneath it. I can't believe I'm smoking when I feel so crappy. This is really sick." She shook her head, dropping her heavy, pale eyelids with an indifferent show of self-disgust, eyeliner smudged in the corner of one eye. "We're really a couple of sick rat-fucks to tromp out here in this freezing cold."

Amy blurted out, "Do people think you're weird spending your lunchtime with me?" The question, which she had not planned on asking, was paid for with an anxious thumping in her chest.

Flicking a piece of tobacco off the arm of her coat, Stacy looked up, surprised. "What people?"

"You know, your friends. Karen Keane and those guys."

Stacy squinted at her. "No," she said. "Not at all." A patch of frozen snow fell from a branch, landing on the ground with a clump. They watched for a moment as the crow darted to another tree. "No one thinks I'm weird because I spend lunchtime with you," Stacy said. "You have a really bad self-image, Amy."

"I guess." With her boot Amy knocked snow off a granite rock that rose up from the ground. Her boots were made of a plastic that was supposed to look like leather. She hated them; hated how they never got scuffed even when she scraped them over a rock, hated how they didn't fit tightly around her foot, the way Stacy's real leather ones did, how they stayed graceless and stiff, indestructible.

"People pay my father tons of money because they have bad self-images." Stacy started to put both cigarettes in her mouth, then laughed. "Can you imagine going to *my father* to feel better about yourself? I mean, that's really funny." She shook her head and lit the two cigarettes, then handed one to Amy. "What a crock of shit. Everything's a crock of shit." Stacy blew smoke through her nose. "You want to know something about those people?"

"What people?" Amy asked. Her fingertips seemed to be burning with the cold.

"Karen Keane and all the rest. They're twits." Stacy closed one eye against the smoke that drifted past her face and gazed with the other one at Amy. "They're twits. Morons. And you're not. You're the only person I know who's not a goddamn moron twit."

AND SO FEBRUARY continued. Many days were dull and white and cold. Often the sky was the same color as the fields of tired snow that lay on the outskirts of town, so that the whole world stretched out, interminable and pale, broken only by the dark frozen trees that lined the horizon, or by a sagging roof of an old red barn. And then would come a sudden thaw; a day of brilliance: blue skies and sunlight bouncing off the dripping trees, a sparkling world where the sounds of shoe heels could be heard clicking along the sidewalk of Main Street and the melting snow caused small rivulets to run alongside the road.

"The kind of day," Isabelle said, "when some poor soul commits suicide." She said this confidently, sitting up straight in the booth, her spoon clicking against the saucer. It was a Saturday afternoon and they were in Leo's coffee shop, next to the foot of the bridge. Sunlight fell through the window, folding itself over the blue linoleum of their tabletop and bouncing off the metal creamer in Isabelle's hand.

"Statistics show," Isabelle went on, pausing to pour more milk into her coffee, "that most suicides occur right after a cold snap. On the first bright sunny day after."

Amy wanted another doughnut. She was eating this one slowly in case her mother said no.

"I knew a man once, when I was growing up." Isabelle nodded

thoughtfully. "Very quiet man. His wife taught school. One day when she came home, she found him dead in the hallway. He had shot himself, poor thing."

Amy glanced from her doughnut to her mother. "Really?"

"Oh, yes. Very sad."

"How come he did that?"

"Well, honey, *I* don't know." Isabelle stirred her coffee. "Made a mess in the hall, though—that's what I heard. A wall had to be repainted."

Amy sucked crumbs off her fingers. "I've never seen a dead person," she said.

On Isabelle's plate was a brown doughnut, and she cut it now with a knife, then picked up a piece delicately with the tips of her fingers.

"Do dead people just look like they're sleeping?" Amy asked.

Isabelle shook her head, chewing. She touched a paper napkin to her lips. "No. Dead people look like they're dead."

"But how is that different from looking asleep? Stacy Burrows's grandfather died in bed and her grandmother left him there all morning because she thought he was asleep."

"Her grandmother needs a new pair of glasses, I'd say," Isabelle responded. "A dead person looks *gone,* not just asleep. Get your finger out of your mouth, please. One should not be picking any orifice in public."

But Amy was happy with the winter sunlight and the taste of her doughnut and the steam on the window and the smell of coffee in the air. She thought her mother might be happy too: the perpetual crease that lay between her eyebrows like the small tracing of a seagull in flight was smooth now, and when Amy asked for another doughnut her mother agreed.

"Have some milk though," Isabelle warned. "Two doughnuts is a lot of grease."

They were silent, eating and gazing around the coffee shop and through the big window at the people passing by on Main Street. What Amy liked about Leo's coffee shop was that it made her feel normal. Both of them seemed normal: a mother and daughter out on a Saturday afternoon. It made Amy feel like one of those girls in a Sears catalogue. And spring was really in the air. The cars parked next to the coffee shop had sunlight bouncing off their fenders and the snow was wet and slushy. Isabelle sat back, fingering her napkin.

"Why would she answer the door?" Amy finally said, finished with her second doughnut now, and pushing back the plate. "If her mother told her not to."

Isabelle nodded. "Well, this is the thing, isn't it. I've told you never to answer the door, but let's say you were home alone and Avery Clark telephoned and said I'd been in an accident, and he was stopping by to pick you up to take you to the hospital. Something like that. You'd go with him, wouldn't you?"

"I suppose."

"Avery would never hurt you," Isabelle said. "Avery would never hurt a fly. I was simply giving an example." She tucked some change under the lip of her saucer; she never cared to leave a tip in plain view. "All set?"

They walked down the sidewalk slowly (so normal!), a mother and daughter peering in shop windows, their heads tilted toward each other, a finger raised to point out a pair of shoes, a handbag, a dress they agreed they would never wear. Oh, such moments for Amy were heaven.

And they were rare.

By the time they were pulling into the parking lot of the A&P, the mood was fading, the moment gone. Amy could feel it go. Perhaps it was nothing more than the two doughnuts expanding in her stomach full of milk, but Amy felt a heaviness begin, a familiar turning of some inward tide. As they drove over the bridge the sun seemed to move from a cheerful daytime yellow to an early-evening gold; painful how the gold light hit the riverbanks, rich and sorrowful, drawing from Amy some longing, a craving for joy.

"Remind me to wash out some pantyhose," Isabelle said.

The A&P had sawdust on the floor, wet and dirty-looking up by the door from the slushy tracks of people walking in. Amy pushed a shopping cart and one of the front wheels wobbled at an angle, making the cart shake and tremble over the sawdusty floor. "Let's get this over with," Isabelle sighed, squinting at the list in her hand. Her mother's mood had changed as well, and Amy felt responsible, as though this sinking of their spirits was somehow her doing. As though having two doughnuts had done them both in.

The grocery store made her want to cry: a strange hope and hopelessness collided here—the hope of all those brightly lit kitchens out there with telephones ringing on the wall, silverware clattering down on tables, steam rising from pots on the stove, and then the hopelessness of these rows and rows of canned beets and canned corn. The tired, unsmiling people pushing their carts.

"Oh, Godfrey," said Isabelle quietly, staring intently at the tunafish can in her hand. "Here comes that dreadful woman."

And there was Barbara Rawley, tall in her long winter coat as she surveyed the salad dressings, a gloved finger to her chin. To Isabelle she resembled a garter snake standing on its tail, to Amy she seemed beautiful; her eyes were large and brown as she turned to them, hair as shiny as a shampoo ad. She wore pearl earrings in her pinkened lobes, and her maroon lipstick made her teeth look very white as she opened her mouth in a smile.

It was not a real smile though, she didn't mean it. Both Isabelle and Amy could tell that. It was the smile of a deacon's wife who had come upon some members of the church, that's all; and some cautious curiosity, perhaps. "Oh, hello," she said, slowly.

"Hello there, Barbara. How are you?" Isabelle's words were noticeably clipped.

"I'm just fine, thanks." Barbara Rawley answered slowly, as if speaking of something particularly meaningful. Her eyes moved from Isabelle to Amy. "I'm sorry. Your name is?"

"Amy."

"Of course. Amy." The smile was still there around the white teeth. "Aren't you in school with my son, Flip?"

"He's in my math class." Amy looked down at the jar of olives Barbara Rawley was holding in her gloved hand.

"And so what do you two ladies have planned for this evening?" Barbara Rawley raised her eyebrows rather extravagantly as she asked this question.

Both Amy and Isabelle felt chided, almost slapped by this inquiry into their evening, and they looked at each other helplessly. For it must have been some kind of slap—how could it be anything else, this woman with her perfect lips, holding a jar of olives as though to taunt them?

"Oh," Isabelle said, "odds and ends—you know."

There was a pause. It was uncomfortable, it really was. And it was their fault. Amy was sure Barbara Rawley could have talked more easily to almost anyone else.

"Well," said Isabelle, "you have a pleasant evening," and she took the carriage from Amy and moved down the aisle.

Following her mother, Amy said, "She's really pretty," taking from a shelf the package of peanut-butter-and-jelly-sandwich crackers that she and Stacy would have for lunch.

Isabelle didn't reply.

"Don't you think she's pretty, though?" Amy pursued.

Isabelle put a package of bloody hamburger meat into the carriage seat. She turned down another aisle. "I suppose," she said mildly, "if one cares for a false, made-up look, one might find her pretty. Personally, I don't."

Amy stood awkwardly while her mother dropped a can of sliced beets into the carriage. She liked makeup, herself. She wanted to wear it, lots of it. Perfume, too—she wanted to be one of those women you could smell when you walked by.

"I just meant she *could* be pretty if she didn't wear all that makeup," Amy said, made anxious by the way Isabelle was frowning at the Raisin Bran.

"She's probably having a dinner party tonight," Isabelle said, squinting at the cereal. "She'll serve those olives in a little silver dish. She can tell her guests how she saw Isabelle Goodrow this afternoon, and they can all have a little laugh about how I decorated the church with autumn leaves and not chrys*an*themums."

Amy had forgotten. Her mother had been really hurt by Barbara Rawley's remarks that day after church, as she stood at coffee hour in the activities room with two bright spots of pink on her cheeks. Her mother had the same bright spots of pink on her cheeks right now as she reached for a jar of applesauce.

"Stand up straight," Isabelle said, scowling at the label on the applesauce jar. "It's terrible the way you slouch. And go up front and get another carriage. This wobbly wheel is driving me nuts."

It was dark out now, the store windows were black except for the square sheets of white paper that advertised products and prices, the automatic swinging doors were humming as people passed through them; boys in their red A&P coats pushed loaded shopping carts over the rubbery mats. Amy took an empty cart, the plastic-coated bar still warm from someone else's hands, and saw Barbara Rawley in the checkout line, her face pleasant and calm as she stared into space, holding the olive jar to her chest as though lost in happy prayer.

Was she having a dinner party tonight? Amy supposed it could be true. Her mother never had dinner parties—and then a thought slipped through Amy's stomach like a hook: Her mother was hardly ever invited anywhere. *What are you two ladies doing tonight?* Nothing. Other people in Shirley Falls would be doing things; Barbara Rawley with a glittering table of china, Stacy out with a boyfriend, maybe off to a party somewhere. (There were references to these sometimes on Mondays in the school, some boy clapping another boy on the shoulder with a laugh, "Guess who puked all over my car.")

Oh, it made Amy sad. Her mother had almost no social life. Here was a fact: Her mother, lonely and alone, with a face earnest and pale, her winter coat shapeless, was bent over the milk, checking the dates on the cartons. "Mom," said Amy, wheeling the new cart up. "You're pretty too." And that was the stupidest thing of all to do, because the words with their awkward falseness seemed to repeat in the silence that followed.

Isabelle, checking her list, finally said, "Go see if you can track down toilet paper, would you?"

The car was cold as they drove home through the back streets. As they got further out of town the houses got smaller and further apart, some of them were dark. They passed a house with a light on over its garage door, the snow-patched driveway in an arc of yellow light, and it made Amy think of Debby Dorne. She pictured the girl falling on her driveway, staying home from school, lying on the couch watching television. Her mother calling at two o'clock, Debby going into the kitchen to pick up the phone.

Amy shifted her feet in the car; the heater was finally making it warm. She thought how Debby had maybe started back into the living room when she heard a car coming up the driveway; maybe she had gone to the window to peek out. Maybe her heart beat fast until she recognized the car, or the person getting out. Maybe she thought, "Oh, phew, it's just him," and opened the door.

Amy stared through the windshield at the dark. A car came toward them, headlights growing bigger, passed them, and was gone. It would have been light out when Debby left her house, but it wouldn't have stayed light for long. Whoever took her away must have taken her in a car; had they been driving in the dark? There were so many back roads, you could drive for miles without seeing a house. Amy chewed her fingernail. Debby would have realized that something was wrong, that she wasn't going wherever the person said they were going. That she wasn't going home. Amy shivered as the heater blew warm on her legs. Maybe Debby had been in the front seat crying. Because she would have finally started to cry, Amy thought. She would have finally pressed her hands to her eyes and cried, "Oh, please, I want my mother."

Amy tapped her fingernail quickly to her teeth. It didn't matter if it was Saturday night and Barbara Rawley was having a party. It only mattered that she was with her mother. It was all that mattered in the whole world—that they were together and safe.

"Stop chewing your fingernail," Isabelle said.

"I was wondering about Debby Kay Dorne," Amy told her, obediently taking her finger out of her mouth and putting her hand in her lap. "I was wondering what she was thinking right now."

"Nothing," said Isabelle, putting on the blinker and turning into their driveway.

The house was cold when they stepped inside. Amy moved through the kitchen with a brown grocery bag held to her hip, the way people sometimes held a small child. There had been times in the past when she pretended that the grocery bag was in fact a child, her child, and she would jostle it gently on her hip, but now she simply set it down on the kitchen counter. She was tired, even slightly dazed.

Isabelle looked at her as she tugged on a sweater. "You need some food," she said.

Bᴜᴛ ᴏɴ Mᴏɴᴅᴀʏ Mr. Robertson said he liked her dress, and how things changed after that! So much for Debby Dorne (who might not be dead—Isabelle and Arlene Tucker didn't know everything), and how gorgeous the gold February sun was that came through the kitchen window as Amy sat at the table doing her homework that afternoon! His intimate, wonderful voice: "A woman should learn to take a compliment gracefully." Amy watched out the window as a chickadee hopped along a pine branch. A woman. That was the best part, the lovely *femaleness* of it implied in the way Mr. Robertson spoke the word; a woman was a lovely thing, and this included her.

It changed everything, in a way. She traced her finger along the edge of the table. Her bra was not some stupid thing from Sears. It was lingerie, a brassiere. And her period, maybe, was not *such* a gross thought. Every woman had one. (Pretty Barbara Rawley.) A woman was a lovely thing to be. Mr. Robertson, his voice gentle and all-knowing, was teaching her. He thought she was worth teaching.

A woman should learn to take a compliment gracefully. She left her homework and went upstairs to her bedroom to practice in front of the mirror. "Thank you," she said (gracefully). "Thank you very much." She brushed her wavy hair back over her shoulders, turning her face one way then the other. "Thank you," she said. "That's very kind."

A rap on her bedroom door. "Are you all right?" Isabelle called. "Who are you talking to?"

"No one," said Amy. "I didn't hear you come home."

"I'm taking a shower," Isabelle said through the door. "Then I'll start dinner."

Amy waited until she heard her mother go into the bathroom. Only she was careful now, she mouthed the words instead. Through her window came the call of a cardinal. A shaft of late-day sunlight fell across her bed. She smiled gracefully into the mirror. *Thank you, yes. That's very kind.* Dropping her eyelids slowly, *Well, that's very kind, what you just said.*

Chapter

5

IT HAD LEFT Isabelle considerably distressed to bump into Barbara Rawley at the grocery store, and she had spent the evening that Saturday fretfully imagining a dinner party in Barbara Rawley's home: wine goblets shimmering in candlelight, soft sounds of laughter—and the horrid thought that her name might be coming up. ("I saw Isabelle Goodrow in the A&P today. She's so odd, I think." And someone poking at an olive with a toothpick would respond, "Decorating the altar with autumn leaves like that." Laughter, the tinkling of glasses. "Didn't the place look like a *barn*.")

Awful.

And all made worse by the fact that on the next day, Sunday, Avery Clark did not show up for church. This was unusual: on most Sundays Avery sat with his wife, Emma, in the third row of pews. Isabelle, who had been taught by her mother years ago that to settle oneself in a front pew meant you were simply in church to be seen, sat discreetly toward the back, peeking past dandruff-flaked shoulders and heads to see if she could find Avery; but she could not.

On the drive home it began to snow. Small flakes, stingy-seeming and gray, spotted the windshield, making the day seem interminable, dull as the road before her. Perhaps the Clarks had gone to a dinner party themselves and had such a merry time that this morning they didn't find it worthwhile to get out of bed. All day Isabelle pondered this, moving through her house. The rooms were dark as evening—even at midday—from the heavy, leaden sky outside, and the snow at one point turned to rain, an uneven wetness dribbling down the windowpanes.

By the time Isabelle stood in her kitchen later that afternoon ironing a pillowcase, the rain having turned to a freezing drizzle and making small shivering sounds against the window, she had found another thought to entertain: Avery Clark was out of town. She ironed the lace edge of the pillowcase carefully and wondered if Avery and his wife had gone to Boston. There were people in Shirley Falls who sometimes went to Boston to see a ballet or visit a museum. There were people who went to Boston simply to *shop*. Barbara Rawley, for one. And some of the other deacons' wives. They made the trip a few times a year, staying overnight in a hotel and returning the next day with new blouses and skirts and strings of beads. To wear to their dinner parties, no doubt.

Why, the dentist's wife went to Boston just to get her hair done! Isabelle remembered this as she folded the pillowcase and started on another. She had learned that news in the dentist's waiting room one day, and it had made her root canal all the more insufferable: lying open-mouthed in the vinyl chair, with that little hose vacuuming up her spit while the dentist's stomach growled beside her head—to suffer such indignity, to stand there afterward in front of the receptionist with a numb and swollen lip (you could never tell if you were dribbling saliva or not) and write out a check for an astonishing sum, knowing that some of it, anyway, was going to pay for Mrs. Errin's next trip to Boston. Just to get her hair done. It irritated Isabelle, and made her sad, too, as she unplugged the iron and emptied the water over the sink, to think of Emma Clark and Avery pulling into their driveway now and unloading their car—he would carry in their suitcases and Emma would follow with a shopping bag of new clothes, expensive perfume, a tasteful pair of pumps.

BUT IT WAS all fruitless conjecture, hours of wasted thought. For when Isabelle arrived at work the next morning and went into Avery's office to inquire brightly, "And did you have a nice weekend, Avery?" the answer was no, he had not.

He had been seized with some kind of "belly bug," he confided to Isabelle, shaking his head, going on to describe how he woke on Saturday morning with excruciating cramps. "Quite nasty," he said, sitting back in his chair, arms clasped behind his head, looking perfectly normal now.

"Well, I'm sorry to hear that," Isabelle said, hugely relieved to think that Avery Clark had not been gallivanting around Boston, or going to some dinner party here in town, but stuck inside his house bent over a toilet bowl instead, a tepid glass of ginger ale left next to his bed. "I hope you're feeling better," she added. "You're *looking* wonderfully well."

If this hadn't been true, she probably would have said it anyway. She believed men were more susceptible to flattery than women, particularly as they aged; she had read in magazines about the private difficulties men often had in later years of life. She doubted Emma Clark was sensitive to this. Emma seemed pretty interested in Emma, and Avery probably suffered. "It can be miserable, can't it," Isabelle said, "that sort of little bug. It can leave one feeling flat. A bit depressed."

"Yes," Avery responded, as though this effect of his belly bug was something he might not have considered. "I'm glad to have it over with." He smiled, clapping his hands down lightly onto his desk. "Glad to be all in one piece."

"Well, nice to know you're feeling better," Isabelle said, "and now I'm going to start my day." She returned to her desk, where she sat tapping some papers together to make their edges even and doubting that really and truly he was very happy with his wife.

Now, if *she* were married to Avery (rolling a sheet of paper into the typewriter and getting rid of Emma Clark with a heart attack that would carry only a few brief moments of panic and pain), Avery might say in response to someone's asking, A nasty bug, but Isabelle took wonderful care of me. Because she would take wonderful care of him, making him Jell-O and wiping his brow, arranging magazines for him on the bed. (Here she made a typo and looked around for her whiteout.) She would sit and talk to him about the hyacinth bulbs to be ordered, how the shower curtain ought to be replaced, she had seen one on sale and what did he think . . . And he would put his hand on hers and say, "I think I'm lucky to be married to you." Yes, Isabelle thought, finding the whiteout and unscrewing the cap, she could make him a happy man.

Amy was in a happy mood herself; Isabelle noticed this as soon as she got home. Her daughter's youthful face was flushed and lovely as she moved about the kitchen helping Isabelle make dinner. The girl's looks could at times be startling; like now, when she positively glowed, when carrying a plate to the table her limbs were graceful and light.

"Today I wore the dress I made in home ec class," Amy reminded her mother as they sat down to eat. "And I got a compliment."

"How nice," Isabelle said. "And from whom did you receive this compliment?" (It pleased her that she knew proper grammar.)

"Oh," said Amy, "you know. Just people." She put meat loaf into her mouth and chewed, her face shiny as she smiled out the window at the last glow of February evening sun. "Everyone liked it," she added. "Everyone."

But still, the moodiness of the girl. Because just a few nights later she was querulous and unpleasant when Isabelle came in. "And how was your day?" Isabelle said, dropping her keys on the table, removing her coat.

"All right," Amy said flatly, closing her schoolbooks, pushing back her chair, preparing to leave the room.

"Just all right?" Isabelle felt a flicker of dread. "What's wrong?" It was impossible to feel any semblance of peace if something was wrong with her daughter; and Isabelle's own day had merely been average, Avery Clark having been busy and distracted.

Amy made a grunting noise and started up the stairs. Isabelle followed her to the doorway. "What's wrong?" she asked again, watching the long thin legs of her daughter in their black tights moving up the stairs.

"Nothing's wrong," Amy said tensely.

"Amy Goodrow, stop right where you are."

Amy turned, gazing at her mother from the stair landing, her face closed off, expressionless, half hidden by her voluminous hair.

"I am your mother," Isabelle said, with sudden despair, "and there is absolutely no reason for you to speak to me that way. Whether you like it or not we share the same house, and I work hard all day at a *stupid* job I am vastly overqualified for simply to keep food in your mouth." She hated herself, saying this. To say she was vastly overqualified for her job was foolishness and they both knew it. Isabelle had never finished college. She could hardly expect a better job than the one she had now. Still—she had not finished college because her mother had died and there was no one to take care of the baby. So really it was because of Amy, this very person who was now staring down the staircase at her with disdain. "And take that look off your face," Isabelle said. "I would appreciate it if you could be pleasant to me. I would appreciate a little common decency in the way you look at me and the way you speak to me, too."

Silence.

"Do you understand?"

"Yes." Spoken carefully—enough coolness to leave no mistake that she found her mother detestable, but not so cool as to allow her mother to continue her accusations of rudeness, and so Isabelle turned away, hanging her coat in the front hall closet and hearing the door to Amy's room shut.

Such moments alarmed Isabelle. It alarmed her that anger could erupt in her so easily, provoked by a simple glance from her adolescent daughter. Adolescents were going to be moody, after all; there was all that business with their hormones.

Isabelle sat down at the kitchen table, holding her hands to her face; such an unpleasant way to begin the evening. She should not have lost her temper. She should have been patient, as the *Reader's Digest* suggested in their occasional articles on teenagers. And then Amy might have told her what was wrong. She wanted to be a patient mother, of course. But it did irritate her to work all day and come home tired and have Amy grumpy. It did irritate her sometimes to think of the enormous sacrifices she had made (really, *enormous*) for this girl, and so of course it made her angry to have Amy close her books and leave the room just because Isabelle had walked in. Was she a shrew simply because she would like a pleasant hello from her daughter? Was she some beast because she longed for a pleasant "Hi, Mom, how was your day?"

from a girl who virtually owned her life? And then Isabelle heard her daughter's bedroom door open and she breathed more easily, knowing an apology was coming, and grateful that it had not taken too long.

For it was true that Amy could not bear to have her mother angry with her. It frightened her profoundly; she had nothing to stand on, it was like swaying in darkness. She walked down the stairs silently in her stockinged feet. "I'm sorry," Amy said. "I'm sorry." Sometimes her mother would say, "Sorry isn't enough."

Tonight, though, she only said, "Okay. Thank you very much." But she did not ask again what was wrong with her daughter, and if she had, Amy would not have told.

It was Mr. Robertson. So he had complimented her dress, but after that—nothing. And now it was like a bug, some infection, this terrible craving to be noticed by him. Every day she brushed her hair before class, pinched her cheeks right before walking into the room. Every day she took her seat carefully, heart beating with hope. And every day when the bell rang and his eyes had not once passed over hers, she would leave the classroom with a disappointment bigger than any she could remember.

"I hate school," she told Stacy in the woods. "I hate my life, I hate everything."

Stacy, puffing dryly on a cigarette, would squint against the smoke and nod. "I hate everything, too," she said.

"But why?" Amy finally asked her. It was the end of February now; the day was colorless but warm; the crusty snow had softened and Stacy's leather boots had stains of wet. "Why do *you* hate everything?" Amy asked. "I mean, you're pretty, and you have lots of friends, and you have a boyfriend. How come you're miserable like me?"

Stacy looked carefully at the end of her cigarette. "Because my parents are rat-fucks and my friends are morons. Except for you."

"Yeah, still." Amy leaned against the log and crossed her arms. Who cared if parents were jerks and friends were jerks as long as you had a boyfriend. Stacy had such a great boyfriend, too. He wasn't mentioned a lot out here in the woods, but Amy knew who Paul Bellows was, that he lived in his own apartment now, over a bakery on Main Street, that when he was in high school he'd been a football champion. The cheer-leaders had a special cheer for him. One time he had broken his leg during a game and there were people who actually cried when he got hauled off on a stretcher. He was tall and big and had brown eyes.

"He's stupid," Stacy said, after considering things awhile.

"He has nice eyes."

Stacy ignored this. She tossed her cigarette into the woods and gazed vacantly after it. "He's boring," she added. "All he ever wants to do is go to bed."

This made Amy feel queer. She inhaled deeply on her cigarette.

"He's all right, though," Stacy decided. "He's nice to me. He bought me eyeshadow the other day." Her face cheered as she thought of this. "A gorgeous turquoise color."

"That's nice," Amy said. She stood up; the back of her coat was damp. A scooped-out impression was left in the snow where she had been leaning against the log.

"It's the expensive kind," Stacy added. "It doesn't cake up. I'll bring it to school tomorrow. I bet it would look nice on you."

Amy stepped on her cigarette. "My mother would kill me if I wore makeup."

"Yeah, well—all parents are rat-fucks," Stacy said sympathetically, as behind them the school bell rang.

ON FRIDAY MR. Robertson said he would see her after school. Amy had maneuvered this. She had become desperate, crazy, somebody else. She had started to wonder, as the days went by, why Alan Stewart, simply by clicking his pen after Mr. Robertson asked him to stop, should be allowed the magnificent event of sitting with Mr. Robertson in his classroom for an hour after school. Why not her? Terrence Landry had been kept after school for blowing up a lunch bag and popping it loudly on his way out of class. Amy could not imagine blowing up a lunch bag and then smashing it (a muffled *whoomph*, as though someone wrapped up in a quilt had been shot), nor did she think she could even keep on clicking a pen, but Maryanne Barmble had been threatened with detention once after whispering to the person next to her.

"Maryanne," Mr. Robertson had said crossly, "if I have to ask you to quiet down one more time, you will be kept after school."

So Amy began to whisper to Elsie Baxter behind her. It took courage, it was not her style. But Elsie, so uncontained and boisterous, was co-operative. Amy whispered that the homework last night was boring, real crap. Elsie said it was pus-colored pee. Mr. Robertson said, "Girls, be quiet please."

The tension got exhausting. Amy's face was moist, her armpits prickled. She turned to Elsie again. "At least it's not home ec class," she whispered, "with that knock-kneed pinhead." Elsie let loose a full-throated giggle. Mr. Robertson stopped the class and stared at them both without speaking. Amy's face burned; she looked down at her desk.

But when it was clear that nothing was to come of this, when Mr. Robertson proceeded with his figures on the blackboard, disappointment made Amy feel crazy again. She turned and rolled her eyes at Elsie. "Amy," came Mr. Robertson's deep voice, "one more time and you'll be staying after school."

The dangers in this! Not the least being that he might keep Elsie as well as herself. But the promise of *one more time* was too great to pass up. Amy glanced at the clock—twenty minutes left. Her heart bounced around inside her chest; the figures on her worksheet were almost a blur. Beside her, Flip Rawley tapped his eraser to his cheek, oblivious. The clock make a click. Amy felt something inside her collapse with despair, and she might have given up on her endeavor completely if Mr. Robertson hadn't at that very moment complimented Julie LaGuinn in the front row for answering some question he had just asked.

"*Good* for you," he said to Julie, rapping his piece of chalk on her desk. "That was very, very good. I'm throwing out something new and you're able to follow."

It made Amy feel crazy. All the times she had sat there knowing the right answer but being too shy to raise her hand, and there was Julie LaGuinn with a pukey, self-satisfied grin on her face, soaking up this stupid man's praise. Amy turned to Elsie. "I guess the rest of us are stupid," and then it happened. His voice: "All right, Amy. I'll see you after school."

Triumphant, successful, she was filled with shame. She thought Flip

Rawley glanced at her. Amy Goodrow staying after school? When the bell rang, she kept her head down as she left the room.

INSUFFERABLE CLASSES: HISTORY as dull as death; Spanish pale and endless. There was no meaning to anything except for the fact that after school she would sit in Mr. Robertson's classroom. And when the final bell rang she was exhausted, as though she had gone for a very long time without food. In the girls' room she studied herself in the mirror above the row of sinks. This was her? This was what people saw when they looked at her? Her hair was nice but her face seemed without expression, and how could it be when so much was going on inside her? She pulled open the door of the girls' room and it swung shut behind her, a tired *thunk*.

The hallway was empty. She had never stayed after school before and it was a different place this time of day. The sun falling over the classroom floors seemed a deeper shade of yellow; the large windowsills and dusty blackboards had a friendly, worn-out feeling to them, the way her clothes sometimes felt at the end of the day. Around her was the silence of an empty hallway, although she could hear in the distance the echo of cheerleaders practicing in the gym.

Mr. Robertson was sitting at his desk in the back of the room, writing, when she came in. "Have a seat," he said, without looking up.

She chose a desk up near the blackboard instead of her usual place, and sat down quietly, unsure of what to do. She squinted toward the window; dust particles hung suspended in the afternoon air, lit by a shaft of sunlight. Down the hall was the metallic sound of a locker being slammed shut and, closer by, the janitor's broom bumping against the stairwell.

She heard Mr. Robertson drop a pencil onto his desk. "Get started on your homework," he said mildly, "if you want to."

"I don't want to," she answered, shaking her head; and then, like that, there were tears in her eyes. Such terrible sadness! Such a sudden collapse; she was worn down by her afternoon of anticipation. She sat with her hands in her lap, away from him. Her hair hung down on either side of her face, and squeezing her eyes she felt warm tears drop on her hands.

"Amy." He had gotten up from his desk and was walking over to her. "Amy," he said again, appearing beside her. He spoke her name gently, his voice a soft strumming, so grave, serious. Had anyone ever spoken to her this seriously before? "I understand, Amy," he said. "It's okay."

He must have understood something, because the tears did not seem to alarm him, or even puzzle him. He sat down at the desk beside her and simply handed her his handkerchief. It was a red bandanna, big as a place mat, and she took it, rubbed her eyes, blew her nose. It should have been excruciating to be crying in front of this man, but it was not. And that must have had to do with his lack of surprise, with the kind weariness she saw in his eyes. She gave him back his handkerchief.

"I know this poem," she finally said, and he smiled at the way she said *poyme,* at the way she sat simply, like a child, her eyes still wet and slightly red. She struck him as something entirely innocent, and bruised.

"It's a poem by Edna St. Vincent Millay," she explained, tucking her hair back behind her ear, "and one time in class I thought of it. The first line is, uhm—is 'Euclid alone looked on beauty bare,' I think that's it."

He nodded slowly, his gingery eyebrows raised. " 'Let all who prate of beauty hold their peace.' "

"You *know* it," she said, amazed.

He nodded again, his eyebrows drawn together thoughtfully, as though he was considering something he had not thought he would be called upon to consider.

"You know it," Amy repeated. "I can't believe you know that poem." For her it was as though some bird had just flown free after being kept in a cardboard box. "Do you know any others?" She turned in her chair so that she was facing him, their knees not far apart. "By Millay, I mean. Do you know any others?"

Mr. Robertson spread his fingers over his mouth, contemplating her. Then he answered, "Yes, I know others. Her sonnets. 'Time does not bring relief; you all have lied . . .' "

" 'Who told me time would ease me of my pain,' " Amy finished, bouncing slightly in her chair, and her hair, tucked behind her ear, slipped loose, catching the slice of sunlight that fell through the window, so that she saw him through a golden haze; she saw the surprise and interest on his face, and then she saw something else, something she would remember for a very long time: a motion deep within his eyes, as though something had just shifted underneath.

He stood and moved to the window, his hands in the pockets of his corduroy pants. "Come look at this sky," he said, nodding his head toward the window. "I bet it's going to snow tonight." He turned in her direction, then back to the window. "Come look," he said again.

Obediently she went to the window. The sky had turned fierce and poignant, dark clouds moving in, and the harsh winter sun, golden at this time of day, as though it had been gathering force since morning, now lit a bank of clouds in the west so that a part of their darkness was rimmed in an almost electrical light.

"Oh, I love it when it's like that," Amy said. "Look." She pointed at the funneled rays of sun splayed down over the snow-crusted street. "I just love that. In real life, I mean. I don't like it in pictures so much."

He watched her, biting down on his mustachy lip.

"This old woman I used to have to clean house for when I was in seventh grade—this old lady from the church," Amy explained, "—she had these ugly old-fashioned paintings in her living room. This girl who looked embalmed. Like a pincushion. Do you know the kind of painting I mean?"

He kept watching her carefully. "Perhaps. Go on."

"It gave me the willies," Amy said. "Dusting the chairs and having that girl stare down at me."

Mr. Robertson moved to lean against the windowsill, facing her, his ankles crossed. He ran two fingers lightly over his mustache. "I had no idea you could talk so much," he mused.

"Me either." Her answer was ingenuous. She looked past him out the window again. The clouds were darker, still competing with the sun; light and dark on the spread-out wintry sky. "Anyways," Amy said (such a tangled bunch of words hopping and bumping inside her), "there was this other picture in the old lady's house that was old-fashioned too, where the sky is all dark but there's bright rays of sun cutting through. And some battle with horses or something—you know, little figures—going on underneath. That kind of picture."

Mr. Robertson nodded. She spoke "picture" as *pitcher,* and he was careful not to smile. Plus how she said *anyways.* "Yes?"

"Well, I don't like that kind of pitcher."

"I see."

"The sky looks so fake and dramatic. But in real life"—Amy indicated with her hand the sky out the window—"it's a different story. Then I love it when it looks that way."

Mr. Robertson nodded again. "Chiaroscuro," he said in a teacherly way.

She glanced at him and looked away, disappointed he would suddenly speak in a foreign phrase. It fuddled her head, made her feel simple and stupid.

"Chiaroscuro," Mr. Robertson repeated. "It's Italian. Lightness and dark. Lightness obscured." He turned to look at the sky. "Like that."

If earlier Amy had had the image of a bird let out of a box, the bird began to falter now. But Mr. Robertson looked at her kindly. "So you no longer clean house for the old woman?"

"No," Amy said. "She got sick and she's in a nursing home somewhere."

"I see." Mr. Robertson sat back on the wide windowsill, a hand on either side of him, his torso thrust forward. "How come you didn't like to clean her house?" The way he asked the question made her feel like he actually wanted to know.

She considered this. "Because it was lonely," she said.

He narrowed his eyes thoughtfully. "Tell me."

"The place was all sterile and icky. Like a museum. I don't know why she had me come once a week, because nothing was ever dirty."

"You did a good job, then," he said, smiling, but she was interrupting him already.

"Like the fireplace. It was never used. She had these birch logs all stacked up in it and she had me wash the logs every week with Lestoil and warm water. Washing those logs." Amy shook her head. "It was weird."

"It sounds depressing." Mr. Robertson nodded.

"It was depressing. That's exactly what it was." Amy nodded quickly. (He understood so *much*.)

"And how did this job come about?" He tilted his head with curiosity.

"An announcement in the church program." Amy held her hands together behind her back and turned slightly to and fro as she talked. It was like drinking fresh water to be able to talk like this. "That she needed someone to help out, so my mother thought it would be nice if I did it. My mother likes to make a good impression at the church."

"Let me guess." Mr. Robertson drew his head back, studying her, contemplating this latest addition to the picture. (For Mr. Robertson, it's true, was a man who enjoyed contemplating things—"an observer of life," he liked to say, observing now how very thin Amy Goodrow's arms were, with her hands clasped behind her back.) "I don't imagine somehow that you're Catholic. I'd say . . . a Congregationalist."

Amy beamed; it was like he was a mind reader. "How did you know?"

"You look it," he said simply. "You appear it." He hopped down off the windowsill and walked to the front of the classroom, where he began to erase the blackboard. "Did you know you looked like a Congregationalist?" His arm worked vigorously.

She moved slowly down the aisle and sat in the seat where Flip Rawley always sat. "No," she said honestly, "because I don't know what I look like." She picked up a few strands of hair from her shoulder and examined them for split ends.

"Like a doe." He dropped the eraser in the chalk tray and dusted off his hands. "A doe in the woods." (It was her skinny arms and legs.) "But then of course there's that hair of yours," he added.

She blushed and peered at him warily, her head ducked down.

"No, really. It's interesting." He swung his leg over the chair where Elsie Baxter usually sat, straddling the chair backwards. "I taught sixth grade in Massachusetts for a while, and then three years later I taught ninth grade there, so I had a lot of the same students again. And it's interesting, girls at that age. Many overnight become bovine."

"What's bovine?" Amy was still studying her hair; his observations on the development of girls made her self-conscious.

"Cowlike. Bovine." He spelled the word. "And then there are others who remain thin and leggy. Like young does."

"A Congregational doe," Amy said, speaking to cover up her embarrassment. She tossed her hair back over her shoulder and breathed in deeply, as though in need of air. She clasped her hands together in her lap.

"That's right. A Congregational doe."

The pleasant, jokey way he said this made her smile at him.

"Tell me what else you don't like, Amy," he said, leaning his arms forward over the back of Elsie Baxter's chair. "You don't like cleaning for old ladies. What else?"

"I don't like snakes. I don't like snakes so much I can't even stand to think about them." This was true. At the thought of a snake she could not bear to keep her feet on the floor out of sight, and so she stood now, walking anxiously to the back of the room and then over to the windows. The clouds had moved in almost completely; just a fragment of setting sunlight showed in one far-off part of the horizon. A few cars driving past had their headlights on.

"All right," Mr. Robertson said. He had turned in his chair to watch her. "We'll forget about snakes, then. What is it you *do* like?"

Being here with you, she wanted to say. She ran her hand over the varnished wood of the windowsill. In places it had risen in thin puckers and cracked; other parts were smooth and very shiny with years of reapplied shellac.

"Poems, I guess," she said after a moment. "The ones I understand, anyway. A lot of poems I don't understand, and then I feel stupid."

"You're not stupid," he said, still sitting in the same position in Elsie Baxter's chair. "You shouldn't worry that you're stupid."

"Thank you," she said sincerely. "But like that Euclid poem. I never knew what that meant until you were talking about triangles that day— you know, the beauty of a triangle or something. I probably still don't know what it means. Like what does *prate* mean? Let all who *prate* of beauty."

Mr. Robertson stood up and walked to his desk. "Come here," he said. He was tapping a dictionary bound in dark green leather; it was the size of a Sears catalogue.

"That's nice," said Amy, coming to stand by him.

"I like words," he told her. "Like 'chiaroscuro.'" He glanced at the window. "No chiar now," he said playfully, "just scuro, I guess. Have a seat."

She sat in the chair next to his desk, and when he handed the dictionary to her, telling her to look up the word "prate," his fingertips accidentally ran across the side of her hand, and for a moment she felt a quick funnel-shaped suction straight down through the middle of her insides, and then they sat together with their heads bent over the dictionary while the last of the February sun faded from the sky, Mr. Robertson with wrinkles springing around his eyes as Amy whispered quickly, furtively, under her breath, the alphabet in order to find out that *P* came after *O,* and then there were more words to look up, and after a while the janitor's thumping broom could no longer be heard, and the cheerleaders who had clapped and stomped in the gym went home.

ISABELLE SWITCHED ON the radio in her car. The dark clouds worried her; they seemed too dark for snow, and yet what other kind of storm were you going to get this time of year? Once in a blue moon you heard of a tornado coming through, although Isabelle's understanding of a tornado was limited—she didn't think it darkened the whole sky: the only story she could recall from her youth was of a man driving down the turnpike when a tornado lifted his car up completely, and not far away the sky stayed blue. She couldn't recall what happened to the man, and doubted now if the story was true. She fiddled with the dial to catch a weather report. Chances were it would be a heavy snowstorm, and that might start the roof leaking again. This thought depressed her. She would have to call up Mr. Crane if this was to be the case.

". . . family has offered a reward for anyone giving information that leads to an arrest in the case of the missing girl, Deborah Kay Dorne, who disappeared from her home on February tenth. So far no suspects have been named."

The poor family. Isabelle shook her head slightly. The poor *mother.* Isabelle switched off the radio as she turned into her driveway. But she felt bumped by chilly silence: the house was dark.

"Amy?" she called, unlocking the door. "Amy? Where are you?" She dropped her keys on the kitchen table and the sound was brief, immense.

She switched on the light. "Amy?"

Into the living room; switching on the light there. "Amy?"

She went from room to room, light switch to light switch, up the stairs. *"Amy."*

The bedroom was empty. The bathroom was empty. Her own bedroom was empty. She opened the closet in the upstairs hall. Folded towels sat quietly, three rolls of toilet paper stared out unperturbed.

And now she felt hysterical. Now she felt as though cold water were pouring through her arms, her legs. She went down the stairs, stumbling at the bottom, bracing herself against the wall. This isn't happening, she thought. This isn't happening. Because clearly whoever had taken away poor Debby Dorne had come now and taken Amy. "Amy!" she called.

She began again. Every room, every closet, every light. She reached for the telephone. Who would she call? The police. The school. Avery Clark. Most likely they would all tell her to check with Amy's friends. They would all say, Oh, give her some time, she'll be home. But she is *never* not home after school, Isabelle wailed silently. I know my daughter, and something is *wrong*. She sat down in a chair and began to sob. Huge, awful sounds erupted from her throat. Amy, Amy, she cried.

And then there she was. First the sound of her boots on the front porch steps, and then the door shoved open quickly. "Mom, are you all right?"

There she was, this daughter. This girl, without whom Isabelle's insides had become the black, deep water of terror, stood now in the kitchen, her cheeks flushed, her eyes huge. "Are you all right?" she asked again, looking at Isabelle as though she were a ghost.

"Where *were* you?" Isabelle demanded. "My God, Amy, you scared me to death!"

"I stayed after school," Amy said. "To get help with math." She turned away from her mother as she unbuttoned her coat. "A bunch of us did. A bunch of us in the class stayed after school."

And Isabelle, with tears still wet on her cheeks, had some incoherent sense that she had just been made a fool.

The days got longer. And warmer, too; very slowly the snows softened, leaving slush on steps and sidewalks and alongside the roads. On days when Amy walked home from school after talking to Mr. Robertson—careful now to leave in time to get home before her mother did—the day's warmth would be over, and though the sun still shone, a white luminescent wafer in the milky sky, she could feel as she walked, holding her books to her chest, coat unzipped, the moist chill that settled over her bare neck and hands and wrists. The late-afternoon sky that spread out above Larkindale's field, the stone wall disappearing over the white slope, the tree trunks darkened by the melting snow— all this seemed to her to promise spring. Even a small flock of birds far away in the sky promised something, in the absolute silence with which they beat their wings.

To Amy it seemed a ceiling had been lifted, that the sky was higher than before, and sometimes—if no car was passing by—she would raise an arm and move it through the air. A mass of joy was in her from the squinting, humorous eyes of Mr. Robertson, and a jumbled, rushing sense from all the things she had wanted to tell him and had forgotten to. But there were small squares of sadness inside her as well, as though something dark and wobbly sat deep within her chest, and sometimes she would stop as she reached the overpass to gaze down at the cars that rushed by on the highway, puzzled by a sense of losing things, and only vaguely knowing this was connected somehow to the thought of her mother. And then Amy would hurry home, anxious to see in the empty house signs of her mother: the pantyhose hanging over the shower nozzle, the baby powder on her mother's bureau—these things would reassure her, as would the sound of her mother's car turning into the gravelly driveway. It was all right. Her mother was home.

And yet the actual presence of her mother provided disappointment— the small, anxious eyes as she came through the door, the pale hand fluttering to tuck up the brown strands of hair that escaped from the tired French twist. It was hard for Amy to match this woman to the mother she had just missed. Guilty, she sometimes ran the risk of being too solicitous. "That blouse looks really nice, Mom," she might say, and then inwardly flinch at the brief wariness in her mother's eye, a wariness so fleeting that even Isabelle was not conscious of having felt it; months would go by before Isabelle recalled those drops of warning that glinted for a moment on the outer edges of her mind.

"I really like poetry," Amy announced to Isabelle a few weeks after the dreadful night Isabelle had come home to find the house empty and had believed for those terrible minutes that her daughter had been taken away like poor Debby Kay Dorne. "I really, really like poetry."

"Well, I think that's very nice," Isabelle said, distracted by the run she had just discovered in her pantyhose.

"I got this book." Amy stood in the doorway to the living room, holding a book carefully in both hands, her face hidden by her hair as she gazed down at what she held.

Isabelle hung her coat in the front hall closet and turned to examine the back of her leg again. "I have no idea when that happened," she mused. "For all I know I've been running around like this half the day." She stepped past Amy to go up the stairs. "What book is that, honey?" she said.

Amy held the book out in front of Isabelle, still holding it with both hands, and Isabelle peered at it as she passed by. "Oh, Yeats," she said, pronouncing it *Yeets,* "Yes, of course. I've heard of him. He wrote some lovely things, I believe."

She was halfway up the stairs when behind her Amy said quietly, "It's Yeats, Mom. Not Yeets."

Isabelle turned. "What's that?" she asked, embarrassment already spreading throughout her throat, her chest.

"Yeats," Amy answered. "You probably just got it mixed up with Keats, which is spelled the same way almost."

If her daughter had spoken this sardonically, with an adolescent disdain, it would have been easier to bear. But the girl had said it gently, with hesitant politeness, and Isabelle was suffering as she stood, half-turned, a run in her pantyhose, awkwardly on the stairs.

"Keats was English," Amy said, as though trying to be helpful, "and Yeats was Irish. Keats died when he was really young, of TB."

"Oh yes. Well, I see." The shame was like a too-tight sweater pressed to her; the moistness of perspiration sprang out on her face, beneath her arms. Here was something new to fear—her daughter's pity for her ignorance. "That's very interesting, Amy," she said, continuing up the stairs. "I want to hear more about it."

That night Isabelle lay in bed with her eyes open. For years she had pictured this: Amy off at college. Not the community college here in Shirley Falls, but a real college somewhere. She had pictured Amy walking on an autumn day, holding notebooks against a navy-blue sweater, a plaid skirt swinging at her knees. Never mind that nowadays there were such grubby-looking girls running around, their unharnessed breasts flopping beneath some T-shirt above a filthy pair of jeans. There were still lovely girls to be seen on college campuses, Isabelle was sure; serious, intelligent girls who read Plato and Shakespeare and Yeats. Or Keats. She sat up, rearranged her pillow, then lay down again.

In all the times she had imagined Amy on some college campus, she had never imagined what she saw now: her daughter would be ashamed of her. Amy, walking across a leafy lawn, laughing with her new, intelligent friends, was not going to say *My mother works in a mill.* She was not going to invite these girls home on weekends or holidays, and neither would she share with Isabelle the wonderful things she was learning, because in her eyes Isabelle was a small-town dummy who worked in a mill. A person to be careful with, the way Amy had been careful with her that evening. It was some time before Isabelle was able to fall asleep.

At the mill the next day, as the women moved into the lunchroom, Isabelle murmured to Arlene Tucker that she was off to the bank for an errand, but instead, buttoning her coat quickly against the March wind, she walked across the parking lot and then drove over the bridge to the one bookstore Shirley Falls had for itself. The thought had come to her that morning as she watched Amy gathering her schoolbooks that she could educate herself. After all, she knew how to read. She could read and study just as though she were taking some course. Why not? She remembered a cousin of her father's, a kindly, pink-faced woman who was a splendid cook. "There's nothing magical about being a good cook," the woman had confided to Isabelle one day. "Get a cookbook. If you can read, you can cook."

And yet stepping into the bookstore, Isabelle glanced around self-consciously, afraid someone from the church might see her—Emma Clark, Barbara Rawley—and say with surprise, "Isabelle Goodrow. What are *you* doing here?" But the place was empty except for a man with wire-rimmed glasses slipping down his nose and another man holding a briefcase. There were a lot of books. She was struck by this as she walked cautiously over the carpeted floor. It's not as though she had never been in a bookstore, for heaven's sake, but it did seem there were a lot of books. She tilted her face sideways to read the titles. She had not realized you could buy Shakespeare in these little paperbacks. Reaching for one, she was pleased with how accessible it seemed, a slim book with a lovely drawing and the elaborately printed lettering: *Hamlet*.

Hamlet. Isabelle nodded as she walked over the carpet. She had heard of *Hamlet*, of course; there was a mother, and a girlfriend who went mad. Although she might be thinking of something else. Something Greek. At the cash register she felt anxious with the enormousness of what she was taking on. But the young clerk, whose chin was covered with a sprinkling of blond whiskers, rang up the purchase with indifference, and this pleased Isabelle. There was nothing in her appearance, evidently, that caused him to find it unusual that she was buying Shakespeare's *Hamlet*. She must look the part. (She smiled, realizing she had made a small joke.) Slipping the purchase into her pocketbook, she crossed the windy street to her car and drove over the bridge, back to the mill.

All afternoon her spirits were high because she was going to become well-read. Typing a letter to Beltco Suppliers, Incorporated, Isabelle thought how she would be able to say lightly to someone, "That reminds me of the scene in *Hamlet* when . . ." Not her fellow workers in the mill, of course (she smiled at Fat Bev, who was just now lumbering back from the water fountain, wiping her hand across her mouth)—no, she wouldn't mention Shakespeare to them. But her daughter, someday, would appreciate this—the two of them sitting in a coffee shop talking about Shakespeare's plays. And meanwhile the women at church—those intimidating deacons' wives who wore their college educations as subtly as they did their expensive perfumes, and with the same confidence— would finally realize that Isabelle was not what they had thought. She was not simply a single mother who worked at the mill but instead a woman of intelligence and stamina who could quote Shakespeare at the drop of a hat.

During the afternoon break, she accepted Arlene's offer of a piece of chocolate candy bar, and even gave Lenora Snibbens a sympathetic nod when Lenora rolled her eyes at the skinny backside of Rosie Tanguay leaving the room. Rosie and Lenora had a long-standing feud. Isabelle could not recall at this point the extensive compilation of details that had gone into this, but she did remember it had begun when Lenora had a dream in which the teetotaling Rosie was very drunk and doing a striptease in the post office lobby. Lenora had made the unfortunate mistake of reporting this dream in the lunchroom, accompanied by a great deal of hilarity, and Rosie had not spoken to her since.

Isabelle, who in all her years at the mill had been scrupulous about not taking sides in any of the frequent disgruntlements that were apt to arise, now, with *Hamlet* in her pocketbook, felt transcendent enough to give Lenora Snibbens that sympathetic smile.

Lenora, after all, was a nice girl. She had buckteeth and a bad complexion, which she seemed to endure with cheerful self-deprecation, and while she may have lacked some common sense in repeating the dream of Rosie, it was tiresome of course to have Rosie get so mean. Although, thought Isabelle, thanking Arlene for the chocolate and heading back to her desk while she touched a tissue to her lips, one could feel sorry for Rosie Tanguay as well. (Rosie had just come out of the ladies' room, her forehead tight with its usual tension.) Isabelle sat at her desk, sharpening her pencil before proofreading the letter to Beltco Suppliers once again. One really should feel sorry for these women in the office room, their tedious days filled with boring work and bath-room jokes and long-simmering feuds. Sad, really. Her tongue moved across the back of her teeth, the final taste of chocolate disappearing now. Gently she blew on her sharpened pencil.

She was different. She was Isabelle Goodrow and she was going to read.

Stacy's eyes were red. It was almost April, but the day was cold, and both girls, their coats open, were shivering. Stacy brought the plastic Tampax holder out of her pocket and removed their cigarettes. "I broke up with Paul," she said.

Amy waited, then said, "You're kidding," thinking that Stacy must be kidding—she had delivered the news so flatly.

And Amy's mind was jumbled. Mr. Robertson had said to her as she left class that morning, "See me after school. I have a book you might like." It was hard to concentrate on anything after that.

Stacy put two cigarettes between her plump lips and lit them while Amy watched. The match went out. "Fuck," said Stacy from the side of her mouth, and tucked her hair behind her ear before lighting another one. "I'm not kidding." The second match was successful. Stacy sucked for a moment while the tips of the cigarettes turned gray. "I told him to get the fuck out of my life." She handed a cigarette to Amy and inhaled deeply on her own.

Amy had no idea what to say. That Stacy, having been so blessed as to have a boyfriend with the status of Paul Bellows, would then tell him to get the fuck out of her life made her appear in Amy's eyes to have a splendor and magnificence, a courage and independence, beyond any she could imagine. "How *come*?" Amy asked.

"His fucking mother accused me of being pregnant." Stacy's eyes moistened, reddening around the edges again. "Stupid mother-fucking cow."

What foreignness to Amy! Boyfriends with their own apartments, and then the mothers of these boyfriends . . . such words said. "She accused you of being pregnant?" Amy asked. "You mean she said that? To you?" It didn't seem polite to take a drag of the cigarette in the face of such a thing. She held it by her side, smoke weaving up her arm.

"To Paul—she said it to Paul." Stacy sniffed and wiped her nose with the back of the hand that held her cigarette. "That I was getting fat."

"Wow," Amy offered. "What a bitch." But she could not stop her eyes from dropping to Stacy's stomach, and Stacy's eyes went there too. For a moment they stood in the silent woods gazing at the part of Stacy's black sweater that could be seen through her open coat.

"You're not fat," Amy said, thinking that she was, just a little. But Stacy had never been skinny; it was hard to tell.

"I think I have a tumor," Stacy said glumly. She looked up through the trees. "One of those stupid fucking tumors women get."

"Then you ought to see a doctor," Amy said seriously.

"So Paul came over last night," Stacy went on, "and I told him that was it. Just get the fuck out."

"What did he say?" The sound of a car made them both turn and duck down, where they stayed squatted, facing each other until the car had driven by. Amy stood, offering her arm to Stacy, who grinned half-apologetically as she hoisted herself up.

"See what a load I am?" she said, squinting at her cigarette before she took a puff.

"You look great," Amy told her, because she did, with her leather skirt and black tights and black boots. Amy would have given anything to look like that; to have a short leather skirt. Her own skirt was a green corduroy that her mother had made, and it was much too long, almost to her knees. "So what did Paul say?" she asked again.

Stacy sighed deeply, shaking her head, her eyes practically closed in recalling this. "You want to know what he did?" She shook her head again. "You won't believe what he did. He cried." She looked at Amy with discouragement, then rolled her cigarette pensively against the tree trunk until it looked like a sharpened pencil. "Christ, he fucking cried." She inhaled and tossed her cigarette onto the snow where it lay silently, a thin waft of gray smoke rising from it, barely distinguishable from the color of the snow.

"Boy," said Amy. "He really likes you."

Stacy made a noise, a grunting from her throat, and Amy saw that her eyes were filled with tears. "These stupid boots are leaking," Stacy said, bending over, poking her finger along the toe's edge.

"I have this dumb hole in the lining of my coat," Amy said, opening her coat wide and twisting her head around to examine the rip in the lining of the armpit, which was of no interest to her at all except for providing her friend with a moment of privacy. "This coat is so old. I never liked it anyway. The plaid looks like a man. I mean something a man would wear." She wanted to make noise so Stacy wouldn't feel watched. "I hate all my stupid clothes."

Stacy was still bent over her boots, and Amy, glancing briefly, saw that she was wiping at her nose. But in a moment Stacy straightened up and said, "The coat's okay. The lining doesn't show."

"I hate winter coats period," Amy said. "I especially hate wearing a winter coat this time of year."

"I know. Me too." Stacy ran her hand over her nose.

"The crocuses next to our house are up," Amy said, taking her second cigarette from Stacy.

"Neat," Stacy answered. She lit her cigarette and held out the match. "Don't burn your hair," she cautioned. "Have you ever smelled burned hair? It's really nasty. And it goes up in a flash." Stacy blew the match out, dropping it on the snow. She snapped her fingers. "Like that. Your whole head of hair could go up in flames like that."

"Great," Amy said. "There's a thought." She tugged her coat around her and leaned back against the fallen tree trunk.

"Well, don't think about it," Stacy said, settling herself on the log as well, close to Amy, so that their shoulders touched through their coats as they shivered and smoked.

"I didn't do my Spanish homework," Stacy mentioned after a while, and from that Amy knew they weren't going to talk about Paul Bellows anymore.

"You can copy mine." Amy pointed up at the spruce tree to a cardinal. "In study hall."

"Yeah, but Miss Lanier will know." Stacy glanced at the cardinal with little interest. "The answers will be right and she'll know they're not mine."

"Screw up a few," Amy suggested, and Stacy nodded. "She's nice, though, she won't say anything." And Stacy nodded again.

Amy tried blowing smoke rings, puckering her mouth like a fish and darting her tongue the way Stacy had tried to teach her, but she was not successful. The smoke came out of her mouth in cylinder spurts. She felt vaguely ill with the anxiety of seeing Mr. Robertson after school. (Once, when she was talking with him last week, he had moved past her to close the window and very lightly, very briefly, touched her on the shoulder.) She wanted to ask Stacy more about Paul, but it would be impolite to push. She wanted to take another look at Stacy's stomach, too, and she was afraid her eyes would go there involuntarily, so she concentrated on her smoke rings. There was a lot she didn't understand. Did Stacy think she was pregnant, or was it just Paul's mother being mean? You could tell if you were pregnant though. Even she knew that.

"It just takes practice," Stacy was saying, having blown a series of perfect smoke rings herself. Both girls watched them float off into the air, getting larger and wobblier and finally losing their shape by the time they reached the spruce tree. The cardinal darted from its branch and flew further into the woods.

"Poor Miss Lanier," Stacy said.

Amy nodded. They liked their Spanish teacher. She wore her dresses very short and it was sad because her legs weren't good; they were all right until you got to the knees, but then the knees came together and right above them her thighs rose up like logs. Also, she wore a lot of nylon-type dresses without any slip, and the dresses stuck to her. You could practically see the outline of her underwear and pantyhose. It was Stacy's theory that Miss Lanier had a crush on the principal, the man they called Puddy, a pasty, homely, middle-aged man.

"He's so shy, though," Stacy said. "I bet he's never even had a date. He still lives with his mother."

Amy gave up on the smoke rings and dropped her cigarette in the snow. "Their kids would be ugly and nice." But her stomach was squeezing in on itself. She thought of Mr. Robertson saying, "See me after school. I have a book you might like." Everything else—Stacy's red eyes, Miss Lanier's unfortunate thighs—all the world seemed faded, with this rendezvous to look forward to. She lived in such an odd, anxious, private world these days; such *pleasure* from the words "See me after school." But always, now, this tumbling anxiety. She eyed the cigarette she had tossed on the ground.

"Poor thing," Stacy mused as the school bell rang and they gathered themselves together. "Someone really ought to tell her about that static cling."

Tucked into bed at night, the lamp throwing a yellow pool across her quilt and the paperback *Hamlet* propped up before her, Isabelle struggled with Shakespeare. The struggle was primarily physical, for her eyelids felt glued together; really, she could barely keep them open. She tried sitting up straighter in bed, and still she couldn't make it through the second page. It was remarkable how her eyes would just flip shut. When she felt sure that Amy was asleep, she got out of bed and went downstairs to the kitchen, where she sat at the table with a cup of tea, housecoat tucked around her, her foot with its terry-cloth slipper rocking up and down as she read the lines again and again.

It was hard. Very, very difficult stuff. She hadn't expected it would be this difficult, and she had to fight a sensation of panic. "Which he stood seiz'd of, to the conqueror: Against the which, a moity competent Was gaged by our King; which had return'd To the inheritance of Fortinbras, Had he been vanquisher . . ." Now what was she to make of that? The kitchen was very quiet.

She sipped her tea and glanced at the window. Where the white curtains parted slightly she could see the blackness of the windowpane, and she got up to tug the curtains together. She was not used to being down here alone at this hour. She sat at the table again, sipped her tea, and skimmed over the lines in her book. "How weary, stale, flat & unprofitable Seem to me all the uses of this world!"

Well, look at that. She could understand that. Isabelle put her finger on the page; it was Hamlet himself speaking. "How weary, stale and flat . . . seem all the uses of the world." Lord knew there were times when she felt the world to be stale and weary, and the way Hamlet said it—it was very nicely put. She felt a genuine prick of delight, as though she and Hamlet were suddenly friends.

Feeling awake now, she whispered the words that began his speech. "O, that this too, too solid flesh would melt, Thaw . . ." (Fleetingly she pictured a rump steak not taken out of the freezer in time for Sunday dinner.) She pursed her lips, sipped some tea, began again. "O, that this too, too solid flesh would melt . . ." (Hamlet was a solid, muscular man, no doubt. In a moment she'd check the drawing of him on the cover of this book.) "Thaw and resolve itself into a dew."

So far, so good; Isabelle nodded. She had certainly experienced in her own lifetime the desire to melt, to disappear. She had never longed to become *dew,* but it was a lovely idea when you thought about it, which was exactly why, after all, she was reading Shakespeare. Because he was a genius and could express things in a way the rest of us would never have thought to. She felt immensely pleased by all of this, and sat up straighter in her chair. "Or that the Everlasting had not fix'd His canon 'gainst self-slaughter! O God! O God!"

She read this over a few times. Because "Everlasting" was capitalized she assumed that Shakespeare was referring to God here, and the business of the canon of self-slaughter must be a reference to suicide: Hamlet wanted to commit suicide but he knew God had a rule against this.

Well. Isabelle looked up. Gazing at her refrigerator she wondered if Hamlet wasn't being a little melodramatic. He was certainly distraught, and of course he had reason to be. But she had been distraught herself, God knew, any number of times, and had never thought she would like to kill herself. She peered back at the book. The tea was causing a pressure on her bladder, but she would try and finish the scene. Apparently Hamlet was very sorry his father was dead. His parents had loved each other . . . but within a month his mother got over it and married Hamlet's uncle.

Isabelle touched her lips; she could see how this would be disturbing. But that line "Frailty, thy name is woman!" She didn't like that particularly; and he was talking to his mother. For heaven's sake. What did Hamlet know about being a single parent, losing the man you loved? Isabelle frowned and pushed on the cuticle of her thumb. Hamlet was pretty offensive there, frankly. Certainly those women down in Boston who had just burned their undergarments on the front steps of some court building (Isabelle had seen this on the news) wouldn't take very kindly to such a line: Frailty, thy name is woman! Isabelle tugged on her robe. Honestly, it did rile her a bit. Men had a lot to learn. There was nothing frail about women. For heaven's sake, women had been keeping things going from time in memoriam. And there was nothing frail about *her*. Nothing frail about a woman who raised her daughter alone through bleak New England winters with the roof leaking, the car needing oil.

Isabelle had to close her eyes for just a moment; she was very tired. And, in fact, she did feel frail. That was the truth, if you really wanted to know it. She sat for a moment, running her finger along the edge of the book, and then she got up and washed out her teacup in the sink, glad enough to go to bed.

BUT A FEW days later she was back at the bookstore. She was not a quitter; it's just that Shakespeare was not the way to begin. She would find other books to read in the section called Classics. This time the bookstore seemed familiar. The young clerk with his facial hair seemed to give her a nod. She perused the shelves for quite a while before deciding on *Madame Bovary*, attracted by its cover. She studied the picture of the dark-eyed woman whose hair was pulled back into a lovely French twist and whose face revealed some inner knowledge, Isabelle decided finally, of the secret sorrows of feminine life.

A SPRINKLING OF burglaries took place in Shirley Falls that last week in March. They were daytime break-ins, all occurring in the Oyster Point section of town. A collection of old coins disappeared from the home of a history professor. Mrs. Errin, the dentist's wife, discovered jewelry missing from her bureau, and in another case—in a rather lovely home down by the river—a number of silver pieces, candlesticks and sugar bowls, were found to be gone; the back door had been jimmied open. There were no witnesses, no clues except for a few footprints in the snow that were muddied by rain before the police could determine anything more definite than the fact that they were probably made by a man of average height and weight; no clues at all, really—no reports of any suspicious characters roaming around, no sense that it was the work of anyone professional, the way it had been a number of years earlier, when two men came up from Boston and emptied out two houses into moving vans before they were finally caught a week later when they came back to try for a third. No, these pilferings had a lighter touch, and before the police could do much more than scratch their heads and file reports, the break-ins seemed to stop.

But Emma Clark, arriving home one afternoon (exhausted, for she had just had an unpleasant altercation at the upholstery store regarding the shoddy job recently done on her living-room couch), found the garage door partly raised, and having heard through acquaintances about the silver taken from the home down on the riverbank, she did not get out of her car but drove straight back into town and called Avery to come home at once.

All his tools were gone, and a spare tire he kept in the garage as well, but the house itself had apparently not been touched. Nevertheless Avery took the rest of the day off from work and had a locksmith come put a double bolt on every door. "I should let Isabelle know about this," Avery said to his wife, distracted by the mud the locksmith was traipsing across the kitchen floor, and Emma nodded. It was true; Isabelle Goodrow lived just a mile down the road, and she ought to be told that someone had come snooping around, stealing tires and tools.

But Emma and Avery had other things to do at the moment, and so Isabelle, sitting in the lunchroom on her coffee break, engrossed in *Madame Bovary*, remained oblivious of anything that was going on out past Route 22. Nor was she aware, as she turned the page, that across town the last school bell had just rung, and that her daughter, Amy, moving through the crowded hallways, was making her way to the girls' room on the second floor to prepare herself for Mr. Robertson.

Chapter

7

WHAT EXCITEMENT! To stand alone in the girls' room, its green walls touched by the milky light that filtered through the frosted window . . . Never mind the sinks were stained and a faucet dripped, for Amy on these afternoons there was an exotic hush, a thrill. But fear, too; remarkable, how it gripped her way down, as though a hand squeezed her tailbone, making her buttocks almost tingle; her hands could have been taken from a refrigerator, they were so cold. She imagined herself a child-bride princess being made ready for presentation to some king.

And it was her hair that seemed most princesslike, falling over her shoulders in long twisted curls, various colors of yellow, light brown, a tendril running alongside her face so blond it seemed almost white. Staring into the mirror with her mouth half parted, she thought she might be beautiful. Then a cramping in her abdomen, a tightening near the tailbone—she had to go into a stall and use the toilet, and when she emerged, checking in the mirror again, she was dismayed to find a plain girl whose lips were pale and dry. She chewed on them and pinched her cheeks, and pulled open the heavy door that had written across it in red ink: *My sister likes her left tit sucked.*

The hallway was empty. The classrooms she passed by seemed gaping in their silence, waiting, chairs vacant, to be filled again tomorrow. In the distance came the faint sound of a trumpet from the music room; descending the stairs, she heard the echo of cheerleaders practicing in the gym.

And then she was there, standing in his doorway. An odd shrinking of her vision made the scene pale and small, a pencil sketch (her large moist hands clutching her notebook were leaving imprints on the cover), but when Mr. Robertson glanced up from his desk his eyebrows rose and his face brightened, and immediately the heaviest part of Amy's anxiety was gone. No one, it seemed, had ever been this happy to see her, unless when she was very small and her mother had sometimes taken her to the mill; then the women would lean toward her and someone like Fat Bev would say, "How's my precious girl?"

Mr. Robertson said nothing, only watched her as she stood in the afternoon sunlight that fell across the floor. "Hi," Amy said, waving a hand just slightly, ducking her head with a quick, self-conscious smile.

"Hi." Mr. Robertson waved back, imitating her gesture so exactly it appeared that he was shy as well. "Come in," he said. "Please, come in."

She walked toward him through the sunny room. To be watched made her uneasy, as though she had to compete with every other person he might gaze upon, and she had known for quite some time that competing was not what she did best. Even as a child this had been true; the game of musical chairs had filled her with panic—that dreadful, icy knowledge that when the music stopped someone would be "out." It was better when she stopped trying. Because there were so many things a young person was required to endure: spelling bees, endless games in gym class; in all these things she had stopped trying, or if she tried, she did so with little expectation of herself, so was not disappointed to misspell "glacier" in a fourth-grade spelling bee, or to strike out in softball because she never swung the bat. It became a habit, not trying, and in junior high, when the biggest prize of course was to be popular among the right friends, Amy found she lacked the fortitude once more to get in there and swing. Arriving at the point where she felt almost invisible, she was aware that her solitude was something she might have brought upon herself.

But here was Mr. Robertson and she was not invisible to him. Not when he looked at her like that—she couldn't be. (Still, there was her inner tendency to flee, the recrudescence of self-doubt.) But his hand came forward and touched her elbow. "I have something for you," he said, and he nodded toward the chair beside his desk.

She sat down, tucking her large feet as far back under the chair as they would go. He had copied a poem for her by Yeats called "To a Young Girl," and she read it in confusion. She had never seen so much of his handwriting before.

I know what makes your heart beat so . . .

She felt he had written her a letter. "I love it," she told him. "I really, really do." She looked from the paper to him. "Can I keep it?"

"Of course. It's for you."

She had to look away because now she knew she loved him, and this changed things.

Before, she had been drawn to him, as though he were a large, dark magnet pulling the nail of herself slowly across a vast room. But here she was, with a soft, imperceptible click; nowhere further to be drawn to. She had arrived and now she loved him.

She slipped the poem inside her notebook. "Well, thank you," she said, and she got up and walked over to the window and saw how the sidewalk was bare and dry in the sun. Through the partly opened window came the sound of a last school bus pulling away, the weary groan of its cumbersome self as it turned into the street. Beyond she could see a smattering of yellow on the south lawn of the school, dandelions growing sturdy and close to the ground. The air coming through the window had a sweetness to it that seemed to cause her physical pain, and looking again at the sidewalk, at the dry parts of it where small flecks on the surface glinted in the sun, she recalled easily the excitement she had felt as a child on such a day as this one. For there had been more, evidently, than the terror of musical chairs—there had been days like this when winter was finally over, and her feet in new sneakers felt buoyantly free as they touched the dry sidewalk. She recalled the weightlessness, the spring in her legs as she walked in her sneakers down a dry sunny sidewalk, and it seemed to her, remembering this, that happiness had been available to her then after all, in the new sneakers, in dandelions to pick (she'd had to be careful though, Isabelle had hated how they could stain her clothes), wearing a sweater instead of a bulky coat—all this had made her happy as a child, had filled her up with hope.

"What are you thinking?" Mr. Robertson asked, and Amy turned from the window.

"I don't know," she answered, because she did not know how to explain about the glinting, dry sidewalk, or about the smell of the air. "I'm glad it's finally spring and everything." She shrugged and looked out the window again. "But it makes me feel weird."

"You know what they say."

She could hear him walking up behind her.

"What do they say?" She turned. He was very close to her and this made her nervous, afraid he would find her unattractive. It was different when you saw a person up close—they sometimes had goopy things in their eyes, or blackheads in their chins. People smelled different up close too. Her mother, for example, sometimes gave off the faint odor of a damp brick when she leaned close to Amy to straighten her collar or to remove something caught in her hair.

"That April is the cruellest month." Mr. Robertson put his hands in his pockets and rocked back on his heels. He jiggled some change in his pocket.

"Who says that?" Amy asked.

"T. S. Eliot."

"Who's that." She thought Mr. Robertson was kind of a show-off. She scowled and sat back on the windowsill.

"Another poet."

"Never heard of the guy." She swung her leg against the radiator screen and was chagrined at the sudden loud metallic reverberation it made. She pressed both legs against it and kept still.

"April is the cruellest month," Mr. Robertson recited, "mixing memory with desire. Or something. I can't remember past that." He walked slowly back to his desk.

Come back, she wanted to say. She got down off the windowsill and followed him. "Tell me that again," she said. "That April stuff."

His eyes were tired, kind. "April is the cruellest month, mixing memory with desire."

She raised her shoulders, dropped them with a sigh.

"What?" Mr. Robertson spoke quietly. The sun had already moved; the bright light in the classroom was gone except for one section of the windowsill that remained in soft yellow, but the spring air was still warm as it moved through the window.

Amy shook her head and shrugged.

"Tell me what you're thinking."

"Oh, you know." Her eyes moved about the room, settling on nothing. "The stuff about April being cruel. It's good. I mean, I like that."

"And what else?"

But it wasn't that she was thinking anything else. It was more that she ached. She ached inside with something and it had to do with the dandelions and the groan of the school bus and the smell of the air and so many things she couldn't name. And of course with him.

"I'm glad I met you," she finally said, not looking at him.

"I'm glad I met you, too."

She looked around for her notebooks, the coat she had put over a chair.

"Could I drive you home today?" Mr. Robertson asked suddenly.

"I guess." She was surprised.

"Do you think anyone would mind?"

She slipped her arm through the sleeve of her coat, giving him a puzzled look as she pulled her hair out from under the back of her coat.

"For example," Mr. Robertson went on, "would your mother mind if your math teacher gave you a ride home?"

"Of course not." But she wouldn't tell her mother.

"I'll get my coat then," said Mr. Robertson, going to a closet behind his desk. They left the room without speaking.

ONCE INSIDE HIS car she was surprised at how close to him she was; the car was smaller than she had thought. When he shifted into reverse leaving the teachers' parking lot his hand briefly touched her leg. "Sorry," he said, glancing over at her.

She nodded, turning to look out the window, her elbow pressed against the door, her thumb against her mouth. She said simply: "Turn left at the light," and then, "The next right," and after that they drove without speaking. When they passed over the wooden bridge the noise was sudden beneath the tires and then just as suddenly gone. Pussy willows appeared and disappeared as the car rounded curves near the swamp on Route 22. They drove past an old farmhouse, where a forsythia bush was just beginning to bloom, a scattering of yellow bits. They drove past Larkindale's field, where patches of brown and light brown mingled in the raggedness of leftover winter. The stone wall rose up a field, weaving into the distance where the spruce trees grew dark as army canvas, their branches bending down as though still encumbered by months of snow. But there was little snow left, really—only dirty hardened drifts by the side of the road—and long strips of the road were dry as the car moved over it, sunlight showing dust on the dashboard in the bright but already fading light.

She was thinking she ought to wear perfume in case she was giving off the same damp-brick odor her mother sometimes had.

"Here on the left," she said, subdued, and Mr. Robertson turned into the narrow driveway, pulling up to the house and shutting the car off; the engine made a series of small pinging sounds as though a tiny rock were being tossed around inside.

Amy, looking through narrowed eyes at the house she lived in, tried to imagine what it looked like to Mr. Robertson, and she thought the house looked like her mother, small and pale, with the white curtain at the kitchen window apologetic, as though its purpose—to appear cheerful, cozy, clean—had failed. Amy closed her eyes.

For years this had been her secret: She had wanted a different mother. She wanted a mother who was pretty, who greeted people warmly. She wanted a mother who looked like mothers in television ads, who mopped large glistening kitchen floors, kissed husbands returning from work, lived in houses with other houses nearby and neighbors running in and out—she did not want the mother stuck out here in the woods in this little place.

"I was brought up in a white house not much bigger than this one," Mr. Robertson said, and Amy, startled, opened her eyes. He was sitting back against his seat, one hand comfortably placed on the steering wheel, the other raised to his chin. "There was a vacant lot nearby." He nodded. "Where kids used to play ball."

To Amy that part sounded like a television ad. She pictured his mother, pretty, wearing an apron and baking cookies in the kitchen.

"But I didn't play ball there much."

Amy pressed her thumb against the dashboard. "How come?"

"I didn't especially fit with the other kids." Mr. Robertson glanced at her briefly. "My mother drank. She was an alcoholic. I used to take long bike rides to get away from home."

An *alcoholic.* Amy stopped pushing her thumb against the dashboard. His mother had not been baking cookies. Probably she had been upstairs drinking gin from a bottle stored under the bed. Amy didn't have a clear idea of what a woman alcoholic (a mother alcoholic) would be like, but her own mother had told her once that such women got very sneaky, hiding bottles under their bed.

"Jeez," said Amy. "That's too bad."

"Yeah. Well." Mr. Robertson sighed and moved down just a little in his seat, spreading his hand over his knee.

Looking sideways through her hair she studied his hand carefully. It was a big hand—a substantial, grown-up man's hand with two veins the size of earthworms running over the top. The fingernails were broad and flat and clean. She minded the thought of his past including a mother hiding gin bottles under her bed. And yet the sight of his hand reassured her. The cleanliness of his fingernails made her admire him, because as a child his fingernails most likely had been dirty. It would be like that if your mother was an alcoholic, Amy thought. But look how strong he was now, so smart, quoting poets and philosophers, his mind full of mathematical theorems, his fingernails clean and trim.

"Tell me more," she said, leaning partly against the car door so she could be facing him.

He raised an eyebrow. "More of the life and trials of Thomas Robertson?"

She nodded.

"I flunked out of college."

That flicker again of almost not liking him, maybe a drop of fear. "You did?" She also felt embarrassed for him—that he would admit to such a thing.

"Freshman year." He thrust out his lower lip, tugged on the reddish patch of beard right underneath. "There were too many things on my mind. So then I worked with handicapped kids for a while, and later on flew out to the West Coast and finished college there." He raised his eyebrows. "With honors, even."

And so he was restored. Handicapped kids; he was even nicer than she had known before. She watched him admiringly, and when he looked at her, she smiled.

"I was going to go on for graduate work in psychology—what a beautiful smile you have" (she blushed) "—but I had a friend who was a brilliant mathematician and through him I got interested in that."

"You mean in college you studied psychology?"

He nodded. "Minored in economics, so I had some knowledge of math."

"My mother says psychology people are crazy." She blurted this out without thinking and then blushed when he burst into a laugh. It was a full laugh, with his head back; she could see the dark fillings in his molars. She felt again that she might not like him as she once had, but when he stopped laughing he said to her sincerely, "I'll tell you something, Amy. Your mother is no dope."

After that it seemed cozy in the car. He rolled his window all the way up and she felt sealed in a bubble with him. Their talking seemed relaxed and sweet, and finally seeing from his watch that her mother would be home in twenty minutes, she gathered her books in one arm, about to open the car door with the other, when she suddenly leaned over and very quickly kissed him on his bearded cheek.

Chapter

8

ARLENE TUCKER'S COUSIN'S son was arrested for selling marijuana. "Fifteen years old and they found him with three hundred dollars' worth." Arlene delivered this with her usual authority, raising one of her penciled eyebrows and leaving it there while the news sunk in.

"Is that so," said Lenora Snibbens. "Fifteen years old. Holy Crow."

"But three hundred dollars' worth," said Fat Bev. "Where'd he get three hundred dollars to buy it in the first place?"

Arlene nodded like a pleased teacher. "He's been selling the stuff. Dealing it. Turns out this has been going on for a number of months."

Isabelle glanced up from her book. "Where do they live, your cousins?"

Arlene eyed the cover of *Madame Bovary*. "Kingswood. About an hour from here."

Isabelle nodded. There was marijuana everywhere these days, it seemed. With the college here in Shirley Falls, Isabelle knew her own town was probably not safe. But Kingswood, just a little spot of a place, and a fifteen-year-old selling it. She closed her book, no longer able to concentrate.

"And I'm telling you," Arlene was saying, picking something from her eye, then blinking the eye furiously. "He's the nicest boy you ever knew."

"See, I just don't buy that," said Fat Bev. She shook her head slowly, unwrapping a sandwich from a great deal of wax paper. "When you've got a fifteen-year-old kid selling drugs like that, something's wrong."

"Well, of course something's wrong," Arlene replied. "I'm not saying something's not wrong. I'm not saying his head is screwed on straight. I'm *saying* you can never tell. Appearances can be deceiving."

"That's true," offered Rosie Tanguay. "I was reading just the other day about some boy in Texas. Good-looking, perfect student, popular, smart—the whole nine yards. Went home one night after a basketball game and stabbed his mother with a fork."

Lenora Snibbens glanced sideways at her. "A fork?" she said dryly.

Rosie ignored this, but further down the table Fat Bev rumbled with laughter. "Really, Rosie. How much damage did this fork do?"

Rosie looked offended. "I believe she was in critical condition."

Lenora turned her face away. "Some forks they have in Texas," she said mildly.

"I guess so," responded Fat Bev, thrusting her head forward to take a bite from her sandwich. A piece of mayonnaisey lettuce slipped onto her large bosom; she plucked it off and ate it, then, frowning, rubbed hard at her blouse with a napkin.

Isabelle winced. It was right on the tip of her tongue to say, Bev, hot water fast. But Arlene spoke up and said she understood the point Rosie was making, that you could never tell who was going to do something nuts. "That's what makes it so scary to live in this world," she said, directing this, for some reason, to Isabelle.

"That's right." Isabelle nodded. She had seen the wary look Arlene gave *Madame Bovary*, and she knew that by bringing such a book to work she might be thought of as a snob. She did not want to be thought of as a snob. She wanted to remain on an even keel with everyone and avoid being involved in any kind of unpleasantness, so she said to Arlene, "Very scary to live in this world." After all, she believed it.

But Isabelle did not believe these incidents simply fell straight out of the blue. She did not believe that the mother of this drug dealer in Kingswood had no warning that her son was behaving in a criminal manner. And as for the perfect boy in Texas, Isabelle was sure there were more facts to the case than Rosie of course knew. "Perfect student," for example. What did that mean? Maybe it meant his homework was very, very neat. Isabelle had gone to high school with a girl like that—her name was Abbie Mattison—and she had copied her homework over three or four times every night until the margins and handwriting were perfect. Everything with Abbie Mattison had to be perfect: hair, clothes, smile. Then she got married and had a baby boy, and Abbie's husband came home one day to find her stark naked, singing, out on the back lawn, hanging up clothes. They took her to Augusta for a while, but according to the latest (Isabelle's cousin Cindy Rae scribbled news at the bottom of her Christmas card), Abbie was negligent about taking her medication and it was a kind of on-again, off-again thing.

Anyway. Isabelle always remembered the way Abbie copied over homework. A little crazy even then. "I'm not sure these things are ever quite the surprise they're made out to be at the time," Isabelle said to Arlene, thinking that by reading *Madame Bovary* all week she had been going too far and ought to display some friendliness now.

Arlene turned her lips down and raised her eyebrows, indicating indifference to what Isabelle had said, and Isabelle considered sharing the story of Abbie Mattison to substantiate her point, but a sense of discretion stopped her. It didn't seem fair to Abbie—wherever she was these days, in the funny farm or out—to have her story gossiped about just so Isabelle could curry favor with her cohorts in the office room.

"I agree," said Fat Bev. "Any parent who's paying attention knows if their kid is smoking marijuana or not. It has a certain smell. And their eyes get red, and they eat like a horse."

Isabelle, who knew of course that Amy would never smoke marijuana, was still pleased to be able to privately acknowledge that her daughter did not have a certain smell, or red eyes, or the appetite of a horse.

"Whenever my girls went to a party," Bev was saying, "Bill and I always stayed up till they came in. One night I remember Roxanne went out with some friends and first thing she did when she came home was to go straight in the bathroom and piss like a bull."

Isabelle tried to smile pleasantly.

"I smelled her breath, and sure enough. We didn't let her out again for a month."

Lenora Snibbens stood up and walked to the vending machine. "I think you were right, Bev," she said, pushing the button for a chocolate bar. "Your girls all turned out good."

"You reap what you sow," Isabelle said. "I've always believed that."

"Probably." Bev nodded vaguely, watching Lenora unwrap her candy bar.

"It's not that simple," Arlene declared. "My cousin didn't know about her son. His eyes were never red and he never smelled funny. He never smoked the stuff."

"Well, obviously he smoked the stuff." Fat Bev tapped her pink-painted fingernail on the table near Lenora. "That kind of chocolate is sixty percent paraffin wax. I read it somewhere."

"No," said Arlene, "he *sold* the stuff. He never smoked it at all. Just sold it."

"Crazy," Rosie said. "Crazy, crazy, crazy."

"What happens to him now?" Lenora wanted to know. "Do they send a kid like that to jail?"

"The judge put him on probation for three years. Has to keep his nose clean for three years." Arlene glanced at her watch and began to gather up the remains of her lunch, pressing down the top of her Tupperware container where the milky shapes of macaroni salad could be seen near the bottom. "And counseling. The judge said he wants him to have some counseling, so the kid goes off each week to talk to a priest."

Isabelle looked at the cover of her book, where the dark-eyed Madame Bovary gazed back impassively. She was awfully curious about whether the greedy Emma was going to be rejected by her lover. (Isabelle hoped so.)

"Then the priest calls up the parents and tells them what the kid says. He's lonely at school. His mother yells at him." Arlene gave a shrug.

"Like all that hogwash means he can go out and sell marijuana," Rosie said.

Lenora was frowning. "That doesn't seem right," she mused, moving the candy bar with her wrist across the table to Fat Bev.

"Of course it's not right," Arlene said. "What about a little responsibility? Your mother yells at you so you go out and commit a crime? What mother doesn't yell at their kid?"

"Well," said Isabelle, drawing her attention away from her book and considering this point of Arlene's. "I doubt it's because his mother yells, although that's a handy thing to tell the priest. But there's something more than that. Children learn things, I think, don't you? He must have learned something that makes him think it's acceptable to take that route. Selling drugs, I mean."

Arlene stopped packing up her things and squinted at Isabelle. "What are you saying, Madame Ovary? That my cousin *taught* her son to go and sell marijuana on the streets?"

"Oh, heavens no." Isabelle flushed furiously. "I only mean our values seem to be disintegrating these days. And that . . . well, when children see their parents cheat on income tax, and things like that . . ."

"My cousin doesn't cheat on her income tax."

"No, no, of course not." Sweat broke out above Isabelle's lip just as the lunch buzzer rang.

"What *I* was saying," Lenora Snibbens said to no one in particular, standing up, "is that it doesn't seem right for the priest to be repeating what the kid tells him. Aren't those talks supposed to be private? Makes me nervous to go to confession. Bev, I think you're right, there's not much chocolate in that," pointing to the candy bar as she passed by.

"I certainly didn't mean to offend your cousin," Isabelle said quietly to Arlene.

"Oh, it's all right." Arlene waved a hand tiredly as she left the room.

Isabelle, still a bit shaken from having suddenly found herself on the verge of an altercation, said to Bev, "I just believe you reap what you sow. As I said."

"Oh, sure. I agree."

"When you get home tonight," Isabelle said, "try soaking that spot in hot water."

In THE EARLY morning it snowed. A sudden April snowstorm that dropped two inches of perfect white snow onto everything; cars, sidewalks, trees, steps—everything seemed rounded and white and edgeless. Just as suddenly the sky became completely blue, and the sun shone so brilliantly that when Stacy and Amy emerged from the back door of the school at lunchtime the brightness was blinding and they both squinted, ducking their heads, holding their hands before their eyes as though to ward off blows.

The snow was melting quickly, making the path in the woods difficult. Neither girl wore boots and they stepped cautiously through rivulets of melting snow and mud, while above them water fell off the trees so steadily that except for the dazzling sunshine it could have been raining instead.

"My father's fucking someone," Stacy said, as soon as they got to their spot. She put a chocolate-covered marshmallow into her mouth and chewed, her jaw working vigorously. "Shit," she added, glancing down, "my feet are *so wet.*"

Their feet were muddy as well, dark edges of mud rising up the sides of their shoes. "Let them dry before you try and clean them," Amy said, but she was worried. Her shoes were suede and Isabelle had made a big deal about how much money they cost.

"Yeah," Stacy said, bringing out the cigarettes. "Well, I don't really give a shit."

Amy watched the melting snow as it ran down the darkened bark of a tree trunk, and then she asked, "How come you think that about your father?" turning back toward Stacy.

"Oh . . ." Stacy sounded like she had forgotten she'd said anything about him at all. "I could be wrong. I don't know. It's just a feeling I have. And I dreamt about it too. Yeah, that's right." She lit both cigarettes and handed one to Amy. "I forgot about that, but I dreamt it. Yeah." She chewed her lip, gazing at her cigarette.

Amy inhaled deeply. "Weird."

"I was in the water or something and my father was on shore with some woman or something." Stacy smoked her cigarette. "Who knows." She shrugged. "Fuck it."

"Those are great." Amy pointed with her cigarette at the half-empty box of chocolate-covered marshmallows balanced on the log. Stacy's mother had bought them for Stacy's little twin brothers' birthday party, but Stacy stole them and brought them to school.

"Help yourself." Stacy waved a hand. "You know, my father gets paid a lot of money to analyze dreams, but whenever I have a dream he couldn't care less."

"You didn't tell him this one, did you?"

"No. But Jesus, what a great idea. I'll wait until we're all eating dinner, then I'll say, Dad, I had a dream you've been fucking some woman other than Mom. Could you tell me what that means?"

Amy helped herself to another marshmallow. She was distracted, only partly interested in Stacy's dream. What was most in her mind of course was the excruciatingly embarrassing memory of the day before, when she had kissed Mr. Robertson on his cheek. What a *stupid* thing to do. And he was married, he wore that wedding ring—so he'd probably gone home and told his wife and they'd had a chuckle. "Normal for girls to have crushes on their teachers," the wife might say. Amy's stomach tightened against the pleasure of the marshmallow. She did not think what she was going through in her feeling for Mr. Robertson was anything like "normal." She swallowed the rest of the marshmallow, thinking the only reason he had smiled at her this morning during class was because he was embarrassed for her acting like a jerk.

A drop of water fell from a branch onto Amy's head and dripped down her forehead. She wiped at it with the arm of her coat. "Where do you think you'll go to college?" she asked Stacy. Mr. Robertson had talked to Amy about going to a good college when they sat in his car in her driveway.

"Nowhere. I'm too dumb. I'm going to New York to be a singer." Stacy peered at the marshmallows and chose one that seemed to have more chocolate. "The trouble with being adopted," Stacy explained, holding her cigarette in one hand and the chocolate-covered marshmallow in the other, "is your parents might be smart, and they're hoping you're going to be smart, but then you turn out dumb. Of course this disappoints them. They can't *say* that, so they keep implying you should be really grateful they took you at all. You should be really fucking grateful they didn't leave you in some gutter."

"You weren't going to be left in a gutter, were you?" This possibility was interesting to Amy.

"Of course not." Stacy nibbled at the chocolate with tiny bites. "That's the whole point. I wasn't anywhere except in some clean hospital getting born and then my parents come in and adopt me and take me home and I'm supposed to act like they saved my fucking life."

Amy smoked her cigarette and contemplated this. "Someone else would have taken you if they didn't," she finally remarked. "I bet a lot of people would have. I bet you were a really pretty baby."

Stacy tossed the half-eaten marshmallow into the woods and then dropped her cigarette on the ground and stared at it for a long time, like behind her open eyes she'd gone to sleep. "Roses are red," she finally said, still staring, "violets are blue, I'm schizophrenic and so am I." She looked over at Amy. "My father thinks that's funny," she said. "He thinks that's just a fucking scream."

Chapter

9

Spring came. Forsythia bushes burst into yellow beside doorways and along stone walls; then daffodils opened, and hyacinths. Narcissus leaned on their stalks, tapping against the bottom shingles of houses as a light breeze moved by. Day after day the sky was blue; the sun fell across brick walls of buildings and baked them warm. By the banks of the river the birch trees stood tentative and skinny with the tender green of their new growth making them seem hesitant, like schoolgirls. The sun danced on the water and warm breezes blew along the banks and people ate their lunches on park benches, reaching out quickly for an empty potato-chip bag scuttling along in the wind.

The evenings grew longer; kitchen windows stayed open after dinner and peepers could be heard in the marsh. Isabelle, stepping out to sweep her porch steps, felt absolutely certain that some wonderful change was arriving in her life. The strength of this belief was puzzling; what she was feeling, she decided, was really the presence of God. God was here on her back steps, in the final patch of sunlight on her tulip bed, in the steady husky chirping from the marsh, in the fragrant damp earth surrounding right now the delicate roots of hepaticas and starflowers. She went back inside, locking the screen door, and felt the certainty again, that her life, because of His love, was finally on the verge of something large and new.

And Amy, thank God (truly, thank Him), was more talkative than she used to be, much more interested in school. She had joined the English Club and the Student Council and often stayed for a meeting in the afternoon. She was good about calling Isabelle at work when this was the case. Sometimes also, Amy explained, she stayed after school to help the other kids from Spanish class. Miss Lanier, the Spanish teacher, had asked her to do this. Stacy Burrows, for example ("She's really nice, we're kind of friends," Amy said), who apparently did not catch on to the conjugation of verbs quickly, stayed after school some days to get help from Amy. Except they spent a lot of time gossiping about Miss Lanier and the principal, Puddy. "We think they have a crush on each other," Amy said, dropping a piece of butter the size of a walnut into the center of her baked potato. "Puddy came in with a note the other day for Miss Lanier, and she blushed and then he blushed."

This all seemed normal to Isabelle: two girls speculating about their teachers' romantic inclinations. And she was grateful for it, because Isabelle had worried that Amy was lonely at school. So now it was pleasant to be able to sit on these lovely spring evenings and listen to the chatter of this growing, happy girl.

"Is he nice? The principal?" Isabelle asked. "I don't know that I've heard you say much about him."

"Oh, he's really nice," Amy said, mashing up the baked potato and butter with her fork. "He's not at all strict. You can tell he hates to yell at anyone." Amy shoved an alarming amount of potato into her mouth. "Except he did suspend Alan Stewart for three days for vandalizing the boys' room."

"Good heavens, I should think so," Isabelle responded. "And please don't talk with your mouth full."

Amy held up a finger of apology and swallowed vigorously, the tendons of her throat springing out. "Stacy thinks," she continued in a moment, "that Mr. Mandel—that's Puddy—still lives with his mother and that he's too shy to ask out Miss Lanier."

"Mandel," Isabelle said. "Isn't that a Jewish name? How old do you think he is?"

Amy shrugged. "Forty, maybe. Fifty. How can you tell he's Jewish?" Amy's head was bent over her plate; her eyes looked up at her mother.

"The name can clue you in. Does he have a big nose? For heavens sake, honey, sit *up*."

"Yeah, he does have kind of a big nose."

Isabelle nodded. "They're apt to. Flat feet too, and maybe Stacy's right about him living with his mother. Jewish mothers have trouble letting go. With their sons especially, I think."

Amy burped, widening her eyes with apology. "Sorry. Sorry, sorry," she said, but Isabelle was enjoying her company and she let it go.

"What does Miss Lanier look like?"

"Kind of plain, but really nice." Amy didn't mention that she wore her skirts quite short, but she did tell her mother about the problem Miss Lanier had with static cling.

"Oh, too bad," Isabelle said, shaking some seasoning salt onto her chicken thigh. "She probably doesn't have a full-length mirror, or she'd see it. Every woman should have a full-length mirror."

Both Isabelle and Amy nodded. A breeze coming through the window over the sink brought with it a moist earthy smell that mingled with the seasoned chicken. "But you see," Isabelle said, aiming her fork at Amy and poking it delicately a few times through the air, "Lanier. I think that's French. Which means she's probably Catholic. Which means Mr. Mandel's mother isn't going to like *that*."

"Why not."

"Oh, honey." Isabelle started eating again.

"Would you care if I married someone who wasn't a Protestant?" Amy asked. The question was an idle one, just friendly.

"No, of course not," Isabelle answered, but even as she said it she felt a tightening within her. "You can marry whomever you choose."

"Like if I married someone Jewish," Amy said, spreading butter onto her potato skin.

"Oh, that would be all right," Isabelle said, relieved. "Jews are very smart. They *think*. They use their heads. They value education."

"What if I married a Catholic?"

Isabelle cut a small piece of chicken in two. "It would be none of my business."

"I probably won't marry a Catholic," Amy said agreeably. "I think it's dumb the way they kneel. I'd feel so queer kneeling in church."

"Well," Isabelle said. "I happen to agree with you there. Although we should respect the differences of others."

And so there was that: the pleasant chitchat between mother and daughter. Isabelle felt redeemed. All the hard work of raising this girl on her own, and just look: they had landed on their feet.

"Say," she said, suddenly remembering, as she cleared away the dishes, that there was something she'd meant to ask Amy about, "that math teacher of yours that took Miss Dayble's place this year. What's his name?"

"Robertson." Amy bent down as though looking for something dropped on the floor. "What about him?" she asked, her head still down, taking her hair from behind her ear so that it fell in front of her face.

"His wife left him." Isabelle had brought a sponge from the sink and was wiping the table thoroughly.

"Really?" Amy stood up, careful to keep her back to her mother. "I thought a pea dropped on the floor but I guess not." But her mother wasn't looking, she was heading back to the sink. "How do you know his wife left him?"

"Becky Tucker took a class with her at the college evidently. Honey, if you think there may be a pea rolling around under there I wish you'd look carefully. I don't want any mice in this house."

"She took a class with Mrs. Robertson?"

"According to Arlene. Here, stick this in the refrigerator if you can't find the pea." Isabelle held out the leftover chicken wrapped carefully in aluminum foil.

Amy waited until she had opened the refrigerator door and then said, "How come she left?"

"Oh, I don't know. Had her consciousness raised, I guess."

Amy poked among the jars of mayonnaise and pickles and ketchup, moved a carton of eggs. "What do you mean?"

"Amy, close that door for heaven's sake. Just stick the chicken in and close the door." Isabelle was filling the sink with hot water, tying an apron around her waist.

Amy closed the refrigerator door. "What do you mean, had her consciousness raised?"

"I don't really know if that's what happened. But you know how all sorts of women are getting together these days in these groups."

"But what are they?" Amy sat down at the table and opened her biology book. She still had homework to do.

"As far as I can tell," Isabelle said, scrubbing a plate vigorously, "women sit around and complain about their husbands and encourage each other to get divorced."

"Mrs. Robertson was in one of those groups?"

"Oh, Amy, I don't really know. I just know that Arlene said she'd gone home to live with her parents."

"But how come?"

"Good heavens, Amy. I really don't know." Isabelle rinsed the plates, then wiped at the faucets.

Amy did not ask anything more.

"Anyway." Isabelle sighed and dried her hands on a towel. "Poor man. To have his wife run off." (She would remember this later—that she had stood in the kitchen and said *Poor man.*)

"Maybe he doesn't care," Amy said, flipping through her biology book. "Maybe he was sick of her."

"Who knows," Isabelle said idly, "the way things are today. But it seems to me being sick of each other is not much of a reason to get divorced." She went into the living room and got out her sewing basket to mend the hem on one of her skirts. It riled her a bit, really, to think of people being so careless with their marriages. "If people remain considerate and kind they don't get sick of each other," she said to no one in particular, measuring off an arm's length of thread.

Amy, sitting at the kitchen table, stared at her biology book. For a while now her homework had not been getting done. Just yesterday she received a poor grade on her biology quiz, and written across the top was a note from the teacher: *Your mind is not on your work.*

ISABELLE HAD FOUND herself so absorbed in the world of Madame Bovary that she long ago stopped congratulating herself for reading the book. When the women in the office room began calling her Madame Ovary ("Here's Madame Ovary," someone might say as Isabelle walked into the lunchroom), she was distressed not so much by the teasing but because she no longer felt comfortable reading the book at work and had to delay the pleasure until she was home. But she kept the paperback with her in her pocketbook, and finding the weather to be once again clear and warm, she slipped quietly out one day at lunchtime and sat in her car in the parking lot, where she chewed her thumbnail till it bled while poor Emma Bovary finally died horribly on her bed.

Isabelle wept. She looked through the cubbyhole for a napkin to dab at her eyes and thought what a mess Emma Bovary had made of her life. Isabelle even spoke it aloud. "What a *mess*," she said, and blew her nose. She was glad it was Emma who had suffered all this and not herself. She was very glad of that. Isabelle took a deep breath and looked through the windshield at the parking lot, where bits of gravel glinted in the sun. It seemed both a relief and just a little bit boring to be in the parking lot of a shoe mill in Shirley Falls in the twentieth century when most of her mind still held the sponginess of the awful mess that had just taken place in a French village a century before: she pictured the small room, bees at the window, Emma's last cries of poisonous pain. . . . Awful, awful, awful. She felt so sorry for Emma. Tears welled in Isabelle's eyes again.

But still. Still and all. (Isabelle took one last look at Emma Bovary and put her in the cubbyhole.) She had brought it on herself. She really had, she just really, really had. Emma had a perfectly decent husband in Charles. If she had been loving to him she would have found that he was capable of growing into a strong and interesting man. Isabelle believed this. As a matter of fact, Isabelle had not been able to shake the feeling that she herself would have been very pleased with a husband like Charles, and so she had some difficulty, of course, seeing things from Emma's point of view.

But it was complicated. Because deep in Isabelle's heart she understood the terrible longings Emma had. There was not a person in Shirley Falls who would have believed this of Isabelle, but she held within her the memories of a devastating physical love with a man, and these memories danced inside her at times like a living thing. It had been wrong, though—as wrong as a thing can be—and her heart bounced furiously now inside her chest; she felt she would suffocate in this car.

She calmed herself by walking along the edge of the parking lot and gazing at two hawks gliding high in the blue sky, and then down at the river, the sudsy, roiling water spewing out from under the mill over the granite rocks. Emma Bovary had been selfish, Isabelle told herself, selfish and unloving, and proof of this was not merely in her indifference to her husband but in the dreadful neglect of her child. No, Emma Bovary was far more evil than Isabelle Goodrow ever had been or ever could be, and if in the end she died a loathsome death, well, she had no one to blame but herself.

Isabelle pulled open the heavy back door of the mill, grateful for the familiar smell of leather and glue, the loud clanking from the machine room she passed, the whirring sound of the elevator as it brought her up and deposited her into the quiet hallway outside the office room. She stopped in the ladies' room to freshen her lipstick and comb her hair, considering as she did these things that she might not read another book for a while, that life was difficult enough without bringing someone else's sorrows to crash down about your head.

"GOING TO STOP by and see me this afternoon?" Mr. Robertson would say quietly to Amy as she left his class, or if he met her during the day in the hallway, and then Amy would go to his classroom after school and they would stand by the windows talking, or they might sit on top of the desks. "Going to let me drive you home again?" he would ask, and so it became a pattern: their walk out to the teachers' parking lot, their drive along Route 22, and then sitting in her driveway in his car.

She had not intended to kiss him again, but the very next time he drove her home, as she prepared to get out of the car, he had said teasingly, "No kiss today?" and leaned toward her, offering his cheek. So that became part of the pattern as well, her lips lightly touching his bearded cheek.

One day he turned his head and kissed her on the mouth. "Have a good evening," he said afterward, with a brief nod of his head.

That night she did not do any homework again. She did not do much of anything except move restlessly about the house, thinking of his deliberate kiss to her mouth. Isabelle felt her forehead to see if she was sick.

"I'm fine," Amy said. "Really."

But it was hard, this whole business of lying to her mother. She said now, sitting down on the edge of the couch and holding some hair up in front of her face, as though checking for split ends. "Tomorrow I'll probably be staying a little bit after school again."

"English Club?"

"Math," Amy said. (There was no English Club. She had made that up on the spur of the moment one day.) "Math help. Well, not *help*. A few of us are really good in math and the teacher's been giving us this trigonometry stuff. Practically college stuff. He said he'll work extra with us sometimes after school."

"Oh, really," said Isabelle, completely fooled. "Isn't that nice. Interesting, too."

"Why interesting?" Amy kept squinting at the hair she held before her face; her eyes were almost crossed.

"Because my father was very good with numbers. Maybe you inherited it from him."

Amy wasn't so good in math. When she saw Mr. Robertson after school they never talked about math. "I like English better," she said, dropping her hair, and thinking again about Mr. Robertson's wife and why she had left him. He must have asked her to leave.

"I finished that book I was reading," Isabelle was saying. "*Madame Bovary,* by that French writer." (She was afraid she would mispronounce his name.) "Really very good. A classic."

"So anyways," Amy said, "if I have to stay after school I'll call you so you won't get worried if you call and I'm not here."

"Yes," said Isabelle, "do that. Please. I would worry myself sick."

Mr. Robertson, meanwhile, seemed no different—with a wife, or without. He still drove her home. They still sat in his car. To the side of the house the tulip bed blazed in yellow and red. He kissed her every day now, comfortably, briefly, on the mouth. But one warm day in May, even though he had just said, "Well, my dear, you'd best be getting out," Amy thought she saw a fleeting difference in his eyes and in the slow way he leaned toward her while looking at her mouth.

Chapter

10

Dr. Gerald Burrows fingered a button on his suit jacket and gazed steadily at the patient before him, a man only slightly younger than Dr. Burrows himself, who, in recounting a childhood fishing trip with his recalcitrant father, was quietly ripping to shreds the Kleenex tissue in his hands. When the man glanced out the window for a distracted moment, Dr. Burrows let his eyes move fleetingly to the clock— a small, gray, discreet clock placed on a table a little to the left and behind the patient's chair.

Dr. Burrows, who prided himself on the meticulous attention he gave to his patients, was having difficulty concentrating on the tale unfolding before him of this sorrowful fishing trip some thirty years ago. While he believed himself to be adequately accustomed to the periods of discouragement his line of work brought with it, Dr. Burrows was particularly aware these days of a pervasive sense of futility. No one got well—almost no one, anyway. The disabilities of the people who came to him were established so young, in such delicate years, that their tender agonies were, by the time they arrived in his office, thickened into a stunned arrangement of expressions, deflections, and shrewd manipulations. No, they did not get well. They came because they were lonely, and because their pain genuinely confused them. At best, he thought, still fingering the button on his jacket, he could provide a refuge from judgment, a moment of collection, of repose.

He could not provide this for himself. Behind the implacable expression on his face right now was the continued, nagging thought of his daughter. Stacy hated him. He could see it in her silent, sneering glances, could detect it in the arrogant slump of her body at the breakfast table each morning. It was frightening how in her momentary, insolent glance at him before she left the kitchen he saw, or felt he saw, a hardened look of knowingness.

Where such acrimony came from he was not altogether certain. But it indicated (it had to, didn't it?) that she had not been raised as gracefully as she might have been. He had been firm about adopting a baby at birth rather than an older child, precisely to avoid this dark imprint of damage—as though *he* could raise the squalling, red-faced baby damage-free! She had been angry even then. Weeks old, she had squinted at them furiously in between her cries; in moments of repose she stared at them with baleful eyes. A difficult birth, they had found out later—she had been stuck in the birth canal with the umbilical cord tightening around her neck. Was it this—the shadowy knowledge, the remnants of this trauma—that the girl rebelled against?

He did not believe it. He knew if some patient in his office tried to pass off an angry daughter as the result of a difficult birth he would not believe it. He would wonder instead what was going on in the home, what was going on in the family's present-day life.

Here Dr. Burrows moved slightly in his chair. He was not going to pretend everything was jolly in their everyday life, but his other children, the twins, were fine—healthy little boys, racing around the house, always glad to see him. (So explain that, he thought belligerently, to no one in particular.) He gazed at the man before him and nodded slightly to make up for the lack of attention. The man had finished his story and was giving Dr. Burrows a look both apologetic and plaintive. "All right," Dr. Burrows said. "This gives us a great deal to think about. We'll pick up on this next time."

The man's face, naked in its hunger for a smile of approbation, hung in Dr. Burrows's mind long after the man had left and closed the door. It bothered him to think how he, too, plaintively wanted more.

. . .

Isabelle's moods began to vary with alarming speed. She wondered if she had always been this way and simply failed to notice. No. Good heavens, you noticed something like this: driving to the A&P feeling collected and cozy, as though your clothes fit around you exactly right, and then by the time you drove home feeling completely undone, because as you walked across the parking lot the smell of the grocery bag you held in your arms had mingled with the smell of spring and produced some scrape of longing in your heart. Frankly, it was exhausting. Because for all those moments of hope that God was near, of some bursting, some widening seeming to take place in her heart, Isabelle had other moments that could only be described as rage.

The sight of Amy's dirty laundry waiting to be done, for example, could make Isabelle feel fury, because it suddenly seemed the mere maintenance of the girl was more than she was up to, and Isabelle did not understand this, for weren't the really difficult years of raising this child behind her? Why did it seem at times that she was losing her footing on this tightrope of *taking care*?

Worry, worry, worry. This is what she was telling Avery Clark one morning as she sat across from his desk, leaning forward slightly as she held the Styrofoam cup of coffee above her knee. "With a child," she said, "it's always worry, worry, worry." But she said this lightly, punctuating it with a self-mocking smile in which the corners of her mouth came down.

"Oh, sure," said Avery with a chuckle. He leaned back in his swivel chair and told a rambling story then about his son going out boating with a friend one day and not getting back until after dark. Avery took such a long time in telling this (including the brief interruption of a phone call) that Isabelle began to wonder what to do with her face; the look of pleasant expectation was actually beginning to make her face twitch, but Avery eventually reached his conclusion.

"And when he finally walked through that door I didn't know whether to kill him or hug him." Avery laughed out loud and shook his head. "Oh boy," he said, "was I upset."

"Of course," Isabelle exclaimed. "Why, there's nothing like it in the world." But Avery was not listening. He was laughing again and shaking his head. "Boy, oh boy," he repeated, "was I upset."

AMY COULD THINK of very little other than the open mouth of Mr. Robertson: the shock of his slippery warm tongue tumbling over hers, the light whisper of a groan that had risen from his throat as he pressed the back of her head with his hand, the cracking sound of his jaw at one point as his mouth had opened even further, thrusting his tongue against her inner cheek, a living warm thing let loose inside her mouth. She was partly relieved when he finally said softly, "Amy, you'd better go in."

She had sat motionless on the living-room couch for many minutes before her mother got home. It was absolutely incredible: Mr. Robertson had French-kissed her. Completely incredible. He had actually done that. So did it mean he loved her? The kiss had not seemed loving. It had seemed, in a way, to have very little to do with her. But that was stupid, because you would only kiss someone that way if you liked them a great deal. Still, sitting in the quiet living room, she felt uneasy, almost sad.

In the morning she didn't feel that way. She woke up with a sense of calm efficiency, as though something central in her life was figured out. She shampooed, brushing her hair while it was wet, something Isabelle told her never to do, and it dried glossy and silky and wavy, looking perfect with the pink sweater she wore over her light-blue dress.

"Oh my, don't you look lovely," Isabelle said, shaking Rice Krispies into a bowl.

But by midmorning she no longer looked lovely; in the girls'-room mirror her face was pallid. Her hair, brushed so extensively that morning, now seemed to have no weight and floated foolishly in all directions like the hair of a child just woken from a nap. Adding to this cumulative disarray was the astonishing fact that Mr. Robertson did not look at her once all during class.

She had not expected this. A knowing glance, a quick warm smile, a surreptitious wink? Nothing. He did not look at her at all. He praised Julie LaGuinn, the quiet plain girl in the front row. "Very good," he said, looking over her shoulder as she worked. "Excellent. Here's a girl who knows how to think." And when the bell rang Mr. Robertson simply walked to his desk while Amy, dazed, moved out into the hall, where a group of boys pushed past her on their way to the gym.

Stacy was absent. She was not in study hall and she was not waiting by Amy's locker at lunchtime either. Once, when it was Amy who had been home with strep throat, Stacy had called her at lunchtime to report on the "fucking morons" she'd had to eat lunch with, and now Amy, finding a coin in the bottom of her purse, went to the foyer, where the pay phone was.

Stacy answered on the fifth ring. "Hello," she said sullenly.

"It's me," Amy said. She saw Karen Keane walking up and down the foyer, hands clasped behind her back, her face tilted upward like one of those girls in a magazine ad who had just emerged from a swimming pool.

"Hi," Stacy said, without expression.

"Are you sick?" Amy asked, still eyeing Karen Keane, who, glancing Amy's way, indicated with a nod of her head that she was waiting to use the phone.

There was a pause, empty space in the phone, then Stacy said, "I have to go to the doctor." She sniffed, and added dully, "Oh, fuck."

"Are you all right?" Amy turned toward the wall, holding the phone with both hands. "Karen Keane is waiting to use the phone," she added softly.

"My mother's taking me to the doctor's," Stacy said.

"Are you sick?" Amy asked again.

"I just have to go to the doctor's," Stacy repeated. "Tell Karen Keane to fuck herself on a flagpole. Tell the whole fucking school to go eat shit and die."

ISABELLE, HAVING FINISHED her coffee, was just bending over to throw the Styrofoam cup into the wastebasket in Avery Clark's office, smoothing her hand delicately over her hips, when Avery said, "Oh, Isabelle."

Isabelle turned to face him, feeling ladylike and pretty (their conversations over the worries of parenthood had been a pleasant one, she thought) and raised her eyebrows in inquiry, pressing her lips together in case her lipstick was smudgy.

"I was wondering. I've had a thought." Avery was leaning forward over his desk, and Isabelle realized that what he was saying was not meant to be heard by the others in the office room.

"Yes?" She sat back down on the edge of the chair, leaning forward, letting him know by her expression that of course any secret was safe with her.

"Well, it's just a thought," Avery said, "but I might be able to use Amy here this summer."

Isabelle's eyebrows went up again; she tilted her head with encouragement.

"It's not something Dottie Brown wants anyone to know at this stage of the game," Avery said quietly, still leaning forward, his eyes briefly looking through the large glass at the women sitting at their desks, "but apparently she may need some time off. She's going to have an operation, it seems." And he mouthed the words "Female trouble."

"Oh, I see. Well, goodness, I hope she's all right."

Avery nodded quickly. "Nothing serious, I think. But she may be gone for the summer. It seems her doctor told her to take off a number of weeks and simply recover. I've told her she needn't rush right back."

"That's awfully nice of you."

"And the thought did occur to me that I could use someone for a little extra help. Simple things, of course. Filing. Checking invoices. Very simple stuff. Tell me, how old is Amy exactly? If she comes in full time she'll have to be sixteen."

"She turns sixteen in three weeks," Isabelle said. "Although, my word, I can barely believe it."

"Well," said Avery, sitting back and looking pleased. "You think about it. But I think if she'd like a summer job here, I can see to it."

"That's really very kind of you," Isabelle responded. "It's almost too good to be true. Last year she baby-sat at the church a few mornings a week, but of course she's old enough to take on more. And it would be wonderful for her to start saving money for college."

"Great." Avery nodded his head. "You let me know. And meanwhile if you could keep this quiet, please. I think Dottie intends to tell people soon."

Isabelle held up her hand. "Of course." She stood to go. "Thank you again," she said quietly, feeling inside her a lovely glow, thinking that if the weather was nice tomorrow she might wear her periwinkle-blue linen dress.

The House was quiet and still. Sitting on the couch Amy did not know what to do. In spite of the vast afternoon sunshine that had poured over her on the way home from school, making the road in places smell tarry and warm, the house was somewhat chilly and dark, built as it was beneath evergreen trees with the front windows facing north.

Entering the unlit rooms—the silent kitchen with its chairs pushed against the table as though they had been standing at attention all day; the living room, which seemed to ache with its own loneliness, the brown afghan folded tidily across the back of the couch, the Boston fern on its spindly black stand—all this added to the heaviness of Amy's heart. She sat for a long time on the couch, not knowing what to do. She could not imagine, upholstery scratchy on her thighs, how it was that for so many years she had managed to come home every day to this emptiness she saw before her. How she had managed to walk through the kitchen door, flip through the cupboards, make herself tea, sit down at the kitchen table with her homework. If her life was to return to this—and apparently it was, because Mr. Robertson had completely ignored her all day—she did not know what she would do.

In the stillness of the house the telephone rang.

Amy got up from the couch. It would be her mother, and she didn't want to talk to her mother, but she went quickly into the kitchen and caught the phone in the middle of the ring.

There was nothing. A pause. Blank air.

"Hello?" Amy said again.

"Hi there," a man whispered.

Amy's heart began to beat so fast she could hear it through her chest. "Who is this?" And then, "Who is calling, please?"

"Hi there," the man whispered again. "Do you like vanilla ice cream?" The voice was low and very husky, sounding faintly southern.

"Oh, please," Amy said, close to tears. "Who is this, please?"

The man whispered slowly, obscenely gentle. "I want to lick vanilla ice cream off your cunt."

Amy put the phone down as though in her hand it had become a snake. "Oh God," she whimpered. "Oh please, God." She dragged a kitchen chair up to the door, tilting its back beneath the doorknob as she had seen her mother do in February after the disappearance of Debby Kay Dorne.

Amy's arms, her bare legs beneath her dress, broke into a mass of goose bumps, her lips, her mouth, immediately became dry. She picked up the phone and began to dial her mother, because all she wanted was her mother. And yet at the last moment, in that split second right before her mother's phone in the office room was to begin to ring, Amy hung up. Across her fear, like the thinnest line of silver, came the knowledge that if she called her mother now, her mother would panic. (Amy was panicking. Her arm on the kitchen counter was shaking.) And then her mother from now on would want to know where she was every single second, even more than she did already, and what if Mr. Robertson started to be nice again?

She did not call her mother.

But she was afraid. She forced herself to go upstairs, to look under the beds, to open the closets. The metal hangers in her mother's closet swung slightly from the motion of the open door, tinging together briefly like a sinister charm.

Oh, she was so frightened! The awful, still, dark house. Running back downstairs, she even checked the cabinets in the kitchen, she even opened the refrigerator door. She was afraid to peer out the window at the driveway or porch, in case some man was standing there. And then she was engorged with terror at the thought of a man peering through the window, trying to find within the shadows of the rooms where Amy might be hiding.

Crying softly, she crept into the front hall closet, sitting down on top of boots, behind the quilted hemline of her mother's winter coat. She thought of Debby Dorne; every detail she had heard or read came back to her. Little twelve-year-old Debby, dressed in a jumper and bright gold kneesocks, waiting for her mother to come home. She had disappeared sometime between two and five o'clock, waiting for her mother to come home.

Amy was too frightened to stay in the closet. She clambered over the boots and emerged, her eyes darting down the hallway. Once again she went through the house checking everything, and then she sat at the kitchen table and waited. She did not know if she was waiting for her kidnapper or her mother, or which one would arrive first. Or if she should just leave the house altogether. She would be safer, she thought, if she left the house completely. But the barren road, the empty stretch along Route 22 . . . So she sat, her palms making damp prints on the kitchen table.

The telephone rang again.

Amy stared at where it sat on the kitchen counter: a black snake once more, coiled, rising with its rattle. She was crying when she answered it.

"So guess what," said Stacy cheerfully, snapping gum. "I'm rolling along at seven months. Can you *believe* I'm pregnant?"

Stacy's parents came to school without her and spent the morning in meetings with the principal and the vice-principal and the guidance counselor, as well as each one of her teachers. Her condition was going to be handled honestly. Amy, having learned this from Stacy's telephone call, caught a glimpse of Mr. and Mrs. Burrows in the guidance office as she passed by on her way to study hall, and she was surprised at the perky smile on Mrs. Burrows's face, the energetic nodding among these adults, as though something had given them cause to celebrate. Later, looking out the window of her English class, she saw the Burrowses leaving school—Mrs. Burrows, very skinny, still smiling and nodding to her husband as they walked across the parking lot, Mr. Burrows with a slump to his shoulders as he opened the car door for his wife, touching her back briefly before she got in. ("My parents are being so nice," Stacy had said on the telephone. "God, they're just being so nice.")

A wasp moved back and forth over the sunny windowsill while old Mrs. Wheelwright, rouge caught in the wrinkles of her cheeks, wrote on the blackboard: *Wordsworth—beauty of the natural world,* and the wasp, making a sudden dart into the classroom, rose up and knocked against the ceiling with a faint click, then in a slower spiral found the window and flew out. "Isn't it nice," Mrs. Wheelwright said (no one was listening; it was the last period before lunch, and the room, on the top floor, was very warm), "to think of daffodils leaning their little heads against the rocks to rest."

Amy, glancing at her, had to look away. Two thoughts arrived at once: She would never be a teacher, no matter how much her mother wanted her to be, and she would go to Mr. Robertson after school and beg him to be friends again, for this morning in class he had ignored her once more. It had made her panic, and now ordinary details of her day seemed altered: Mrs. Wheelwright was a corpse raised from the dead; her classmates (Maryanne Barmble in the seat next to her writing on her desk in capital letters WORDSWORTH FUCKED HIS SISTER) were a separate species altogether. There seemed little left to Amy except for some all-consuming dread.

But there were people in the town of Shirley Falls who were perfectly happy that day. The Spanish teacher, Miss Lanier, for example, right downstairs from Amy in the teachers' room was smiling broadly as she filled her coffee cup: the principal, Lenny Mandel, had invited her to have dinner with his mother that night. "You're both nice people," he had said. "I'm sure you'll get along." And Avery Clark's wife, Emma, having received the news that morning that her eldest son had been accepted into a graduate program at Harvard, was now—the appropriate calls having all been made—lying on her bed with her arms outstretched, wiggling her toes in their pantyhose. Mrs. Errin, the dentist's wife, was happy because she had found some shoes on sale, and because her husband—having met with his accountant—was in a cheerful mood.

So there were a variety of joys, large and small, taking place throughout the town, including a hearty laugh between Dottie Brown and Fat Bev as they sat at their desks in the office room, the kind of laugh (in this case regarding Dottie Brown's mother-in-law) that comes from two women who have known each other for many years, who take comfort and joy in the small, familiar expressions of one another, and who feel, once the laugh has run its course—with an occasional small giggle still left, and a tissued patting of the eyes—a lingering warmth of human connection, the belief that one is not, after all, so very much alone.

. . .

SHE WENT TO his classroom after school and discovered Julie LaGuinn standing at the blackboard.

"Amy?" Mr. Robertson said. "Did you want to see me?" She didn't answer, and he said, "Have a seat. We're almost through."

When Julie LaGuinn left, casting an impassive glance in Amy's direction, Mr. Robertson sighed deeply and sat down in a chair near Amy. "So," he said, crossing his arms and leaning back, "how are you, Amy Goodrow?"

"Good."

They sat silently, not looking at each other. The large clock on the wall made a tick. Through the open window a school bus groaned, and the breeze brought with it the smell of lilacs that were now blooming grandly by the school's front door. Finally Mr. Robertson said quietly, "Come on, I'll drive you home."

And when it seemed that all in fact was probably lost—that whatever had changed between them was going to stay that way—Mr. Robertson had pulled the car off the road and parked beneath some trees. "Let's take a walk," he said.

They walked down the faint imprint of what had once been a lumber road, both keeping their eyes on the groove of a tire track now overgrown with weedy vines, until Mr. Robertson said, "To kiss you like that, Amy, was not a good idea."

"You mean because you're married?" (She had come here with her mother. They had looked for wildflowers each spring when she was little; hepaticas, trillium, jack-in-the-pulpit. Once they found lady's-slippers, which Isabelle said should be kept a secret, since people might come and pick them—they were that rare.)

Mr. Robertson was shaking his head, poking at a small rock with the tip of his shoe. "No, we've separated. My wife's gone back to live with her folks."

Amy fingered the sides of her dress; she wasn't going to tell him this was something she already knew.

"No." Mr. Robertson walked again, and she followed. "It's because if people found out we were kissing each other they wouldn't really understand."

"But why would anyone find out?"

He turned his head and glanced at her briefly, carefully.

"How could anyone find out?" she asked again, looking at him through her long coils of hair. "I would never tell anyone."

"I don't know," he said. "You might."

They stopped walking. Amy stood silently while a whippoorwill called. Mr. Robertson crossed his arms and gazed through half-closed eyes at his young protégée.

A FTER THAT IT rained for three days—a steady, unpleasant rain that beat against rooftops and cars and sidewalks; pools of water gathered in parking lots, their surfaces breaking continually from water landing on water so they seemed like small ponds filled with fish in a biting frenzy. A torrent of water fell from the edge of the school building where a gutter pipe was broken, and the ground beneath it was no longer grassy, or even muddy; all its color had been beaten away, and there was only the collection of soggy wetness where that part of the lawn had been.

Stacy came out of the building quickly, then stopped, saying "Shit," and touched Amy's sleeve. "Just run for it," she directed, and they ran, splashing across the lawn and then the parking lot, getting their shoes soaked, the front of their thighs and shoulders drenched, until they reached the car they were headed for and piled into the back seat, saying with reckless laughter "Oh shit, oh Christ, oh my God, am I wet!"

The car, a dented yellow Volkswagen, belonged to a senior named Jane Monroe who was letting them smoke in it these rainy days. The girls moved to the center of the seat to avoid the water that slid in and dripped down, and lit their cigarettes. Stacy's parents had given her money to buy little "treats": makeup, jewelry—whatever, they said, would help make her feel better about herself. She bought two cartons of cigarettes, one to keep at school, one stored beneath her bed, as well as a big bag of candy bars. Now the girls smoked with one hand, eating candy with the other, while the rain smashed against the windshield. "I'm happy," Amy said, and they smiled at each other.

"Oh, yeah," Stacy said, "this is great. If this car had a bathroom things would be fucking perfect."

"You sure Jane doesn't mind her car getting all wet and smoky." Amy peered through the bag of candy and poked around.

"Doesn't give a shit," Stacy said. "She's out in some truck getting stoned with her boyfriend."

Stacy had become a celebrity. The school, having been presented with the situation in such a straightforward manner, was anxious to appear modern, enlightened, accommodating. Even the teachers indifferent to these qualities possessed compassion in their hearts for such a young girl (only fifteen!), who, they decided, had clearly been taken advantage of. Among the older teachers (kindly Mrs. Wheelwright) there was talk in the teachers' room of how this always happened to the "nice girls," meaning that any girl capable of cold-bloodedly taking precautions must be a whore.

But something else was involved here, an element of the situation that was left unsaid but that played a big role in the accommodating attitude of the school. And this was the fact that Stacy Burrows lived in the Oyster Point section of town. Stacy did not live in the Basin, her parents did not work at the mill, or run a gas station, or live on a farm. Stacy's father was a college professor, a psychologist; her parents were "intellectuals," and they lived in one of those new homes with a mansard roof to prove it. True enough that eyebrows were raised in some parts of town, but the fact remained: Stacy's father had a certain kind of status, and if he and his wife were going to be breezy and up-front about their daughter's pregnancy, no one wanted to be caught looking down their nose.

This feeling extended to her classmates as well. Far from having to endure whispers or sneers, Stacy was treated like a hero. Kids looked kindly at her in the hallway, standing back as she moved to her locker, saying, "Hey, Stacy, how you doing these days?" Older girls befriended her—Jane Monroe, generous with her car. And one of the snobbiest girls in the senior class, whose father was head deacon of the Congregational church, spoke with Stacy at great length one morning in the girls' room, confessing that she herself had had not one but two abortions in New York, and still owed money for them.

Stacy glowed beatifically through all of this. She also looked suddenly and absolutely pregnant, as though her body, with the acknowledgment of its condition, had finally been released; her spine swayed backward to accommodate the protrusion, round as a basketball, that showed its outline beneath her baggy sweaters.

The sweaters belonged to her father. On warm days she wore her father's shirts, which came almost to her knees, so that at times she looked like an innocent redheaded milkmaid wearing a cotton frock. Beneath these capacious tops, however, she had the same pair of old jeans on every day and simply left the fly unzipped; her parents, in spite of their gift of cash for little treats, had decided they would not be buying their daughter any maternity clothes. Stacy didn't seem to find this odd, and moved contentedly through the rainy days with the bottom inches of her jeans soaking wet; they were bell-bottoms, and the torn hems flapped across the wet pavement.

In the car with Stacy's leg draped over hers, Amy pulled at a thick wet thread falling from the jeans and listened while Stacy reported on the people who had been nice to her that day. "Puddy Mandel fell over trying to get the door for me in the gym. He blushes whenever he sees me." Stacy paused to drag on her cigarette. "A kick about Sally, isn't it." (Sally being the deacon's daughter who had two abortions under her belt.) Stacy leaned forward to toss her cigarette out the car window and then broke open the carton of her milk, which she was drinking every day at lunch now. "Walks around like a little Girl Scout and she's out there spreading her legs." Stacy leaned her head back, drinking and laughing silently, so that milk spilled down her chin.

"Don't laugh when you drink—it can come out your nose."

Stacy nodded. "One time I was chewing on a Tootsie Roll lying down—" Amy wiggled her fingers to indicate Stacy had told that story before, and Stacy swallowed her milk and said, "Hurt like a motherfucker. One of the guys that knocked Sally up was a black man she met hanging out at the college. I told you that, right?"

Amy nodded. It was amazing, really, the secret, busy underworld of the school. It would have depressed her if her own life did not include Mr. Robertson, but it did, and while she did not confide this to Stacy, the fact was like a pillow right next to her in the car whose casing was soft and warm and redolent of the scent of skin.

"The black guy took her on a Greyhound bus to New York. She told her parents she was at Denise's, and then she had cramps all the way back. Is there any gum in there?"

Amy peered into the bag of candy bars and shook her head.

Stacy lit another cigarette and dropped the match out the window. "What would your mother do if you got pregnant?"

Amy looked at her. "*My* mother?"

"You're not going to get pregnant. But let's just say you did. You know. What would your mother do?" Stacy spread her fingers over the ball of her stomach and blew a flattened stream of smoke from between her pressed lips.

"Send me away."

"Yeah?" Stacy raised an eyebrow.

"She'd send me away." Amy nodded. She could not explain the certainty she felt about this, but she knew such a crime would result in banishment.

"I don't think your mother would send you away," Stacy said, dismissively, evidently bored already by the question she had raised, and by the vast unlikeliness of Amy Goodrow's getting pregnant. "I'm sleepy," she added, closing her eyes comfortably, leaning her head against the back of the seat.

"Me too." But through the sound of the rain beating on the car came the resolute drill of the school bell.

"Shit." Stacy opened her eyes and inhaled twice, intensely, before dropping the cigarette through the crack in the window. They packed themselves together, rolled up the windows, then ran back across the rain-soaked parking lot.

"Did I tell you about the vitamin pills I have to take?" Stacy shouted, leaning against a gust of wind that was blowing the rain straight into their faces. Amy shook her head. "They're huge," Stacy called out. "Big as fucking footballs." She started to jump over a puddle, thought better of it, and simply walked through, dragging the wet bottoms of her jeans.

B Y AFTERNOON AMY was sitting again in a car parked in the rain watching through the streaming windshield as the lilac bush by her front porch wavered and bounced beneath the steady downpour. The new petunias in the window boxes seemed beaten beyond repair, their crepey lavender blossoms smashed closed. Only the marigolds appeared resilient and unperturbed, solid buttons of yellow lining the walkway to the house.

" '*Sorrow like a ceaseless rain beats upon my heart,*' " Amy recited slowly.

"Really?" Mr. Robertson had turned his back against the car door so that he was facing her.

"Not really," Amy said, smiling, and he watched with his slow gaze, his eyelids slightly dropped, for he knew of course that she was not sad. They had only now just finished their first kiss of the afternoon, which had begun as soon as Mr. Robertson turned off the engine of his car.

"I wouldn't want you to be sad," Mr. Robertson said, almost sleepily, his eyelids still slightly dropped in that knowing, intimate way he had.

Amy turned to watch the rain again, wondering how people lived without this kind of love. Yesterday he had studied her fingertips one by one while she told him about the man who called and said he wanted to lick ice cream—"off my body" is how she put it to Mr. Robertson, because she wasn't going to say that other word—and Mr. Robertson had said to tell him if it ever happened again.

Turning her face away from the rainy windshield, she was hoping he would kiss her more, touch her hair again. But he stayed where he was, looking sleepy, his back against the car door, running a finger idly along the edge of the steering wheel. "Tell me about your friend Stacy," he said.

"What do you want to know?"

Mr. Robertson watched his finger trace the steering wheel and said in a lazy, quiet way, "She likes some action, does she?"

Amy shrugged.

"Who's the boyfriend?" Mr. Robertson asked.

She told him how Paul Bellows used to be a football star and how he pumped gas now at the Sunoco station on Mill Road. "He cried when Stacy broke up with him," she added, and wished immediately she hadn't said it. It made Stacy seem very attractive.

"His treasure trove gone." Mr. Robertson, unsmiling, ran his fingers lightly through Amy's hair, looking at it with half-closed eyes.

"I shouldn't have told you that part," Amy said. "It's not that Stacy asked me not to—"

He cut her off, taking her wrist. "Your secrets are safe with me." He put Amy's finger into his mouth and she did not think about Stacy or Paul anymore.

Chapter

12

M<small>ISS</small> D<small>AVINIA</small> D<small>AYBLE</small>, the math teacher whose earlier fall down the cellar stairs had precipitated the hiring of Mr. Robertson, had recovered from the crack to her skull, and having spent a bored and fretful spring cooped up at home, she was looking forward to and planning on the return to teaching high school in the fall. This Robertson fellow would have to move on.

But celebrating her birthday on a windy day in the first week of June, Davinia Dayble coasted down her driveway on a contraption amounting to, in essence, a very large tricycle, and turned over on the blacktop, breaking her hip. Her brother, a pale, startled-looking man of sixty-three, was horrified; the bicycle, or tricycle, really, for it had one very large wheel in front and two smaller ones in back, had been a gift from him; he had thought on summer days she might pedal into town, using the straw basket attached to the handlebars to bring home small items—books from the library perhaps, or a loaf of bread. But there she lay, sprawled on the driveway, her shoes flung into the grape hyacinth bed.

So Emma Clark, Avery's wife, made a visit to the hospital. Emma Clark was on the Sunshine Committee at the Congregational church, and it was now her duty to call upon the ill. She stood with bored graciousness at the foot of the hospital bed, commenting on flowers and hospital food; all the while an unpleasant odor was filling the room.

Davinia Dayble appeared overheated; her forehead glistened and her cheeks were red. But she talked without pausing about how she had missed being at school this year, at which point Emma Clark thought to tell her there was a girl who was now attending school well into a pregnancy—the psychologist's daughter, Emma believed—and the school didn't seem to be making any fuss about the situation at all.

Davinia shook her head. She had heard about it already, and who could believe such a thing? But the psychologist's daughter—that was interesting, didn't Emma think so? (Emma nodded. She thought so.) Amazing, Davinia said, when you thought about it, how times had changed—she found it all disgusting.

Emma Clark, tired of nodding, got ready to leave.

Oh, then—Davinia wondered if on her way out she could please find a nurse. She gave Emma a triumphant nod. "I'm finished with this bedpan now," she said.

Driving home, Emma Clark could not prevent certain unpleasant images from coming into her mind regarding the now obvious fact that Davinia Dayble had been using a bedpan full force throughout their entire conversation. Emma frowned into the clear June light; it riled her how Avery expected her to do these churchy things. She was going to drive home and tell him in no uncertain terms that she was *damned* sick and tired of the Sunshine Club.

B UT THE WEATHER was perfect. "Perfect weather," people said to each other, shaking their heads. The sky was vast and blue, lawns vibrant with their tender shoots of grass. Barbecue grills got rolled out of garages, and people ate supper on their front porches; there were the summer sounds of screen doors banging and ice cubes clinking, while children called out as they rode their bicycles in zigzags on the street.

Isabelle, living in her little house beneath the pines, heard the peepers in the marsh nearby and loved how long the evenings were. Poking through her window boxes, or crouching pensively as she tended the marigolds that lined the front walk, she often found herself thinking of Avery Clark's long and slightly crooked mouth, and what it would feel like, with great tenderness, to press her mouth against it. She was certain that Emma Clark had not kissed her husband tenderly in years. (Older people tended not to, she thought, just as Amy yelled out the window, "Mom, have you seen my yellow blouse? The one with the buttons in the back?") Perhaps, Isabelle considered uncharitably, Emma wore dentures that produced an awful smell. In addition to the fact, of course, that she was simply a cold fish. ("In the ironing basket," Isabelle answered. "And for heaven's sake, don't shout.") She stood, brushing a few loose strands of hair from her face, listening to the peepers and smelling the fragrance of the crushed marigolds still on her fingers. Gifts from God, she thought, picturing again the tender mouth of Avery—all these gifts from God.

But that night she had a bad dream. She dreamed that Amy took off her clothes in a field filled with hippies and walked into a muddy pond, where a man with filthy long hair embraced her, laughing. In the dream Isabelle ran through the field and frantically called her daughter's name.

Waking, she continued calling out, and found Amy standing in her nightgown by her bed. "Oh, honey," Isabelle said, confused, embarrassed, still distressed.

"You're dreaming," Amy told her, and from the light in the hallway Isabelle could see the face of her daughter, her long body in its pale nightgown leaning over the bed. "You scared me, Mom."

Isabelle sat up. "I had a terrible dream."

Amy was nice; she went into the bathroom and got her mother a glass of water.

Isabelle tightened the sheet around herself, thinking it was good to know she had a nice girl like Amy and not the dirty hippie in the dream. And to know that a mile down the road Avery Clark lay sleeping. Still, it took her a while to get back to sleep. There was a queer, unpleasant feeling that wouldn't go away, as though something lay undigested right below her ribs.

It took Amy a while to get back to sleep, too, but for her it was okay, because in the dark she smiled slightly, thinking of Mr. Robertson. They went into the woods each day now, leaving his car parked beneath the trees on the old lumber road. After the part where they walked down the path, sometimes holding hands, and after the part where Mr. Robertson talked, they would sit with their backs against the big gray rock and he would kiss her face, or sometimes after studying her lips he would kiss her hard and strong right away in the mouth, and then, rather soon, because there was never the taking-off of any clothes, they would be lying down, him moving on top of her, clothing rumpled and pressed together, while she, filled with some inner singing, damp between her legs and at the roots of her long hair, would look at the blue sky laced above the pine boughs; or if her head was turned to the side, the yellow, dancing spots of buttercups.

All this was happiness—to run her open mouth across his face, to have his dark curly hair mingled with her own, to sometimes slip her skinny fingers into his mouth and press her fingertips against his gums; oh, it was joyful heaven, to have this man *so near*.

A FEW NIGHTS later the weather turned muggy, and by morning it was very hot. The next day was hotter and even more muggy. The following day was worse. In a few more days the river smelled. The sky was pale white, indifferent. Yellow jackets hung over garbage bins in the hazy air as though too stunned to land. This was the start to what was to be one of the hottest summers in the history of Shirley Falls, but nobody knew it then. Nobody gave it much thought, except to pluck at their shirts and say, "It's the humidity that gets you, I think." It was still early in the season; people had their minds on other things.

Dottie Brown, for example, lying in her hospital bed (one flight up from Miss Dayble), staring blankly at the television set hanging from the ceiling, had survived her hysterectomy and was grateful—privately she had feared she would die. But she felt odd. On a tray beside her sat her dinner: a warm can of 7-Up, a melting scoop of lemon ice, and a Styrofoam bowl of beef broth that looked like day-old dishwater and whose smell made poor Dottie almost gag. She wondered where her husband was. The doctor said she could go home in a few days—as soon as she had a BM.

And Barbara Rawley, the deacon's wife who had annoyed Isabelle at church, and later in the A&P, was now annoyed herself. Her best friend, another deacon's wife, named Peg Dunlap, was having a disgusting affair with the psychologist Gerald Burrows, and Barbara was forced to hear about it more and more. On the phone this afternoon the woman had gone so far as to imply that their adulterous lovemaking was even better in this heat. "When his daughter got pregnant I was afraid he might call it quits with me. But, no"—a happy sigh. "*Quite* the opposite, if you get what I mean."

Barbara said she had chicken to defrost and hung up the telephone. It offended her profoundly. She knew marriage wasn't perfect; life wasn't perfect. But she wanted it to be.

THE LAST DAY of school was a Thursday, the twenty-fifth of June. Because dismissal was early and because the weather was terribly hot, the students had been told they could wear shorts if they wanted to, and now the school was filled with an anxious, festive feeling, teenagers moving about the hallways in long T-shirts and cutoff dungarees, many wearing baseball caps, or floppy denim things covering an eye. The effect was odd, as though it were a Saturday and the school building had been opened only to accommodate an overflow of the town's exuberant youth. Some students left the building and draped themselves along the front steps, or sat on the lawn, leaning back on their elbows with their faces tipped toward the sun, which baked down through a white sky.

Amy was not wearing shorts, because Isabelle that morning had not allowed her to leave the house in cutoff jeans. Only a navy-blue pair of shorts from Sears would meet with her approval, and Amy had refused them. She wore a plain white blouse and a lavender skirt and felt miserably foolish, while her classmates appeared more confident than ever, even insolent. When old Mrs. Wheelwright wished the class a very pleasant summer, few people bothered to answer. Instead students snapped gum with abandon and called out loudly to each other. To Amy it seemed that everyone had a party to go to as soon as they were released, and so it was a good thing when Mr. Robertson confirmed, murmuring to her on the way out of their final class, "I'll see you after school?"

At lunchtime she went with Stacy to their spot in the woods. Stacy, squinting into her pocketbook for the cigarette pack, said, "Shit, am I glad this year is over. What a stupid, fucking school."

Amy held a cigarette in her lips and twisted her hair off the back of her hot neck. "It's probably better than working with those farty old ladies all day in the mill," she said. "I start on Monday, you know."

"Oh, yeah," said Stacy. "What a drag." But Stacy didn't seem particularly concerned with Amy's prospects for the summer. Instead she tilted her head back, blowing up a great stream of smoke, and said, "My father's being a prick again. He was nice for a while, but now he's a prick again."

"How come?" The air was motionless, hot as an oven.

Stacy shrugged. "Made that way, I think. Who knows." She tried fanning her neck with the cigarette pack. "When you're pregnant, your body temperature rises ten degrees." With her other hand she wiped at her face. "He's always writing papers for these stupid journals and stuff."

Amy nodded, although she did not know what journals or papers Stacy meant.

"He should write one called Why I Am a Prick: A Psychological Study by Gerald Burrows, Pukehead, Ph.D." Stacy held her hair off her neck. "It is *so* fucking hot. You're lucky your hair looks pretty in this heat. Mine looks like something tacked onto the rump of a circus horse."

Amy wished she could invite Stacy to come to her house some Saturday during the summer, but what would they do at Amy's stupid, small house? Look at her mother's marigolds?

Stacy opened her carton of milk and leaned her head back. She swallowed a number of times and then said, "I met Maryanne Barmble in the store the other day with her mother. Ever seen her mother?"

Amy shook her head.

"*Just* like Maryanne. Spacey, nice. Waved her hand around in front of her face just like Maryanne does."

"Weird."

"Was weird. This milk is warm." Stacy made a face.

Amy smoked, watching Stacy pour the milk onto the ground, a white puddle separating into tiny rivers creeping over the dirt and leaves, darkening as it seeped into the soil. She missed Stacy already. Already Stacy seemed gone.

"I wonder if I'm like my real mother." Stacy smoked pensively.

"Because if everyone just turns out like their mother, then what's the rat's-ass point?"

O NCE AMY WAS in the car with Mr. Robertson, things seemed a little more normal, although it was earlier than usual, since the school day had been shortened. The sun was high and very hot in the white sky. "Am I going to see you this summer?" she blurted out, not long after they left the school parking lot.

Mr. Robertson glanced at her as though mildly surprised. "I certainly hope so," he said.

"Because on Monday, you know, I start my stupid job at the mill."

He nodded, pulling up to a stop sign. "We'll work it out," he said, touching her arm lightly.

She turned her face away, letting the air from the open window move across her neck; she held her hair in a loose fist, the tips of it tapping lightly against the window frame. For the first time she felt on the verge of a quarrel with him. Such a thing had not seemed possible before.

Nor was it possible now, for she could not find the words, could only feel a dismal petulance as she gazed out the window of the moving car and thought how he, after all these weeks of kissing in the woods, had not told her anything more about his wife, or about himself, for that matter (except for stories about his past, she thought crossly), nothing of how he felt about *things,* his plans or hopes for the future.

Finally she said, "Are you all right?" as he turned off Route 22 and parked the car under some trees partway up the old lumber road.

"I'm fine," he said, touching her hand as he pulled the key from the ignition.

But in fact he seemed distracted and silent, and things didn't go the way they usually did. When he kissed her, she felt only flatly and lucidly conscious of the pine needles beneath her bare legs and of the short, deep breathing of this man rhythmically pushing against her. She was very warm and so was he; clutching his back she could feel the moistness of his wrinkled shirt.

Finally he rolled off her and said, staring at the sky, "I guess we both knew this probably wasn't the day."

She said nothing. In a while he reached for her hand and helped her up. They walked back to the car. "You should go to college in Boston," he suddenly said. She didn't answer but instead brushed the pine needles off her leg and got into the car.

He examined a scratch on his door and then got into the car too, leaning his back against the open window, one elbow propped against the steering wheel. With his other hand he touched the inside of her arm and smiled when he saw goosebumps springing up. "You're shivering," he said, "and it's so warm."

She almost didn't like him. She dropped her eyes, shrugging slightly. The dashboard was dusty in the milky light. Her skin felt oily, not clean.

"Amy," he said. "You know you'll always be loved, don't you?"

She looked at him. For a long time she didn't say anything, but then because of the expression in his kind, sad eyes, she said, "Oh, God, that sounds like a good-bye."

He pulled her head toward him, murmuring, "No, no, no," as he stroked her hair by the side of her face. "We'll work something out, little Amy Goodrow."

She straightened up, ready to kiss him, but he seemed content to simply gaze at her, and so she sat shyly looking down at her hands in her lap.

"Amy," he said quietly, "take off your blouse."

She glanced up, surprised. He was watching her impassively through half-opened eyes.

Slowly she undid the buttons, flat, shiny buttons; one glinted in the muted sun. "All the way," he said, because she was hesitating once the buttons were undone.

She leaned forward, tilting first one shoulder, then the other one, removing the wrinkled blouse, two pine needles stuck to it. He took it from her and picked off the pine needles, and then very elaborately folded the blouse before he turned and placed it on the back seat.

She sat there in her bra from Sears, a plain white bra with a tiny appliqué of a daisy between the pointed cups. She was perspiring, and when he looked at her she wiped her hand across her mouth and looked away.

"Take that off, too." He said it very quietly, in his low, rumbly voice.

She flushed in the heat of the car. It was like her eyelids were sweating;

her eyes felt almost swollen. She hesitated, and then leaned forward and unhooked her bra; her fingertips were cold. He held out his hand and she gave him the bra. With his eyes still on her face, he dropped it onto the back-seat floor.

She looked away, at the gearshift that was there between them with its dark lump of a leathery top. He would have to be looking at her now. She blinked at the gearshift and started to raise a hand to press a finger to her mouth, but she stopped, and pressed her lips together instead. So that her hair would hide her face, she tilted her head down, and saw between the roundness of her breasts, the pale pink tips as excruciatingly exposed as something newborn, a trickle of sweat run down her stomach into the waistband of her lavender skirt.

"You're so pretty," Mr. Robertson said conversationally, but softly. "Honestly, Amy, you really are beautiful," and after that she was all right. A tiny flicker of a smile shot across her face and she looked at him, but he was looking at her there.

"Would you mind doing certain things?" he asked quietly.

She said nothing, not knowing what he meant.

For example, would she mind putting her hand under her breast and holding it toward him? She blushed and gave a small laugh, rolling her eyes quickly, embarrassed, but she did what he asked, and he looked so pleased that she didn't mind after all. She didn't mind doing more; like holding both of her breasts together, and then having her hair fall down over them with her nipples peeking through. He asked if she would mind spitting on her fingers and then touching the nipples, and she was surprised, but she did that too.

He asked her to turn one way, then another. He asked her to raise her arm and hold her hair up and tilt her head. The longer he looked at her, the more she liked it. She wished he had asked her to do these things before. With her arm raised she could smell the sweat of herself, the lilac smell of the deodorant mixed with herself. Her nose itched, and rubbing her arm across it she could smell that too, the smell of her arm.

"Touch them again," he directed, and she did.

He had her put the seat back after that, so that, really, she was lying down. Her breasts flattened out, spreading over toward her arms. It was very hot in the car.

"Close your eyes," he said.

She felt a tiny, unexpected breeze come through the window, and her eyes flickered open.

"Are you worried?" he asked gently. "I'm not going to hurt you."

She shook her head.

"I don't want you to be frightened."

"I'm not frightened. My eyes won't stay closed, though."

"That's okay. Lift up your skirt, honey. Around your waist."

She was embarrassed again, and smiled slightly, blushing, and then obediently she tugged at the lavender skirt until it was bunched at her waist, showing her white cotton Carter underpants and the slight rising from her pubic hair.

"I don't want you taking your panties off," he said. "Do you understand?"

She nodded, looking at him, her mouth parting with some deep emotion at having heard his husky, soft voice speak the word "panties." His face seemed slackened; he was staring at her down there.

"Let's just stay like this awhile," he said. "Let's just enjoy the warm summer day." A bead of sweat ran down the side of his face, disappearing into his beard; another followed. "Lie back," he said. "Try closing your eyes again. Enjoy the summer day."

He smiled at her, leaning his head back against the window frame, closing his own eyes. She closed her eyes too.

"A very beautiful girl," she heard him say quietly, and she smiled a little, her eyes still closed.

And then he had his mouth to her breast and was sucking on it, her eyes opening in amazement to see his furry mouth working, sucking slowly at first but then with greater urgency, so that in a few moments he was not just moving the hardening nipple through his mouth, but was biting it with little bites, pulling on it with his teeth. She let out a small cry, and then it really was like she was crying because the sound she made became continuous, as a series of sobs would be, but it was not a sobbing, it was an odd cry of begging, and the more she cried the more fervently he sucked on the hard nipple, and the funnel-shaped thing in her middle swirled, tugged her down there, every squeeze of his mouth made her ache down there so that her hips began to move, her middle arching up and the sound of begging filling the air.

And then he stopped, sat back. His forehead was red, the cheeks above his beard flushed with a deep red. He took his glasses off almost sternly, tossing them onto the dashboard. She thought he was angry, but he said, "Christ, you're amazing," and she closed her eyes, aching down there, her mouth dry from the quick breathing of her cries.

"Pull your pants down," he said, almost whispering. "Pull your pants down to your knees." She hesitated. "Do it," he said.

And she did, her nipples bruised and rigid in the hot air, her skirt still bunched at her waist. "They're wet," she murmured, blushing deeply, almost ready to cry with embarrassment.

"You're supposed to be wet," he told her softly, kind now, leaning over to touch not her, but the wetness of her underpants. "Because you're great. You're every man's dream. A horny girl," he was saying, running his fingers through the gumminess on her underpants and then to her amazement suddenly slipping those same fingers into her mouth, so that she tasted the odd deep saltiness of herself. "You're so fucking horny," he repeated, murmuring, and then whispered, "I want you even hornier," so that once again when a terrible embarrassment might have overtaken her completely she felt instead the thrill of pleasing him, of being encouraged, almost commanded forward—this is what he wanted, for her to be this way. He sucked her breasts again, hard, and with her nakedness exposed there in the middle, that curly pale hair just lying right there out in the open, her naked legs shiny together, the wetness of her underpants touching against her knees, she murmured, her voice halting, "I don't want to get pregnant."

Her breast still in his mouth, he said, "You won't," and while he kept on sucking her she felt his hand very lightly, so lightly, move across the top of her leg and then touch her there—his whole palm at first covering her hair, so lightly that it seemed like a faint breeze—and then with a gentle, slow deliberateness his fingertips touched her, slipping just the littlest bit inside her, and oh, the *sweetness* of this, how *sweet* of him, such sweet kindness!

He stopped sucking on her breast and smiled at her. She slipped her fingers into his mouth, ran her moist fingers across his ear. "You're not to worry," he whispered, his eyelids half lowered, his fingertips still so gently, slowly moving, and then one a little more than the rest moved into her with a sweet boldness, a knowingness. And then he leaned his head forward to watch himself do this to her down there, and she caught a glimpse of her undone self: her naked breasts wet from his mouth, still glistening, her naked middle, and right there, his large hand—oh, it was terrible how wonderful he was—this wonderful, wonderful man!

HAVING BEEN TO the dentist, Avery Clark drove home to get some papers he needed for a meeting later that afternoon, and happened to turn his head and see, as he drove down the wooded area of Route 22, the fender of a car glinting in the sun, parked under some trees down the old lumber road. It bothered him; he remembered the burglaries of winter.

Emma was not home, and he expected this. She had told him earlier she would be shopping with a friend. He found the papers he needed and scratched her a note in the kitchen, telling her he needed bridgework— darn—and he would see her at five. (It was a habit to leave her a note whenever he came home at an unaccustomed time.) Again he wondered about the car parked in the woods. It could very well belong to Hiram Crane; there was a rumor he planned on selling some land. Taxes were getting too high. But if the car was still there on his way back to work he would call Hiram just to see.

The car was still there. Avery Clark pulled over a little further up ahead and then got out and walked back. Most likely it was Hiram out with a surveyor. If not, he would get the license plate, at least, and let Hiram know what he had seen. It was decent for neighbors to keep their eyes on things. He took a few cautious steps down the lumber road. There did not appear to be anyone in the car. He mopped his brow with his handkerchief, his large shoes moving forward through the glinting buttercups, stepping on the delicate, tiny bluets that grew in patches among the blades of grass.

ISABELLE, SITTING AT her desk tired and hungry this time of day, had just straightened up her paper clips and let out a deep sigh, when glancing over at the clock she saw Avery Clark stride into the room and thought: Someone important has died.

Chapter

13

DAISIES AND PINK clover grew alongside the back roads of Shirley Falls. There were wild sweet peas too, tangled among the lupine and timothy grass, and the bramble of raspberry and blackberry bushes, as well as the large-leafed carrion twisting over stone walls, and in the fields Queen Anne's lace. But all of it had a faded, washed-out look this summer, the way weeds and wildflowers do when they grow next to a dirt road and get covered in a layer of dust; although now it was the weather doing this, the awful heat and mugginess, the unrelenting white sky stretching high around that seemed determined, somehow, to block out any of the world's usual colors.

It was June, and in June the world was supposed to be green and firm and vigorous, but this time some element had been left out, as if (thought the dairy farmer's wife, Mrs. Edna Thompson, as she hung up clothes out back one day) God had forgotten this year to fertilize his great window box of New England; the daisies grew tall but skinny, their heads not much to boast about; the petals ripped easily as children plucked at them, "Loves me, loves me not." The timothy grass rose in blades of pale green but then bent over wearily, brown at the tips. And the clusters of Queen Anne's lace that grew throughout the pastures seemed webby and gray, or not noticeable at all, just blending in with the pale white sky.

Farmers who had been working the land for many years, who had in themselves a stoic ability to endure whatever variations of the seasons Mother Nature brought, now stood in their fields fingering the pole beans that were shriveled on the vines and casting an uneasy eye at the acres of corn a good foot shorter than it should have been; for there were fields of cow fodder that seemed barely able to grow, and this is what disturbed the farmers most of all—how the spontaneous effortlessness of growth seemed gone, or stunted, anyway. In trouble. The earth seemed to be in trouble.

But generations of hardship and survival stood behind these fears. Old gravestones by the river dating back to the 1600s attested to this: mothers who had lost baby after baby, some buried without even receiving a name, though many had lived, and carried throughout their lives the names Reliance, Experience, Patience. There were families in Shirley Falls whose ancestors had been scalped by Indians. (Mrs. Edna Thompson, for example, had a great-great-great grandmother, Molly, who had been kidnapped by the Indians in 1756 and taken on foot to Canada, where she was sold to a Frenchman before her brother came to rescue her.) Homes and crops had been set fire to again and again in the early years of settlement. Such endurance—one headstone showed the name of Endurance Tibbetts—had bred men and women whose Puritan features and pale blue eyes even now remained; they were not alarmists.

Still and all, people were worried that summer, and when rumors spread that UFOs had been sighted in the northern part of the state— that the government had even sent officials up to investigate—there were people in town who refused to discuss this, who only frowned more deeply as they went about their work. Church attendance rose; without exactly forming the thought, people were praying for the appeasement of God. One glance at the river offered proof of a higher displeasure, for it lay in the middle of town like something dead, that putrid yellow foam collecting at its edge, as though a snake lay flattened in the road with its insides seeping out, infected and nasty in the colorless sun. Only the tiger lilies seemed indifferent. These bloomed along the river the way they always had; they rose up next to houses and barns and along stone walls, their tawny orange petals opened like mouths, speckled and fierce compared to everything else.

So people waited. In spite of their misgivings, the farmers, some of whose progenitors had carried the name of Patience, knew what patience was. Mill workers, too, had long ago learned to tolerate the less tolerable periods of life. It was at the college, actually, where a great deal of the complaining took place. Many of the teachers there—most of them—had not grown up in Shirley Falls; many were not even from New England. What had seemed, under the coating of soft winter snows, the succulence of spring, to be a quaint, provincial place, now, in this particular summer's stagnant heat, appeared to be only a poor New England mill town with faded brick buildings and a river that stank. So in parts of the Oyster Point section of town a certain impatience took hold. In other areas, however—the outskirts of Shirley Falls, as well as the Basin—an uneasy listlessness had settled in.

The office room at the mill certainly held the unmistakable sense of lassitude. Here large fans whirred steadily on the windowsills while invoices were slowly separated, envelopes slowly addressed. The air was thick, and the invoices, four layers of a tissuelike paper, seemed almost moist as they lay on the desks. Chairs were scraped tiredly over the wooden floor, a box of paper clips got spilled into a filing cabinet's metal drawer. Fat Bev, sitting at her desk with her legs apart, sharpened a pencil, blew the tip clean, then folded her arms and fell asleep.

Moments later she snored, waking herself, and jerked her head back. "Jesus," she said, foggy-eyed and startled. "You can get whiplash working here."

But the girl across from her in Dottie Brown's place only gazed at her briefly before pushing a number on the adding machine. Fat Bev (constipated now for an astonishing seventy-two hours) considered this and decided she found it rude. The girl had been on the job three days and hadn't said a word.

"Cat got your tongue?" Bev said loudly, and the girl blushed so hard her eyes watered.

"I'm sorry." The girl almost whispered. "I never know what to say to anyone." She looked at Fat Bev with plaintive eyes, tears brimming at their red edges, and Bev felt alarmed.

"It's okay. Hell." Bev stuck a cigarette in her mouth and lit a match.

"You haven't got anything to say—nothing wrong with that." The cigarette bobbed between her lips. "I'd be a lot more pleasant myself," she added, "if I could manage a crap."

This caused the girl to blush again, and Fat Bev watched her cautiously. What a skinny-necked, big-eyed thing she was, sitting there like some weirdo bird, her hair cropped off at her ears, tufts sticking out this way and that. "Long as you don't mind me talking like a magpie," Fat Bev told her. "I can't shut up for five minutes, unless I'm asleep."

"But I *like* that," the girl said, with such spontaneous feeling that she seemed surprised at herself and so blushed again.

"Well, good. Then we're all set." And it was somehow understood they were now friends.

Isabelle, walking back from the large metal filing cabinet, could not keep herself from glancing toward her daughter, and so happened to witness a smile passing between Amy and Fat Bev. She looked away quickly, but not quickly enough; Amy, mid-smile, glanced across at Isabelle and let her eyes go dead.

AT LUNCHTIME ROSIE Tanguay said she really should go to the optometrist with the prescription for ironing glasses she had been given by her doctor, but it was too darn hot to move.

Fat Bev hiccuped and pushed aside the celery sticks she had brought from home wrapped in wax paper, hoping no one would bother to respond to Rosie's remark, spoken as it was with that tone of self-importance. Bev didn't give a damn if Rosie's doctor had prescribed horse pills or eyeglasses, but Arlene Tucker said, "What do you mean ironing glasses, Rosie?"

So Rosie explained how every time she ironed for more than five minutes she got a terrible headache, and when she reported this to her doctor he said he had heard of it before, although it was very uncommon, and it had a name. What Rosie suffered from, she said, nodding and raising her eyebrows with a gesture of resignation, was an eye disease called "spasmodic accommodation."

Fat Bev groaned as Arlene Tucker said loudly, "What?"

"Spasmodic accommodation—a condition whereas a person's eyes switch from farsightedness to nearsightedness about every three seconds."

A few of the women exchanged puzzled glances (Lenora Snibbens rolled her eyes and didn't glance at anyone), and Arlene said, "What do they want to do that for?"

"They don't *want* to," Rosie said. "They just do that on their own, switch back and forth like that."

People seemed to lose interest. Isabelle Goodrow was smiling in her odd, vague way, taking a delicate bite from her sandwich with a look of embarrassed apology, as though to be caught eating was very shameful. Arlene Tucker (whose interest Rosie had been counting on) was rummaging through her purse now for change, evidently with the vending machine in mind, and Fat Bev was turning a celery stick in her fingers, as though considering whether such a thing was worth eating or not.

"I've always had perfect vision," Rosie continued, "so it came as some surprise." The young Goodrow girl was gazing at her with those very large eyes, and Rosie ended up delivering this last comment in her direction, but the girl looked away quickly, ducking her head.

Crunch. *Crunch.* An enormous sound, really, as Fat Bev devoured the celery stick. *Crunch,* crunch. She chewed slowly and swallowed with deliberation. "I don't get it," Bev finally said.

Arlene was peering into her purse. "Who has change for a dollar?"

"The machine will give you change." Lenora Snibbens yawned loudly and blinked her eyes.

"Supposed to but it doesn't."

"Five minutes ago," Lenora said, "it gave me change."

"Then you must have the touch. I don't have the touch. Vending machines hate me and I hate them." Arlene cast a wary eye at the large contraption looming silently against the wall. "Hears me talking like this, you watch, it won't give me *nothing.*"

"Here." Rosie reached around for the pocketbook that hung on the back of her chair. "How much do you need?"

"I don't get it," Fat Bev said again. "I don't get why your eyes suddenly do that over the ironing board if they don't do that flippy-flop stuff right here at work."

"They probably do," Rosie said, coloring slightly and looking through her purse. "But it has something to do with the distance from things. Up close, for reading or whatever, they're okay, I guess. Ironing, it's a little further away and they go all funny. So he's given me ironing glasses. Don't ask me, that's all I know." Rosie handed Arlene some change and then touched her forehead with a paper napkin.

"Too hot for ironing," Fat Bev said, feeling slightly ashamed of her mean-spiritedness now that she had managed, as she intended, to get Rosie upset. "What're you doing ironing in this heat anyway? Stupid as me eating celery sticks."

"They're very healthy for you," Rosie responded.

"Roughage," Bev said. "Good God, do I need roughage." She rolled her eyes meaningfully and dumped the contents of her lunch bag onto the scratched linoleum tabletop just as Arlene Tucker slammed her palm against the vending machine and shouted, "Goddamn it to hell!"

The women all turned to look at Arlene. "Hey," a few admonished, raising their eyebrows toward the Goodrow girl.

Arlene held up a hand in Amy's direction. "Pardon my French," she said.

It was hot, and stayed hot. The sky stayed white. July arrived with a sense that it had always been July and always would be. Even Fat Bev's Fourth of July barbecue (which Isabelle for the first time in years did not attend) lacked its usual boisterous luster; all afternoon people drank beer that seemed warm in spite of its being packed in two large garbage bins of ice, then went home early with headaches. Back in the office room a sense of being hungover lingered; even women like Rosie Tanguay who had drunk nothing but Pepsi appeared exhausted, almost queasy, from the continual humidity and heat.

Isabelle herself was stunned. She remained stunned as the colorless days rolled by. The same mugginess that hung in the air seemed to be inside her head; there was the sense of being suspended above the earth, unrealness, disbelief. If at times in the lunchroom it seemed to the women, munching tiredly on their sandwiches, that a spasm of pain was suddenly running across Isabelle's face, making the pale features tighten and shiver ("Are you all right?" Arlene Tucker wanted to ask more than once, but she refrained; one didn't ask Isabelle Goodrow that question), it was, in fact, that one more detail, one more lie told to her that spring by her duplicitous daughter, had suddenly slipped into place.

For Isabelle it was like a jigsaw puzzle. Her mother had derived real enjoyment from doing jigsaw puzzles, and Isabelle's childhood had included a card table in the corner of their living room that more often than not held a spread-out puzzle on its top. Her mother worked slowly; sometimes the haphazard skeleton of a puzzle would remain on the table for months, and Isabelle, who lacked her mother's interest in this pastime, would nevertheless occasionally stand at the card table and idly hold up different pieces—part of a blue sky, the tip of a dog's ear, the petal of a daisy (her mother had been partial to pastoral scenes)—and sometimes find the piece's proper place.

Even in her halfheartedness Isabelle had been struck with the pleasure of this; had been especially interested in the fact that often what appeared to be one thing was actually another. For example, the tip of the dog's ear had been thought in many attempts to be part of the bark of a tree. But once it was correctly placed in a whole different part of the puzzle—to the left of the dog's face—once it was seen in this context, then of course it all made sense. One could see that it didn't belong on the tree trunk at all, that in fact it wasn't even the same color.

But this summer there was, of course, no accompanying sense of pleasure in the jigsawed rearrangement of Isabelle's memories. The feeling was one of breathlessness. Those dinners in the kitchen together as the days had grown longer—"So what's new with you?" she had said smilingly to her daughter, unfolding her napkin on her lap.

"Nothing really, I guess. Some of us stayed after school for math help." A shrug. "He's teaching us new stuff." The sweet face, the luminous eyes.

Oh my God. Isabelle wanted to cry.

THERE REALLY WAS, when you thought about it, an awful lot for Isabelle to take in. Not only had all the memories of that happy spring now become pernicious and sly as her mind flashed before her scenes of what in truth had actually been occurring, but there also seemed no resting place from them. For example, doing the laundry, Isabelle might stare in wonder as she pulled her daughter's undergarments from the washing machine. Was this a bra the loathsome man had touched? This pair of pink panties she now held in her hand? Was this a blouse the man's head had leaned against in some embrace, his fingers on these buttons? If there had been any way of knowing exactly what pieces of clothing the odious creature had touched, Isabelle would have thrown them right away. But there was no way of knowing, and so the clothes, the panties, remained in her house, contaminated, in the laundry basket, the bureau drawers; her home was invaded.

But everything was invaded—that was the thing. Her workplace certainly was. She was stuck in the same room with her daughter—and Isabelle felt the presence of Amy seated at Dottie Brown's desk every single minute of the day—but also Avery Clark, the one part of Isabelle's life that had seemed sweetly and privately hers, had now been removed, for Avery in his embarrassment would not look at her.

She knew, at least, that he would be discreet. He was that sort of man. And she was hugely grateful that the women working with her, eating lunch with her right now, did not know of the events that had transpired. She sat nibbling on her peach. But when Fat Bev, squinting at an Avon magazine, said, "Two lipsticks and a face cream; I need a pen to do this, I've always been a dunce in math," Isabelle's lunch was through. She couldn't eat anything more. "A dunce in math" was all it took. Isabelle, hit in the stomach with the mere word "math," began remembering that winter night she had arrived home to an empty house, had searched through it frantically, thinking her daughter had been kidnapped, like Debby Kay Dorne. And to see now that her daughter had been lying! (Hadn't Amy said, "Some of us stayed after school because we're good in math"? And hadn't Isabelle said another time, chatting like some idiot, "My father was good in math, maybe that's where you got it from"?) To think Amy had lied to Isabelle not that once, but many times. It was stunning. Isabelle was stunned. She put the peach into her lunch bag and threw the bag away.

"Hey," Lenora Snibbens said to Arlene, as the women glanced at their watches and began in a desultory way to tidy up their things. "How's your cousin's boy doing? The one selling all that marijuana. He still talking to the priest?"

"Far's I know," Arlene answered. Isabelle quietly excused herself, squeezing past Arlene's chair with an apologetic smile. She remembered too well the day Arlene had reported on her cousin's son. Isabelle had said these things didn't happen right out of the blue. She remembered the confidence with which she had said this, and the memory lapped inside her stomach like a dark, oily wave.

Seating herself at her desk she tucked at her hair, returning some fallen strands to the flattened French twist. It was true. If Arlene Tucker had chomped on a carrot stick and said, "You know, my cousin up in Orono has this teenage daughter who for months and months it seems was carrying on with her teacher," Isabelle would have thought to herself: *And where was that girl's mother? How could that mother not have known?* They all would have thought that most probably. All the women would have sipped their sodas and shaken their heads and said with a certain knowingness, Of course these things don't happen in a vacuum. If the mother had wanted to look . . .

Now Isabelle wanted to run back into the lunchroom and cry out: You really *can* not know!

But who would believe her? She had become pitiable, and sometimes it exhausted her too much. The hideous jolt as each little jigsaw piece took its place in the puzzle—what did it all matter now? The whole arranged jigsaw of her life had been swept to the floor. She wished she could stop the part of her mind where the hidden pieces about Amy lay. She wished she could stop picturing certain things. Sometimes sitting at her typewriter she would squeeze her eyes closed and pray.

She felt in some real way (though it was an odd, bewildering sensation, one she would not have been able to explain to anybody even if she had allowed herself to try) that she had died. Her body of course stupidly lived on, because she ate—not much—and slept—at times curiously well—and rose and went to the mill each day. Her "life" went on. But she felt little connection to anything, except for the queasiness of panic and grief. And increasingly she realized that what lay beneath this "incident" went back years and years, to a mendacity at her very core. What she faced, really, she sometimes thought, was a crisis of almost a spiritual nature for which she understood herself to be profoundly unprepared.

AMY SAT AT Dottie Brown's desk continuously fighting tears. It was an exhausting physical battle, like trying not to throw up in the back seat of a car, managing to suppress one swelling of nausea only to swerve around a corner and feel another surge roll up; or like trying not to cough in church, clamping one's throat hard against the fiendish tickle.

Once or twice Amy got up to go to the ladies' room, but she suffered from excruciating self-consciousness each time she left her desk. Should she announce to Fat Bev that she was going to the bathroom? Murmuring, she got up from her seat and blushed. Walking through the large room between the rows of desks, she sensed the women's eyes upon her and felt ten feet tall, and naked.

Once in the stall, she sat on the toilet seat weeping silently, frightened that any moment someone might walk in (the click, click, click of Rosie Tanguay's beige pumps, the locking of the stall next to hers, the whispering sounds of a skirt being hiked up, the momentary pause before the spray of urine). Amy would blow her nose hard and return to her desk, and within minutes the urge to weep, to bawl loudly, would rise up in her again.

And her hand, with some reflexive tenacity of its own, would rise to touch her hair over and over again. Each time bewilderment poured through her at the bluntness that stopped now right below her ears. She was hideous. This had been confirmed once more in the ladies' room, no matter how quickly she had looked away from the mirror. She wanted to claw her cheeks, to disfigure herself completely. She imagined using a razor blade to cut long streaks across her face so that her face would be covered with blood, and maimed.

They sent you to Augusta, though, if you did things like that. To the funny farm. Her mother used to talk about some old woman, Lillian, who'd been sent off to the funny farm; the people who worked there weren't nice because they didn't get paid much, and Isabelle said sometimes Lillian sat in her own feces because no one felt like cleaning her up. That she just sat there, staring at a wall.

"Yoo-hoo. Earth to Amy. Yoo-hoo."

Amy glanced at Fat Bev quickly.

"You all right?" Bev asked. "You look like your battery's gone dead."

"How do you know if you're crazy?" Amy blurted, leaning forward over her desk.

"You're not," Bev answered calmly, as though the question were completely expected, "as long as you think you might be."

Amy considered this, chewing slowly on the tender skin inside her cheek. "So crazy people think they're normal?"

"That's what they say." Fat Bev held out a roll of Life Savers toward Amy. "I'll tell you"—Fat Bev sighed, raising her eyebrows with a kind of tender and complete exhaustion—"sometimes I think I'm nuts. Or awfully close to it."

"You don't seem crazy to me," Amy said. "You seem incredibly normal."

Fat Bev smiled, but almost sadly. "Nice girl." And then she said, "Oh, we're all nuts, probably."

Amy chewed her Life Saver hard between her molars; it made a sound Isabelle could not stand, and remembering this, Amy stopped, putting her hand to her mouth apologetically. But Fat Bev gave no indication of having heard it at all. "Except if we're all crazy," Amy persisted, still leaning forward over her desk—Dottie Brown's desk—"then how come some people get sent to the funny farm and other people don't?"

Fat Bev nodded, as though she had already given thought to this as well. "They *act* crazy." She nodded again. "Doesn't matter if you *feel* crazy. Long as you don't *act* crazy." She rapped her pink fingernails on the desktop as a kind of punctuation. "Don't talk to yourself in public. Take baths once in a while. Get up in the morning, get dressed. That's the way I see it. You keep jumpin' through the hoops, you're all right. Nobody's going to cart you off long as you're still jumpin' through the hoops like you're supposed to."

Amy nodded slowly. What occurred to her was that she ought to avoid, these days, seeing her reflection. She pictured herself after work standing in the parking lot next to the car waiting for her mother to unlock the doors: she would turn her head and gaze out over the dead brown river rather than glimpse herself in the car window. And in the morning she would get up and get dressed and come to work again. She would do that every day until enough time passed to make it different. Until she and Mr. Robertson were together again. She smiled tentatively at Fat Bev.

"Another thing," Bev said, turning back to her typewriter but stopping a moment to raise a hand instructively. "Never get lipstick on your teeth. If I see a woman with lipstick on her teeth, I always think to myself, She's probably crazy. Probably nuts."

Amy nodded seriously. "Well," she said finally, with a sigh, "I don't wear lipstick all that often."

"You should," Fat Bev said, her fingers with their colorful nails tapping comfortably on the typewriter keys. "Could be lovely, you know."

AVERY CLARK DID not like coming to work now that Amy Goodrow was there. It was awkward. For example, just that morning he was walking through the hall to take the elevator down to Shipment, when Amy emerged from the ladies' room and there they were, alone in the hallway, walking silently toward each other. He might have felt compassion for her—in fact he did feel the faint stirrings of this as she blushed and ducked her head (her hair was strange, he thought, she looked almost ill)—except for the fact that as she neared him, raising her eyes and speaking an almost silent "Hello," he saw, or thought he saw, a flicker of a sneer in the midst of her discomfort, and this angered him.

"Hello," he responded stiffly, and when he reached the elevator he banged the button with his fist.

Nasty girl. Filthy thing.

When he thought of her, of what he had seen that day (and he tried hard not to think of this, but it would come to him again and again), he felt the same anger. At times with his wife in bed he felt that anger too. It seemed to him that he was old and much in life was denied him.

He had thoughts that included vulgar language, and he knew if he were a different sort of man he would have told his men friends what he had seen that day in the car parked out in the woods. "A terrific set of knockers," he might have said. "A great pair of tits." But he was not that kind of man, and he did not say those things to anyone.

When he told his wife, he told what he had seen in careful, general terms. They had shaken their heads all evening, discussing the little they knew of Isabelle's life. Avery Clark cautioned Emma: "For the sake of Isabelle we won't repeat this," and Emma said of course not, it was really such a shame.

Chapter

14

So for Amy and Isabelle—their lives had changed completely. When they spoke to one another, their words seemed pushed through the air like blocks of wood. If by chance their eyes should meet—while stepping out of the car, or leaving the lunchroom—they glanced away as quickly as they could. In the small house they moved past each other carefully, as though being near one another was a dangerous thing. But this only made them more aware of each other, joining them in a perverse intimacy of watchfulness, so that they learned more accurately the sounds of the other's quiet chewing, noticed more astutely the moist smell of the bathroom after use, were aware even of when the other was or wasn't sleeping by the quiet turning over in their beds at night, separated only by the thin Sheetrock wall.

Isabelle was not sure how long this could go on. It seemed ludicrous that they should eat a meal across from each other every night, should live together, work together, arrive at church together on Sundays, sitting in a pew so close that when they rose and sang the Doxology they could smell each other's breath. It had crossed Isabelle's mind to send the girl up the river to live with Isabelle's cousin, Cindy Rae, but such an act would require an explanation to others that Isabelle was not prepared to give, and, more important, she was not prepared, even now, to release her daughter from her.

So they were stuck with each other. Each felt her suffering was greater than the other's. In fact, each felt at times that perhaps her suffering was greater than the suffering of anyone, and so when it was reported on the news one night that a kneesock belonging to Debby Kay Dorne had been recovered in a field by a farm dog, and that the girl was now officially presumed to be dead, both Amy and Isabelle—not looking at each other, watching the television silently—actually allowed themselves the indulgence of thinking their own situation was somehow worse.

Amy thought: At least Debby's mother loved her. At least everyone feels sorry. At least the girl is dead and doesn't feel things anymore. (And *everyone* felt sorry.)

Isabelle, who was old enough to know better, to know, really, that what the mother was feeling must be the worst feeling of all, could nevertheless not stop herself from thinking: At least the girl was sweet. At least the girl hadn't been cold-bloodedly lying to her mother for weeks and weeks and weeks.

Isabelle got up and turned off the television. "I'm going to bed," she said.

Amy stretched her feet out in front of her, putting her hands behind her head. "Night," she answered, staring straight ahead.

ISABELLE, LYING ON her bed in the summer darkness, a darkness that seemed porous and soft and something you could almost put your hand into, found it necessary, as she did on some of these nights, to go over it all once more in her head, as though this dreadful and wearying process of repetition was the only way she could absorb her—and her daughter's—present state.

The day Avery Clark had discovered Mr. Robertson and Amy in the car parked in the woods, Isabelle had driven home from the mill believing it was not true. Her mind had been oddly lucid, although her body gave all the signs of having come upon a crisis: a tingling in her chin and fingertips, a shaking in her legs so marked that she had trouble driving, her breathing accelerated and shallow. Still her mind said: There has been some mistake, and this is not true.

But when she stepped through the door calling "Amy!" and found her daughter sitting on the edge of the living-room couch with her knees pressed together, Isabelle saw in the paleness of Amy's face, particularly in the girl's lips, which were absolutely drained of color, that what had just been so bizarrely reported to her by Avery was, in fact, all true.

Still, Isabelle didn't get it right away. She didn't get the whole thing right away. In her mind something terrible had happened to Amy *that day.* Isabelle did not comprehend the full implication of what must have happened in the days before, or even thoughts of what might still happen in the days to come; she was filled with the queasiness of the moment.

The midafternoon light that filtered through the window seemed to hang suspended in a living room vaguely unfamiliar—they were not used to being together there this time of day except on weekends, and that was very different. So right off the scene carried with it the oppressive feeling of a sickroom; and four o'clock had always been the saddest time of day for Isabelle anyway, even in the spring, or especially in spring.

She had walked slowly to Amy and knelt down so that she could look into the girl's pale face. "Amy," she had said, "this is very serious. What Avery Clark has just told me is very, very serious."

Amy stared straight ahead, her eyes vacant, almost flat.

"When a man drives a girl out into the woods and makes her—when he makes her do certain things."

"He didn't." Amy turned her head to her mother quickly, and then away.

Isabelle stood up. "Avery wasn't . . ." She saw Amy's eyes begin to travel sideways, and then return to their vacant stare. "You mean he didn't make you," Isabelle said.

Amy didn't answer, didn't move.

"Is that what you mean?"

Just slightly Amy's face tilted upward.

"Amy, answer me."

"No, he didn't make me, Mom."

Isabelle sat down on the arm of the couch, an indication that they had found themselves in a genuine state of emergency; she never sat on the arms of furniture.

"Amy."

But she could not now, weeks later, actually remember it all; there were only particular images that stayed with her: herself sitting, temporarily, on the arm of the couch, the sickroom pall of the afternoon light, the dreadfully pale face of Amy, her closed-off expression, the terror in the room.

Isabelle had experienced, nevertheless, an odd, initial period of great calm. If you could call it that, for her mouth was very dry and her leg began to tremble so that she had to rise from the arm of the couch and walk about the room. But something inside her had expanded, initially, so that later, contemplating this, she understood better the expression "rising to the occasion," for certainly something inside her had expanded and risen. Something in her had taken over at first, rather amazingly and admirably, as though perhaps she had been preparing over many years for just this sort of crisis.

So there was tenderness in the voice she used with Amy, getting whatever information she could, and while Amy's lips remained extraordinarily pale, and while she still did not look at her mother directly, she answered with enough scorn ("No, of *course* not"), with just enough derision to be believable, to her mother's question—made with particular tenderness and calm—if intercourse itself had taken place.

"You're very innocent," Isabelle said, kneeling once again in front of Amy so as to try once again to look directly into the girl's pale face. Amy turned her head slightly upward and back, and then away, with much the same silent expression that she had used as a small child in her stroller, when Isabelle had bent over to wipe some kind of food from her mouth. "And it's possible that someone could take advantage of you this way," Isabelle continued, as though she might actually be speaking to that small child, "without your even knowing exactly what was going on."

It was then that Isabelle had her first real sense that her daughter had somewhere slipped beyond her grasp, that things were far murkier than she had originally imagined; for the expression on the girl's face, the flicker of muted disgust at her mother's words, the arrival and then disappearance of an expression Isabelle recognized immediately to be one of condescension, jarred Isabelle with a sickening wave of foreboding. The sense of calm that had taken her this far began to give way.

She stood and retreated to the window, where she leaned against the wall. "In the car today was not the first time you were with him," she stated, and Amy's silence appeared to acknowledge this as true.

"Was it."

Just barely Amy shook her head.

"When did it begin?" Undoubtedly Isabelle had been in shock; had been in shock from the very moment Avery Clark had called her into his office. But it was not until this point in her conversation with Amy that the measurements of the room seemed altered; she felt an odd inability to judge distances, she had to squint to focus on her daughter.

The girl raised her narrow shoulders tentatively. "I don't know."

"Don't do that, Amy."

Amy looked at her quickly; Isabelle saw how her eyes had become wobbly with fear, and it was this fear that made Isabelle realize further that much was being hidden. Some indefinable feeling of knowledge planted itself in Isabelle's mind as she absorbed the glimmer of superiority that had crossed Amy's expression only seconds before, when Isabelle called her innocent.

Isabelle repeated, "When did this begin?" Her right leg suddenly jerked uncontrollably and she leaned against the sill, pressing down hard with her leg.

Amy stared down at the braided rug. She moved a hand to her mouth, a gesture of shyness she had developed as a small child. ("Get your hand away from your mouth," Isabelle would admonish relentlessly), and said, "We got to be kind of friends this winter."

"Since *winter*?"

"No, I mean—"

"What do you mean?"

The girl seemed unable to answer; beside her hand her lips opened and partly shut again.

And so it went. Isabelle's attempts to get information from Amy, her rising sense of hysteria . . . At one point she went to Amy quickly, sitting next to her on the couch, taking her hands in her own, and said,

"Amy, sweetheart. A man like this . . . Oh, Amy. A man like this is troubled. My God, when you think . . ."

But Amy was already shaking her head, pulling her hands from her mother's. "It's not like that, Mom. It's not like what you think." Color had come back to her lips.

"Then what is it like, Amy." The pulling-away of her daughter's hands, when Isabelle had taken them in her own with such love just seconds earlier, seemed not only rejecting but profoundly unfair, and so Isabelle found herself standing up and moving through the room once again, this time landing in the green upholstered chair, where for more winters than she cared to remember she had often sat on weekend afternoons and watched the chickadees at the feeder.

"He's not a nice man, Amy," she said, trying again. "He doesn't care for you. That kind of man never does. He *says* he cares for you because he wants what he wants."

Her daughter's face turned from the rug to stare at her, a look of growing alarm on her face. "He wants me," Amy blurted out, childish tears of defiance coming to her eyes. "He likes me, he does so."

Isabelle closed her eyes and murmured, "Oh God, this is sickening." And she did feel sick; her stomach was hot, her mouth felt coated, as though she had gone a week without brushing her teeth. When she opened her eyes Amy was staring once again at the braided rug, but now her face was squeezed with crying, her nose dribbled shiny mucus down over her mouth.

"You don't know what the world is like," Isabelle told the girl gently, almost crying herself, leaning forward slightly in the green upholstered chair.

"No!"

Amy spoke suddenly, loudly, turning her wet face toward her mother. "*You* don't know what the world is like! You never go anywhere or talk to anyone! You don't read anything . . ." Here she seemed to weaken momentarily, but moving a hand sideways through the air as though propelling herself forward, she continued. "Except for the stupid *Reader's Digest.*"

They stared at each other, until Amy dropped her eyes. "You never even go to the movies," she added, angry tears still sliding down her face. "How do *you* know what the world is like?"

It changed everything, her saying that. For Isabelle it changed everything. Remembering it weeks later, in the soft darkness of night, it brought to her the exact intensity of silver pain rippling through her chest that it had delivered at the time it was spoken; without moving, she seemed to stagger, her heart racing at a ridiculous pace. Because the humiliation was hideous. Mispronouncing the name of that poet might not be a moral shortcoming, but in the end, so what. The truth is that Amy had scored accurately, had delivered a blow more powerful than she probably ever intended or imagined she could do.

Isabelle, who had received this shattering while sitting in the green upholstered chair (it would be a year before she sat in that chair again), had remained silent for quite some time, as though in order to absorb this her body needed to remain still, and then she finally said quietly, "You have no idea what it has been like raising a child on my own."

What she did not do, and wanted to so badly she could almost feel the shape of the words in her mouth already formed, was to shout: *You weren't supposed to even be born!*

Whenever she went over the dreadful scene in her mind, the way she was now in the darkness of her room, she allowed herself a moment of approval, because it was, really, very good of her not to have said such a thing.

But she hurt. She hurt remembering all this, and even though she could not remember everything that had taken place that afternoon, she remembered well enough that sickening and growing realization that she had been living with a daughter she barely knew. She remembered how they had sat in silence and then how she, Isabelle, rose and opened a window; the air outside had struck her as stagnant and warm as the air in the room, and she had leaned against the windowsill. "Who is this horrible Robertson man, anyway," she finally said. "Where did he show up from?"

"He isn't horrible."

These words infuriated Isabelle. "What he did," she told her daughter in a scathing voice, "was, to *begin* with, illegal."

Amy rolled her eyes, as though this was further indication of how foolish and provincial her mother really was.

"You don't need to roll your eyes at me, young lady," Isabelle had said, anger shooting through her. "You go right ahead and tell yourself that your mother is an illiterate moron and that she's too stupid to know anything about real life, but I'm telling *you* that *you* are the one who doesn't know anything!"

It had become that senseless and awful, yelling at each other about who was the most stupid.

Tears ran from Amy's eyes. "Mom," she pleaded, "I just mean you don't know about Mr. Robertson. He's a *really* nice man. He never wanted to . . ."

"Never wanted to what."

Amy picked at the skin around her thumbnail.

"He never wanted to what? *Answer me!*"

Amy clamped a fist around her thumb and looked in anguish toward the ceiling. "I was the one who kissed him first," she said, her face pale again. "He didn't want to. He said not to do it again, but I did."

"When?" Isabelle's heart was racing.

"What?"

"When. When was that?"

Amy lifted her shoulders tentatively. "I don't know."

"Yes, you do."

"I don't remember."

It was sinking in—trying to, as she watched her child's pale face, averted eyes—the sense that this girl had been living a separate life, the sense that her daughter was strikingly different from what she had thought, that the girl *hadn't even liked her.* ("You don't read anything except that stupid *Reader's Digest.*")

What followed was something that Isabelle would speak of only once, years later, when her life had become a very different one. Amy, on the other hand, would later on in her adulthood tell a number of people, until she realized finally that it was one story in a million and ultimately didn't matter to anyone.

But it mattered a great deal to them, to Amy and to Isabelle, and while over time they would forget parts and remember parts differently, both remembered and would always remember certain aspects of the scene. How, for example, Isabelle began throwing the couch pillows across the room, screaming that this Mr. Robertson creature was nothing more than a pimp. One of the pillows knocked over a lamp, smashing the bulb into little bits against the floor, and Amy began to cry out "Mama!"—a child terrified.

The cry brought with it the sudden memory of Amy as a little girl, a blond, curly-headed little girl sitting in the front seat of the car next to Isabelle as they drove to Esther Hatch's house each morning. "Mama," Amy had sometimes said in a querulous voice, trying to hold her mother's hand.

This memory was anguish now, and while part of Isabelle wanted to rush to the side of this tall, pale, teenage child, instead she brought her hand down hard on the back of the couch, and this hurt her and made her cry out the word "God*damn*!" She saw how this caused her daughter's thin shoulders to jerk with fear, and that her daughter was afraid of her only enlarged Isabelle's fury; she felt something very big had been released, something that must go back generations and had been gaining speed for years, she didn't know—but something terrible inside her was being released.

She went to find Mr. Robertson.

THE MAN'S NAME had not been in the phone book, and so Isabelle had picked up the telephone and, in a bizarrely cheerful voice, obtained from Information the telephone number and address of one Thomas Robertson.

She was curiously aware of the car as she drove, the rumbling looseness of its metal construction as she sailed up a hill and rounded a curve, that tiny momentary gap in space between the turning of the steering wheel and the answering move of the car, as though it were a living thing, bewildered and old, but obedient. Shuddering, bouncing, tires squealing slightly, the car did what she wanted it to do.

The man lived in the sort of apartment complex that Isabelle scorned; cheaply constructed and painted gray, it was a phony attempt at New England attractiveness and included a gratuitous white picket fence—stiff and plastic—leading up the walkway to the main door. The interior hallway smelled like a hotel, and rapping on the door of Apartment 2L, Isabelle could hear the rattle of pots and pans from the place directly across; she reminded herself at all costs to keep her voice low.

Apparently he was expecting her. This did not register until many days later when, reviewing the scene in her mind, she saw that he had answered the door with a certain hostile complacency; that Amy had undoubtedly called to say her mother was on her way. What did register, however, was some immediate sense of conspiracy that this man had with her daughter.

He was short and barefoot.

"I'm Amy Goodrow's mother," Isabelle had said, hearing how brisk and tart her voice sounded, and how it was all quite wrong somehow, right away. "And I would like to talk to you. Please." This she said quietly, aiming in her tone for a superior detachment, which was ludicrous of course; she was in agony.

"Won't you come in." A very slight bow, a slow dropping of the eyelids beneath the rimmed glasses, as if he were mocking her. Later she realized he probably was. He appeared both somnambulistic and wary; his bare feet, flat and white at the end of his jeans, offended her in their nakedness.

Stepping past him into an angular and barren living room (there were no pictures on the wall, a small TV was placed upon a crate), Isabelle, before she turned back to face this man, caught briefly the view in the partly opened window. It was merely a tree. Part of a tree, a maple close enough to the building so that the leaves, green and thick and dappled by the early-evening sun, appeared to be pressing toward her through the open window. She heard for a brief moment their gentle rustling.

Why this particular glimpse of a tree with early evening beginning to settle upon it should present to her the most awful feeling of sadness and utter loss she had ever in her life experienced she was not able to precisely understand, but for a moment she thought she might crumple to the floor. Instead she turned to the man and said softly, "You *are* Thomas Robertson?"

He blinked his eyes slowly, not seeming to close them all the way. "I am. Would you care to sit down?" His jaw moved like a puppet's when he spoke; his full beard made it impossible to see his mouth.

"No. No, thank you." Her fatigue made her almost smile. In fact she felt, just slightly, the corners of her own mouth turn up, and even experienced, bizarrely, briefly, the sensation that they were working together, united in some understanding of catastrophe.

She no sooner felt this than she realized of course it was completely untrue; there was no hint of an answering smile from him. Instead she perceived in his gaze the watchfulness of someone encountering instability in another. She said, "But please. You sit down."

He sat on the edge of a gray vinyl couch, resting a forearm on each knee, still watching her, his neck thrust forward.

"Let me tell you what I know of certain laws," she said, and she proceeded to recite, rather quickly, what she knew. At the time she felt he had been impressed, though later, remembering it (there was a great deal she could not seem to remember), she felt that to proceed that way had been a terrible mistake, that she never ought to have exposed herself in such a way to him.

Because in the end he "won." In the end he had retained his sense of dignity and managed somehow to destroy hers. This was unspoken, but they both knew. And she was not able to remember or figure out exactly how he had done it.

She had stated her case concisely: she wanted him out of town. "Of course I would like to go to the police," she said quietly, "but my main concern is Amy, and I won't have her put through any of that."

He had not said anything. He gazed at her with a curious indifference and eventually slid himself further back into the seat of the vinyl couch, crossing one leg over the other's knee, so that he seemed audaciously at ease.

"Have I made myself clear?" Isabelle asked. "Is there anything I have said that you don't understand?"

"Not at all," the man replied. "The picture is perfectly clear." He glanced around the living room, which seemed more and more to Isabelle to have the sort of temporariness in its decor that one would find in the dwellings of a college student (a spider plant sat on a bookshelf near the door, many of its fronds brown and bent at the middle), and then, running a hand slowly over his head, the deep brown waves of hair rising off his forehead making Isabelle inwardly shiver, said that he could, if it pleased her, leave town tomorrow.

"Just like that?" she asked.

"Sure." He stood up then, and walked a few steps toward the door, as though to indicate their interview was over. "I have no reason to stay," he added, turning his palm upward, as though both the words and the gesture would reassure Isabelle that he was telling her the truth.

But she heard in his remark the disposability of her daughter; and while she would have been mightily offended had he attempted to say he *cared* for the girl, she was even more offended that he did not.

"Have you any idea," she said, her eyes narrowing, taking a step toward him, "have you any idea how you have injured my child?"

He blinked rapidly a moment, then tilted his head slightly. "Excuse me?"

She could have harmed him, ripped his hair from his head and clenched it in her fist with little pieces of skin still clinging to its roots, she could have twisted his arm through the cotton shirt until she heard it snap inside the skin, she could have killed him easily. Her eyes blurred, making things sway.

"You have taken a very, very innocent girl and put your handprint on her forever." Horribly, she saw two drops of saliva shoot from her mouth and land on the sleeve of his cotton shirt.

He glanced at his arm, letting her know by his expression that he considered himself to have just been spit upon (which was incredibly unfair, Isabelle felt, her head roaring every time she thought of this).

He placed his hand on the doorknob. "Mrs. Goodrow," he said, and then he cocked his head. "*Is* it *Mrs.* Goodrow? I'm afraid I was never quite sure."

Her face burned. "It is Mrs. Goodrow," she whispered, because her voice seemed to have given out.

"Well. Mrs. Goodrow. I'm afraid you take a dim view of the situation. Amy may very well be underage, and in that I'm not without some respect for your position, but I'm afraid you've been a tad naive about the nature of your passionate and unusually attractive daughter."

"What is it you're saying?" Isabelle asked, her heart thumping ferociously.

He paused, his eyes moving about the room. "Mrs. Goodrow, Amy did not need a good deal of teaching, shall we say."

"Oh," said Isabelle. "Oh, you are horrible. You really are a horrible man. I'm going to report you—you're loathsome. Do you know that about yourself?" She leaned forward peering at him, asking this question with her voice raspy, tears in her eyes. "A loathsome man. I'm going to report you to the superintendent, the principal, the police."

He was more than willing to hold her gaze, and she saw no indication in the brown eyes, seeming all the more impenetrable behind the lenses of his glasses, that her threat had intimidated him at all; it was her own eyes that glanced aside—she had never, even as a child, lasted more than two seconds in any kind of confrontation that required a stare-down with another person—and it was then she saw the books on the shelf beneath the moribund spider plant. *The Works of Plato,* she read, and next to that a white book with a circular coffee stain over the title *On Being and Nothingness.* Right before she looked away she saw *Yeats: The Collected Works.*

Thomas Robertson watched her glancing at the books, and when she met his eyes she read in them his final victory, for in a moment he said, "I think it would be best if you didn't report anything. I'll be gone tomorrow."

At the door she turned and said, "I find you contemptible."

He nodded just slightly. "I understand you do." He closed the door slowly; it clicked.

As she drove home Isabelle thought she ought not to be operating a motor vehicle. These were the words that came into her mind, as though lifted in fine print from the back of a box of decongestant tablets—*Do not operate a motor vehicle*—for it seemed her ability to judge distances, curbs, stop signs, was greatly impaired. There was no sense, as there had been on the way over, of having power, control, over the car. There was barely a sense of the car at all. There was only the image of Thomas Robertson, his eyelids blinking slowly, the stinging echo of his words, "I understand you do."

She hated that he was smart. He was smarter than she was and she hated that. He was some kind of smart hippie, had undoubtedly been a hippie, had probably lived in a commune at some point along the way, smoking marijuana, taking anyone he cared to into his bed.

(What was worst of all, of course, was what he had said about Amy, what he had implied about Amy.)

And they had discussed her. She realized that driving back home, that they had discussed her at times during their horrid little rendezvous. Because that was there in the slow lowering of his eyes (Is it *Mrs.* Goodrow?). That he knew things about her. But what would he know? That she was strict? That she had few friends? That she worked in the mill? That she had said Yeets instead of Yeats? (Yes, he probably did know that, and her face burned.)

What she felt, turning into the driveway, was a fury and pain so deep that she would never have believed a person could feel it and still remain alive. Walking up the porch steps, she wondered seriously, briefly, if in fact she would die, right here, right now, opening the kitchen door. Perhaps dying was like this, those final moments of being rushed along by some powerful wave, so that at the very end one did not actually care, there was no reason to care: it was just over, the end was there.

Except she wasn't dying. Tossing the keys onto the kitchen table, she felt the everydayness of life reappear. This was hers to bear. She felt she could not bear it, and so anger pulsed through her; her legs were shaking as she climbed the stairs.

Chapter

15

AMY HAD—JUST as Isabelle later surmised—telephoned Mr. Robertson, once her mother left the house. Standing by the kitchen window, she had watched to make sure her mother's car did not suddenly return. It did not, and Amy, beginning to cry as soon as Mr. Robertson answered the telephone, told him what had happened since her mother came home. "I *hate* her," she finished. "I hate her *so much*." She squeezed her wet nose with her fingers.

There was a long pause on the other end of the telephone, and Amy, wiping her nose again, asked, "Are you still there?"

"I'm still here," Mr. Robertson said, though surprisingly he said no more.

"But what are we going to do?" Amy asked. "I mean what are we going to tell her?" She turned the mouthpiece upward so he wouldn't hear her crying; tears slipped down her face.

"Don't tell her anything else," Mr. Robertson advised. "Leave the rest to me. I'll handle it. When she comes home don't tell her anything more." His voice, though, was oddly expressionless; he could have been talking in his sleep. Even when he said, "It'll work out, Amy. It will all get worked out in the end."

A new kind of fear spread through her as she hung up. In her mind now was the brief image of a huge, black sea; she and Mr. Robertson bobbing separately on black waves in a black night.

But no. When he said it would get worked out, he meant he loved her. And that he would stand by her. He had said that just today: "You know you'll always be loved, don't you?" He loved her. He had told her so. She ought to have told her mother this, because her mother didn't understand.

Amy walked up the stairs. Maybe Mr. Robertson would tell her mother, "I love your daughter and we want to be together." Would he say that to Isabelle? And what words, exactly, would he use? Anyway, he was a grown-up and he would know what to do, Amy reasoned, tripping suddenly on the last stair; thinking there was one more stair, she had put her foot down too quickly. She steadied herself against the wall and went into her bedroom.

She sat waiting for her mother to return. She sat on the skirted vanity stool in front of her mirror, and after a while she began to brush her hair, and the thought even occurred to her that Mr. Robertson might return here with her mother. The early-evening sun, which at that time in June always passed for a few minutes through Amy's room, sent through the window a haze of pale light that touched Amy's hair, so it seemed at that moment like spun gold from a fairy tale. (She thought this as she gazed at herself.) But she felt unwell. She felt like she had just thrown up, with more left back inside her.

And it was so odd: the white hairbrush she was holding, a school notebook tossed onto the bed—these familiar things seemed to belong to a life she could now only faintly remember. Now that Isabelle had found out that some man loved her, everything was different.

He did love her. He had said, "You know you'll always be loved, don't you?" She could tell by the way he smiled whenever she walked into his classroom after school, but especially from the way he had touched her today in the car, from the things they had done. It was indescribably private what they had done. When people did that kind of thing . . . well, they loved each other incredibly. You had to be together after that.

Mr. Robertson would tell her mother it couldn't be helped: people fell in love. Maybe he would even tell Isabelle that in a few years—his wife had left him, after all—he would like to marry Amy. (She pictured living with him, how he would empty out some bureau drawers for her to put her clothes in, how on their first day he would hand her a clean towel and washcloth and say, "Here, Amy. These are for you.")

The kitchen door slammed; car keys flung onto the counter; then her mother's footsteps on the stairs.

Amy put the brush down quietly, as though by merely holding it she had been doing something wrong. The sun, just now leaving the room, touched Amy's hair one final time as she turned to see her mother, appearing out of breath, standing in the doorway. "He's leaving town tomorrow," Isabelle said, her chest rising and falling, rising and falling. "He should be thrown in jail."

Amy opened her mouth. They stared at each other until her mother turned and stepped across the hallway into her own room.

Amy looked around confusedly. She should run downstairs and out into the road, because she had to get to Mr. Robertson. She pictured herself stumbling down the road past the pine trees and the swamp, seeing his car coming toward her, waving her arms desperately to him. It filled her with panic to think of him leaving—except he wouldn't do that without her.

"Look at you." Her mother was standing in the doorway again. She held the black-handled sewing shears at her side. "Look at you sitting there like that," her mother said quietly, moving into the room.

Amy thought her mother intended to kill her. She thought her mother was walking toward her to stab her with the shears, because it seemed her mother had gone crazy, become somebody different. A blank, white hatred on the face of her mother coming nearer, her mother's arm reaching up, Amy's own arm reaching up, ducking her head ("No, Mommy"), her arm knocked down, a fist grabbing her hair, the sound of cutting, more hair grabbed, her head jerked one way, then another. An avalanche of terror dropped down through Amy, carrying with it a swirling debris of long-forgotten smells, the couch in Esther Hatch's house, the car rides there, rotting apple cores and gritty sand, the unyielding hardness of a plastic doll's head, stale radiator heat, and melting crayons.

Leaning forward, half standing, jerked back by each handful of hair her mother grasped, the sharp pain of her scalp as though the skin could be peeled right off, Amy heard her own half-whispered screams, her cries of "Mommy, *don't*!" "Oh, Mommy, please," then a sudden deep guttural sound, "Oh *don't.*" The scissory sound of the shears cutting again and again (she would remember the sound of the shears perfectly, would experience it in dreams for years to come), a metallic flash in the mirror as the silvery blades briefly caught a shaft of the disappearing sunlight, then the peculiar sense to Amy that she wasn't balanced right, her head was weighing less.

"Clean it up." Her mother stepped back, panting. Screeching suddenly: *"Clean up the mess!"*

Sobbing, Amy stumbled down the stairs and took a brown grocery bag from where they were folded beneath the kitchen sink. She returned to her room (climbing the stairs on all fours like some intoxicated animal, dragging the brown paper bag with her as it scraped lightly against the wall), where she put the hair into the grocery bag, and in doing so began to scream, because picking up in her fingers the long curls of hair was like picking up some amputated leg with its shoe still on—this stuff was separate from her now (screaming louder)—what was still *her*?

Isabelle, who was sitting on her bed across the hall, rocking forward with her fist to her stomach, kept saying, "Oh please stop making that noise." Her own room was almost dark by now, the sun having left it some time ago. The thickening dusk that gathered first in the corners and grew steadily until it filled the room enough so that the thin outline of the bluebirds on the wallpaper could no longer be seen, brought with it the sense of something dangerous and final.

Later Isabelle wanted to take the shears and cut her own hair off. She wanted to cut up the bedspread she sat on, and all the clothes in her closet. She wanted to go into the bathroom and cut up the towels, to make cuts in the upholstery coverings downstairs. She wanted to be dead and she wanted her daughter to be dead too so that neither of them would have to face the unbearable business of continuing on. It even went through her head to open the stove and keep the gas running all night while upstairs she held Amy in her arms, rocking her to sleep.

(Who was Amy? Who was the person that man, that stranger, had made such innuendoes about? Who was the girl Isabelle had just found this evening when she came home, sitting before the mirror with her hands folded in some kind of mocking childlike obedience, but with a vividness, a luminosity; the streaky hair all messy and bright, falling over her shoulders and partly in front of her face, that certain look in her eyes, a certain kind of knowingness? Who was her daughter? Who had she been?)

"Please, God," Isabelle whispered piteously, kneading her face with her fingers. "Oh God, please." Please what? She hated God. She *hated* him. In the darkness she actually shook her fist into the air, oh, she was sick to death of God. For years she had been playing some kind of guessing game with him. Is this right, God? Am I doing the right thing? Every decision made on what would please God—and look where it had gotten her: no place. Less than no place at all. "I hate you, God." She whispered this between gritted teeth, into the darkness of her room.

IN THE EARLY morning, as the sky against her window was whitening and the birds increased their noise, Amy woke from where she had fallen asleep on the floor, her hand wet from saliva that had been seeping from her mouth. She sat up and almost immediately began to cry, and then stopped soon, because what she was feeling was so much worse than that; the tears, the crunching of her face, seemed futile and insignificant.

"Amy." Her mother was standing in the doorway.

But it went no further. Amy did not look into her mother's face. She only glanced in her direction long enough to see that her mother had apparently spent all night in her clothes. And she didn't care. She didn't care what words might be stuck right now in her mother's throat; they were as futile as the puny tears she herself had just shed. She and her mother were stuck together, sick and exhausted with their stupid lives.

On Monday Amy started her job at the mill.

Chapter

16

MORNING BREAK, AND Arlene Tucker was saying, "There was a fountain in the middle of the cake."

"Charlene had a bridge," another woman joined in, referring to a daughter whose wedding and divorce had been discussed in the lunch-room now for a number of years. "I said at the time, Charlene, are you sure? But she was set on that bridge."

"This one had a bridge." Arlene nodded. "Wide enough for the lit-tle bride and bridegroom figures. The bride had a parasol. I thought it was nice."

"Who's this again?" Lenora Snibbens took a compact from her bag, and squinted at a blemish on her chin.

"A cousin. One of Danny's up in Hebron."

"You've got more cousins," said Lenora, powdering her red-ended nose.

"Do you have any idea," Fat Bev said, entering the lunchroom, "how *awful* that river smells?"

"It's awful," Lenora agreed, moving her chair forward to make room for Amy Goodrow, who had wandered into the lunchroom and was gaz-ing vaguely at the candy in the vending machine.

"It does seem worse this year," Isabelle said, from the far end of the table, where she sat stirring her coffee with a plastic straw. She shook her head at Lenora. "Does seem to be worse," she repeated, her eyes following the exit of her daughter, for Amy, having glanced at the vending machine, was now wandering back out of the lunchroom.

"Oh, it's something." Lenora let out a fast sigh.

"It really is." This remark seemed to require Isabelle to nod her head after having just shaken it back and forth, and the switching of the motion made her feel spastic, unhinged. She disliked these morning breaks that she no longer shared with Avery Clark in his fishbowl of an office. And she didn't care if the river smelled; she barely noticed. What she noticed was how Avery never looked up from his desk anymore when the buzzer for morning break bleated throughout the building. She noticed how he never caught her eye anymore when he passed by her desk, and she wondered if the other women noticed too.

"It's never made sense to me," said the woman who was the mother of the much-discussed Charlene, "spending all that money on a wedding."

"Oh, I don't know." Arlene Tucker gave a pouty shrug. "It makes sense to me."

"Why?" Charlene's mother blinked once her almost lashless eyes, looking for that moment something like a toad.

"It's the most important day in a girl's life," Arlene said. "That's why." She added (unnecessarily, most of the women present later agreed), "It's *supposed* to last forever."

"Was Charlene *supposed* to get slapped around by her husband? Was she *supposed* to put up with that?" The poor mother of Charlene had gone pink in the face, her lashless eyes blinking rapidly now. Clearly, umbrage had been taken.

"Relax, please." Arlene Tucker looked embarrassed and resentful at finding herself the recipient of these charged statements.

Tensions had been rising for some time now. All the women (except for Isabelle) had been increasingly aware of that. It was the heat, of course, the stagnant, awful, cloying heat. Still, they did seem unable to help themselves, for suddenly Arlene Tucker said, "Well, the *pope* would say that in the eyes of God, Charlene is married forever."

"Damn the pope."

This was astonishing. Rosie Tanguay, just back from the ladies' room, actually had to cross herself. To make things worse, Charlene's mother, having damned the pope, now began to laugh. She laughed and laughed, red in the face, and just as she seemed to slow down she started up again, until tears ran down her face and she had to blow her nose. Still she laughed.

The women exchanged looks of concern, and Lenora Snibbens finally said, "Maybe get some cold water and throw it in her face." Rosie Tanguay, with a look of self-importance, took her empty coffee mug to go fill at the water fountain, but the gasping mother of Charlene held up her hand. "No," she said, winding down, mopping at her face, "I'm okay."

"It's not funny, you know." Arlene Tucker delivered this flatly.

"Oh, Arlene, shut up." Fat Bev rapped her fingernails on the table as she spoke, and seeing Arlene's mouth opening indignantly in her direction, Bev cut in again, "Keep it shut, Arlene. Just this once."

Arlene stood up. "You can go to hell," she said, apparently to Fat Bev, but her eyes flickered briefly to include the mother of Charlene. "And you know you will, too," she added, leaving the room.

Fat Bev waved a hand lazily through the air. "Hell, I'm in hell," she said, and this started Charlene's mother laughing again. Rosie Tanguay reached for the coffee cup of water, but Fat Bev shook her head; the woman had run out of energy and didn't laugh for long this time. When she had settled down, an uncomfortable silence fell over the room as the women looked at one another cautiously, uncertain what lines had been drawn and where.

"So," Fat Bev said, slapping her hand down onto the table. "Happy day."

"What about you, Isabelle?" Lenora Snibbens suddenly asked. "Did you have a big wedding?"

Isabelle shook her head in a rapid, dismissive way. "Small. Just family." She stood and walked to the trash can by the door, pretending she found it necessary to throw the plastic straw away, but she was really checking on Amy, to see if she had overheard this. The girl was far across the room, however, by her desk, running her hand along the windowsill.

AMY DID NOT believe that Mr. Robertson had actually left town. She knew he was still around. She could feel it. What he was doing, she had concluded, was biding his time, waiting for the right opportunity to get in touch with her. And so she was waiting for a sign from him. Even standing in the office room right now, her eyes searched the parking lot below, half expecting to see him sitting in his red car, his own eyes covered with sunglasses, looking toward the building for some glimpse of her.

He wasn't there.

The fan blew hot wind over the side of Amy's face. She had thought he might call her here at the mill. Or at home even, where he could tell her to pretend it was a wrong number if her mother was standing there. When he did not call, she realized that of course he could not. There was no way he could get a message to her without her mother knowing. He would have to wait and so would she.

For how long? She imagined it all the time: Her hair would be grown out just enough so she looked like herself again, and he would run his hand through it, saying, "Oh, poor Amy, how you suffered." He would kiss her, and she could undress and feel that flood of warmth that came from having his wet mouth attached to her breast. Standing here in the stifling office room, she could close her eyes and almost feel that feeling again as it streamed up through her body, remembering the particular look in his eyes as he bent his head over her that last day together in his car.

The buzzer suddenly blared through the office room, and Amy's eyes flew open. She looked over her shoulder toward the fishbowl and watched Avery Clark bending over his desk; the hair that he combed across his bald spot had parted slightly in the middle, one side of it moving away from his head.

He glanced up and saw her. For a startled minute they held each other's gaze, and then it was Avery Clark who looked away.

"So, ho," said Fat Bev, who was just taking her seat. "The winds begin to blow."

"What do you mean?" Amy sat down.

"The winds in here," Bev said, leaning forward, wagging her head once to indicate the women behind her. "Some discord in our happy little family." Bev hit the desk with her fist. "Left my soda." She rolled her eyes at Amy and heaved herself up again, moving back off to the lunchroom, her huge heart-shaped bottom rocking up and back, up and back as she lumbered down the aisle between the desks. Watching her, Amy was seized with love for her very massiveness. She could picture men and children clinging to this woman, pressing their heads against her solid bulk.

And she wondered, too, where Fat Bev got her underwear. Amy had never seen in stores underwear that would fit someone who was the size of Fat Bev. Before, she would have asked her mother, because it was the kind of thing that Isabelle would know. Now, however, she wouldn't even glance in the direction of her mother's desk, but instead punched numbers onto the adding machine and let her mind return to Mr. Robertson.

I'm thinking of you, she thought, closing her eyes tightly for a few seconds, her hand resting on the adding machine. *I'm waiting for you.*

He was there nearby. She could feel this, could feel his comings and goings, his solitary meals. She knew at night when he stretched out on his bed, removed his socks, took his glasses off, and lay in the dark thinking of her. This much she knew, and as the days went by she seemed to know it more.

BUT POOR ISABELLE knew nothing. Certainly not herself. She knew nothing except the aura of disbelief that surrounded her as the days rolled by. She had done that to Amy, grabbed her hair and cut it off.

It was like she had done a murder—it was like that.

You read about such a thing occasionally, an ordinary citizen murdering someone. A normal, pleasant, churchgoing man suddenly stabbing a knife through the chest of a wife, stabbing again and again, the knife hitting bone, blood spurting, sinewy sounds, pulling the knife out, plunging again—and then standing there—all of it unbelievable. But true, because you have just done that.

Only in Isabelle's case the corpse got up and walked around, drove to work with her each morning, sat across from her at dinner each night, the red bloodstains still there in the form of that terrible hair, the changed face, its pale angularity, the stunned, naked-looking eyes. She had disfigured her daughter. But hadn't she *intended* that when she walked into her bedroom, holding the shears?

It didn't seem possible. Because who was Isabelle Goodrow? She was not a murderer. She was not one of those monstrous mothers you sometimes heard about who disfigured their children, putting them in tubs of scalding water, pressing burning cigarettes or hot irons onto their small, precious hands. And yet she had clutched the hair of Amy that night, had seized the yellow curls of her own daughter with a colossal desire to destroy bursting from within.

She didn't know herself. She didn't think this was Isabelle Goodrow.

The hot days passed. When she glanced at her daughter across the tired office room (the girl sitting hunched over the adding machine, her skinny neck, white as paper, seeming so long), Isabelle's eyes would fill with abrupt hot tears and she would want to run across the room and throw her arms around the girl's neck, to press the pale face against her own, and say, Amy, I'm so sorry. I'm so sorry, Amy.

Oh, the girl was not going to let her do that. Not then, not ever. No sir. You could see in the blank, unforgiving eyes that something irrevocable had been snipped with those shears; the hair might grow back but not this other thing, whose loss Amy clamped down upon with absoluteness. Forget it, Amy's blank eyes, never quite looking at her mother, said—forget it, you're gone.

The hair, in fact, was growing back and within a few weeks' time it didn't seem quite as bad, as wild as it had at first. Still, it needed to be trimmed and shaped. But Isabelle could not bring herself to say this, could not imagine herself speaking to Amy the word "hair." Arlene Tucker spoke it instead. "This heat," she said in the lunchroom one day, "is hell on hair. Everyone looks like shit." And whether she intended it or not, her eyes happened to pass fleetingly over the bent head of Amy Goodrow, who was sitting across the table with a peanut-butter sandwich lifted to her mouth.

"God Almighty," Fat Bev responded, "speak for yourself, Arlene." She shot Arlene a look. Isabelle's face flushed red.

"I am speaking for myself, God Almighty," retorted Arlene, putting her fingers into her own dark hair and plucking at it. "I went to have my roots done and the color came out wrong." This was true enough, if anyone cared to look closely. The crown of Arlene's head seemed a deep shade of orange while the rest of her hair remained chocolate-brown. "And the girl said she'd given someone a perm that morning that didn't take in this heat. Came out all wacky, sticking out in all directions on this woman's head—"

"I read there's a new beauty shop opened in Hennecock," offered Isabelle, anxious to get off the subject, specifically, of hair. "They're giving free makeovers for the month of July. I guess to drum up business." And then, recklessly, "I sometimes think that would be fun. Walk in one person, walk out another."

She thought she saw in the quiet drop of Amy's eyes an expression of disgust.

"Those never work," Arlene said dismissively. "They just paint you up like a dead person to sell you all the products."

"All right, then," Isabelle said. "So much for that. Forget I mentioned it."

AT THE CHURCH a tall fan blew in the middle of the activities room, but it didn't seem to be doing a bit of good. The room was stifling and smelled old, as though the heat had released years' worth of people's sweat that had previously settled into the floorboards and walls and wooden windowsills, as though the countless meetings held there in the past—troops of anxious, noisy prepubescent Girl Scouts (little Pammy Matthews, who had one day wet her pants, pee trickling down her leg and into her red shoe while hands were raised solemnly in pledge to God and country); the countless coffee hours after church, when deacons stood politely in dark gray trousers, eating doughnut holes as their wives chatted to one another; the many meetings of the Historical Society (Davinia Dayble had once given a talk on the first flush toilet in Shirley Falls, which according to her research had been on the Honorable Judge Crane's estate)—all these past activities in the activities room seemed now in this heat to emit their own memorable scents of anxiety, and the effect was cloying, nostalgic, muffled.

Isabelle walked to the back of the room, the floor creaking beneath her black pumps, and took hold of a metal foldout chair. She stood for a moment, uncertain where to place it.

A few other women had already arrived. They stood by a card table that held a large thermos bottle with the word LEMONADE printed on it in black Magic Marker, a tilting column of Styrofoam cups placed alongside. The women had nodded in Isabelle's direction, wiggling their fingers in a casual hello, but they were engrossed in their conversation and no one said, "Oh Isabelle, come and get yourself something cold to drink."

She unfolded her chair not far from them and sat down, arranging her face in what she hoped was a pleasant smile, although to her it felt strained, and she worried she might appear crinkle-eyed and foolish.

She had come here to change her life. She intended to be forthright and friendly, to make her way into the social world of the Congregational church; for it had occurred to her as she dwelled on this for the last number of days that in the past she had simply not tried hard enough. Having friends meant being friendly, her father used to say.

But as she sat on the metal chair, her perky smile feeling undirected, if not ridiculous in this awful heat, it seemed she suffered from some disability, for if only she could sail over to Peg Dunlap right now and say breezily, "Goodness, warm enough for you tonight, Peg?" these women would see how she was ordinary and pleasant like them.

But she was not like them. She worked in the mill, to begin with. And she lived in a small rented house, and she had no husband.

She crossed her ankles carefully. She didn't fit in at the mill, either— that was the thing. Dottie Brown, Fat Bev, Arlene Tucker, Lenora Snibbens, they were all Catholic, of course, their backgrounds were French Canadian, and that was simply a whole different kettle of fish. She had nothing against them, but they were not women she wanted to mix with outside of work. She had gone every summer except this one (claiming illness, which was true enough—she was ill with life) to the Fourth of July barbecue at Fat Bev's house, and watched the men drinking beer, wiping their mouths with the backs of their hands, and listening to the jokes they told. "What do you get when you turn a blond bimbo upside down?"

Arlene Tucker might laugh and say to her husband, "Now, don't go being disgusting," but nobody really seemed to find it disgusting except for Isabelle. She tried to be accommodating; she didn't want to be a spoilsport, but it simply wasn't funny. *A brunette with bad breath.* That really was not funny. And another joke concerning flatulence and pantyhose that even right now brought color to Isabelle's cheeks as she remembered herself standing tense and anxious, eating Bea Brown's potato salad off a paper plate.

She was absolutely certain these women here, Clara Wilcox and Peg Dunlap and the others, would never in a million years enjoy a joke like that. She thought, and not for the first time, that if she had become a teacher, the way she had planned, it would all be very different. These women here would know that she belonged. They would call her on the telephone, invite her to dinner, talk about books.

Although they weren't talking about books now, Isabelle noted. They were talking about some person, she felt quite certain of this, the way their hands were held to their mouths, their voices low and confidential. Peg Dunlap caught Isabelle's eye and stopped midsentence in her talk with Clara Wilcox to say, "Some lemonade, Isabelle?"

Gratefully Isabelle rose to her feet. "It's really something, isn't it," she said, touching her perspiring forehead. "This heat."

"Really something."

She clutched her Styrofoam cup and the women smiled vacantly, their conversation interrupted. She sipped her lemonade, holding the cup to her lips, and glanced at the women with shy expectancy. But the women's eyes remained averted, and Isabelle returned, rather awkwardly, to her seat.

Peg Dunlap said something to Clara Wilcox and Isabelle heard the words "straight for a mammogram" and felt so relieved to know at least they hadn't been talking about *her* that she almost got up to rejoin the group and tell them whoever it was that had to go straight for a mammogram shouldn't worry too awfully much because nine out of ten lumps were benign. She thought that's what the *Reader's Digest* had said anyway. (Suddenly remembering Amy's voice: "You never read anything except that stupid *Reader's Digest*.")

She took a rather large swallow of her lemonade. Perhaps if she finished it she could return to the card table for more and mention then the business of nine out of ten. Still, she didn't want to appear piggish with the lemonade, the thermos was not that big. While she contemplated this dilemma, Barbara Rawley, the deacon's wife who had made the unpleasant remarks last fall about Isabelle's choice of colored leaves and bittersweet in decorating the altar, now walked into the room and began to clap her hands. "Okay, girls. Let's begin."

It did seem preposterous to be discussing the Christmas bazaar in such heat. But, as Peg Dunlap reminded them, the bazaar was their biggest event, and there was no getting started too soon. The women nodded, touching their brows with tissues and fanning themselves with church programs that had been left on the windowsills the Sunday before. Volunteers were needed for the baked-goods stall, and Isabelle raised her hand; her telephone number was written down on a list. "I'd be happy to make a few chocolate cakes," Isabelle said, smiling. "A wonderful recipe of my mother's. Sour milk, you know."

No one smiled back. Clara Wilcox vaguely nodded her head, and Peg Dunlap, in charge of the list, simply said, "Isabelle Goodrow, two cakes."

Isabelle pretended to look through her pocketbook for something, finally snapping it shut. Picking a piece of lint from her skirt, she bobbed her foot.

"Paper goods," said Barbara Rawley, who in this heat did not look quite as pretty as usual, a grayness showing beneath her eyes. "Last year we forgot that entirely." She and Peg Dunlap discussed briefly in low tones the need for subcommittees.

"Oh," said Clara Wilcox," extending her hand toward them. "I spoke to Emma Clark. She wasn't able to come tonight, but she's ready to sign on for wreaths again."

Peg Dunlap nodded. "I spoke to her," she said, and Isabelle, who had experienced some feeling of agitation at hearing the name Emma Clark, now saw Peg Dunlap look up quickly and glance into her eyes—an involuntary glance—then just as quickly look away.

Peg Dunlap knew. Isabelle saw this instantly: in that one quick, reflexive glance, she saw that Peg Dunlap knew.

It was dark when she drove home. Through the open windows came the sound of crickets; passing over the wooden bridge by the marsh, she heard a bullfrog, throaty, deep. The night air was just beginning to seem cool as it moved through the open car windows, and passing by a farm the smell of mowed field filled Isabelle with some tremor that was almost erotic, some confluence of different longings; and then tears came down her face, dripping steadily off her chin, and she just let them come, steering the car slowly through the dark with both hands on the wheel.

She thought how Avery Clark had told his wife, after all, what he had discovered in the woods that day, even though he had promised Isabelle he would not tell anyone. She thought of her daughter, and of her mother, who was dead, and her father, who had died when she was a young girl, and her father's friend, Jake Cunningham, who was also now dead. She wondered when it had been determined that her life would turn out this way.

"Belle, Belle, the miracle," her father used to say, opening his arms for her as she sat on the couch. He meant it: Isabelle's mother, having been told by doctors she would most likely not be having children (for what reasons Isabelle never learned), had therefore, producing Isabelle, produced a miracle; but there were responsibilities in being a miracle, and some little stone—smooth, dark, heavy for its size—had sat inside Isabelle from early on. She had never given it the name of fear, but fear is what it was. Because her parents' joy, it seemed, rested in her hands alone. As a result, they seemed awfully vulnerable to her and required, without knowing it, the same kind of dotingness they offered.

Isabelle was twelve years old when her father sat behind the wheel at a gas station one morning and died while his car's tank was getting filled. Her mother cried easily after that. Sometimes her mother would cry just because the toast got burned, and Isabelle felt sorry and would scrape the burned edges into the garbage with a knife. Her mother cried every time the roof leaked, and Isabelle would scurry around the living room with pails, watching through the window for a letup in the rain.

She loved her mother. She was devoted to her. Isabelle's friends were starting to sneak cigarettes, or drive around after school with boys, but Isabelle didn't do that. She went home after school to be with her mother. She couldn't stand to think of her mother unhappy, and alone.

But they *were* lonely, the two of them, living there like orphans. So that day in May when the magnolia was blooming by the porch and the first bees were banging into the screens, they couldn't believe how wonderful it was to have Jake Cunningham show up at their door. Her father's best friend, and they hadn't seen him since the funeral. He must stay for dinner, Isabelle's mother said, bringing him into the living room. Sit down, sit down. How were Evelyn and the kids?

Everyone was fine. Jake Cunningham's eyes were gray, extremely kind. He smiled at Isabelle.

He also fixed the roof. He went to a lumber store and bought tar paper and shingles and climbed up onto the roof and fixed it. Later he sat at the kitchen table while Isabelle and her mother cooked. The bulk of him was lovely; he sat with his shirtsleeves rolled up, his forearms placed across the table. And he smiled whenever Isabelle glanced at him.

Otherwise it was just the two of them, she and her mother, spending quiet evenings together. Her mother was proud of her, really proud that Isabelle was going to be a teacher, that she graduated first in her high school class. She had sewn a white linen dress for Isabelle to wear while she read her valedictory speech on that hot day in June. (And then when they got home Isabelle vomited, ruining the dress forever.)

Isabelle, driving through the dark now along Route 22, was weeping hard. She shook her head back and forth, and ran her arm across her eyes.

The amazing thing was, she had actually thought she'd managed things with Amy. She had actually thought, if the truth be known, that she had been stronger than her mother. Isabelle turned the car into the driveway and sat in the dark, leaning her head in her hands on the steering wheel, shaking her head slowly back and forth. And how had she thought that? Just last winter, when the snow melted and leaked through Amy's ceiling, she had wrung her hands and carried on, frantically sending Amy down to the kitchen to get the yellow mixing bowl. Hadn't she known at the time that her reaction was way out of proportion? Hadn't she seen Amy's eyes go a little bit dead?

Isabelle rubbed her face and groaned softly in the dark. She thought of what Amy had hurled at her only a few weeks ago: "You don't know anything about the world." It was an accusation she could have made against her own mother. (Except she wouldn't have because of that smooth heavy stone of fear.)

But it was true. Her mother had not known much about the world. Her mother had not been comfortable with much of anything. She had not, for example, told Isabelle anything at all about the mysteries of her body. On the day of her first menstruation, Isabelle assumed that she was dying.

So she had done it differently. She had bought a pink booklet for Amy; she had said, "Let me know if you have any questions."

Isabelle got out of the car and walked quickly up the steps of the porch. There was a light on in the living room. Her heart beat fast with the need to talk to her daughter, to kiss her daughter's face.

But Amy had evidently gone to bed; there was no sign of her downstairs. Isabelle went up the stairs to Amy's room and stopped by the closed door. Tears had started down her face once more. "Amy," she whispered loudly, "are you asleep?"

She thought she heard Amy turn over in bed. "Amy," she whispered again; it pained her to think that the girl might be feigning sleep.

Isabelle knocked lightly on the door and when there was no response she pushed it open across the carpet. In the dim light that shone from the hallway she saw her daughter lying on her bed with her face to the wall. "Amy," she said. "Amy, I need to talk to you."

From the bed there came the quiet sound of Amy's voice. "But I don't want to talk to you. I don't ever want to talk to you again."

Chapter

17

THERE WAS ALL sorts of unhappiness in Shirley Falls that night. If Isabelle Goodrow had been able to lift the roof off various houses and peer into their domestic depths she would have found an assortment of human miseries. Barbara Rawley, for one, had discovered in the shower the week before a small lump in her left breast, and was now, as she waited for arrangements in Boston to be made, in a state of panic the proportions of which she had never thought possible; for alongside the dark terror of waiting for the future (was she actually going to *die?*) was the private realization that she had married the wrong man: her husband, lying next to her in their dark bedroom while she spoke quietly of her fears, had had the audacity to fall asleep.

And the principal of Amy's school, Len Mandel (whom the students called Puddy because of his pockmarked face), was sitting right now in the half-darkened living room of the Spanish teacher, Linda Lanier, feeling absolutely miserable himself. His mother, having invited Linda to dinner weeks ago, had kept postponing the date. Tonight the event had finally taken place, and it had not gone well. Linda's dress was too pink and too short; his mother had not approved. You could see it on her face as soon as Linda walked in. And now, having driven Linda home, he knew that in her smiling anxiety she was waiting for a kiss.

And that his mother at home was waiting also, glancing at the clock while she cleaned up the kitchen, imagining that he had succumbed like some schoolboy. He touched Linda's shoulder and left, but the image of her stayed with him as he drove—standing by the door in her bright pink dress, smiling gamely through her disappointment and surprise, blinking her small, contact-laden eyes.

And there was more: Across the river in a sprawling old house past the outskirts of the Basin, Dottie Brown sat in the dark in her kitchen, smoking cigarettes and listening to the intermittent leak of a dripping faucet. One hand rested on her abdomen; the incision from her hysterectomy was no longer sore, but the skin along each side of it was queerly numb; even through her cotton nightgown she could feel the oddness of it. The cigarettes were a comfort. She was surprised to remember what a comfort they could be. When she gave up smoking, seven years earlier, she had not been able to conceive of a situation that might cause her to start up again. But here she was. Icing on the cake, she thought, salt in the wound.

Half a mile away, unnoticed, the river moved slowly; on the languid, brownish surface, twigs and small sticks turned in slow circles. In the deeper parts the water moved more quickly, dark currents swirling in silence around unseen rocks. The moon, indistinct behind the night clouds, gave off a round spread of some ill-defined lightness in the murky sky, and part of this came through the window of Amy's room, where poor Amy right now lay awake in her bed.

She would never have thought that he'd go. She never would have thought it.

When Isabelle had driven off earlier in the evening to go to the meeting at church, Amy went to the telephone and dialed Mr. Robertson's number. But a recorded voice said the number had been disconnected, and when Amy dialed it again, and again, the same thing happened each time. Finally she had looked up the number for the gym teacher at school because Mr. Robertson had kind of been friends with him. She told the gym teacher she had one of Mr. Robertson's books and wanted to get it back to him, but the gym teacher said he didn't know exactly where Mr. Robertson was. He'd gone back to Massachusetts, the gym teacher thought, and Amy said, When? Oh, back in June sometime, right after school got out.

Amy could not believe it. She could not believe he would leave town without letting her know.

She walked into the living room, and then back into the kitchen. Then she went upstairs and got into bed with her clothes on. Her mother had done it. This presented itself suddenly with a new clarity. Her mother had said, "He's leaving town tomorrow. He ought to be thrown in jail." And she had meant what she said. How could Amy have thought otherwise? How could Amy have missed that her mother was more powerful than Mr. Robertson?

When Isabelle ventured out to the bathroom in the morning, passing Amy in the hall, she saw that her daughter's face was already set in its immovable manner, there was only the veil of contemptuous anger to trail behind her in the hall, and Isabelle realized that she could not mention the words spoken last night, *I don't ever want to talk to you again,* that things had changed that much. She could not say, "Amy, you should apologize for speaking to me that way."

They dressed for work in silence, and neither of them ate anything.

In the car Amy said, "Stacy Burrows wants to know if I can come over on Saturday." They were driving into the parking lot of the mill.

"All right," Isabelle said, simply. And then self-consciously, "When is her baby due?"

"Soon." Amy had expected resistance from her mother, and she had been prepared to fight, to tell her mother she was going to Stacy's house whether she wanted her to or not.

Turning the car slowly into a parking space, Isabelle asked, "She's giving the baby up for adoption?"

Amy nodded.

"Yes?" Isabelle turned the car off and looked at her daughter.

Amy scowled. "Well, what is she supposed to do?"

Isabelle's face went blank; she sat motionless a moment, her hand still on the key in the ignition. "Nothing," she finally said, with a genuineness that surprised Amy. "I'm just wondering if someday she'll be sorry."

"She won't be sorry." Amy opened the car door and got out. Walking across the parking lot next to her mother, she felt compelled to add,

"The social worker said she has a nice couple lined up. They like the outdoors. They like to hike."

"Hike?" Isabelle looked at Amy as if she had never heard the word.

"Climb mountains and stuff," Amy said irritably. She had experienced a strange jealousy when Stacy told her this, had pictured a man looking like Mr. Robertson, a couple active with their child, not living isolated the way Amy and Isabelle did. "They really want a baby," Amy added. "So they'll be really *nice.*"

She stepped in front of her mother to pass through the door; without expecting to, she briefly caught her mother's reflection in the glass and was so struck with how awful her mother looked—her face seemed actually old—that Amy wondered fleetingly if her mother might not be seriously ill.

BUT THINGS WERE hopping in the office room that day. A great deal of commotion was caused by an announcement from Avery Clark: Dottie Brown was coming back to work. The women sat in the lunchroom discussing this in detail, going over the reports that had come in from Fat Bev and Rosie Tanguay, both of whom had spoken to Dottie Brown on the telephone that morning. While Avery Clark, as everyone knew, had generously given Dottie the entire summer to get over her hysterectomy, she wanted to come back earlier than planned. She wanted to come back the very next week. She didn't want to be home alone anymore while her husband was at work. She had seen a UFO.

This caused some real turbulence among the women, and they became divided rather quickly between those who believed her and those who did not. Why this split of opinion should cause *such* bitter discord no one seemed to care or know, but Fat Bev found herself in a difficult position. Being Dottie Brown's best friend for almost thirty years, she was forced to defend her with vigor. But she herself believed the story was a puzzling fabrication, that it couldn't be true.

The story went like this: Dottie Brown, sick to death of soap operas, had gone out on her back porch to lie in the hammock. It was the middle of the afternoon and she brought with her a glass of pink lemonade, which she held listlessly against her stomach. She may have dozed off. In fact she was rather certain that she had dozed off, the heat being what it was, but she woke to see the lemonade trembling in the glass and right away this puzzled her. She didn't know why the lemonade should be moving like that when the glass, propped up there on her stomach, wasn't moving at all.

Suddenly the glass broke. She hadn't knocked it over, it simply broke. As she sat up, confused, of course, and frightened, she saw this thing in the sky. This "thing" was big and silver and shaped like a flying saucer and it was coming closer and closer, moving in over the back field until it was right there in her backyard. (What was she *doing* all this time, different women demanded.) She was simply watching, unable to move, half sitting, half lying, in the hammock her husband had bought for her earlier this summer, soaked in pink lemonade and broken glass, her heart beating so fast she fully expected to die.

When the spaceship landed on her back lawn—taking up the entire area—a door on the spaceship opened, and a figure, olive-skinned with a very large head (no hair or clothes to speak of), came out onto the ground and walked toward her. He-she-it didn't speak but rather "put thoughts into her head." Like: They didn't want to hurt her, they needed to study her, they had come from a planet far away to research what was going on with the earth.

She didn't remember anything after that. (Oh, that's convenient, the nonbelievers said, shooting Fat Bev a look of disgust, as though she might be the one responsible for this.) When her husband got home from work about five-thirty, there she was, just lying on the hammock, still covered with lemonade. *But.* Her wristwatch, a nice little Timex she got from Sears at last year's Christmas sale, had stopped at exactly three-thirty, which she thought was just about the time she had woken up to find the lemonade slopping about in the glass.

"Well, maybe," said Lenora Snibbens loudly and slowly, and not altogether nicely, "she forgot to wind it."

"Of course she thought of that," Rosie Tanguay retorted. "But she wound it first thing that morning. That's what she does every morning. And furthermore," Rosie went on, growing red in the face, having for whatever reasons become an immediate and ardent defender of the Dottie Brown cause, "the watch doesn't work anymore. Ka-put."

"Oh, for God's sake," said Lenora, rolling her eyes, "I have never heard such horseshit."

"Isabelle, what do you think," demanded Rosie Tanguay.

Isabelle, feeling somewhat alarmed, realized a kind of poll was evidently taking place; teams were getting drawn. "Oh, heavens," she stammered, attempting to bide her time. "Well, my goodness. Anything's possible, I suppose."

"But do you *believe* her," said Rosie Tanguay, and Isabelle felt all eyes upon her, including Amy's, which bothered Isabelle the most—she hated having her daughter witness her uncertainty.

"I've never known Dottie to lie," said Isabelle.

"People lie all the time," Arlene Tucker said. "Honestly, Isabelle. Where have you been?"

Isabelle felt her face grow hot; she must be turning crimson. "I don't believe people lie all the time," she retorted. "But if you are forcing me to take a stand"—her voice trembled, and attempting to cover this, she spoke her last line rather loudly—"then I will stand behind Dottie."

It was the strongest statement Isabelle had been known to make in her many years in the office room, and the toll it took on her was evident in her still-burning face. "Now, if you will excuse me," she said, rising. "I have work to do."

She was afraid she might stumble on her way out of the lunchroom. At the last minute, as she moved successfully through the blur of women and chairs, she caught Fat Bev's eye, and it was a jolt in the midst of chaos, for on the face of this woman she had known for years she saw a look of such clarity and understanding that for the first time in a long while the thought passed through Isabelle's mind, *I have a friend.*

Chapter

18

A̲VERY C̲LARK̲ WAS more concerned with keeping peace in the office room than he was with whether or not Shirley Falls had been visited by a UFO. He tended to think it had not been, although he was experiencing some apprehension about the matter, because Dottie Brown had never in seventeen years shown signs of being prone to hysterics. However, the point was, if she wanted to return to work earlier than planned, then by all means she ought to come back. But it meant the Goodrow girl would have to go. This actually brought Avery a sense of relief; the girl's presence had been a thorn in his side all summer, but he did not look forward to telling Isabelle, whom in some portion of his heart, he realized now, as he asked her to step into his office, he felt quite sorry for.

She had lost weight. Avery Clark, standing back to let her pass through his doorway, was struck with how Isabelle's arm looked like a piece of kindling. And he saw as she sat down across from him that her face was unevenly colored; her eyes appeared bald, exposed, as they blinked in what seemed to be self-conscious confusion.

Politely, speaking slowly, he leaned across his desk and presented to her the situation with Dottie Brown and Amy.

She took it well, as he should have known she would. "Of course," she said simply. "I understand." It appeared she had nothing more to say, and Avery felt slightly caught off guard to think the job had been so easily accomplished. But then Isabelle added kindly, "I appreciate what you've done for Amy already, letting her work here the way you did."

"Oh, sure." It made him very nervous to think she might in any way mention what he had witnessed that day.

"The money has been helpful," Isabelle was saying. "Her paychecks go straight in the bank and then she'll have it for college when the time comes."

"Good. That's good." He nodded with some tentativeness at the small, complaisant woman sitting before him, her pale hands folded on her lap. She seemed only half there, like a beach ball that had steadily been losing air through some slow, invisible leak. A slackening. Her eyes, small, a little shiny, met his glance briefly, and he saw that behind her ever-present politeness her mind was not fully on him.

"You surviving this hot summer all right, Isabelle?"

She seemed startled by the question, her eyes moving back to his, blinking twice, as though she had come from a dark room into bright sunshine. He saw how she hesitated before answering, and he hoped again she would not mention the business with Amy.

But she said only, "I'm tired, Avery. I feel very tired."

"Of course," he said hurriedly. "This weather is perfectly awful. And not a break in sight, I guess, if you're going to believe the weatherman."

"Everyone's upset," Isabelle said quietly, almost indifferently, indicating with a slight motion of her head that she was referring here to the women in the office room.

"Yes." Avery sighed through his nose, giving Isabelle a grim smile of acknowledgment which included in it some degree of camaraderie: they were parents faced with a roomful of unruly, petulant children and would have to do the best they could. "We'll get through it, I suppose." Avery placed his hands down flat on the desk in his characteristic, conclusive way. "But listen, Isabelle. I appreciate your cooperation. With everything. I most certainly do."

She nodded and stood up, returning silently to her desk in the stifling office room.

. . .

THE CAR SMELLED. Left in the parking lot all day with its windows rolled up, it turned into a kind of vile hothouse, a nasty implosion of unseen fungi or bacteria, and Isabelle always opened all four windows and all four doors for a few minutes before stepping inside to take her place behind the steering wheel; a procedure Amy found profoundly embarrassing. She didn't know why her mother couldn't be like most people, who simply left their cars unlocked with the windows down. But to Isabelle, who had been raised in a very small town, Shirley Falls appeared to be a city, and so she locked her car up every day, and every day now it needed airing out, sitting on the tar like some mechanical bird with wings extended while Isabelle made ineffectual waving motions with her pocketbook and Amy sat slumped in the front seat, a hand to her forehead.

Today Isabelle proceeded with listlessness, opening the back doors for only a moment, and soon they were driving home.

"You don't believe the UFO thing, do you," Amy finally said.

Isabelle glanced at her briefly. "No."

They drove in silence past the trailer park, the swamp, past the old logging road where Amy had been discovered with Mr. Robertson.

"It could be true, though," Amy said, squinting slightly in the heat, her elbow resting on the open window, her fingers tugging compulsively at her hair. When her mother didn't respond to this, Amy added, "I think it *is* true."

Still, Isabelle didn't answer.

"Why wouldn't it be true?" Amy persisted. "We're not the only stupid little planet, you know."

Isabelle simply kept driving.

"So why couldn't there be life on some other planet?"

"I suppose there could be," Isabelle answered.

"Well, don't you even *care*? You sound like you don't even *care*."

For a moment it appeared that Isabelle wasn't going to bother to answer this, but then she said with little expression, "I have other things on my mind."

Amy slumped further down into her seat and rolled her eyes with disgust.

Awful, Isabelle thought, feeling lightheaded—everything is awful. "Anyway." She drove carefully with both hands on the wheel, looking straight ahead through the windshield. "Dottie Brown is returning to work on Monday, so you're out of a job."

She turned to glance at her daughter, who seemed to have nothing to say to this.

Isabelle added, "Avery told me this afternoon. With Dottie coming back there's not enough work to keep you busy. And not enough money to pay you. Apparently."

Amy remained silent, turning her head to look out the open window beside her. Isabelle, glancing at her again, could not see her face.

"What will I do?" Amy eventually asked. The question seemed genuine and Isabelle could not guess her daughter's thoughts. Was she worried about being lonely, bored? (Was she thinking of running away?)

"I don't know."

"Maybe I'll get lucky and be kidnapped by a UFO," Amy suggested, with real nastiness, as they pulled into the driveway.

Isabelle turned the car engine off and simply closed her eyes. "Who knows," she said. "Maybe you will."

Still, there were things that had to be said. If they couldn't immediately decide upon the rest of the summer for Amy, Isabelle at least needed to know what time on Saturday Amy was expected to be at Stacy Burrows's house, whether or not she was to have dinner there, and how she would get home.

To all these inquiries Amy responded that she didn't know. Isabelle found this irritating, which in turn irritated Amy, and the outcome was that Amy, late Saturday morning, took off on foot, telling Isabelle if she was going to be later than five she would call. "I'd be happy to drive you there," Isabelle offered one more time, following Amy out the door.

Without turning around, Amy said loudly, "No."

In order to walk into town she had to pass by the logging road where she had gone with Mr. Robertson, and she turned her head away now, as she did every time she passed by. (Driving with her mother she would simply close her eyes.) In her head she told this to Mr. Robertson. In her head she imagined his kind eyes watching her. Only it was somewhat different now, ever since she found his number disconnected, found out that he had *gone away*; she could not stop her inner trembling.

She was glad when she came to the center of town—the cars, the shops, the people on the sidewalk. She crossed Main Street, then cut through the parking lot of the post office and came out onto a sidewalk that led eventually to the neighborhood where Stacy lived. The street names were wonderful: Maple Street, Valentine Road, Harmony Drive, Appleby's Circle. Nothing plain and ugly like Route 22. The houses were pretty and clean-looking too; some were gray, others white, a few maroon. They had bay windows in their living rooms and curtains hanging in their upstairs rooms. There were front lawns, side lawns, sometimes a white picket fence.

Stacy's house was different. It was part of a new development built down by Oyster Point, where the houses were bigger than in other parts of town. Stacy's house was the biggest of all. It had huge windows and a mansard roof. The driveway was glinty with white chipped rock that crunched beneath Amy's sneakers. Amy had never been in Stacy's house before. Without admitting it, Amy shared her mother's distaste for modern architecture; she liked houses to look traditional. And this one, in addition to the queer slope of the roof, had a front door painted bright yellow, which made Amy feel uneasy, and which seemed fleetingly in her mind connected to the fact that Stacy's father was a psychologist. But she was uneasy anyway: Stacy had invited her over so they could watch a film on childbirth that her father had gotten from the college. Amy had not told that to Isabelle.

She hesitated, then rapped on the door.

From inside came the muffled sound of motion, then Stacy's voice as she approached the door—"Get out, you little buggers. Stay away"— and then the door opened and there was Stacy, red-haired and beautiful and very, very pregnant. *"Hi,"* Stacy said, raising both hands as though she might be going to take Amy's face between them. And then: "Jesus, what happened to your hair?"

Amy, stepping through the door, looked down at the straw mat under her feet and tried to smile, but her mouth could not seem to manage; the corners turned down jerkily.

A child partly hidden behind a closet door peered at Amy, and Amy turned her back, wiping her nose quickly with her arm. "Get out of here, you little pieces of shit," Stacy said. A scuffling sound by the closet, a wail.

"Mom," cried the boy, running off down the hallway, "Stacy hit me and called me a piece of shit." Another little boy dashed out and ran after him, calling out, "Stacy hit us!"

"Cockroaches!" Stacy called after him. "You *are* little pieces of shit. Quit spying on my friends or next time I'll kill you." She took Amy's arm. "Come on." And Amy followed her down a flight of stairs into Stacy's bedroom. It had never occurred to Amy that people might speak to one another this way in their home, and the sense of foreignness brought on by the yellow front door increased as she went into Stacy's bedroom and Stacy slammed the bedroom door.

"So what happened?" Stacy asked cautiously, once they were seated on her bed. It was a double bed and seemed huge to Amy, with its four high posts of dark wood and tumbled, unmade flowered sheets.

"This is a great room," said Amy, looking around. Next to the bed was a large window that went almost to the floor; trees were visible, sloping downhill toward Oyster Creek.

"It's okay," Stacy said, indifferently.

Amy pulled at her hair and shrugged with embarrassment. "Uhm. My mom. She got mad at me."

She dropped her eyes, fingered the flowered sheets. She was afraid of having to explain, but Stacy only said after a while, "Don't you just hate parents?"

Amy looked up, and Stacy held out both arms. "I love you," Stacy said simply, and Amy, too embarrassed to answer, closed her eyes briefly against the smooth, slightly warm feel of Stacy's hair.

MR. BURROWS FUSSED a great deal with the film projector. "It's going to take me a few moments here," he told his wife, a scowl causing ridges to rise across his forehead. Mrs. Burrows, recognizing vaguely that some aspect of his manhood seemed at stake here (he was a person who liked to "run the show"), went into the kitchen and made popcorn, the smell soon wafting into the living room, where Amy and Stacy sat waiting—with some degree of anxiety themselves—on the living-room couch.

The couch was made of brown leather and to Amy it seemed enormous. If she leaned back it was almost as though she were lying down.

And yet sitting up straight she looked like a jerk, she was sure—as though she had never been invited to someone's house before. Stacy herself sat cross-legged, her bulbous stomach before her, squinting her eyes furiously at her little brothers whenever the children came into the room. "I'm warning you, rat-fucks," she murmured.

It took some doing to get everything arranged—Stacy needed more salt on her popcorn, which Mrs. Burrows hurriedly brought her; the children had to be sent downstairs, the blinds on the huge windows drawn—but eventually Mrs. Burrows settled onto the couch next to Amy, and the movie whirred away in black and white, blurry at first; a pregnant woman walked into a hospital while a male narrator spoke about the miracle of life.

Amy did not like popcorn. Years before, sick with a stomach virus, she had noticed how similar the taste of her vomit was to the taste of popcorn. Even her burps had tasted that way, and she sat now on the ocean of this leather couch with a large mixing bowl of popcorn placed on her lap, the inside edges of her mouth every few moments breaking out with a watery secretion that she knew often came right before upchucking. Her palms were moist from the fear of being sick on the Burrowses' leather couch. "Try not to get butter on the leather," Mrs. Burrows had said to the girls just moments before, handing them both a napkin.

On the screen now was a diagram; little tadpole-looking things moving toward an "egg," which in this case was a smiley face with eyelashes blinking flirtatiously at the tadpoles.

"How's the popcorn?" Mrs. Burrows asked.

"Good." Amy blushed and put a piece of popcorn tentatively into her mouth.

"More salt?"

"No, thank you."

Without moving her head Amy tried to survey her surroundings. The ceiling of the living room was so high it could have been a church, and on the white walls hung an assortment of carved masks, the expressions on some of them fierce and foreign-looking. It surprised Amy that people would want faces like that on their walls.

The pregnant woman was lying down now on a bed, her stomach rising in a fearsome mound under the hospital cloth, her eyes, it seemed to Amy, flickering with terror, while the male voice of the narrator continued, speaking calmly and knowingly of cervical dilation.

Amy shut her eyes, praying not to vomit. She thought of daffodils, fields of daffodils. Blue sky, green grass, yellow daffodils.

"Gross," Stacy exclaimed. "God."

Amy opened her eyes: the woman's water had broken. A dark wet head was emerging from an opening that Amy could not imagine was actually between the woman's legs. The camera moved to the woman's face—her contorted, sweating, horrible-looking face; it embarrassed Amy far more to see this woman's face than to see between her legs, where, according to the camera now, shoulders were emerging, a body, tiny arms and legs tucked up like a turkey packaged in a grocery store.

"Ugly," Stacy said. "God, is that baby *ugly.*"

"All babies look that way at first," Mrs. Burrows said cheerfully. "They have to get washed off. Mother cats lick their babies clean. They lick all the mucus and blood right off—the afterbirth, it's called."

A wave of nausea rolled up from the back of Amy's throat. Daffodils, she thought. Blue sky. She put the bowl of popcorn onto the floor by her feet.

"Thank God I'm not expected to lick the baby clean," Stacy said, rearranging herself on the couch, tucking a leg up under her, stuffing a handful of popcorn into her mouth.

"It's supposed to be high in protein—isn't that right, Gerald?" Stacy's mother directed this question to her husband, who was scowling at the projector again; the film was coming to an end, with the baby being placed in the mother's arms.

"Protein. Yes. I had a patient who cooked the placenta in a soup afterward, and she and her husband and friends ate it—a celebratory event, I believe, is how they viewed it."

Amy pressed her lips together.

"Oh, *gross,*" Stacy said. "That is really fucking gross. Your patients are *so* crazy, Dad."

Mr. Burrows was trying to rewind the film without tearing it; it kept coming unthreaded, and he felt everyone was watching him. "Stacy," he said. "The language has got to stop. It has simply got to stop. And it's entirely inappropriate to refer to neurotic people as 'crazy.' We've been through this before."

Stacy rolled her eyes at Amy while Mrs. Burrows said, "Well, that was a very interesting film. That was *very* helpful. Now Stacy will know what to expect."

"I expect to die," Stacy answered. "Did you see that woman's face?"

"Thank your father for bringing home the film, please. It wasn't easy to get the projector here from the college." Mrs. Burrows was smiling as she stood up; she took Amy's bowl of popcorn from the floor and returned it to the kitchen without saying anything about its still being full, and Amy, relieved at this, said boldly, "Thank you for inviting me."

"Oh, yes. You're welcome." Mr. Burrows, still scowling, with his head bent over the projector, did not look up at her. In fact Amy wasn't sure he had looked at her once since she arrived. He seemed to her a nervous man with a wide, flat bottom. Amy, glancing with private disgust, remembered Stacy's report on his "fleshy white stupid-looking ass." Amy did not miss having a father when she saw fathers like that.

"Yeah, thanks, Dad." Stacy sounded subdued. "I'm scared," she finally said.

Amy, her nausea subsiding, looked carefully at her friend. "It'll be okay," she said, lamely. "I guess."

"Oh, it will be fine," Mrs. Burrows said, emerging from the kitchen. "They'll give you an epidural, sweetheart. You won't feel a thing."

"What's that?" Stacy looked confused.

"A big injection in the spine," Mr. Burrows responded, with ill-concealed impatience. "They just discussed it in the film."

AMY WALKED HOME through the woods by the river. It was muggy and horrible, as though cobwebs pressed against her, not at all what she had imagined—saved herself with—sitting on Stacy's brown couch. Here the sky was not blue, there was no green grass, there were no daffodils. The pine needles were tired and spongy, the sky, what could be seen of it through the trees, just an everlasting white. She sat down on an old stone wall that seemed to rise up gradually from the pine needles until a number of yards later it disappeared again.

The woods were full of stone walls like this one, moss-covered rocks falling away from each other, making way here and there for a tree trunk that had fallen in a storm and now lay rotting, covered in vines; beyond, the granite stones emerged in a line again, no longer the property boundaries they once were but only faint reminders of a time when other people (not Amy or Stacy) had lived there, a time presumably so difficult that merely withstanding the seasons and surviving childbirth were triumphs in themselves.

None of this occurred to Amy now. When she was younger she would walk through the woods imagining Indian girls and men, white settlers frightened in their log homes, closing their thick shutters at night; it had interested her then: how women lived in long skirts without toilets or running water, how they baked bread in the large Dutch ovens. Amy didn't care about it now. She just wanted to have her cigarette, to try to get rid of what the popcorn had started, what had turned since into some queasiness of her heart. Stacy, with her swollen stomach and her leather couch, and her queer parents—Stacy seemed gone.

And Mr. Robertson was gone. This of course made her the sickest, the dull pain always with her. Where had he gone to?

Later, crossing Main Street, she heard someone call her name. Amy was not used to having her name called out in public, and because the man who called to her was handsome, and looked genuinely glad to see her, it took her some moments to figure out that he had not mistaken her for somebody else.

It was Paul Bellows. Stacy's old boyfriend.

Chapter

19

ALONE.

Isabelle sat in the armchair by the living-room window, watching the sparrows that hopped and darted by the bird feeder, every one of their motions seeming compact, nimble, deliberate, but also the mere result of being startled. If this was the case, their existence was a tense one, Isabelle considered. Still, they had each other. Hadn't she heard that birds mated for life? She watched as one sparrow hopped from the feeder to a small branch in the spruce tree; in a moment the other followed, the branch bouncing slightly beneath their delicate double weight. Birds of a feather.

And people, too—lots of people were together right now. Her own daughter visiting her pregnant friend . . . (Briefly Isabelle closed her eyes.) Women from church—Barbara Rawley, Peg Dunlap. Perhaps they were out shopping together right now. On the other side of town, across the river, Fat Bev might be sitting on Dottie Brown's porch, sharing a laugh about Arlene Tucker. Birds of a feather flock together. *Why am I alone?*

But what about Avery Clark? Here Isabelle shifted slightly in her chair and rested her chin on her fist, as though she had something to contemplate that could take a very long time. Was Avery Clark alone right now as well? She preferred to think he was, but he did have a wife; Isabelle necessarily had to consider that. Perhaps Avery was doing yard work out behind his house, Emma rapping on the window, calling out that whatever he was doing wasn't being done right.

Yes, this was where Isabelle's mind wanted to be. She pictured Avery in his back garden, wearing gardening gloves, a rumpled canvas hat on his head. Weeding, perhaps—tugging out weeds from the rock garden (she had no idea if he had a rock garden), then raking the weeds up. She pictured him leaning for a moment on the rake, wiping his brow. . . . Oh, how Isabelle longed to reach out and take his hand, to press his hand to her cheek. But he didn't see her, didn't know she was there, and he moved past her into his house, the afternoon stillness hanging over the heavy dining-room furniture, the carpeted staircase, the overstuffed living-room couch. He would go to the kitchen and pour himself something cold to drink, then take it to the window, where he would stand looking out.

Sitting in her armchair, Isabelle sighed deeply. It surprised her sometimes how absorbed she could become in something that was not happening. (What *was* happening? Nothing. She was sitting in a chair in a silent house and had been sitting there for quite some time.) But he had been so kind the other day in his office, so concerned as he sat at his desk. "You surviving this hot summer all right, Isabelle?" So she let herself continue to picture him leaning against the windowsill, drinking something cold. He would stand gazing through the window, looking past the rake he had left propped against the garden wall, and then he would return the glass to the kitchen sink and climb the stairs, because he would have to take a shower after gardening.

His secret parts—oh, the incredible privacy of them, moist and warm at the very inner tops of his legs. There were times when Isabelle pictured this part of him as it would be in a state of excitement; but now she saw it in its complacency, moist and warm and pale tucked up there in his undershorts. She loved him, and it moved her that he carried with him this private, intimate aspect of himself.

How terrible, how ironic, that someone existed in this world (she, Isabelle Goodrow) who would, given the chance, gladly touch with extraordinary delicacy and love these aging parts of this aging man. Surely every man longed to be touched that way, with tender, tender love, and surely that stiff Emma, who walked around like she had a bad smell in her nose, and who lived with no regard for the privacy of people's sorrows (spreading gossip about Amy to Peg Dunlap), was not a woman who would love a man with delicacy and tenderness.

The way she would, the way Isabelle would.

So that was life. You lived down the road from a man for years, worked with him daily, sat behind him in church, loved him with an almost perfect love . . . and nothing. Nothing, nothing, nothing.

Through the trees there was a motion, a person walking on the road. Isabelle watched as the girl—it was Amy—moving slowly and with her head down, came up the gravel driveway. The sight of her pained Isabelle. It pained her terribly to see her, but why?

Because she looked unhappy, her shoulders slumped like that, her neck thrust forward, walking slowly, just about dragging her feet. This was Isabelle's daughter; this was Isabelle's fault. She hadn't done it right, being a mother, and this youthful desolation walking up the driveway was exactly proof of that. But then Amy straightened up, glancing toward the house with a wary squint, and she seemed transformed to Isabelle, suddenly a presence to be reckoned with. Her limbs were long and even, her breasts beneath her T-shirt seemed round and right, neither large or small, only part of some pleasing symmetry; her face looked intelligent and shrewd. Isabelle, sitting motionless in her chair, felt intimidated.

And angry. The anger arrived in one quick thrust. It was the sight of her daughter's body that angered her. It was not the girl's unpleasantness, or even the fact that she had been lying to Isabelle for so many months, nor did Isabelle hate Amy for having taken up all the space in her life. She hated Amy because the girl had been enjoying the sexual pleasures of a man, while she herself had not.

It was awful how it rolled up to her: the memory of that day in June when Avery, averting his eyes, told her he had discovered in the woods her daughter "partly undressed." And here Avery's face had become terribly red as he added, "Completely so, on top. Beyond that, I didn't see." (Which was not true, Avery Clark had seen the bunched-up skirt, the long pale expanse of thin white thighs, the patch of hair, had seen how, upon being discovered, the girl's hand scrambled to her lap—details that Avery often dwelled upon and that he had not mentioned to Isabelle, or even to his wife.) And then he had said to Isabelle, "The man was having his pleasure there. Above her waist, I'm referring to."

Oh, poor Avery! His face so red as he stammered these words.

But it made Isabelle sick; it made her want to vomit. Amy exposed like that, offering her breasts like that . . . enjoying it, *liking* it. Not that it would have been better if the girl had not enjoyed it—but that wasn't the case. Isabelle was quite certain somehow that Amy had been actively, happily involved, and it made her want to cry.

In spite of Arlene Tucker's remark—delivered a number of years ago with great authority, and Isabelle had never forgotten it—that teenage girls who had sex didn't enjoy it because they were sexually too young (where would Arlene Tucker get this information from, anyway?), Isabelle knew it was not true.

She knew because the touch of Jake Cunningham's hands years ago had filled her with desperate sensations. She knew because over the years she had remembered the feeling exactly—the extraordinary joy of it. As she rose from the armchair with agitation, a fleeting knowledge came to her—that she had lived ever after with a sense of continually pressing down, pushing back inside, the billowing bursts of longing she had; that she had been longing, longing, longing for a man, to have those insane, desperate sensations again.

And Amy had had them instead. (To avoid the approaching girl, whose footsteps could be heard on the porch, Isabelle went hurriedly up the stairs.) Amy had so vehemently defended that man. You did not defend a person that way if you had not responded with desperation to the touch of his hands. And then the nasty innuendoes the man made about how Amy hadn't needed much teaching, or whatever dreadful thing he had said that day in his wretched bare apartment. Implying what? What was he implying? That Amy was a "natural"?

Oh, Isabelle hated her. (She closed her bedroom door, seated herself on the edge of her bed.) It wasn't fair!

It wasn't fair either to have to hear about all this free-love business these days, young people living together without marriage, moving on to someone new when they got tired, these filthy, dirty hippie girls with flowers in their hair. Isabelle had read that on some college campuses now they had doctors just handing out the pill to any girl who wanted it; all these girls using their young bodies like they were mere toys.

It pained her.

It pained her to see billboards, television commercials, any advertisement that made use of seductive young women. And it seemed they all did. It seemed that no matter what was being advertised, it all came down to sex. Everyone was having sex—it was there for the asking.

Downstairs the kitchen door could be heard opening and then closing. "Mom?"

Isabelle remained where she was on the bed, listening as Amy's footsteps came slowly up the stairs.

"Mom?"

"I'm resting," Isabelle called out from behind the closed door. She could hear Amy stop on the landing.

"I didn't know if you were home or not," Amy said.

"I'm home." Isabelle could hear in the silence that Amy was still there. "Did you have a good time?" Isabelle eventually asked, her face, in the privacy of her room, tight with fury.

"It was okay." Again there was the silence on the landing, as well as the silence in Isabelle's bedroom; both poised, waiting. Then Amy crossed the hall and went into her room.

Iᴛ ᴡᴀs ᴛᴇʀʀɪʙʟʏ hot up here. Amy closed the door and turned on the fan, aiming it toward her bed, where she lay down with one leg flung over the edge, her foot on the floor. In a way, she had been hoping to talk to her mother. After the strangeness of Stacy's house, to walk up the driveway and see her mother—it was a relief, almost, to be home.

Except it wasn't. Forget it. Her mother was still awful. But what had she expected? That her mother would greet her at the door and say, "Sweetheart, I love you, come give me a kiss?" That was not her mother. Even when Amy was small and came to her crying with a skinned knee, Isabelle would tell Amy to stop crying. "Grit your teeth and bear it," she would say. And now she was lying in her room "resting," which was a crock of shit because Amy had just seen her at the window a few moments ago.

So there was no point in being glad to be home. She wasn't glad to be home. Although thinking that made her wonder about Debby Kay

Dorne, made her wonder again why the girl had just vanished from her house that day, why she was still missing, why she hadn't been found. The newspaper hardly bothered mentioning her anymore. On TV last week the guy only said, "The search continues for Debby Kay Dorne"—and that was all. Amy turned over on her stomach. It was pretty creepy, it really was.

And it just showed how stupid Isabelle was being. Anyone *else's* mother would be glad to have their daughter around, would be happy to sit and talk right now instead of scuttling off upstairs to "rest." She might as well have stayed longer with Paul Bellows. Or longer at Stacy's. Except she had felt really depressed at Stacy's, especially after the movie, when they went back down to Stacy's room and Stacy showed her a book about sex that Stacy's new boyfriend had bought her. Amy hadn't even known that Stacy had a new boyfriend, but she did, a guy named Joshua who was going to be a senior. He had bought her this book on sex. It had drawings to show you ways to do it, and it made Amy miss Mr. Robertson almost unbearably. The guy in the book had a beard like Mr. Robertson's, and the woman he was doing it with had long straight hair. It made Amy feel just terribly lonely to see the drawings in the book. (And anxiously curious too, because that's what Mr. Robertson's thing must look like—with the bump on the tip of it, and the little pouches at the other end; and the hair.) She told Stacy she had to get home before her mother got mad, but it was really because she wanted to leave and have her cigarettes in the woods, sitting on the stone wall by herself.

And then she'd run into Paul Bellows, which was weird, because she hardly knew him, and he acted like they were friends. He wanted to know about Stacy, of course, since her parents wouldn't even let him call. Amy didn't say anything about the new boyfriend; she just said that Stacy was doing okay.

"Good," Paul said, nodding. "Because I really care about her, you know."

"Sure," Amy answered. "I mean, sure you do."

He took Amy for a ride in his new car. "How do you like it?" he asked, smiling. His teeth, as well as his big eyes, seemed moist, his large hands caressed the gearshift as he drove.

"Oh, it's great," Amy said. "It's nice." She didn't know, really, what a person said about a new car. The car was small, a little sports car; it was blue on the outside, gray on the inside. "I like the color," she added, tentatively, touching the gray vinyl upholstery next to her leg.

"Purrs like a baby, doesn't it," Paul said.

She nodded, seeing how his mouth was like Stacy's, full in the same way, his lips blooming outward, his cheek smooth with an inner dark glow, his wet teeth very white.

He drove out onto Route 4 to show her how the car had great "pickup," which evidently meant it could go very fast, for he tapped the speedometer for her to look as the car went seventy miles an hour, then eighty, then ninety. It was the blacktop of the road that seemed to be moving as she stared terrified through the windshield, some ferocious conveyor belt gone out of control, hurtling beneath them.

"There we go," Paul said, grinning at the speedometer that now showed the needle shaking over the number one hundred. "It's a beauty, this baby."

He slowed. "You ever go that fast in a car before?"

Amy shook her head.

"Scare you?"

Amy nodded.

"I won't do it again." He seemed genuinely sorry. "Just showing off," he said, and the color in his cheek seemed to deepen.

"It's okay," Amy said, her relief at going slower making her loquacious. "It's a new car and stuff. Whenever I get new stuff I always like to, you know, play around with it."

He glanced at her as he drove down an exit ramp, heading back to town. "You're nice," he told her simply. "I want to buy you something."

"Oh, that's all right," she said, embarrassed. "No, that's okay."

But he really did want to, she could see that, and in a few moments they went into a drugstore, where he bought her lip gloss and mascara. The lip gloss was the expensive kind. "Jeez," she said. "Thank you."

Back on the sidewalk she stood self-consciously, looking around to see if, God forbid, her mother might be driving by. "I'll walk home from here," she said. "I need the exercise."

But Paul seemed happy, excited. "Hold on one minute," he told her, and he disappeared into the florist shop that was there next to the drugstore. In a moment he walked out with a bunch of daisies wrapped in a big paper cone. "For you," he said, beaming at her with his white teeth. "Because you've been so nice to Stacy. And to me. You're a nice person, Amy."

Here Amy sat up and put her perspiring face directly in front of the fan. It was nice to have someone say you were a nice person. It really was. She didn't know why the whole thing made her sad in a way. Amy closed her eyes against the fan. Her bedroom was hot and smelled like an attic; where her scalp was moist at the roots of her hair, she felt a faint chill.

What she had done was to walk to the high school, and finding the back door open by the gym, she had moved through the silent hallway and left the daisies by Mr. Robertson's door.

AUGUST ARRIVED. THE sky was pale and seemed higher each day, some increasing sense of a domelike membrane swelling with its own exhaustion.

Peg Dunlap, the woman from church who was on the Christmas Committee and who was having an affair with Stacy's father, spent one of these hot afternoons in the A&P, where it was cooler, and where she could follow the unsuspecting Mrs. Burrows as she pushed a cart up one aisle and down another. Wearing sunglasses, Peg Dunlap peeked around the lettuce and watched the wife of her lover study the jars of jellies and jams. She could not have said why doing this filled her with such excitement, and an excruciating pain.

In a top-floor apartment a few miles away was Linda Lanier, the Spanish teacher, who at that very moment of the monstrously hot August afternoon was in her bed naked with Lenny Mandel, the two of them grunting and sweating vigorously as they moved about the twisted sheets; daisies discovered in the corridor of the school by a surprised Lenny Mandel now jiggled in a milk jug next to the bed. (Mrs. Mandel, calling her son at the high school to ask him to bring mustard on his way home from work, was told he was already gone for the day.)

Across the river in the office room Fat Bev was having trouble with her stomach, her digestion. Right after she got to work these days she would start to cramp and then have terrible gas. Walking carefully through the office room, squeezing her sphincter to save her life, she sometimes felt as though her entire lower region was about to explode—only to land finally and safely on a toilet seat and find there was nothing to emit but a loud blast of air. Absolutely nothing more.

At least it gave her something to talk to Dottie about. She sure wasn't going to talk about UFOs. "Honest to God," she said now, settling herself back in behind her desk. "So much rumbling in my innards down below."

Dottie Brown looked up, her forehead furrowed. "Really?" she asked, and Bev saw that Dottie had not absorbed what was just said, that something stood between Dottie and the rest of the world; the distance flickered there in her eye, which did not quite land on Bev; it was there in the slight overexpressiveness of her response "Really?"

It made Bev tired, as though she had been swimming after someone, as though she herself needed to talk louder, faster, more expressively, in order to keep Dottie afloat. Typing, Bev watched her friend from the corner of her eye. Dottie's face held the expression of someone in physical pain; this is what dawned on Bev as she watched and typed. A memory from years ago came to her—an aunt who had died of cancer had the same expression that Dottie had now, as though something behind the eyes were getting tugged back, a bit on a horse's mouth, something like that. . . . Bev was alarmed.

"Dottie," she said. She stopped typing and squinted at her friend.

Dottie looked up, surprised.

"Dottie Brown, are you okay?"

Irritation seemed to flicker briefly on Dottie's face. "Why do you ask?"

"Because you seem different," Bev said forthrightly. "I've known you a long time and you seem different to me."

"For heaven's sake," Dottie answered softly. "If some spaceship had landed in your backyard you'd seem different too."

This put them in choppy waters; Bev's stomach cramped. She didn't believe Dottie's UFO story and she thought probably Dottie knew that. But when Dottie was faced with a disbeliever (Lenora Snibbens was the worst, being as vocal about it as she was), her eyes would fill with indignant tears, and she would say quietly that no one could understand anything in this world until they had actually experienced it themselves. "True enough," Fat Bev would say in support of her friend, and there the matter would drop.

"But I mean physically," Bev said now. "Are you physically okay? You still bleeding at all? The incision still sore?"

"Tender," Dottie said, and lit a cigarette.

"Hate to see you smoking again," Bev added, lighting up herself, and Dottie simply tossed her a disparaging look that said clearly she was one to talk. "You were my inspiration," Bev explained. "I always figured when the day came to quit I could do it because you had."

"Well, I'm not inspiration for anything," Dottie said, placing her cigarette carefully in the glass ashtray, then touching her finger quickly to her tongue before flipping through a stack of invoices. "You can forget that, thank you very much."

Fat Bev exhaled slowly and studied her fingernails. "How's Wally? He being nice about all this stuff?"

"What stuff?"

"You having a hysterectomy and everything. You hear sometimes about how men get queer. I knew a man who actually cried when the doctor said he'd taken out his wife's ovaries. Great big brick of a man actually broke down and cried. And then never slept with her again."

"They're babies, all of them." Dottie reached for her cigarette.

"Yuh, I guess that's true." She ought to come right out and tell Dottie that she was having trouble believing the UFO thing, and that she felt bad about it. They'd been friends so long they ought to be able to talk this one through.

"Whew," said Bev, leaning across her desk toward Dottie. "My insides are going bonkers." She scraped her chair back and stood up. " 'Scuse me," she said, "while I try and shit a watermelon."

She saw tears spring to Dottie's eyes, and if it weren't for the fact that she feared this watermelon might explode, Bev would have sat back down.

"Stacy had her baby," Amy said.

Isabelle looked up from her plate and gazed open-faced at Amy. "She did?"

Amy nodded.

"She did?" Isabelle repeated. "She had the baby?"

"Yes. She had the baby. Her mother called." Amy stood up and began clearing away the dishes.

"Tell me." Isabelle's eyes followed Amy back and forth, her face pale and importuning.

"There's nothing to tell," Amy responded with a slight shrugging of her bare young shoulders, which glimmered as she reached forward in her sleeveless shirt. "She had the baby. The end." It was odd, speaking to her mother the way she sometimes did these days, openly rude, contemptuous. Before this summer she would not have dared.

"It's hardly the end," Isabelle said. "Hardly that."

Amy didn't answer, hating the way her mother could make pronouncements this way—smug, know-it-all remarks dropped casually into the humid air of the kitchen. "I know a thing or two that you don't know," her mother would sometimes say when Amy was growing up, then leave it at that—as though, in the superiority of knowledge and experience that was rightfully hers, Isabelle found Amy not worth explaining things to.

"Does Stacy ever talk about it?" Isabelle asked tentatively, twisting part of her paper napkin into a tight roll, glancing from the corner of her eye at Amy, who continued to clear the table.

"Talk about what."

"Giving the baby up."

Amy's face went blank for a moment, as though she couldn't recall what Stacy might have said. "I think she was scared about the birth part," she admitted, moving the plates into the kitchen sink. "She never exactly said it, but I think she was scared it would hurt. Her mom told me she did okay, though." Amy pictured the woman in the movie that Stacy's father had brought home; a face twisted ferociously, the deep grunts of pain. "*Does* it hurt that much?" Amy turned from the sink, asking her mother this question with sudden sincerity.

"It's uncomfortable, certainly." Isabelle stopped twisting the napkin and looked out the window. Her face—in the glance Amy had of it before she turned away—looked troubled and exceedingly vulnerable; Amy felt a jolt of anxiety: her mother was trying not to cry.

For a brief while there was only the sound of dishes being washed, water running, the squeak of the faucet as it got turned off, silverware dropped into the dish drainer.

Isabelle spoke. Amy, standing at the sink, could tell from the sound that her mother was still looking out the window. "So Stacy never talked about what it felt like, that she was giving the baby up?"

"No." Amy did not turn around. She rinsed a cup under the faucet, put it in the drainer. "But I sometimes wondered," Amy added truthfully. "I mean, she might walk past it on the street when she's forty-five years old and not even know it. That's pretty weird, I think. But I never asked her if she thought of that."

There was no answer from Isabelle.

"I just didn't think I should ask her, you know." Amy turned, her hands still soapy in the water. Her mother was still looking out the window, her flattened French twist losing its shape at this time of day, straggles of hair slipping from it down her long white neck.

"Mom?"

"No. I think you were right not to ask." Isabelle turned, smiling apologetically, for there were indeed tears on her cheeks. She patted her face quickly with the napkin that was still in her hands. "No, you were quite right," she repeated. "One doesn't ask needless questions that might cause people pain." She seemed to be recovering herself now, blowing her nose, rising from the table, dropping the napkin into the wastebasket.

"You should go visit her," Isabelle stated, clearing the few things that had been left on the table. "What hospital is she in?"

"You mean visit her in the hospital?"

"Well, yes. I think so. I really do."

"She's in Arundy. Not Hennecock." Amy rinsed another cup, moving her body aside as her mother placed more silverware in the sink.

"Call up and see about visiting hours," Isabelle said officiously, wiping at the counter with the sponge. "I'll drive you over tonight. Don't worry," she added, as though reading Amy's mind, "I won't come in with you. I'll stay in the car."

"You sure?" Amy asked. "You wouldn't mind?"

"Go." Her mother motioned with her head. "Change your shirt, that one looks a little grimy." (In fact it revealed the young glimmering shoulders of the girl in a way that made Isabelle slightly uncomfortable.) "I'll call the hospital for you."

When Amy descended the stairs a few minutes later with a fresh blouse and her hair combed—it had grown just enough now to curl below her ears—she found Isabelle standing in the kitchen going through the cupboards. "Eight o'clock," Isabelle said. "But you need to take her something."

"Like what," Amy said. "I don't know what to take her."

"Here it is." Isabelle brought a small basket from the cupboard. "Let's take some flowers from the garden and bring her this."

For the next few minutes they worked together; or rather Isabelle worked while Amy watched. Isabelle lined the basket with aluminum foil, and then taking a trowel they went down the back steps to the garden, where Isabelle knelt and dug up a small clump of marigolds and bluebells, tucking the soil tightly into the basket. She worked with a certain fervor, sweat stood out above her lip and also in the pockets below her eyes; Amy, watching her mother's face, had to look away.

"They'll last a little longer this way," Isabelle said, straightening up, wiping her face with the back of her hand, "than if we just picked them."

"Plus it looks nicer." Amy gazed at the basket, impressed.

"Does look nice, doesn't it." Isabelle squinted at the basket as she turned it slowly around. They went back inside the house, where Isabelle found some white ribbon that she tied in a bow around the basket's handle, and then with the shears (neither she nor Amy remembered at the moment that these were the shears that had cut Amy's hair) she curled the ends of the ribbon, so that two white springy curls dangled above the blue and yellow flowers.

THE HOSPITAL WAS private and not old. It looked more like some discreet modern office building than a hospital. Sprawled back from the road, it was only two floors high and a series of small windows ran in straight lines across its cement walls. The front doors were made of glass, but darkened, and to the anxious Amy peering through the windshield, they appeared somewhat formidable. Isabelle parked in the corner of the parking lot.

"What do I do?" Amy asked, holding the basket of marigolds and bluebells on her lap—a moistness was beginning to creep through and be felt on her thigh. "I've never been inside a hospital before."

"Just tell them you're here to see Stacy what's her name."

"Burrows. Do they let kids in?"

"You're sixteen," Isabelle said, her eyes running lightly over Amy, appraising her. "But if anyone asks I suppose you could try and say you're eighteen. You could pass."

Amy glanced at her mother; it was unusual for Isabelle to suggest any kind of lie. She started to open the door, then hesitated. "What if in Stacy's case—I mean because she had a baby and she's not supposed to—they don't allow her any visitors?"

Isabelle looked blank. "That would be wrong of them," she said.

"Yeah, but what if."

"Then say you're family. If you have to."

"Okay." Again Amy hesitated. "What're you going to do? Do you have anything to read?"

Isabelle shook her head. "Go on."

Watching Amy walk across the parking lot (the navy-blue shorts from Sears looked nice with that white blouse) Isabelle suddenly recognized in Amy's step a certain tentativeness that had been there even as a small child. In the pleasing symmetry of the legs walking now away from her, Isabelle saw the familiar slight turning-in of Amy's right foot; a whisper of shyness emerged—as it always had—with this barely noticeable imperfection of gait, as though the girl carried with her the delicate, unspoken words "I'm scared." It caused a shiver to pass through Isabelle, for it was odd to see momentarily both images at once: the back of the full-grown person with a basket of flowers in her hand, and the small, curly-haired girl walking up the driveway to Esther Hatch's house, clutching in her tiny fingers the head of a plastic doll.

No one asked Amy anything. In the quiet corridors the nurses seemed sleepy, indifferent, waving a hand vaguely to give directions.

Stacy was alone. She sat propped up in bed with a blank, expectant look on her face, which broke into amazement at the sight of Amy. *"Hi,"* Stacy said. "Oh my God, *hi.*" She reached her arms out like a child asking to be picked up, and the basket of flowers risked getting crushed in a jumble of nervous laughing and bending and kissing but was saved at the last minute and made it safely into Stacy's lap. She examined the basket with shining eyes.

"Amy, it's so pretty."

Together the girls looked at the little garden there in Stacy's lap, the vigor of the marigolds, the vaguely-beginning-to-droop reticence of the bluebells. "My mother made it for you," Amy said.

"Your *mother?*"

Amy nodded.

"That's pretty fucking strange."

Amy nodded again.

"Parents are so weird." Stacy shook her head slowly, placing the basket on her bedside table. "My parents were real nice when I went into labor, and then this afternoon when I started to get bored—because these fuckhead doctors make you stay here three days—I asked my parents if I could rent the TV here and they said no, they didn't think so."

"How come?"

"Who *knows.* Look, they bind your breasts." Stacy opened her hospital gown to show Amy how beneath her nightgown her breasts had been wrapped in strips of white cloth. "Hurts like piss."

"Your *parents* did that?"

"No, the nurses. Because my milk will come in or something."

Amy turned and looked around the room; it was angular, sterile, disappointing. She sat tentatively on the edge of a blue vinyl chair that was pushed against the wall, but Stacy said, "No, no. Sit here," patting the bed and moving her legs over.

Amy got up and sat down on the bed. "You look the same," she said, studying her friend. "But you still look pregnant." Through the sheet there was the visible rising of Stacy's abdomen.

"I know. It takes a while for the uterus to go back down, or something. I'm having these un-fucking-believable period pains. A couple hours ago I had to pee so they put me on this bedpan and this whole clump of bloody stuff came slipping out the size of a grapefruit. I figured I was dying but the nurse says it's just afterbirth. I guess that's the stuff the cats eat. I mean, you know, if I was a cat."

They were silent for a moment. Then Amy said, "Well. It's good you're not a cat."

"Really." Stacy fiddled with a button that hummed when she pressed it, making the head of the bed rise higher so she was almost sitting up. "Here," she said, moving over more so that Amy now sat (or half lay) on the bed beside her.

"Let me do it." Amy pressed the button herself and their torsos moved downward. She pressed again and they came back up. "Where're your parents?" she asked.

"Home, I guess. I think my mother was drinking all day." Stacy gazed at Amy's feet on top of the sheets. "She was supernice and then she fell asleep in that chair. My father dragged her home, stumbling out of here. I think she was really drunk."

Amy pressed the button and their feet rose slowly. "I didn't know your mother drank. Mr. Robertson's mother drank."

"Who's Mr. Rob— Oh yeah, that substitute guy. My mother drinks on special occasions."

Amy sent their feet back down and looked at the ceiling; it was made of white cardboardy stuff with little holes in it. "Anyone tell Paul yet?"

"My mom. He wanted to come to the hospital but we said no way."

"I saw him the other day," Amy offered. "He gave me a ride in his new car."

Stacy waved a hand tiredly in the air. "Paul," she said. "I don't want to think about Paul."

"Okay." Amy still looked at the ceiling. "I stopped working at the mill. The boss, this asshole Avery Clark, hates me, so he said they ran out of money. You should see him, Stacy. He's like the most boring guy. You *know* he hasn't had sex except maybe once or twice in his life, just to have a kid."

"You might be surprised," Stacy said. "People are weird. People have all kinds of secrets you'd never dream of. My father had a patient once— not in Shirley Falls—who was like Mr. Proper, Mr. Normal. He owned a bank or something. And he used to pay really expensive prostitutes just to get naked and roll an egg down a hallway toward him."

Amy turned her head toward Stacy.

"Weird, huh," Stacy said. "No sex, just roll an egg down this hallway. I heard my father tell my mother about it one night."

"I thought psychiatrists weren't supposed to tell anyone what gets told to them."

"Bullshit," Stacy said. "Never trust a shrink. I like your sandals. I've always liked those sandals."

Together they gazed down at Amy's feet. "I've always hated them," Amy said. "I hate all my clothes. Like these queer shorts from Sears just because my mother won't let me wear cutoffs."

"Clothes," Stacy mused. "In a little while I can wear normal clothes."

"I hate my mother," Amy said, suddenly overcome with intense dislike for her shorts. "I mean it was nice of her to make you the basket of flowers, but she's really a queer. I hate her."

"Yeah," Stacy said casually. "I hate my mother too." She turned her face toward Amy's. "You know what?" she whispered. "One of the nurses let me hold the baby. I wasn't supposed to but one of the night nurses really early this morning snuck him in for a while and let me hold him."

Stacy's blue eyes stared into Amy's.

"He's beautiful," Stacy whispered. "On your way out take a peek through the glass into the nursery. He's in the back row, right-hand corner. The nurse told me. You'll know which one he is 'cause he has this huge head of reddish hair." Stacy shook her head. "He's really beautiful."

THEY DROVE HOME in silence. "She's fine," Amy had said when she stepped into the car, and after that nothing. Amy kept her face turned toward her window, and Isabelle, who opened her mouth once or twice to ask something, closed it instead. It was dark now. They passed by houses, back lawns, above-ground swimming pools seen dimly through the hazy glow of streetlights and headlights and lights from the windows of the houses themselves.

Where was Mr. Robertson?

The car ahead of them put its blinker on and turned off at the next exit, the small red light still winking as it went down the ramp. Then for a while there were only trees they drove by, spruce trees and pines standing there in the dark. In this milky evening darkness Amy sat silently next to her mother and imagined herself naked, rolling an egg down a long pine-floored hallway where a normal-looking man in a business suit (like one of the deacons who passed the collection plate at church) crouched with desperate longing on his face. "One more," he whispered, begging her, "roll one more," and she would; she would be good at it, taking her time, gazing back at him indifferently. The smell of the river came to her then; they were entering Shirley Falls.

"I saw the baby," she told Isabelle. "I wasn't allowed to but Stacy told me where he was, so I peeked at him on the way out." She did not tell her mother that she had stood in the hospital corridor whispering a prayer through the glass, giving the sleeping red-haired baby a blessing that he would never in his lifetime know about, telling him that she had watched him grow in his mother's stomach out in their lunchtime spot in the woods, and pledging her love to him forever.

Isabelle said nothing. They drove up their dark driveway in silence.

Chapter

20

AVERY CLARK TOOK a week off. This was something he did every August, renting the same cabin each year on Lake Nattetuck, in the mountains, fishing with his sons, swimming with Emma from a narrow dock, roasting hot dogs, lying on a canvas hammock hung between two Scotch pines. These happy times were recorded yearly in a stack of photographs that, with a certain contained enthusiasm, Avery would show to Isabelle after he picked them up at lunchtime from the pharmacy across the street.

It always broke her heart. Standing at his desk, peering at these pictures (holding them carefully by the edges so as to not place a smudge print on the backsides of Emma stepping from the dock into a canoe), Isabelle would say, "Oh, Avery, this is especially good, I think—this one of you," and she would smile at a shot of Avery bent over a rowboat, reeling in a fish. A perch. She nodded as he explained how long they had been fishing that day, two full hours without so much as a nibble. "Oh my," she would say. "Imagine."

Now, this particular hot and horrible August, with the river lying dead and smelling to high hell and the sky without color, her daughter barely speaking to her, Avery himself saying very little ("Hold the fort down, Isabelle" was all he seemed able to come up with when he left on

Friday), she wondered if this year he would show her any pictures of the lake when he got back. She knew, because she had heard Bev ask, that his sons were joining him there again, even though they were both out of college by now. "Oh yes," he said. "I suspect we'll have grandchildren there with us someday. Lake Nattetuck's a family tradition."

"Isn't that nice," Bev had responded, nodding lazily, and Isabelle envied her indifference.

To her there had only been the cheerful "Hold the fort down, Isabelle." Although in his eyes of course was the brief understanding that such a thing was no easy matter these days, what with new feuds and old ones simmering in the office room, alliances arranged and rearranged. Rosie Tanguay and Lenora Snibbens, who had not been speaking to one another for well over a year, owing ostensibly to Lenora's public reporting of her dream in which Rosie had done a striptease in the post office lobby (the true offense to Rosie lying not so much in the telling of the dream as in the extreme hilarity displayed by Lenora), had at the beginning of the summer shown signs of putting the matter to rest, agreeing one day—in mild, pleasant tones—that the heat made them both very sleepy. But with the arrival of Dottie Brown's UFO, the old animosity came back.

It was not only Rosie that Lenora seemed ready to take on. For whatever reasons, Lenora could not abide not only the idea of a UFO in their midst but, apparently, anyone who chose to believe such a thing might exist. If some woman standing in the lunchroom should look around tiredly and say nothing more than, "Where did I put my Pepsi?" Lenora felt compelled to answer with a sarcastic, "Maybe some alien took it."

While neither Fat Bev nor Isabelle was inclined to believe Dottie's story, both had aligned themselves on "Dottie's side." And both were distressed at Lenora Snibbens for continually rocking the shaky boat. "Why can't she just shut *up*?" Bev murmured to Isabelle one day as they left the lunchroom together. Lenora had, in a momentary silence that fell over the stifling lunchroom, said without looking up, "Seen any more spaceships, Dottie?"

It was cruel; there was no way around it. Unnecessary. One might expect this from Arlene; a mean streak was there (some felt) beneath her painted eyebrows, but Lenora—ordinarily good-natured, bucktoothed, and talkative—her insistence about this matter was a surprise.

Dottie Brown turned red, then her face simply crumpled and she began to cry. "Oh, come on, Dottie. Jesum Crow." Lenora rapped her fingers impatiently on the linoleum tabletop. Probably Lenora was faced here with more than she had bargained for, but in her discomfort she unfortunately added, "Come on, Dottie. Give it up."

Dottie pushed back her chair and left the room. It was then that Fat Bev, following her, had murmured loudly to Isabelle, tossing her head back in Lenora's direction, "Why can't she just shut *up*?"

And it was true. Lenora ought to just shut up. If Dottie Brown, or any one of them, for that matter, wanted to come in to work and say they had just seen twelve white kangaroos walking over the bridge—well, that was their business. You might think they were nuts, but a decent person would simply keep quiet.

Isabelle settled herself behind her desk. "I agree, Bev. Completely agree."

Bev headed off for the ladies' room to tend to her friend, and Isabelle began typing a letter, making a number of mistakes along the way. She felt a certain panic flutter through her chest, as though she were a substitute teacher whose classroom had suddenly become unruly, and the principal was away. What if these women went crazy? (And why shouldn't they, Isabelle thought, her own hand shaking a bit; it was so awfully, awfully *hot*.) What if they just went bananas and Avery returned to find the place in complete disarray? "Hold the fort down, Isabelle."

It wasn't her responsibility, for heaven's sake! Avery was paid to maintain order in the office room; she was not. Isabelle pulled the sheet of paper from her typewriter and started the letter again.

In the ladies' room, meanwhile, the unthinkable was taking place: Lenora Snibbens, having followed Dottie Brown into the bathroom with some vague apology forming in her head, was aghast to have Dottie turn from the sink and strike her on the upper portion of her bare arm. The blow was fairly soundless as Dottie used the side of her hand, but there was the immediate shriek from Lenora, who backed away, then suddenly stepped forward again and spit in Dottie's face. It was not much of a spit. Lenora was too upset to have collected any real quantity of saliva in her mouth, but the gesture was clear, and a few drops sprayed across the air, arriving on Dottie's cheeks, which Dottie immediately rubbed with great vigor, sobbing, "You *disgusting* pimple-faced pig!"

This reference to her unfortunate complexion caused Lenora to spit again, resulting, in her frenzy, in little more than her lips buzzing together ferociously in a childish raspberry sound.

Fat Bev, standing by the sink and witnessing all this with horror, roused herself to step between them and bellowed in a voice she had not used since the adolescence of her daughters, *"Stop it right now, you two."*

Moments later Fat Bev leaned over Isabelle's desk to inform Isabelle that she would be driving Dottie home, and that she herself might not be back to work that afternoon.

"Certainly," Isabelle said, alarmed, and having no idea what had precipitated such measures. "Of course, Bev."

Lenora Snibbens returned to her desk and sat with tears brimming in her eyes, refusing to talk. The office room was very quiet. There was only the whirring of the fans in the windows, although even that sound seemed subdued, as though the fans themselves had become cautious and wary as well. Occasionally a chair squeaked, a filing cabinet clicked shut. Twice Lenora blew her nose.

Isabelle, glancing up, saw Bev in the hallway gesturing to her. She took her pocketbook from the drawer in her desk and walked quietly out into the hall, as though she were simply going to the ladies' room.

Bev's car wouldn't start. It had something to do with the heat, she thought, baking all day in the parking lot. She usually tried to park in the corner beneath the tree, but today the place was taken. None of this mattered, she told Isabelle (a fat hand wiping at her perspiring lip), except that she had Dottie out there in that car right now and Dottie needed to get home. She, personally, thought Dottie was having a breakdown, but the only thing at the moment was to get her home. When she told Dottie that she'd call Wally at work—

Here Isabelle held up her hand. "Come on," she said. "Let's go."

The heat shimmered before them as they drove out of the parking lot, Dottie sitting up front next to Isabelle, docile and expressionless. Fat Bev sat in the back seat, her legs spread, her hand holding a cigarette hanging out the window. Isabelle drove self-consciously, as though all aspects of her driving skills were being judged. It reminded her of the few times in Amy's childhood when she had volunteered to drive on school trips; how monstrously self-conscious she had felt behind the wheel, driving a carload of weary, truculent kids.

"I hit her," Dottie said tonelessly, turning her face partway to Isabelle.

"Excuse me?" Isabelle put her blinker on. The car behind was following too close; Isabelle hated it when cars followed that close.

"I hit Lenora. In the bathroom. Did Bev tell you?"

"No. Goodness." Isabelle glanced in the rearview mirror; Bev caught her eye and gave her a look of laconic defeat. "Really? You hit her?" Isabelle turned her head toward Dottie, who nodded.

"Slapped her arm." Dottie patted her own upper arm to indicate where, then rummaged through her pocketbook for a cigarette.

"Well." Isabelle thought about this while she turned right at the stop sign. "A person reaches a point," she said generously, unexpectedly.

"So Lenora spit at her." Fat Bev offered this from the back seat, as though encouraged by Isabelle's accommodating attitude.

"Oh, my *Lord*."

"You can't blame her," Dottie eventually said, sighing. "I did hit her."

"It's different though," Isabelle responded, still feeling nervous about her driving skills, particularly since thinking of grown women hitting and spitting left her somewhat shaky. (Good *Lord*, she thought.) "Hitting seems slightly different somehow. Of course it's wrong to hit," Isabelle added quickly, the image of driving small children again going through her head as she turned down the road that would lead to Dottie's house. "But at least"—she hesitated, searching for the words—"at least it's clean. But *spitting*. My word."

"Dottie called her a pimple-face," Bev reported from the back seat, and Dottie, without looking at Isabelle, nodded glumly to confirm this.

" A 'disgusting pimpled-faced pig,' " Dottie said, as though to make the record accurate. She dragged deeply on her cigarette.

"Oh dear," Isabelle said. "Oh my." She steered carefully down the narrow, rural road. "Oh my," she said again.

"Next left," Dottie directed.

The driveway was long, winding its way down toward the river. It was a nice spot, really, with the fields all around and the clusters of maple trees before the house. The place had been in the family, Isabelle knew; Dottie couldn't afford a house like this now. It needed some work, she saw, pulling up toward the front door. The porch railing on one side was actually falling down; the gray paint had been blistering long before this summer. That disturbed Isabelle, as did the sight of a rusty truck that appeared not to have moved in years, settled in among the weeds further down beyond the house.

"Let's just sit for a moment," Dottie said, with a shy, questioning look at Isabelle.

"Sure," said Isabelle. She turned the car off.

They sat quietly in the baking, colorless heat. Sweat beaded on Dottie's face, and Isabelle, glancing at her cautiously, said suddenly, "Dottie, you've lost weight." It was herself she recognized as she said this, the way Dottie's arm took up so little space coming from the sleeve of her blouse; Isabelle had noticed this about her own arm recently in the reflection of the window of the A&P.

Dottie nodded indifferently.

"I thought people gained weight after a hysterectomy," Bev said, from where she sat confined in the back seat. "When Chippie got spayed, she blew up big as a table."

Dottie leaned her head far back on the car seat, as though she were in a dentist's chair and resigned to it. "I've been spayed," she said. "Oh God." She began to rock her head slowly back and forth.

"Dottie. I'm awful sorry." Bev tossed her cigarette out the window onto the gravelly driveway and leaned forward to touch her friend's shoulder. "Shit," she said, "the stupid things people say." And then to Isabelle: "Pardon my French."

Isabelle gave a tiny shake of her head, a little tightening of her lips to indicate, Don't be silly, Bev—for heaven's sake, say whatever words you like. (Though she did somehow, *really*, not like the word "shit.")

But Dottie was crying. "It's okay, really," she said, tears running down beside her nose. "I don't care, really."

"Oh Godfrey, I could kill myself," Bev said, genuinely distressed at having used the word "spayed"; sweat broke out anew along her neck and face. She sat back, plucking the front of her blouse away from her skin. "Dottie Brown, you needed that operation. You couldn't continue your life bleeding to death every month. That cyst in there was the size of a cantaloupe."

Dottie kept rolling her head against the back of the car seat. "It's not that," she said. "It's more than that."

Bev and Isabelle glanced at each other, then both looked vacantly out the windows, eyed their fingernails, snuck a peek at Dottie again; they waited patiently. Bev, sweating profusely now, did not dare open the car door, did not dare interfere with whatever Dottie might have to say, though Bev's legs inside her slacks felt drenched, and she suspected when the time came to get out of the car it would look as though she had wet her pants.

"It could have been a dream," Dottie finally said. "I don't know if I saw it. I'd just been reading about someone over near Hennecock who said they'd seen a UFO, and then I fell asleep. In the hammock that day. It could have been a dream."

Bev leaned forward again. "That's okay," she said. "Dreams can be awful real." She was hugely relieved to have Dottie make this confession, but Isabelle, who had a better view of Dottie's face from where she sat in the driver's seat, felt a wave of foreboding pass through her.

"It's all right," Fat Bev said earnestly, continuing to pat Dottie's shoulder.

Dottie closed her eyes. The eyelids, to Isabelle, seemed very naked, as though some private part of Dottie was being exposed by their thin fleshiness there on her face. She said, "Nothing's all right."

"It'll blow over," Bev assured her. "Everyone's cranky with this heat. Few more weeks no one will mention it again. Those dodos in the office will find something else—"

Isabelle held up her hand, shaking her head to Fat Bev. Dottie's eyes were still closed; she was rocking her body slowly back and forth. Isabelle exchanged a look of alarm with Bev; then she leaned over and placed her hand around Dottie's thin wrist.

"Dottie, what is it?" Isabelle whispered this.

Dottie opened her eyes and looked into Isabelle's face. Her mouth opened, then closed; two gummy white bits of saliva clung to her lips. Again Dottie opened her mouth, again it closed, again she shook her head. Isabelle moved her hand slowly up and down the distressed woman's arm.

"It's okay, Dottie," Isabelle whispered again. "You're not alone. We're right here." She said this because it was her own greatest fear—to be alone with grief; but why it was she said anything, why, after having known Dottie Brown for years at a polite, unwavering distance, she had now succumbed to a position of such intimacy as to be stroking this poor woman's arm in a car that was virtually an oven on this workday afternoon, she could hardly have said. But the words seemed to have an effect, some plug in Dottie seemed loosened, for she began to sob softly and instead of shaking her head, she nodded. After a moment she wiped her face with her hand, tears smeared childishly across her fingers. "Do you have any paper?" she asked. "Paper and pen?"

Both Bev and Isabelle immediately rummaged through their purses and in a moment a pen, an old envelope, and a tissue were collectively produced and placed in Dottie's moist hand.

As Dottie wrote, Isabelle exchanged a surreptitious glance with Bev, and Bev nodded slightly as though to indicate that this was good; this terrible anguish, these labor pains, really, were finally producing . . . what?

Dottie stopped writing and lit a cigarette, then handed the envelope to Isabelle, who didn't want to usurp Bev's position as the "real" friend and so made sure to hold the envelope in a way that Bev could see it also. It did not take long to read.

Bev sucked in her breath; a chill wrapped itself around her sweating body. Isabelle, with her heart beating very quickly, folded the envelope in half and then in half again, as though to hide the offending words. Tears tumbled down Bev's face. "I hate him," she said, quietly. "Sorry, Dottie, but I hate him."

Dottie turned partway around to see Bev.

"I'm sorry," Bev repeated, when she saw Dottie looking at her. "He's your husband, and I've known him for years, and you're my best friend so I have no right to say it, no business saying it, but I'm going to say it again. I hate him."

"It's okay," Dottie said. "I do too." She turned forward in her seat again. "Except I don't."

Isabelle was silent. She stared at the dashboard, at the radio dial. Dottie, she knew, had three sons. They must be in their twenties by now; she knew they no longer lived at home. One of them, she remembered, had gone down to Boston and was thinking of marrying some girl. Isabelle gazed through the windshield at the house spread out before her and pictured Dottie as a young wife and mother many years ago, a home full of noise and activity, Christmas mornings with the five of them (no, six of them at least—she supposed that Bea Brown was present quite often), Dottie busy, always so much to do.

"That's your whole life," Isabelle said to Dottie.

Dottie looked at her sadly, and in her moist blue eyes there seemed to be something extraordinarily lucid as she gazed at Isabelle. "That's right," she said.

"And while you were in the hospital," Bev said with quiet awe. "Oh, Dottie. That's awful."

"Yes." Dottie's voice sounded vague and transcendent now; although most likely it was simply fatigue.

Bev herself felt ill. "Let's go in," she said, opening the car door. (Finally.) "Sitting in this heat we might die." She meant it; she was fully aware of certain facts regarding her health: she was fat and she smoked; she never exercised; she was not exactly young anymore; and she had just in this terrible heat suffered a shock. It would not be any great surprise to the universe if she did keel over and die right now, and if she did, she thought bitterly, heaving herself from the car and seeing little black dots swim before her eyes (her pants were indeed wet) she would blame it entirely and exactly on Wally Brown.

Oh, she felt sick.

"I don't care if I die," Dottie said this in the same transcendent voice, still sitting in the car.

"I know." Bev opened Dottie's door and took her arm. "But you might care later on. And besides . . ." Here tears came from Bev's eyes again as she felt the lightness of Dottie's weight, the astonishing thinness of her arm, saw the red-rimmed blue eyes of this woman she had known for so long, and it was suddenly Dottie's death that seemed real and near and possible, not her own. "I would miss you like hell," Bev finished. "Would miss you like shit, Dottie Brown."

All of this was awkward for Isabelle. She had no idea if it was intended that she would go inside the house, or if, most likely, Bev would take over from here. Yet it seemed impolite to simply drive away, having witnessed something so personal.

"Isabelle," said Dottie, outside the car now, standing next to Fat Bev and peering back through the open window to Isabelle. "Come in the house. I'd like you to."

Bev's voice overlapped Dottie's. "Yes, Isabelle. By all means you come on inside too."

The kitchen confused her; Isabelle's immediate reactions were confused. On one hand, the room was lovely; the big windows over the sink showed pale fields in the distance, and closer up a row of geraniums sat on the windowsill. A collection of hand-painted mugs on a shelf seemed familiar and homey, and so did the rocking chair that sat near a cluttered bookshelf, where the long vines of philodendron leaves spilled down. The gray cat sleeping in the rocking chair fit the picture as well, and yet Isabelle could not help but be, on some level, put off. For the room smelled "cattish" to her, and sure enough, there was a litter box (a quick glance left the afterimage of brown clumps right there in the gravelly rocks—how could someone *live* with such a thing in their kitchen?). Almost as disturbing was the fact that the plaster walls of the room had holes in them. And ragged strips of wallpaper showed. Surely they were renovating this room, Isabelle thought, looking around discreetly, though no mention of this was made by either Dottie or Bev.

Dottie had gone straight to the rocking chair and dumped the cat out, and then seated herself with a kind of finality, immediately lighting a cigarette and flicking the match into one of the geranium pots. "Iced tea's in the fridge," she murmured, closing her eyes and exhaling.

Fat Bev, clearly at home here (and Isabelle was envious of this, of a friendship so intimate that one moved about someone else's kitchen as if it were one's own), produced a glass of iced tea and handed it to Dottie. "Drink," she commanded. "Drink fluids, Dot. Keep yourself hydrated." Dottie opened her eyes and took the glass wearily.

"He says think of all the good times we had together." Dottie looked confused. "But he doesn't understand. There are no good times now. There are no *good memories*."

"Of course," said Bev, placing a glass of iced tea in front of Isabelle, interrupting herself momentarily to admonish Isabelle with the use of a quick, authoritative expression, that she ought to be drinking fluids as well. "I can see that. Of course. Just like a man not to get it. They're morons, they really are."

Isabelle sipped her tea. (It needed sugar but she'd never ask.) After a moment she said slowly, "I can see how it would spoil all your memories." And she could. She could easily see that. God knew she could see how one's entire life could be taken apart, and that Dottie's life was being taken apart right now, almost in front of Isabelle's eyes. It's what Isabelle had meant, really, when she said in the car to Dottie, "That's your whole life." And that was why Dottie's blue eyes had been so lucid for a moment in their answer, because it was true. A whole life built together with this man, every year a new layer added—until what?

"You must feel gutted," Isabelle said quietly, and here Dottie shot her a look of earnest gratitude, but Isabelle was suddenly thinking of something else, picturing something she had not pictured before (not really): a woman, a mother, standing in a kitchen in California on a hot summer day, planning her weekend, perhaps, baking a cake for her husband, living the normal life she had lived for years—the telephone ringing—and then the roof of her life collapsed.

Isabelle touched her mouth, perspiration breaking out over her face, under her arms. She gazed at the stupefied Dottie in her rocking chair and had the sense of visibly witnessing a disaster, a house left in shambles, as though an earthquake had struck.

But it wasn't any earthquake, it wasn't any "act of God." No, you couldn't blame these things on God. It was people, just ordinary, regular people, who did this each other. People ruined other people's lives. People simply took what they wanted, just as this Althea who worked at Acme Tire Company wanted Wally Brown and got him.

Isabelle uncrossed her legs so quickly the chair beside her almost fell over, and she lunged forward to grab it, steadying it with both hands, giving a quick apologetic look to the two women. Althea was twenty-eight years old, Isabelle told herself—a fully matured woman, old enough to know what wreckage her actions could leave. Didn't that make a difference?

"Wally and I were friends," Dottie was saying, with bewilderment. "I said that to him. I said, Wally, I know we've had our differences over the years, but I always thought we were friends."

"What did he say?" Bev wanted to know. She was drinking a beer herself, straight from the can. She leaned her head back to drink again, then placed the beer on the table, turning it slowly in her hand.

"He said I was right, that we *were* friends." Here Dottie looked beseechingly at Isabelle and Bev. "But friends don't do that to each other."

"No," Bev said.

"No," Isabelle said, more quietly than Bev.

"So then we weren't friends."

"I don't know," Isabelle said. "I don't know anything."

"I don't know anything either," Dottie said.

Then you're both stupid, Bev wanted to say. Because there's no mystery to this. Some men, and some women (picturing the tall, sallow-faced Althea), are simply pieces of shit. Bev didn't say this; she finished her beer and lit a cigarette.

Chapter

21

It was still hot, and everything still seemed colorless, or at least not colorful the way it was supposed to be. Goldenrod growing alongside the road looked dirty and bent over, not yellow at all, more a soggy orange in the nubbliness of the drooping stems. Fields filled with black-eyed Susans had a blighted look where the petals of these plants had not grown to their full size, or in some cases not even unfolded, leaving only a brown eye on a hairy stalk. Vegetable stands by the road competed with each other by advertising WE HAVE CORN!!! on hand-painted signs, though actually the ears of corn tossed into weathered bushel baskets were often the size of slim garlic pickles, and customers who had pulled over feeling hopeful stood fingering the small ears uneasily. There was something vaguely obscene and disquieting about the inability of these ears of corn, wrapped tightly in their pale green husks, to reach the fullness that was meant to be. People either bought them or didn't, though; the farmers' wives either commented or didn't; life was either going to continue or not; people were awfully tired of it by now. Tired and hot.

But sometimes, with all the windows rolled down, a breeze could be felt passing through the front seat of Paul Bellows's new car, especially when Amy was riding down narrow, out-of-the-way roads with him, where the spruce trees and pines pressed in from both sides; then there might actually be a breath of cool dampness, a quick pungent smell of earth and pine needles that gave Amy a queer thrill straight down into her middle. It was Mr. Robertson she wanted of course.

But what impressed her about Paul was the freedom he brought, the way he drove around without any plans. And he was kind to her. "You like doughnuts?" he asked her one day.

"I love doughnuts," Amy said.

His smiles appeared genuine, boyish, and always a bit disconnected, as though they came a split second late. This seemed true of most of his reactions—a little schism, a tiny pause—and it was this that prevented intimacy. What they had instead was an arrangement, an unspoken acknowledgment that their minds were on other people.

In a doughnut shop at the traffic circle on the outskirts of town, Paul smoked Marlboros and drank coffee and watched with his pleasant, disconnected smile as Amy finished her second doughnut. Because Marlboros were too strong for her (she shuddered as she inhaled), he bought her at the cash register a pack of the kind she used to smoke in the woods with Stacy, and he said Amy could keep them in his cubbyhole since she was afraid to take them home and have them discovered.

"I can pay you back," she said.

"Don't worry about it." He touched her back lightly as they walked across the parking lot.

Once in the car he put the key in the ignition and then reached beneath the seat and brought out a box, an old-fashioned cigar box with a top that flipped open. "Look at this," he said, and she leaned toward him. It was a collection of foreign coins and jewelry, but what caught her eye especially was a pair of women's earrings; on each gold wire was a small strip of gold, inlaid with pearls and pale green stones, and then at the bottom of this strip a small red stone, so that the earrings looked like a pair of exquisite exclamation marks.

"Oh, those are gorgeous," Amy said, picking them out of the box, turning them slowly in her hand.

"You want them?" Paul asked. "Take them."

She shook her head, dropping the earrings back in the cigar box. "Where did you get this stuff?"

When he didn't answer, when he half-smiled and gazed down at the box, she realized he must have stolen it.

"You know anything about old coins?" he said, picking one of them up. "Or whatever these things are."

She took it from him to be polite, turning it over in her palm. "No, I don't know anything about stuff like this."

He took the coin back, looked at it indifferently, then dropped it in the box. "I thought maybe I could sell them, except who buys this shit?"

"Take it to Boston," Amy suggested. "Maybe some place down there."

He stared at the box in his lap. There was fatigue in his face, as though the contents of the cigar box were burdensome. "Sure you don't want these earrings?" he asked again. "They'd look real nice on you."

Again she shook her head. "I don't have pierced ears," she explained. "Those are for pierced ears."

"Oh, yeah." He looked from the earring to her earlobe, leaning forward to look carefully. "How come? You scared it will hurt?" The question was sincere, nonjudging.

"My mother won't let me."

"Oh." Paul put the cigar box back under the seat and started the car. Then he pushed in the cigarette lighter and tapped out one of his Marlboros, so she opened the cubbyhole and took one of the cigarettes from the pack he had bought for her. They sat with cigarettes in their hands waiting for the lighter to pop out. She thought it was wonderful, being able to do that. Just have a cigarette when you felt like it.

He lit her cigarette first, which is what he always did, and then drove out of the parking lot, his own cigarette placed between his full lips. Back on the highway he drove fast.

"She thinks if you get your ears pierced you might as well get your nose pierced too," Amy said, speaking loudly against the wind. "Something like that—I don't know." She dragged on her cigarette and exhaled, the smoke flying from her mouth. "She's an asshole," she concluded. "Is your mother an asshole?"

Paul shrugged. "No." He rested his elbow on the open window and took his cigarette between his thumb and index finger. "She gets on my nerves though."

Amy held her cigarette the way Paul did, stuck her elbow out the window the way he did.

For a long while they didn't talk, until Paul said simply, "Stacy has pierced ears."

When he kissed her she was not sorry. He had pulled into her driveway to drop her off, and she was aware as he leaned toward her (the kindhearted, disconnected smile on his full lips) that she had kissed Mr. Robertson in the very same spot. She experienced a fleeting sense of pride, not unlike when years earlier she had earned her Girl Scout badges—a kind of anxious relief that she had "collected" one more.

So now she was a young woman that men wanted. Not just one man but *another one* too: witness this in the full lips of Paul Bellows moving right now over hers. And witness too how she knew what to do; there was nothing tentative about her as she closed her eyes and accepted his tongue—old pros, both of them.

But it was different. Paul's mouth was fleshier, softer, than Mr. Robertson's had been. And there was not the hard urgency of desperate exploration, it was a much more leisurely thing, a friendly "swap of spit." These words passed through her mind as she sat kissing him, and she wondered where she had heard the phrase. In the hallway of school probably, and then she pictured the hallway at school, the beige metal lockers all lined up; she thought how peculiar it was to be kissing someone while picturing a row of beige metal lockers. (Here she turned her head obligingly as Paul turned his.) And then she thought of those words again, "swapping spit," and pictured being in the dentist's chair when all the spit was collecting in her mouth and she was waiting for the dentist to use that little vacuum hose to suction it out. (Paul's tongue moved back into his own mouth and in a moment they both sat back.)

"Sure you don't want those earrings?" he asked. "Someday you might get your ears pierced."

"Okay." She felt bad she had been thinking about the dentist while kissing him.

IN THE EVENING she sat on the couch watching television and waiting for the evening to go by. She had thought that kissing someone else would be the same as kissing Mr. Robertson. That it would feel the same. She had thought that tongues and teeth and mouths touching each other would make her feel all dizzy and wonderful again. She had thought that while Mr. Robertson *himself* might not be available right now, at least the fun of making out with someone else could be.

She looked out the window. It was almost dark—the flickering of the television reflected in the windowpane.

"Really and truly," Isabelle said from where she sat in the armchair, tugging on a ball of yarn, "I've never seen things at work this unpleasant before."

Amy glanced at her briefly, not believing her. But she started thinking about the office room. She missed Fat Bev. She missed the lazy, jokey way the women in the office room had talked with one another.

"How unpleasant can it be?" Amy asked unpleasantly.

A different show came on the television set; Isabelle was allowing more and more TV. When the news was over, instead of turning off the set, as she usually did, she would watch whatever show came on next. Amy would usually sit in a corner of the couch, the way she was now, with her knees tucked up beneath her, a sullen scowl on her face. ("Get your feet off the couch, please," Isabelle would say, and Amy would move her feet a few inches.)

Isabelle worked on her afghan, knitting needles flying, half-glasses perched on her nose as she stopped occasionally to peer at the magazine on the side table that contained the directions. Her legs were crossed and one foot bobbed constantly. In between glancing at the yarn or the directions in the magazine, she would give the television sidelong looks.

Amy couldn't stand it. The stupid half-glasses, the bobbing foot, the pretended disdain for the television show when she was clearly watching it.

"I'd say pretty unpleasant," Isabelle was answering now. "When Dottie Brown and Lenora come to blows in the bathroom. I'd call that pretty unpleasant."

Amy picked at her toes and cast her mother a wary glance. "What kind of blows."

Isabelle tugged at her yarn. "Physical blows."

Amy picked her head up. "You're kidding."

"No. I'm not."

"They were *fighting* in the bathroom?"

"I'm afraid so."

"Like pulling each other's hair and stuff?"

Isabelle frowned. "Oh, Amy. For heaven's sake, no."

"Then what were they doing? Tell me."

"It was simply unpleasant, that's all."

"Oh, come *on,* Mom." Her mind went over faces from the office room. "I can't see Lenora slugging anyone," she said in a moment.

"No one *slugged* anyone," Isabelle replied. "Dottie felt insulted by Lenora. And Lenora has been pretty nasty about the whole UFO business, I must say. So in the ladies' room Dottie was apparently beside herself, and slapped Lenora on the arm."

"A little slap?" Amy was disappointed.

"And then Lenora spit at her."

"Really?"

Isabelle raised an eyebrow. "That's what I was told. I didn't witness it myself."

Amy pondered this. "It's pretty queer," she concluded, "for a woman to go around slapping the people she works with. You know what I think?"

"What do you think." Isabelle sounded tired now; the perfunctoriness of her tone insulted her daughter.

"Nothing," Amy said.

THE RAIN BEGAN during the night. It began softly; so softly that at first it did not seem to be falling from the sky as much as simply appearing in the darkened air. A man lurching from the doorway of a hotel bar on Mill Road swatted his hand in front of his face a few times as though finding himself in a cobweb. By the early hours of morning, though, the rain was tapping gently and steadily onto the open leaves of maples and oaks and birch trees, and those people—particularly the elderly, and the anxious—who each night woke about three, and often stayed awake until the sky began to lighten, found themselves wondering at first what that sound was; raising themselves onto an elbow, sitting up against the headboard of the bed, why it was *rain,* of course, and they lay back down, expectant and pleased, or fearful, depending on how they felt about thunderstorms, for it promised to be grand, this storm, huge, climatically complete after a summer as stultifying and humid as this one had been. The sky would crack and split and thunderous crashes would rearrange huge blocks of air as though the universe itself were in the throes of some vast quake.

But instead the rain simply fell more steadily, tapping down now on rooftops and cars and pavement, and those people who had woken in the night fell back asleep and slept deeply, for the sky did not lighten the way it usually did; it became only as light as evening. By morning there were puddles beneath gutter pipes, small pools in gravel driveways. The rain was dark and heavy and rattled down onto porch railings, front steps. People ate their breakfasts by lamplight, or in the kitchen light of overhead fluorescent bulbs. For some it was reminiscent of times when they had woken early to travel somewhere far that day; it held that same kind of anticipatory air, although they were not going anywhere but to work on this dark August morning.

Isabelle, having been one of those who woke briefly in the night, had slept again deeply and soothingly. Though now awake in the kitchen with the windowpanes a darkened wet, she felt phlegmy and stunned, as though she had taken sleep medication that had not worn off yet. She sat with her fingers lightly placed around her coffee cup, thinking how strange it was that she had slept soundly when she had gone to bed with disturbing thoughts shooting across her mind. How strange to have been sitting in her baking car yesterday with Dottie and Bev, and then in Dottie's kitchen—how strange that had been. Strange to think of Avery Clark waking in a cabin right now on Lake Nattetuck. Strange, in fact, to think that both her mother and father were dead, that perhaps this very rain was pelting down on their graves, which were only two hours away; that the small farmhouse she had been raised in belonged to another family, had belonged to them for years.

Strange to think her daughter lay upstairs right now in bed, her full-grown limbs sprawled across the sheet, when for so many, many mornings (it had seemed) little Amy had woken before Isabelle, padding across the hall in her pajamas with their plastic-soled feet, the snapped waistband moist from the diaper that sagged soggily beneath; she would stand patiently, so little that her head was even with the bed, and wait for Isabelle's eyes to open. How strange when you were not beautiful yourself to have a beautiful daughter.

Here Isabelle drank her coffee down quickly. She needed to wake herself up, get to work. Carrying her cup to the sink, seeing through the window the dark trunks of the pine trees glistening with rain, she was aware of anticipation making its way through the blank odd "strangeness" that had enveloped her since getting up this morning.

What was it? she wondered, placing her coffee cup carefully in the sink, tightening the cloth belt of her bathrobe. It was not that she was looking forward to going back to work (why would she, when everyone there was losing her mind, and Avery was still away?), but there was some—well, "eagerness" was too strong a word—but some desire to bathe and dress and leave the house, as though another place waited where she belonged.

AND THERE WAS no doubt about it: Bev and Dottie were her friends. Every time Dottie walked by Isabelle's desk she would reach down and lightly touch Isabelle's arm. At lunchtime Fat Bev saved Isabelle a seat in the lunchroom, indicating with a nod that Isabelle should sit in this particular chair; and once seated, with Dottie on her other side, Isabelle found herself offered a stunning assortment of foods.

"Got to fatten you two up," Fat Bev murmured. "So pretend we're having a picnic." And she spread out on the table an array of hard-boiled eggs, pickles, carrot sticks, fried chicken, two small packages of cookies, and three brownies in a wax-paper bag.

Isabelle looked from the food to Fat Bev. *"Eat,"* Bev said.

Isabelle ate a drumstick and a pickle. Dottie eyed one of the hard-boiled eggs and said she might be able to manage that. "Be good if you could," Fat Bev said, peeling it for her.

"True," Isabelle agreed, wiping chicken grease from her mouth. "Eggs are a great source of protein. Put a little salt on it, Dottie, and in three bites you'll have it gone."

But halfway through Dottie started to panic, and it was Isabelle who saw this and understood; she knew how quickly a stomach could feel full, how resolute the gullet could become in shutting down, and when she saw Dottie gaze with a certain horror at the half-eaten egg in her hand—teeth marks streaked across the greenish yellow of the cakey yolk—Isabelle tapped her wrist with a carrot stick and said quietly, "Eat this instead."

The carrot stick made it down, and Isabelle, watching carefully, slipped her another, and that one went down too. Fat Bev observed this with approval, and when Dottie later ate a chocolate chip cookie and said how chocolate always made her want milk, Isabelle and Bev exchanged a look and Bev lumbered right over to one of the vending machines to push the button for a carton of milk. Dottie managed to drink half of it before getting full, and Isabelle, who had also eaten one of Bev's chocolate chip cookies and was also feeling a desire for milk, in spite of her aversion to sharing drinks this way, poured the remainder in a paper cup and finished it off.

Bev was delighted. "I'll keep you two skinnies alive if it's the death of me," she said, lighting up a cigarette, inhaling with satisfaction, and something about this made all three of them laugh.

"What's the joke?" Arlene Tucker, from across the room, wanted to know.

"No joke," Bev said, one final chuckle moving her huge chest, from which she brushed some brownie crumbs.

"Life," Dottie Brown said, lighting her own cigarette, "the joke is life." And they laughed again, though not so loudly as they had before.

(At home, while the rain beat steadily against the windows, Amy watched, dull-eyed, the game shows that were on TV.)

Down the road a mile Emma Clark stood in her hallway holding the telephone and motioning with her other hand for Avery to take the duffel bag of dirty laundry straight to the basement; she had to snap her fingers and point before he seemed to understand.

"Of course they don't care," Emma said into the telephone, nodding yes to her husband that the brown suitcase could go upstairs. "They only care about the dollar bill," and then she winced, because she was speaking to Carolyn Errin, the dentist's wife, who herself, Emma thought, cared only for the dollar bill. But apparently Carolyn Errin had not taken umbrage at Emma's remark about insurance companies, for she was already agreeing in her steady, irritated voice that the earrings were priceless because her father gave them to her the night before he died and who could put a price on that ("No one," said Emma

Clark, who had a headache, and hated arriving home from vacation in the rain), and the insurance company should only now be telling them these items weren't covered, when the earrings had been stolen last *March*.

"Oh, such incompetence," said Emma, sitting down in the black chair by the telephone and thinking that Avery, like her, was subdued because of the girlfriend that John had brought to the cabin, brown-eyed Maureen, thin and intelligent and halfway through medical school. All very impressive, but something was not right.

"You can't believe anything the insurance company tells you," Emma said to the dentist's wife, "but I'll have to call you back. Avery's unpacking and I need to supervise."

But Carolyn Errin had one little question before she hung up: How did the visit with John's new girlfriend go?

"Lovely," said Emma, standing up now, and leaning her head toward the phone in preparation for hanging up. "Lovely girl. She's in medical school, you know."

Well, if they got married they'd have quite an income, wouldn't they.

"I'm sure that's a long way down the line," Emma said. "Bye, bye."

She was not the least bit sure it was a long way down the line. And this Maureen was simply not what Emma had in mind for her son. Emma opened the closet door and hung up a shirt. One would assume that a woman in medical school hoped to be a pediatrician, or go into obstetrics and deliver babies. But Maureen planned on being a gastro-enterologist. Emma sat down on the bed. That kind of doctor looked at people's rear ends all day long. And did more than look, Emma thought, moving the suitcase aside.

"Tell me, Avery," she said, as her husband came into the bedroom, "as a male."

He looked at her with wariness.

"Would you go to a woman gastroenterologist? If you needed one, I mean."

"Oh, Lord," he said, looking slightly abashed, sitting down on the bed beside her.

Emma sighed, and they watched while the rain slid down the windows in front of them. "Why would *anyone* be that kind of doctor?"

Emma demanded, thinking how they both felt invaded by a chilliness, an uneasiness, how their entire future seemed rocked somehow by this vigorous, slender Maureen.

But then Avery said there was probably some canned stew they could heat up for dinner tonight, since the rain made it bothersome to go to the store. And they were making too much of the Maureen business; she was a nice girl. Besides, who said that John was going to marry her?

Emma stood up. "Oh, he'll marry her," she said. "You wait and see." She did not add that the children would be raised by a housekeeper and would therefore grow up anxious, or that John himself would be neglected over the years. No, she wasn't going to say another word. Avery could just wait and see.

ACROSS TOWN BARBARA Rawley, the deacon's wife, sat down on her bed. The rain tapped steadily against the windowpane. From the family room below came the sounds of the television, and her son, Flip, hooting as he watched the baseball game.

What she couldn't get over was how the breast was gone. How simple it was. Just gone.

She heard her husband speak to Flip, the footrest of his recliner squeaking into place. All that mattered was this: the happiness of her family.

But still. Her breast was gone. She couldn't seem to get over this, to believe it. She opened her bathrobe slowly, and stared. She stared and stared. The breast was gone.

In its place was a long, red, raised line. The breast itself was simply gone.

IN THE MORNING the rain let up slightly but it didn't stop. Drivers still needed their wipers as they drove across the river—the squeaky rhythmic back-and-forth over the windshield, smearing, clearing; the rumble of the bridge beneath the tires; and beneath that the brown river, hard and unrelenting as it swerved around the rocks, as though the days of rain had returned to it some long forgotten arrogance.

The sky, which since dawn had stayed an unvaried galvanized gray, now darkened perceptibly, and the rain tapped down steadily again, but faster. For anyone driving over the final pinning of the bridge and onto Mill Road it could easily seem the world was underwater; cars nosing down roads and turning into parking lots like so many slow-moving fish; clogged drainpipes on the edge of the road causing large and shallow ponds to form in places; trucks driving through sending up a sheet of spray. In the parking lot of the mill, people hurried through the rain wearing plastic hats, or holding umbrellas, their shoulders scrunched forward as they ducked inside the door.

In the office room the lights were on, casting a yellowish hue onto the old wooden floor, and because the windows were shut against the rain, the room had a wintery feel to it, which was peculiar after a summer that had seemed it would never end, and in fact had not yet done so.

Avery Clark did not show Isabelle any photographs of his week in the mountains on Lake Nattetuck. Nor did he offer any other accounts of his family's vacation, except to acknowledge, rather dismissively, that yes, indeed, it had been raining there as well.

"Oh, what a shame," Isabelle said, from where she stood in the fishbowl doorway.

"So you managed all right?" Avery said. He was poking around in a desk drawer. He glanced at her quickly. "No problems, I hope."

"Well . . . no." She said this slowly, stepping inside his door. She was ready to tell him softly how there had been a bit of trouble with Lenora when she saw, or rather felt, that he was not interested. He was more than not interested—he did not want to know.

"Good, then. Glad to hear it." He tapped the edges of some papers on his desk, while his eyes glanced over his appointment book. "I'm sure with this break in the weather, everyone's feeling better."

"Oh, I think so. For the most part. You know." Through the glass wall of his office Isabelle could see Dottie Brown sitting at her desk. Not engaged in work or conversation, unaware of being observed, Dottie's face had a fragile, naked look, like that of a child who had been everlastingly stunned, and it sent a shiver through Isabelle's bones.

Chapter

22

It RAINED LIGHTLY for two more days and then the sky suddenly cleared just as darkness fell, leaving for a few moments a strip of luminescent afterglow along the horizon from a sunset that had not been seen. That night the stars came out, the whole array of them: Orion's Belt, the Big and Little Dippers, the smudgings of the Milky Way, all were reassuringly there against the deep ocean of quiet sky.

By early morning a delicate strip of clouds high overhead looked like a thin layer of frosting spread across the side of some blue ceramic bowl. Mourning doves cooed unseen in the fine light; cardinals and hermit thrushes darted from one tree to another, calling out. The dairy farmer's wife, Mrs. Edna Thompson, stood on her back steps saying to no one in particular, "Listen to those birds," and it did seem their morning chatter was more noticeable in this soft, surprising air.

Still and all, it was remarkable after a summer of constant complaining how few people mentioned this change in the weather. It might have been because things simply seemed normal again, for lawns that had been tired-looking patches of brown had, in this week and a half of rain, found something green in themselves again; even the bark on the birch trees appeared refreshed and tender and clean, the leaves calmly hanging in the windless sun.

By afternoon mothers could be found sitting on their front steps while children ran bare-legged down the sidewalks. Fathers arriving home from work felt like barbecuing again, and did, then sat on their porches till evening. In short, the traditions of summer were available again, and they brought over the next number of days certain combinations of comfort in the loamy smells of earth and in the wafting of barbecued meat, and in the ever-hopeful nostalgia that is felt sometimes in the scented air that hovers over newly cut grass.

Barbara Rawley, breathing in this freshness as she stood in the kitchen doorway watching her husband return the lawn mower to the garage, thought of all the brave women out there in different parts of this vast country who faced each day wearing a gelatinous prosthesis tucked into their bras, and she thought it might be possible that she, too, could accept living this way.

Lenny Mandel, driving down Main Street toward the apartment where Linda Lanier continued to entertain him so generously, felt capable of things decent and good, envisioned a future strolling the corridors gray-haired and with a commanding presence, principal of a school that would improve greatly under his concerned and sensitive care.

It was the air, really—the clear brightness of the air that in the evenings now held the first chilliness of autumn, and brought with it that subtle undercurrent of old longings and new chances which autumn often brings. It was this, combined with the confidence given by her deepening friendship with Dottie Brown and Fat Bev, that started Isabelle thinking how she might invite Avery Clark and Emma to her house one evening for dessert.

The thought, coming to her one night as she stood at the sink finishing the dishes, noticing with surprised satisfaction how very nice the kitchen looked with the geraniums on the windowsill, the patch of marigolds seen through the window catching the last of the evening's sun—this thought, having arrived, grew larger, more prominent, and pushed other thoughts away. What she wanted, really, was to "look good" once again in Avery Clark's eyes, which is why the sight of her attractive kitchen that night prompted the idea; she wanted to open herself, her life (even her house), to his inspection, to say, in effect, Avery, see how clean I have managed to be? See how, in spite of everything, I have survived my struggles? But she had to approach the question on its face: Was inviting the Clarks to her house an acceptable thing to do? At times it seemed it was; they were neighbors, they went to the same church; it would be a merely friendly gesture. Perfectly all right.

Other times it seemed ludicrous. (*Was* it ludicrous to invite your boss to your home?) She thought of telephoning her cousin Cindy Rae two hours away, but in order to have the situation weighed honestly she would have to include the sordid little piece of history involving Avery and Amy—and Emma's subsequent gossip—and of course she wasn't going to do that. No, she was on her own with this one, and she sat in the office room typing at her desk, losing her confidence, gaining it, losing it again.

But leaving the ladies' room one afternoon and unexpectedly finding herself alone in the hallway with Avery Clark, who was bending over the drinking fountain, Isabelle blurted out quietly, "Avery, I wondered if you and Emma would care to come over for dessert one night?"

Avery straightened up and stared at her, a bit of water still clinging at the edge of his long, crooked mouth.

"It was just an idea," Isabelle said, faltering. "I just thought . . ." and here she raised her hand as though to stop the thought, or conversation, from going further.

"Oh, no, no. No." Avery wiped his mouth briefly, nervously, with the back of his hand. "Very hospitable of you." He nodded, so clearly caught off guard that Isabelle, to her horror, felt her face grow red. "Very nice thought," he said. "Let's see. What night did you have in mind?"

"Saturday. If you're free. Around seven o'clock. Nothing very elaborate of course."

"Seven o'clock," Avery said. "I think that's fine. I'll just check with Emma, of course, but that sounds fine." They nodded to each other rather excessively until Avery walked away. "Thanks very much," he added.

So there it was.

Isabelle barely looked up from her desk for the rest of the day.

ACROSS THE RIVER in Oyster Point the school was being made ready for a new year; the floors were waxed and buffed, the gymnasium floor especially glowed a honey gold; graffiti in the bathrooms had been scrubbed off, the walls repainted, a leaky faucet in the upstairs girls' room fixed. The supply closet next to the teachers' room in the basement was filled with boxes of brown folded paper towels, toilet paper, erasers, and chalk. Mrs. Eldridge, the school nurse, came in to go through her files and draw up her requisition list: alcohol, bandages, iodine; she put a plant on the windowsill.

There was a pleasantness to all of this: without the disarray of an anxious student body the building seemed to hold the promise of what it was meant to be, the benevolent center of learning run by capable adults. The principal, Puddy Mandel, worked steadily, rearranging last-minute kinks in the scheduling and being, his secretary reported to a lunchroom worker, nicer than he had been before.

The janitor, a man named Ed Gaines, who had worked for the Shirley Falls school system for twenty-eight years, stepped out the side north door for a moment to have a cigarette and saw a young girl walking past the school slowly. She turned her head frequently to gaze at the windows of a first-floor classroom. Ed Gaines recognized her at once, although she looked different. She was the girl he had seen leaving the building often with the Robertson man. (Here the janitor exhaled, shaking his head, flicking the ash from his cigarette.) He had seen plenty of things in this school over the years, but he kept his judgments to himself. He was a quiet, solitary man who preferred to believe the best about people, though perhaps because of this his presence was frequently discounted. Teachers, for some reason more than students, tended to ignore him, and he had often been privy to salacious, surprising remarks made to one another by members of the faculty. He had seen things as well: the biology teacher—a heavy, married man of fifty with thick glasses that enlarged and distorted the pupils of his eyes—had, on the stairwell one late afternoon, actually slipped the librarian's woolen skirt clear up over her bottom when below them Ed Gaines had finally bumped his broom, scaring them like birds. (He graciously pretended not to see them as they fled.)

Yes, he had had time over the years to come to one conclusion: The behavior of human beings was a curious thing. Ed Gaines could not recall ever having seen that biology teacher laugh, for instance, and why the librarian, a pleasant woman with four children of her own, would allow, or even desire, this particular man's hand to run itself over her ample thigh was, to Ed Gaines, a curious thing. There was no accounting for taste, his sister always said, and he could only think that she was right.

The girl had seen him. She ducked her head in embarrassment at having been watched. Ed Gaines thought she was shy—you could see it in the way she walked: pigeon-toed, with her long skinny legs and big bare feet. She glanced up again, as he knew she would, and he waved this time in a friendly, easy way.

She waved back, a slight, tentative raising of her hand, and then unexpectedly she turned and walked across the lawn to him.

"And how are you?" Ed Gaines said, while she was still some yards away.

She gave him a wan, apologetic smile; up close she looked quite different from how he remembered her.

"Got your hair cut," he said, and seeing how she seemed to flinch at this, added, "Looks good, like a real grown-up lady."

Her smile grew fuller, relaxed; she dropped her eyes. Kids, he thought—just wanted to be treated nice.

"Do you know where Mr. Robertson went?"

Ed Gaines nodded, dropping his cigarette onto the cement step and grinding it hard beneath his dark work boot. "Back to Massachusetts, I believe." He kicked at the flattened cigarette butt, sending it sailing a good two feet across the weedy lawn. "He was in here just last week, cleaning some things out of his classroom."

"Last *week*?"

Her look made him feel careful. "Believe it was last week I saw him about the place. He only had a year contract, you know, on account of Miss Dayble's broken hip."

"Oh, I know." The girl spoke this in a murmur, looking down, turning away.

"Or was it her skull. Cracked her skull first, I guess, then broke her hip." Ed Gaines shook his head with lingering wonder over this.

"But I thought he was already gone. He was in last *week*?" The girl turned back to him, her large eyes were just faintly red-rimmed.

It was making her feel bad, this news—maybe he ought to take it back. But it was not in the nature of Ed Gaines to lie, and so he said kindly, "You ask in the office and maybe they'll give you his address if you want to send him a letter."

She shook her head, looking down again. "It's okay. Well," waving her hand slightly, "see you around."

"See you around. You enjoy your last days of summer now." He watched her walk away.

ISABELLE WAS HAVING some doubts, of course. But she imagined herself in conversation with her cousin Cindy Rae, and Cindy Rae told Isabelle it was an excellent idea, inviting the Clarks to her house, that Isabelle had always been too shy, people responded to friendliness; frankly, Isabelle didn't realize this, but shyness was often mistaken for unfriendliness, and maybe the women at church—including Emma Clark—had for these number of years thought Isabelle was snubbing *them,* instead of the other way around.

All this imagined advice Isabelle agreed with, was inspired by. Still, she had expected Emma Clark to call her on the telephone, to thank her in person for the invitation that Avery had relayed.

But never mind.

Avery, at least, was practically his old self at work, giving her every morning a cheerful wave, though he was busy catching up on things after his vacation and didn't have time for long chats. But that was all right; after his initial surprise at the drinking fountain that day, there was nothing to indicate she had blundered by inviting him to her house.

Her mind was busy with the planning, though she did not tell Dottie and Bev that she was entertaining Avery Clark this weekend because they might read into it some snobbishness. Besides, it seemed rude to be anticipating some happy event while Dottie was still struggling with her newly realized misery; skinny as a rail, she continued sucking the life out of her cigarettes while Bev kept watch, plying her with brownies and fruit. For Isabelle, whose own vigilance she understood was being counted on in this camaraderie, there was an uneasy sense of lying, because, truth be told, it was a terrible thing to have to watch Dottie's pain, to have to think about that pain—much nicer to dwell on the possibility of Avery's liking her once more, and because at the same time she was exchanging glances of approval with Fat Bev over the unremarked-upon consumption of a peach by Dottie, she was wondering if instead of making chocolate cake for the Clarks she might not do better with a peach Melba instead. Or both. No, both would be excessive, but a nice bowl of fruit perhaps to go with the cake.

"I'd like to wring her husband's neck," Bev was murmuring as she watched Dottie, who, in making her way out of the lunchroom, was being forced to stop and listen to Arlene Tucker's latest pontification on whatever it might be (Dottie was gamely nodding her head), and Isabelle herself nodded at Bev, feeling again—reeling in her thoughts of fruit bowls for the Clarks—that she was, on some level, lying. Still, Isabelle had been living with variations of this feeling for a very long time, and would have been astonished had anyone described her as "cagey"; she thought of herself as *discreet*.

On Friday afternoon when it was time for Isabelle to leave work, Avery was on the telephone. She waited to speak to him, but having used up ways to linger—straightening all the paper on her desk, fussing with the plastic typewriter cover—she finally ducked her head through the doorway of the fishbowl and said softly, "Are we all set then, Avery?"

He nodded, briefly turning the phone piece upward from his mouth. "All set," he said, giving a thumbs-up sign.

She waited until they were almost finished with dinner before saying to Amy, "Avery Clark and Emma are coming here tomorrow for dessert."

Amy, who had been silent for most of the meal, looked up with surprise and said, "Here? They're coming *here*?"

"Yes," Isabelle responded, the level of the girl's surprise making her uncomfortable, "and after saying hello very nicely, you might want to go upstairs and read in your room."

"Forget it." Amy spoke flatly, pushing back her chair. "I don't want to see them at all."

Isabelle said, "Amy Goodrow, so help me God, you will do as you are told."

But Amy, placing her dishes into the sink, said a few moments later in a conciliatory tone, "I'm supposed to meet Stacy at the library tomorrow. She wanted to know if I could have dinner with her, maybe spend the night. Since you're busy, that's probably what I'll do."

She turned from the sink. "If that's all right."

It was a problem these days, worrying as to Amy's whereabouts, now that her job at the mill was through. Except the girl had relatively few options of places to go to; Isabelle recognized that. The library, or sometimes Stacy's house, and Isabelle was not inclined to deny her access to either. She had made a few discreet calls during the summer, both to the school and to a certain apartment complex, and she was sufficiently convinced that Mr. Robertson was gone. That, obviously, was her main concern. Beyond this, however, she remained uneasy—and who wouldn't—whenever Amy was not at home. But there was not a lot of summer left; soon she would be back in school.

"We'll see," Isabelle said now to Amy. "If Stacy has invited you to dinner, well, yes, I guess so. That may be all right."

ISABELLE SLEPT POORLY that night and was embarrassed by the fact. She doubted that Barbara Rawley (Isabelle could still recall the woman standing in the A&P, a jar of olives in her hand—"And what are you two ladies doing tonight?") had trouble sleeping before her dinner parties. Isabelle would have to leave time in the afternoon for a little rest. She had once read in a magazine that one should always leave time, after bathing, for a nap on the day you planned to entertain.

But first she baked the cake, hoping the warm scent would linger throughout the day so that when the Clarks stepped through the door the smell would be inviting.

Then she dusted. She dusted all the furniture, including the legs of the table and chairs. She dusted window sashes, lampshades, the light-bulbs themselves, the mop boards, the banister. She washed the windows, the floors (at some point Amy left the house, saying she would call when she knew if she was spending the night at Stacy's), vacuumed the rugs, and spent an inordinate amount of time scrubbing the sink in the tiny bathroom off the kitchen, because that was the bathroom Emma Clark would be using if she needed to use one at all.

"Oh, certainly," Isabelle would say, "right around the corner there. It's awfully small, I'm afraid." Pause. "But it's clean." This last phrase would be spoken with some degree of merriment, and Emma, being friendlier than Isabelle ever gave her credit for, would answer, "Well, that's all that really matters, isn't it." And then she'd duck into the bathroom—and see what? See this. Isabelle, a number of times, tried to pretend she had never seen her own bathroom before, and opened the door again and again to see if the impression was a good one, or bad.

She couldn't tell. Still, it seemed the bathroom needed something. And then she realized: of course, it needed flowers.

WALKING INTO THE florist shop, Isabelle passed by her daughter, who was standing barefoot in a phone booth, smoking a cigarette. Isabelle did not see her. If she had, if she had lifted her eyes just slightly, or if she had not been so preoccupied with her own excitement and vague sense of shame over purchasing flowers (something she never did) to beautify her surroundings for her guests that night, then events might have been altered; for it is hard to imagine that the discovery of her barefoot daughter, whose lips were covered now with a purplish frosted lipstick, the smudged circle of which was present on the cigarette she held in her hand—who was not in the library after all, or even in the presence of Stacy—would not have precipitated some sort of scene, resulting in Amy's being returned to her house and stored safely away in her bedroom upstairs.

But it did not happen. Isabelle stepped inside the florist shop, a bell tinkling on the closing door behind her, only moments before Amy stepped squinting from the phone booth, tossed her cigarette into the street, and walked up the sidewalk in the other direction, toward the apartment of Paul Bellows, her sandals held loosely by their straps in her fingers—for Amy could not, when she did not have to, bear anything on her feet.

Before making this phone call, Amy had been experiencing an odd period of panic: she had nothing to do for the day. Nothing at all. She had been aware all along that Stacy had gone off for two weeks with her parents, to some farmhouse somewhere, and when she told her mother she would spend the day and possibly the night with Stacy, it had simply been a lie—because she had no desire to observe her mother's anxious preparations, and no desire *at all* to be present for the arrival of Avery Clark and his queer, stupid-looking wife.

So Amy had left the house with only a few dollars and no plans, and by the time she reached town and bought a pack of cigarettes and shoplifted the purplish lipstick (her first try at this, and it was surprisingly easy), she was beginning to have serious doubts about how exactly she would spend her day. And she did not know what to make of the fact that the janitor at school had said Mr. Robertson had so recently been in town. Mr. Robertson would have called her—she was certain of that. Which meant (and it was so distressing to think) that the telephone on the kitchen counter had been ringing while she sat in a doughnut shop with Paul Bellows, smoking her cigarettes. Or, not knowing of course that Dottie Brown had seen a UFO and come back to work early, perhaps he had tried to reach her at the mill. Although that seemed risky and unlikely.

The thought that Mr. Robertson had returned to town and *not* attempted to find her did not stay long in Amy's mind. Instead she became more and more certain that this man who loved her ("You know you'll always be loved, don't you?"), who had touched his mouth to her newborn breasts with such loving and exquisite tenderness, gazed at her naked middle with such *seriousness,* had returned to town not to clean out his classroom (which made no sense, he would have done that earlier) but to *find her.* It seemed to Amy, whose mind was always filled with him, and who assumed his mind was filled with her, that Mr. Robertson had gone to the school in hopes of finding her there, or near there, because she had in fact walked by the school compulsively since being released from the mill, the way one is compelled to return again and again to scenes of earlier exaltations.

She had gone there today even, after buying her cigarettes and lifting the lipstick, walking past the brick building cautiously, for she did not want to be observed again by the kind janitor, Mr. Gaines. But it was Saturday and Mr. Gaines would not be working. No one would be working, Amy thought, walking up the south lawn toward the school's front door; but there was Puddy Mandel walking across the parking lot, and so she had hidden herself behind the lilac bushes, peering toward the windows of Mr. Robertson's classroom—and had seen nothing.

Finally she had walked back into town and then over the bridge toward the Basin, feeling exposed on the sidewalks of Oyster Point, feeling on some instinctive level that the broken, tarry sidewalks of the Basin provided greater anonymity, as well as the chance of running into Paul Bellows, who might at least be free to drive her around in his car. She couldn't rid herself, however, of the thought that if she walked around the back roads enough that day, Mr. Robertson, driving by, would find her. But by four o'clock she was tired and hungry, and she stepped into a phone booth to call Paul Bellows.

It turned out to be the right thing to do. Paul was just headed out the door—he had to drive to Hennecock to see some insurance guy about his car; he'd be glad to have her come along. "I'm kind of hungry," she confessed, pressing her fingers against the glass of the telephone booth while the cigarette she held sent a spiral of pale blue smoke directly toward her eyes, so that she turned her face away and therefore just missed her mother walking by, "but I don't have much money on me."

"No problem," Paul said. "We'll stop somewhere."

Hanging up, Amy thought maybe Stacy had been too hasty in dumping the guy.

ISABELLE HAD DELIBERATELY gone to the rather dingy florist shop on Main Street in the Basin rather than the more open, lovely one in Oyster Point in order to avoid the chance of bumping into Emma Clark. She had a horror of being "witnessed" in her hostess preparations. It was Emma, after all, who had to be won over. It was Emma who might say (if all went well, God willing), driving home tonight, "Really, Avery, what a shame we never paid more attention to Isabelle all these years." And it was Emma who might get on the phone tomorrow and say to whoever it was she gossiped with that they had misjudged Isabelle Goodrow; that having spent a lovely evening in her home, she realized that Isabelle was actually an awfully nice woman, she'd made that Crane cottage a sweet little home and . . .

And what? Isabelle was tired from having slept poorly the night before. She was making far too much of this, she thought, nodding a greeting to the old man who ran this dingy florist shop, and there was very little here to choose from—*plastic* flowers, for heaven's sake; she ought to have simply snipped a few flowers from her own back garden.

But there by the cash register was an abundance of yellow tulips. What a surprise so late in the summer. Isabelle reached her hand toward them; yes, she would take six of these. They were terribly expensive. She stood silently while the man rolled them with great elaborateness in two sheets of flowered paper, and then she carried them to her car carefully in the crook of her arm, as though holding a newly swaddled baby.

But what a smart choice after all! When she was through arranging and rearranging, taking down from the cupboard all the vases she owned, pewter, cut-glass, china, the tulips were a sight to behold. For there on the kitchen table three of them sang out cheerfully; two more on the mantel in the living room, and in the little half-bathroom Isabelle placed the slender pewter vase with one yellow tulip on the back of the commode.

The telephone rang. A sudden fear that Avery would be calling to say Emma wasn't feeling well—oh, it seemed unbearable.

But it was Amy, who said, "Hi, Mom," snapping her gum.

"Please, Amy." Isabelle dropped her eyelids, pressing a finger to the bridge of her nose. "If you're going to chew gum, do it with your mouth *closed*."

"Sorry." A car honked.

"Where are you?" Isabelle asked.

"Outside the library. With Stacy. How late are the Clarks going to be at our house?"

"Well, I don't know. Ten o'clock maybe? It's hard to say." Isabelle herself had been wondering how long the Clarks would stay. How long did people stay when they went for dessert? Certainly if they left by nine o'clock you could count the evening a failure.

"Anyway," Amy said, "I'm staying at Stacy's house tonight. We're probably going to a movie."

"What movie."

"I'm not sure. Some kid movie for her little brothers in Hennecock, I think."

"But Amy. You didn't take anything with you. A nightgown, underwear. What about your toothbrush?"

"Mom," said Amy, with obvious annoyance. "I won't die, you know. Jesum Crow. Look, I'll call you in the morning."

"Please. Please do." Isabelle turned her head to glance at the tulips on the table. In the warmth of the kitchen they had opened further. "And please don't snap that gum, Amy, in front of Stacy's parents."

She hung up feeling uneasy. Shaking confectionery sugar into a bowl for the frosting, Isabelle pressed her lips together. It would take time, trusting Amy again. That's what happened when you lied to some-one; you forfeited their trust. Amy knew that, and it's why she was an-noyed. Anyway, it would be—to be honest—a relief not having her around when the Clarks showed up.

Chapter

23

$A_{T\ A\ DINER}$ in Hennecock Paul Bellows ate a plateful of fried clams and said he hoped they didn't end up making him shit his brains out later. "It's happened before," he said, without elaboration.

Amy sat back while the waitress filled her cup with water. She had finished her hot dog and now ran her fingertip over her plate. With a wave of his hand Paul offered her some of his fried clams, but she shook her head. "Do you mind if I smoke while you're still eating?" she asked. She had been smoking all afternoon and had gone past the point of enjoying it; still, she felt compelled.

"Nope." Paul tipped the bottle of ketchup over his plate, whacking it hard. When a mound of ketchup slid onto the edge of his plate he licked the top of the ketchup bottle and screwed the top back on.

Up front the cash register rang. Steam rose from the coffeepots, dishes clattered as a table was cleared. Paul ate his clams, smothering each one in the mound of ketchup before pushing it into his mouth, ketchup remaining on his lips as he chewed. He paused to drink from his Coke, ice cubes clunking as he tipped the cup, then returned to his clams. This steady, indifferent way he attacked his food was almost mesmerizing to Amy. She reached over and took one of the clams, dipping it in the ketchup as he had done.

"I would have married her, you know."

The clam belly, beneath its fried batter, squished unpleasantly in Amy's mouth.

"Her parents think I'm dumb."

Amy spit into her napkin. "Her parents are kind of queer," she offered, tucking the napkin under her plate.

"Her father's a rat-fuck, the mother's just spacey and weird." Paul finished eating and tapped a cigarette from his pack. "What do you want to do?"

"Drive around I guess."

Paul nodded. She thought he looked kind of anxious and sad.

ISABELLE LAY ON her bed, showered and powdered, her eyes closed. Outside her window the birds sang. She opened her eyes and closed them again, remembering how when Amy was very small and sometimes had trouble with her afternoon nap, Isabelle would bring her into this room and lie with her on this bed. "Mommy's going to sleep too," she would say, but Amy had never been fooled. When Isabelle opened her eyes the little girl would be lying quietly, staring at her. "Close your eyes," Isabelle would say, and Amy always did, her tender eyelids quivering with the effort of this obedience. In a few moments they would open once more, mother and daughter caught looking at each other in the silent room.

ON THE TOP floor of an apartment house on Main Street, Lenny Mandel was once again undressing. He had not intended to come here today; it was Saturday, and his mother expected him home to help with her bridge club tonight. He had gone into school to do some work and then stopped here afterward to say a quick hello. But when Linda reached into the refrigerator, the sight of her thighs, pale and bare emerging as her red cotton dress tugged up over her rump, caused him to inwardly moan; seeing the expression on his face when she turned, Linda smiled shyly and walked toward him.

His constant need to insert himself in her—penis, fingers, tongue, it hardly mattered—was baffling to him. (He would have put his fingers down her throat if he could have done so without hurting her.) With his eyes shut now, squeezing her, running his face down over her middle, he wished he could unzip her skin, place his entire self inside her body, make love to her like that, inside out instead of from the outside in. It wasn't normal, he thought, to desire a person so much; his world felt crazy and dark now, he was in a frenzy all the time.

She moved with him to the bed, spreading her legs wide—such open generosity. He gazed at this magnificent gift on the flowered sheets; he wanted to split her open, crack her up the middle like a lobster claw.

Afterward he apologized. He always did. She shook her head gently. "Lenny," she said, "you're just a very passionate guy."

He wondered why it no longer made him happy, and why he continued to crave it in the face of this.

AT THE SAME time that Lenny Mandel was buttoning his pants and Isabelle Goodrow was descending the stairs to eat a light and early supper so she wouldn't be dizzy or have a headache by the time the Clarks arrived, Dottie Brown, on the other side of the river, was following her husband mutely from room to room watching as he put things in a duffel bag. In the hallway he stopped and looked at her, a muscle twitching in his cheek. "I'll wait and go in the morning," he said, "if you want me to."

THERE WAS PLENTY of light left in the sky, but already the day was beginning to end. They had been driving without speaking for quite a while, listening to songs on the radio, played loudly, when Paul reached over to turn the radio off and in the sudden silence that followed said, "It gets me how her parents think I'm some dumb-fuck jerk."

Amy turned her head to look at him.

"My uncle might make me part owner of the business someday," he said, and then dragged deeply on his cigarette. He glanced over at Amy and she nodded.

"Hey, fuck it." Paul tossed his cigarette out the window.

The road they were on had become dirt, and they were bumping past fields on one side, woods on the other. "Where are we?" Amy asked.

"I was wondering myself." Paul squinted past Amy, looking through her open window. "This probably belongs to one of those farms we passed. Doesn't look like it's been farmed though."

"They rotate fields," Amy said. "The soil gets tired. That's why farmers need so many acres. Half of them just sit and rest every few years."

Paul grinned at her. "You do good in school?"

"Okay. Not great."

"I did okay in school," Paul said. "I never flunked anything."

The road was getting narrow. Branches were scratching the car at times; a rock clunked up against the bottom. Paul drove more slowly, then stopped. "Gotta look for a place to turn around. It's not like this baby is some jeep, you know."

Amy nodded, sticking her head out the window. "Can you back up?"

Paul turned to look behind him. "Guess I'll have to." He said this tiredly. "Jesus, we're in the middle of nowhere." He moved back around and switched the car off, then looked at her, hanging his head. "Want to give me a little kiss, Amy?"

She leaned her face forward, feeling sorry for him, feeling some shared shadow of desolation; she thought of Hansel and Gretel, two kids lost in the woods.

It was his breathing that alerted her, and the way he began twisting his head, turning his mouth back and forth over hers. She didn't want to be rude.

He pulled back and gave her that disconnected grin. He cocked his head, looking down at her hand. "So, Ame," he said, "you want to . . ."

Her heart flipped steadily, quickly. The air from the open car window smelled wet, autumnal. She felt responsible; she was the one who wanted to drive around, wanted to kill the evening until the Clarks went home—then she could walk in late and just tell her mother she wasn't staying at Stacy's after all. Or maybe Paul had a couch she could sleep on—she hadn't really thought it through. But now he wanted . . . to do stuff . . . and she felt suddenly that maybe she had been using him. His car might be scratched up right now on account of her too.

"Oh," she said, faltering, "see, well. I like you and everything. But it's weird because—"

"It's not weird," he said, his grin spreading now, "it's pretty natural, if you want to know the truth." He leaned forward and began to kiss her again.

Amy turned her face away. "See," she said. "I just wouldn't feel right. I mean, you know, I'm Stacy's friend and everything. Oh God, I'm really sorry."

"It's okay. Hey, don't worry about it." He touched her face, spread his fingers through her hair. "You're a nice person, Amy." He exhaled loudly, raising his eyebrows. "I'm just dying to . . . it would've been nice, but it's okay." He moved back, opening his door. "I gotta piss bad. By the way," he added, sliding out of the car, then leaning back in through the window. "Didn't you used to have really long hair?"

Amy nodded.

"Thought so. I'm going to be just a couple of minutes—I gotta go find a place to piss." He started walking up the narrow road. "Don't go anywhere," he called back.

She watched as he stepped through ferns and undergrowth, holding back branches, ducking his head. She lit a cigarette, wondering where Mr. Robertson was, her desire for him rumbling through her as though she were, all of her, nothing more than an empty stomach. She closed her eyes, leaning her head back, thinking of her breasts bare before him that day in the car, her legs bare, the feel of being touched by his slow fingers. He must think about it too. She knew he did. She knew he had come back looking for her.

"Amy!"

She opened her eyes and looked toward the woods. In just these few minutes evening had arrived, the air cool with autumn smells.

"Hey, *Amy!*"

She got out of the car hurriedly, slamming a stalk of goldenrod in the door behind her.

"*Amy!*"

Paul came crashing through the branches, his face glistening. "Jesus, Amy." His tanned arm had small fresh scratches across it as he reached for her wrist. "You gotta see this. Holy shit."

"What," she asked, following him. Her legs were being scratched by brambles, a branch of a fir tree snapped in her face.

"Holy shit," Paul said again, ducking forward, his sneakers flattening two pale Indian pipes that had pressed up through the pine needles, "I found this car—come here, look."

He pointed. They had reached a clearing, and a small blue car was on the edge of the field near the woods. Paul took her arm again, tugging her toward it. "I figure, abandoned car, you know, maybe tires or parts I can sell, so I pop the trunk and you won't fucking believe it."

She thought he had found money, maybe a suitcase of money.

They had almost reached the car when a smell rose up, something gone bad, like passing by a garbage bin that had been sitting for days in the sun. "It stinks," she said, making a face at Paul.

His face was shiny with sweat as he motioned for her. He raised the trunk. "You won't believe it, Amy. Look."

ISABELLE HAD FINISHED washing the fruit. The plates were ready, the teacups out. The Belleek china creamer that had belonged to Isabelle's mother, and that Isabelle loved so much (she gave it a quick intimate smile right now, as though its delicate shimmering were a whisper of good luck from her mother), sat complacently on a silver tray next to the sugar bowl. The cake was in the center of the table with the bowl of fruit beside it, the tulips nearby.

Lovely. Just lovely.

The Clarks would be here any minute. In the Oyster Point section of Shirley Falls people did not arrive late. At five past seven Isabelle filled the creamer; she had bought real cream for their tea. Or coffee, if they preferred. She was going to offer both.

At seven-fifteen her head ached. She took two aspirin and stood eating a cracker by the kitchen sink. Then she went into the living room and sat on the edge of the couch flipping through a magazine. Twice she thought she heard a car in the driveway and got up to peer cautiously through the kitchen window, not wanting to be seen looking out. But there was nothing.

It was getting dark now. She switched on another lamp in the living room. She thought: I will go upstairs and turn on the lamp by my bed, and when I come back downstairs they will be here.

They were not. Descending the stairs, moving through the living room, the kitchen, she felt that the house itself was watching her like some expectant, well-behaved child waiting for a performance to begin. At quarter to eight Isabelle washed her hands and dried them carefully, then dialed the number of Avery Clark's house. It rang four times, and in her legs she could feel the relief: they were on their way over, of course.

"Hello?" said Avery. In the background was the unmistakable sound of people talking.

"Oh," said Isabelle. "Yes, hello. Ah, this is Isabelle."

"Isabelle," said Avery. "Hello."

"I wondered if there might be a problem." Isabelle looked around the kitchen, the teacups ready, the tray laid out, the tulips rising up behind the bowl of fruit.

"A problem?" Avery said.

"Perhaps I made a mistake." Isabelle squeezed her eyes shut. "I thought you and Emma were going to drop by . . ."

"Tonight?" said Avery. "Oh, gosh, was that tonight?"

"I thought so," Isabelle said, apologetically. "Perhaps I got mixed up."

"Oh my goodness," said Avery, "this is my fault. I'm afraid I clean forgot. We have some friends in tonight."

Isabelle opened her eyes. "Well, another night," she said. "That's quite all right."

"I apologize," Avery said. "Boy, I'm awful sorry. There's been so much going on. Church get-togethers and whatnot."

"That's quite all right," Isabelle repeated. She had not heard of any church get-togethers. "Really. No problem at all. We'll try some other time."

"Some other time," said Avery. "Absolutely. And Isabelle, I'm very sorry."

"That's all right," she said. "Please don't even think about it. It was hardly anything. Hardly a big event." She tried to make a sound like laughter, but she felt disoriented. "Good night."

She put the teacups away, the plates, the silverware, feeling as though her eyesight had been affected by the moisture that was springing out over her face.

The tulips mocked her.

Everything did; the cake seemed to sag in its heavy roundness, the fruit bowl gazed with dry superiority. She took a brown grocery bag from beneath the sink and into this she dumped the cake, its frosting smearing down the side, and then the contents of the fruit bowl. Quickly she twisted the tulips, hearing their stems snap, and the sugar cubes from the sugar bowl as well, because they had been bought specially.

Everything had to be put away, put out of sight. She poured the cream down the sink and washed the Belleek creamer and sugar bowl. She was drying the creamer—her gestures were jerky and quick—when she heard a car pull into the driveway, its headlights momentarily lighting up the front porch.

"Oh *no*," she said out loud, thinking Emma and Avery, in their embarrassment, had decided to arrive after all, and here every single thing had been thrown out. How could she explain this? How could she possibly say, "Oh, I'm sorry. I just threw the cake away"?

Two car doors slammed, one right after the other, and she realized immediately that it was not Emma Clark out there slamming her door with such heftiness. Then Isabelle's heart pounded even faster, for this was some nightmare coming true: she was to be attacked in her own home, in the dark, with no neighbors in sight.

Moving quickly to push a chair against the door, her elbow swept the Belleek creamer to the floor, where it shattered with one quick, light sound. It lay like little broken seashells on the linoleum floor.

A strong knock on the door actually caused the blind that was drawn over its window to move, and Isabelle called out shrilly, "Who is it? Go away! I'm going to call the police!"

"We are the police, ma'am," came a deep, steady voice from behind the door, sounding both authoritative and slightly bored. "The state police, ma'am. We're looking for a girl named Amy Goodrow."

FOR AMY, WHAT happened that evening remained for a long time a dark compression of scattered images and sensations: the acrid,

salty taste in her mouth, for example, which she could not get rid of;
even stepping into the alley behind the Laundromat to thrust her head
forward and spit, to gather saliva and spit again. No, the peculiar saltiness of what (emptying her mouth in a fist of toilet paper in Paul's tiny
dark bathroom) had appeared as some kind of globular pus had seemed
to find its way into the tiniest, farthest-back crevices of the soft mem-
branes of her mouth. She had not been prepared for that, for that especially, and later, spitting behind the Laundromat, smoking a cigarette
there, she could not rid herself of this taste, or how it mingled in her
mind with the image (much of it immediately forgotten except for the
kneesock, and the teeth, and one gold earring) of a small dead person
in the trunk of a car, only not a person anymore—she wouldn't have
known, right away, what it was if Paul hadn't pointed to the teeth lined
up that way; and then the oddness that followed, the silent escalation
of—of what?

Climbing the stairs to his apartment behind Paul (the dark calves of
his jeans moving up the stairs), she knew she would ask him for money,
because she needed money now—there was something she suddenly realized she had to do. He would have given it to her regardless, she was
almost sure of that. But she was desperate for money, and he, in some
queer, agitated state, was desperate for her (not *her*, she knew, but for
her mouth, her hands), and how could she say no and then ask him for
money?

In the dark he unzipped his pants and then held her head, one large
hand on either side, and she had liked it, the way he held her head, but
when her face, her mouth, was pressed up to him there, she smelled how
he was unclean, the pungency of those secret smells, fetid, sweaty. She
was certain she could smell in this the faint and cloying smell of his
latest crap—small streaks left, maybe, from when he had last wiped
himself—and it was this that made her want to cry, how her face was
pressed into that part of him that went to the bathroom, and how hard
the thing was in her mouth; she was uncertain exactly what to do.

But it was like he couldn't help it. It was like this thing had to be
done, and she, being there, assisted him. He was nice. He even apologized afterward. And then he kept saying that if you found a dead body
you had to call the police, that he was going to call the police.

But she just wanted money. He gave it to her and she left.

She had gone into the Laundromat because it had a change machine; whether other people had been there she was never able to remember; she only remembered standing there with her hands trembling as she fed dollar bills into a small conveyor belt that made a whining noise and hesitated, drew back, went forward, finally tumbling out coins for her. Then spitting in the alleyway, trying to get that taste from her mouth.

And then there had been the desperate long walk to the college, because the library at the college would still be open on a Saturday night and she had to get there, and the car that had pulled up, offering her a ride; in the mottled darkness she saw the face of a heavy older man who did not smile. No, Amy shook her head, No thank you; still, he had not driven away, his car creeping slowly along beside her. *No thank you!* She had screamed the words, started to run, briefly seen on his shadowy face how her scream had made him nervous; he pulled back onto the road, drove away.

In the quiet, high-ceilinged library at the college she felt that people watched her. Silent faces above the wooden tables watched her carefully, their expressions the crest of a silent wave of disapproval; she ducked her head.

The man behind the reference desk had that watchfulness too—he had warned her that the library was closing soon. But he had helped her with a politeness she was to remember for years, and when he presented her with a huge atlas, finding on one of the huge pages a map of Massachusetts, she thanked him three times in a row. She needed paper and a pen; this sudden realization brought tears, and the reference man helped her out again.

And then finally she was in the telephone booth on the basement floor. It was a closet, really, with nasty things written on the walls. SUCK MY COCK was written there, and this made her start to cry, sitting in the telephone closet of varnished wood that gleamed almost golden from the light, holding the list in her hand of towns in Massachusetts that began with the letter *P*, because he was from a town that started with *P*—she remembered that, dialing Information.

How many numbers did she call asking for Mr. Robertson? Maybe five? More than that. Ten? But then: an older woman's voice, her hello delivered not very pleasantly, it seemed to poor Amy, exhausted, almost out of her head.

"I'd like to speak with a Thomas Robertson," Amy said. "Is this the right number?" And when the woman didn't answer, when there was that momentary silence, Amy knew she had found him. "Please," she begged. "It's very important."

"Who's this."

"A friend. It's really important I talk to him." Amy closed her eyes; was this the alcoholic mother?

"Hold on." A muffled clatter, murmuring, then a presence drawing nearer to the phone, the murmuring sounds of a man's very deep voice coming close; a sound Amy recognized. Tears of relief slipping from her eyes, she leaned her head against the wooden wall of the telephone closet; finally, finally, finally, she had found him.

The phone picked up: "Hello?"

"Oh, Mr. Robertson. It's me. It's Amy Goodrow."

A pause. "I'm sorry," said Mr. Robertson in his lovely deep voice, "I'm afraid you have the wrong number."

"No, I don't. It's me, it's *Amy.* In Shirley Falls. *You* know."

"I'm afraid not," Mr. Robertson said slowly. "You have the wrong number." He hesitated before adding firmly, in a slightly different tone, almost southern-sounding, it seemed, "I don't know who you are. And there is no need for you to call me here again."

Chapter

24

By MIDNIGHT THE house was quiet. A small lamp on the kitchen table cast a glow through the downstairs hallway, but the living room was dark, and the dining room, and it was dark on the stairs except for where a strip of light fell across the landing. The light, dim enough to make the darkness nearby seem a deep-green hue, came from Isabelle's bedroom, where a towel had been placed over the lampshade in order to keep the light low. Beneath the folds of a loose blanket lay the figure of Amy, sprawled on her back like some oblivious sunbather, fast asleep. In the muted light her face appeared neither peaceful nor distressed—a result, probably, of the sedative now moving through her bloodstream. Still, there was in the way her lips were parted, her nose thrust slightly upward on the pillow, a look somehow of tender openheartedness.

To Isabelle the girl looked separate. That was the word that went through her mind as she leaned forward to tug lightly on the blanket, rearranging how it fell over Amy's arm and neck. Separate from her— Isabelle. Separate from everyone. Sitting in the ladder-back chair that she had drawn up close to the bed, Isabelle studied the different shadows and shapings of this face; at some point in these recent years the features of the girl had moved into their final place. And who had she become?

Someone separate, Isabelle thought again, touching tentatively a lock of hair that fell across Amy's cheek. Someone who could not even inherit the Belleek china creamer of her grandmother; and here Isabelle sat back, the memory of the delicate shattering of the creamer bringing tears to her eyes, for the pale china had represented to Isabelle her own mother, delicate, impractical, sweet. And now gone. That its ending should have coincided with Avery Clark's forgetting to come to her house brought Isabelle a pain so extensive as to not yet be fully absorbed; his words, *"I'm afraid I forgot, Isabelle,"* were harsh white spotlights lining the circumference of her mind.

But there in the center was Amy. Unknown Amy, who had been out in the woods with Paul Somebody (Isabelle's stomach floated and swayed, although she had believed Amy when she said there was nothing between them—"Nothing, nothing, nothing"), stumbling across dead bodies in the trunks of abandoned cars; oh, horrible for a young girl, to discover the body of another young girl! Poor, poor Amy, coming into the house, her face streaked and darkened, her eyes queerly small, as though looking out from the depths of a cave. Really, she had not been recognizable, staring at the policemen as if they had come to arrest her—when in fact they had only come to check out Paul's story, to ask her, perfectly nicely, what details she could add—and then, later, Amy had burrowed her face into the crevices of the couch, reminding Isabelle of a frightened dog in a thunderstorm, pure animal fear. Awful, guttural sounds she had made. "It can't be real," she kept crying into the couch. "No, I don't believe it, no I don't."

The policemen, particularly the older one, had been very kind. It was the older one who had suggested Isabelle might call a doctor if the girl did not calm down. The doctor had been kind as well, telephoning in a prescription to the only drugstore open late on a Saturday night—in Hennecock, half an hour away. In the drugstore, with her arm around a huddling Amy, Isabelle had looked into the kind eyes of a tired pharmacist and said, "My daughter has suffered a bit of a shock," and the pharmacist only nodded, his bearing exuding the suspension of all judgment, and in four years' time, when Isabelle was to meet him again, she would have no memory of him (though he would remember her, would remember the touching femininity of this small woman whose arm was tightly around her tall, frightened girl); for Isabelle tonight the world was shapeless and whirling.

The telephone rang.

"Isabelle?" A woman's voice, familiar. "Isabelle, it's Bev here. I'm sorry if I woke you up."

"Oh, yes," Isabelle said, breathing quickly, for she had stumbled hurriedly down the stairs. "Yes, hello. No, you didn't wake me."

"Isabelle, we got a problem here." Fat Bev spoke softly. "I'm at Dottie's. Wally's gone off to shack up with his girlfriend—he's moved out."

"Oh, Lord," Isabelle murmured, stepping toward the stairs to hear if the ringing phone had woken Amy.

"Dottie didn't want to be alone, so I came over. But just being in this house is too much for her. I'd bring her home with me except Roxanne's got two friends sleeping in our living room right now, and that's the last thing Dottie needs."

"He's gone to live with his girlfriend?" It was the only thing Isabelle could think to say.

"He's a fool," Fat Bev said. "Making a fool of himself." She paused. "Dottie's having a hard time, Isabelle. She doesn't want to stay here tonight."

It had not occurred to Isabelle that Bev was asking something of her. She had been certain when the telephone rang that it would have to do with Amy again. But now she pictured, briefly, Dottie Brown sitting in the rocking chair in her kitchen, blank-eyed, a cigarette dangling from her hand.

"Would you hold on just one minute, please, Bev? Just one minute. Hold on." She placed the receiver carefully down on the kitchen counter, then climbed the stairs. Amy was still asleep, in the same position. Isabelle squinted, leaning forward to watch for the rise and fall of the girl's chest. She went back downstairs.

"Bev?"

"Yuh, I'm here."

"Do you want to bring Dottie over here for the night?" It seemed ludicrous, really. Of all nights, when the inside of her head was so dazzled by those white spotlights of Avery Clark's voice: *I'm afraid I forgot, Isabelle.* With Amy in such a state . . .

"Would that be okay, Isabelle? I'll stay too, if that's all right—be more comfortable for her. Probably for both of you. Just give us a couch to curl up on would be good. I know you're kind of pinched for space."

"Please," said Isabelle. "Come."

AND THEN HOW odd it was. How queer to have the three of them, grown women, sitting in the living room with the mattress from Amy's bed right in the middle of the floor, complete with sheets and a blanket and a pillow. And the couch too had sheets and a blanket and a pillow. At first it promised to be awkward: Dottie being steered through the kitchen like a stunned child, Isabelle squeezing her hand, murmuring condolences as one would in the case of a death, Fat Bev following, lugging a large brown purse, the skin of her heavy face drooping like a tired dog's, and then all three of them sitting in the living room, tentative, uncertain. But Isabelle said, "Amy found a dead body tonight. She's upstairs asleep on my bed."

That seemed to break the ice.

"Father of Jesus," said Fat Bev. "What are you talking about?"

Isabelle told them. Of course they remembered the girl, Debby Kay Dorne—yes, they did. Remembered her picture on television, in the newspaper. "Cute thing," Bev said, shaking her head slowly, pulling down on her heavy cheeks.

"An angel," said Dottie. New tears seeped from her eyes.

"What do you mean Amy found her?" asked Bev, opening her large leather purse and producing a roll of toilet paper, which she handed matter-of-factly to the weeping Dottie. "What do you mean she *found* her?"

"She was driving around with a friend of hers. Would you like some Kleenex, Dottie?" Isabelle started to rise, but Fat Bev waved her back down.

"Used up all the Kleenex in town tonight—right, Dottie? Go on."

"She was driving around. Her friend Stacy recently had a baby, you know. I don't know if you know. Dottie, let me get you some Kleenex, it won't be so rough on your nose." Dottie's nose was awfully red, you could see that from here.

But Dottie was shaking her head. "I don't care if my nose falls off, I just don't care. Get to the body, please."

"Really," said Fat Bev.

So Isabelle repeated what she knew of the evening (leaving out anything about Avery and Emma Clark), finishing up with the kind doctor, the drive to the pharmacy for tranquilizers. "Amy was almost hysterical," she said. "Otherwise I wouldn't believe in giving children tranquilizers—"

Bev cut her off. "Isabelle. She found a murdered girl. I guess if there's a good time to pop a pill that would be one of them."

"Well, yes," said Isabelle. "I thought so."

"Could I have one, Isabelle?" Dottie asked from where she half lay on the couch. "Could I have one the tranquilizers? Just one so I could get to sleep?"

"Oh, good idea," said Bev. "Lord, yes, Isabelle, can you spare one of the pills?"

"Certainly," said Isabelle, rising, going into the kitchen, and returning with the bottle of pills, which had a sticker on it prohibiting by federal law the transfer of them to anyone else. "You won't have a bad reaction will you?" she asked. "I know when people are allergic to penicillin they're supposed to wear a dog tag around their necks."

"These aren't penicillin. They're Valium." Bev had taken the bottle from Isabelle and was peering at the label. "No one's going to arrest you for giving your friend a Valium."

Isabelle returned with a glass of water and Dottie swallowed the pill, then took Isabelle's hand, her blue eyes with their red rims looking pathetically into Isabelle's face. "Thank you," Dottie said. "For letting me come here tonight. For not asking me anything."

"Of course," Isabelle murmured. But she said it too quickly, moved away too quickly, and a fog of awkwardness rolled back into the room. Isabelle sat down in her chair. The women were quiet. Intermittently glancing at Dottie lying on the couch with the afghan pulled over her, Isabelle had to keep looking away, for she was struck with the extreme ease with which lives could be damaged, destroyed. Lives, flimsy as fabric, could be snipped capriciously with the shears of random moments of self-interest. An office party at Acme Tires, whiskey flowing, and in one series of groping moments, Wally Brown's life had changed, and Dottie's, and even the lives of their grown sons, she supposed. Snip, snip. All undone.

Isabelle said, "Dottie, I need to tell you something." Both women turned their heads to look at her, their faces expectant and cautious.

Isabelle wanted to cry, the way someone sick would want to cry, frustrated and weary at simply, for so long, *not feeling well.* "Amy," Isabelle began. But no, that wasn't right. She traced the arm of her chair with her finger. Dottie was looking down at her lap now; Bev kept her eyes on Isabelle.

"When I became pregnant with Amy I was seventeen," Isabelle finally said. "I wasn't married."

Dottie stopped gazing at her lap and looked over at Isabelle.

"I have never been married. That's one thing." Here Isabelle had to pause, staring vacantly at her hands, which she kept squeezing into fists and then unsqueezing, before she said, almost loudly, "He was a married man, Dottie. A married man with three children of his own." Isabelle looked in earnest at her friend whose pale face revealed blank surprise in the midst of its fatigue.

"I would love to be able to tell you I was innocent," Isabelle continued, "ignorant of . . . things. I guess in a way I was. I had never experienced it before, been with anyone. But I knew what we were doing. I knew what we were doing was wrong. I knew that, Dottie." Isabelle looked at the floor. "I went right ahead and did it anyway, because I wanted to."

For a long while no one said anything, and then Isabelle added, as though she had only just remembered, "He was my father's best friend."

Fat Bev breathed in loudly, moving back further in her chair, as though she needed to spread her weight more comfortably in order to contemplate this. "Some friend," she said.

But it was right then that Dottie leaned forward and said softly, "Isabelle, I hate Althea Tyson. I don't hate you. If that's what you're afraid of."

It was, on some level, what she had been afraid of. And more. She was afraid—had been afraid, ever since the day she drove Dottie home from the office room and sat with her briefly in her kitchen—that she, Isabelle Goodrow, had brought this sort of pain upon another person.

And it had never occurred to her before.

Not really. She had not really given Evelyn Cunningham too many thoughts over the years, at least not sympathetic ones. This was stupefying to Isabelle now, unbelievable. How could she have gone so long without recognizing what this might have—must have—done to the life of Evelyn Cunningham? How, year after year, had Evelyn Cunningham remained as unreal to Isabelle as a picture of some person in a magazine would be?

Because the woman was blood-and-bones real; she had, presumably, risen in the night to attend to a sick child, had piled into a washing machine the dirty clothes of her husband, had made lunches, dinners, had washed dishes, and had had to picture (in the middle of the night, undoubtedly) her husband unzipping his trousers and climbing onto Isabelle Goodrow in some potato field. Had lived, perhaps, with these thoughts for years. Had known, as her husband died and her children grew, that another woman was raising a child of this man that she, Evelyn Cunningham, had loved and lived with day after day for years. What could that have been like?

"Tell us more," said Dottie.

But Isabelle didn't want to. What words would she use? She glanced from Dottie to Bev, and both of them, she realized with great surprise, were looking at her kindly.

"Does Amy know?" Bev asked, when it seemed that Isabelle, after all, was not going to continue. "Amy know any of this?" Bev raised her eyebrows, scratching her head with one fat finger and rearranging herself once again in the chair.

Isabelle, shaking her head, felt as though some illness had left her battered, that if the house began to burn down she would not be able to move. Her shoulder blades ached, and her arms sent pains down to her wrists, her knuckles; her fingers lay spread on her lap. "If I could explain . . ." she faltered, and both women nodded.

Her parents were good people, she finally said, as though speaking through the depths of this illness that made her mouth dry, horrid, unfamiliar. She was not one of these people who had complaints about her childhood. She really wanted to stress that, she said, suddenly blinking away tears. ("It's okay," Fat Bev said kindly, "just go on.")

Her parents worked hard, they went to church every Sunday. She was taught right from wrong. Her mother was shy and they didn't have a lot of friends, but they did have some friends, of course (Fat Bev nodded encouragingly)—the Cunninghams, for example. Like she said, Jake

Cunningham was her father's best friend. They had grown up together, two boys, in the town of West Minot. Jake married a woman named Evelyn, who worked in a hospital there. She was not a nurse—well maybe she was; Isabelle wasn't sure how much training she'd had—but she worked for a while after they got married, and then she quit at the hospital and had three babies right in a row. Isabelle was around ten, something like that, and the Cunninghams would show up sometimes on a weekend afternoon, driving down from West Minot with all their babies in tow. Isabelle wondered now if her mother had been jealous of that, since her mother had not been able to have more children; but she couldn't say—she hadn't thought about it then.

The Cunninghams had moved to California. Jake joined a roofing business out there, and apparently it went well—Isabelle couldn't really remember. They got Christmas cards.

Then, when Isabelle was twelve, her father died ("Is that so," murmured Bev. "I had no idea"), sitting in his car at a gas station while his tank got filled. ("I'm so sorry," Dottie said, blowing her nose.) Yes, it was hard. You don't think when you're a kid how awful something is, you just take it as it comes, but you stay in shock at first; the funeral was beautiful, she always remembered that. A lot of people showed up. Jake Cunningham came from California—Evelyn couldn't come with all the kids to take care of, of course—and people were very nice to Isabelle. She felt special on the day of the funeral. And they played "A Mighty Fortress Is Our God," which was still Isabelle's favorite hymn—she took such comfort in the words of that hymn—but she was getting off the track; it wasn't really her father she meant to dwell on.

So. She took a deep breath. So anyway. After the funeral was when it got hard. The months after, when people stopped calling, when people didn't mention it anymore. ("Yes," said Bev, nodding, "it's always that way, isn't it.") She took care of her mother, and her mother took care of her. But they didn't go many places—to church, of course, and her cousins lived up the road. Isabelle worked hard at school and got good grades. She wanted to be a teacher. First grade, because that was the year children learned to read, and a good teacher could make a difference, you know. Her mother was proud of her. Oh, she and her mother loved each other very much, Isabelle said, her voice rising slightly, her eyes blinking again, and yet to tell the truth, to tell the sad real truth, in her

memory those years stretched out like one long dreary Sunday afternoon, and she didn't know why, because she would give anything to be
with her mother again. It wouldn't seem dreary at all.

She had broken her mother's Belleek china creamer tonight, hitting
it off the kitchen counter by mistake. ("What's that, hon?" Fat Bev
leaned forward. "Broke what, hon?") It had always been like having a
piece of her mother tucked away safe in the kitchen cabinet, and now it
was gone. (Tears were rolling down Isabelle's face.) She'd always thought
Amy would have it someday in her own home, but now it was gone.
("Better pass that toilet paper around," Bev said, reaching an arm
toward Dottie, and Dottie obeyed, unwinding a long strip of it for
Isabelle.)

Well, so anyway. Isabelle blew her nose hard, wiped at her eyes. So
anyway, she got good grades and ended up valedictorian of her class, actually, which made her mother proud. ("As it well should," said Dottie
generously, handing over another strip of toilet paper in case it was
needed.) There were only thirty-three people in the class, though—a
small school. ("Doesn't matter," Bev said firmly. "Everyone knows
you're smart. You should be proud.")

Her mother liked to sew. Her mother made her a beautiful white
linen dress for graduation day. Except she was getting ahead of herself
here. Because six weeks earlier, on a nice day in May (the magnolia had
been blooming by the front door—she remembered that—and bees
were knocking into the porch screens), Jake Cunningham showed up
out of the blue. He'd come east on business and stopped by to visit
Isabelle and her mother, and oh, they were happy to see him. Come in,
come in, her mother had said. How are Evelyn and the kids? Fine, all
fine. Jake Cunningham's eyes were gray and extremely kind. He smiled
each time he looked at Isabelle. And he fixed the roof. He went off to a
lumber store and came back with supplies and climbed up a ladder and
fixed the leaks in the roof. It was wonderful to have a man in the house.

He sat in the kitchen while they made dinner, his arms there on the
table, big arms covered with blond curly hair, and Isabelle, popping
rolls from the oven into a basket, was happy. She hadn't known until
that day how unhappy she had been, and now she wasn't unhappy, and
his eyes, she thought, were a little bit sad, and very, very kind. He still
smiled every time she looked at him.

Her mother was tired from all the excitement and went to bed early that night. Isabelle and Jake sat in the living room. She would always remember that. That time of year, the evenings were getting long, and it had just been getting dark when her mother went to bed. "Turn on the lamp," her mother said to them innocently, as she left the room.

But they didn't. They sat there on the couch facing each other, their elbows hanging over the back, talking quietly to each other, smiling, looking down, glancing out the window, as the room filled with that soft, springtime darkness. Jake was wearing a striped shirt—well, that didn't matter, she supposed; it's just that she couldn't help remembering. Anyway, there was a full moon that night, and the night sky through the open living-room window had a wonderful, hazy glow.

So.

They went for a walk. They walked through the neighboring potato fields, and there was that earthy smell of a greenhouse. The full moon was low in the sky, like it weighed a great deal.

She wished she could say she didn't know . . . but she couldn't say that. She knew it was wrong. And she didn't even care—that was the thing. Well, she did, but she didn't. Because she was so happy! She didn't care what it cost! She was happier than she had ever been.

The next night they went for a walk again. Afterward, he kissed her on the forehead and said that no one must ever know. She loved him. Oh, goodness, did she love him! She wanted to tell him how much she loved him, and she thought in the morning she would tell him that, but in the morning he was gone.

(Toilet paper was passed around; all three women blew their noses.)

She didn't tell anyone. Who was she going to tell? But then she was valedictorian and she had to give her little speech, which she did, standing on the school lawn on a hot day in June, wearing her white linen dress. When she got home she vomited, upchucked right down the front of that white linen dress, ruining it forever. Her mother thought it was nerves and was nice about the dress. Her mother was very nice. (More toilet paper was passed to Isabelle.)

But she vomited again the next day, and the next, and finally confessed the whole sorry business to her mother, both of them crying, sitting in the living room holding hands. The next afternoon she and her mother went to see the minister, sitting on his plaid couch while the sun fell over a gray carpet that Isabelle always remembered was remarkably dirty—isn't it funny how you remembered certain things? In the middle of everything she wondered why no one had vacuumed the minister's rug. The minister walked back and forth with his hands in the pockets of his seersucker trousers. God worked in mysterious ways, he said, and His will would be done.

Her mother took care of the baby while Isabelle drove each day to the teachers' college in Gorham. And that was strange, too, because after class when some classmate asked if she wanted to have coffee, she always said no and just hurried home. No one at the college knew she had a baby. ("Did Jake Cunningham ever know?" Bev asked. "Yes," said Dottie, who was completely sitting up now, "did Jake Cunningham ever know?")

He knew. Her mother had called him in California. Evelyn answered the telephone. Imagine Evelyn that day.

She *had never* really imagined—that was the thing. But imagine it now, standing in your kitchen, wondering what to make for dinner that night, checking the refrigerator—and the telephone rings. One minute your world is one way, the next minute it's all caved in. ("But what did this Jake fellow say?" demanded Bev. "What did the creep have to say?")

He was sorry. Oh, he was terribly sorry, of course. If money was ever a problem they should please let him know. But they weren't going to take money from him. ("Of course not," said Dottie, looking wide-awake and lucid, as though the tranquilizer had perked her up instead of sedating her. "Bullshit," said Bev. "I would have taken every dime.")

No, it was her responsibility—Isabelle's. And her mother's, which didn't seem fair. None of this was fair to her mother; she hadn't done anything to deserve it. ("Well, life isn't fair," observed Dottie.) But that January her mother died. She went to bed one night not feeling quite right in her stomach—a little queasy, she had said—and then she passed away in her sleep from a heart attack. Isabelle always thought it was the stress that had killed her. ("People with worse stress live to be a hundred," Fat Bev assured her.)

And so she had dropped out of college. She panicked, is what she did. She had a baby to take care of, and she really wanted a husband. There were no husbands available in her small town, so she sold her mother's house and moved down the river to Shirley Falls. Even the minister had told her not to do it. But she thought she had a better chance of find-ing a husband in Shirley Falls.

It was a mistake, though. She got nervous and bought a wedding band at Woolworth's; she did that on the spur of the moment, but then she ended up wearing it for almost a year—and when anyone asked, she said she was a widow. (Dottie and Bev both nodded. They remembered this.) It really was a terrible mistake to lie like that. But once you're in the middle of a lie it's hard to get out of, even if you want to. (Dottie nodded again, more quickly.) Growing up, she had always thought she'd get married and have a nice little family. It was still strange some-times to think it hadn't happened that way.

But that was it.

That was her story.

The three of them sat in thoughtful silence, nodding almost imper-ceptibly to one another and to the floor. In the distance a car could be heard passing by on Route 22. "Jake died right before I moved to Shirley Falls," Isabelle added, as an afterthought.

"Not another heart attack, I hope," said Fat Bev.

Isabelle nodded. "On a golf course."

"Jesum Crow, Isabelle," said Dottie. "Don't you know anyone who gets hit by a car? Drinks poison? Falls out of a boat and drowns?"

They all looked at each other; Bev widened her eyes.

"But I never thought of Evelyn," Isabelle continued after a moment. "I never *really* thought of her." She looked at Dottie apologetically.

"Well," said Fat Bev, lighting a cigarette finally, "it's Amy you'd bet-ter think of now."

ISABELLE ENDED UP being the only person in the house that night not on Valium. Bev, at the last minute, decided too many things had transpired over the course of the evening for her fuddled mind to ever manage to fall asleep naturally, particularly in this itsy-bitsy living room of Isabelle's, and so when Isabelle finally said good night, cheeks coloring because both women had leaned forward to give her a kiss, and leaving behind the bottle of pills next to the couch where Dottie sat, Bev helped herself to one of them. And then, thinking that she and Dottie would whisper—very softly, of course—for a few moments about what Isabelle had just told them, Bev came out of the bathroom to find Dottie so deeply asleep you'd have thought she'd been hit on the head. She was still sitting up, in fact, and didn't bat an eye when Bev tugged her down gently on the couch, sticking a pillow beneath her head, pulling the afghan over her.

Bev got herself arranged on the mattress that Isabelle had brought down earlier from Amy's room—there in the middle of the living-room floor—and found herself surprisingly comfortable. Within minutes it seemed she could feel the lull of Valium at work; God, it's a good thing she didn't get her hands on these things too often. They constipate you, though. Who would have thought Isabelle Goodrow—life was a funny thing. Wally Brown after all these years. Making such a fool of himself.

Upstairs, Isabelle lay awake on the bed next to Amy, listening to her breathe. The smell of cigarette smoke that lingered from downstairs, reminded her, not unhappily, of church suppers she had attended with her parents as a child, when after eating at card tables in the church basement the men would gather and smoke their cigarettes, talking of crops, of tractors, while the women made coffee in the big silver urns and laid out the different cookies and cakes. These were the same women who a few years later would bring casseroles for her mother in the days following the funeral. That had been kind of them, Isabelle thought now. It seemed to her (What was that sound? Only Fat Bev snoring) that kindness was one of God's greatest gifts: the fact that people, so many people, held within themselves the ability to be kind, really, was the work of God. How kind those women downstairs had been to her tonight! How kind the policemen had been earlier, the doctor on the telephone, the silent pharmacist (remembering only a large, white-coated bulk of a man). Yes, how kind people could be.

She would not let herself think right now of Avery, his wife, Emma—she could not bear right now the scraping harshness of those thoughts. She would think about her friends downstairs, how at one point tonight they had *wept with her* as she told of her love for Jake Cunningham. Isabelle could not get over this. These women had wept with her. They had heard her story of a life falsely lived, of other lives hurt by her own actions, and they had then with tender kindness kissed her good night.

She did not deserve it. For years, after all, she had held herself apart from them, thinking she was better, thinking she ought, really, to be with the likes of Barbara Rawley and Peg Dunlap and Emma Clark. *Who did I think I was?* she asked herself, bewildered. *Who did I think I was?*

She slept lightly but smoothly, as though she were not lying on a bed but on warm air, as though through some peculiar osmosis she had partially absorbed from the other bodies in the house the remnants of Valium doing its job. At times during the night Amy twitched, jerked a leg, called out, and Isabelle would wake without a sense of having been asleep. "I'm right here," she said each time, touching the girl's arm. "I'm right here, Amy. Everything's all right."

She opened her eyes one time and it was light, early-morning light moving into the room. Amy, lying on her side facing Isabelle, was looking at her with large, lucid eyes, an expression in them impossible to read. And it was so like when the girl had been little, when Isabelle had lain in this bed with her for an afternoon nap, trying to get her to sleep. But now her body was longer than Isabelle's, blackheads were pressed in the crevices of her chin and nose, an angry pimple had pushed itself out on the top of her cheek. Still, her eyes contained the same enigma that Isabelle had seen there when the child was less than two years old. *Amy,* Isabelle wanted to say, *Amy, who are you?* Instead she said quietly, "Sleep."

And the girl did. Closing her eyes, her lips parting slightly, she fell back into sleep.

THE LIVING ROOM looked vandalized. A bare mattress half covered with a sheet lay in the middle of the floor, the couch had blankets and sheets falling off in a tumbled mass, pillows were knocked about, the lampshade tilted at an angle; a saucer of cigarette butts sat precariously on top of the television set, gray ashes having spilled over onto the floor. Toilet paper stretched from the end of the couch to the coffee table, where a half glass of water was leaving a mark on the mahogany finish.

In the bathroom off the kitchen the toilet flushed and Fat Bev could be heard singing, "You're yesterday's doughnuts, love, and I'm moving onnnn . . ." The bathroom door opened and Bev greeted Isabelle with a sweep of her hand, indicating the mess before them. "Some party last night."

Isabelle nodded, moving a pack of cigarettes off the seat of the armchair before sitting down.

"I'm sorry we made a mess," said Dottie, from where she sat in the corner of the couch, her knees drawn up beneath her chin, smoke from her cigarette rising past her face, spreading into a widening gray haze as it neared the ceiling.

"How's Amy? She all right?" Fat Bev picked up a roll of toilet paper, wrapping it around itself, then put it back down on the coffee table.

"She slept." Isabelle nodded. "She'll probably be down in a minute. She had some bad dreams, I think."

"Sure. Did you dream, Dottie?"

Dottie shook her head just once, tiredly. "Except everything's a nightmare. It all feels like a nightmare."

Bev sat down on the couch and picked up Dottie's hand. "You take it a day at a time, Dottie."

"My cousin Cindy Rae," Isabelle said from the armchair, "used to say the way to eat an elephant was one bite at a time."

Bev lit a cigarette, using Dottie's. "I like that. One bite at a time."

Isabelle's head ached. Whatever nighttime protection she had had from Avery Clark was gone. He was real once more—a real man who lived down the street, a man who with his wife had forgotten to come to her house. She pictured his mild face moving across the office room and felt a cavernous yearning; she hated him, too, picturing his crooked mouth, his tall thinness (*high heinie,* she suddenly thought). It hurt.

The girl stood in the doorway ducking her head, gazing into the room with a kind of startled tentativeness.

Fat Bev couldn't help herself. She said, "Amy Goodrow, you come over here and let this fat old woman give you a hug."

But the girl just looked at her; her expression didn't change.

"Come on, now," Bev commanded. "Do it for me. I bet you don't believe it, but I've missed you." She held her arms out, wagging her wrists, turning to Dottie for confirmation. "Haven't I, Dot? Haven't I said every day at work, Dottie, it's nice to have you back but that Amy Goodrow was one little love?"

"It's true," Dottie agreed.

Now the girl smiled, a shy smile, tugging at her mouth self-consciously. "C'mon now."

And the girl went to her, bending down awkwardly while Bev squeezed hard with her big, soft arms. Isabelle, watching from the arm-chair, grimaced inwardly, partly at the girl's clumsiness, and mostly because the girl, she knew, had terrible breath this morning, which Isabelle had smelled lying next to her on the bed—an unfamiliar, powerful, and pungent accumulation of nighttime fears.

"Thank you," said Bev, finally releasing Amy. "My girls think they're too big for hugs" (a lie) "and it's going to be a few years before I have grandchildren around. God, I hope it'll be a few years. I worry about Roxie, that she'll marry the first foolish fellow comes along."

"No," said Dottie. "Roxanne has sense." She moved the afghan so Amy could sit down on the couch. "I bet you wonder why your house is full this morning," she added apologetically to Amy. "I'm having some problems at home, and your mom was nice enough to let us have a little pajama party here last night."

Amy nodded tentatively. When she had woken this morning, the second time, her mother had whispered to her of Dottie's troubles, and in her own cottony state of anguish Amy was comforted to know she was not the only person in the world whose heart had so recently been punched at, broken, pulled.

"Your mom was real kind," Bev agreed, retrieving a pillow from the floor.

"No," said Isabelle. "Actually you two were very kind to me."

Yes, there had been and still was kindness in this room of ship-wrecked women, but secrets remained nevertheless that would have to be borne alone. For Amy, of course, there was the astonishing voice of Mr. Robertson: *"I don't know who you are."* For Isabelle, there was the private removal of Avery Clark from a position that no one, including him, ever knew he occupied. And even Dottie had not given all the details of her grief to Bev (recurring thoughts of Althea's vagina being fingered—a dark moist tunnel that led to her very insides, instead of the dry butchered thing that stopped short, sewn at the top now, in Dottie); and Fat Bev herself had private concerns she could not put into words, some heavy blanket of dread pressing down on her.

But what could you do? Only keep going. People kept going; they had been doing it for thousands of years. You took the kindness offered, letting it seep as far in as it could go, and the remaining dark crevices you carried around with you, knowing that over time they might change into something almost bearable. Dottie, Bev, Isabelle, in their own ways, knew this. But Amy was young. She didn't know yet what she could or could not bear, and silently she clung like a dazed child to all three mothers in the room.

"We've destroyed your living room," Fat Bev said to Isabelle. "We might as well make pancakes and wreck your kitchen."

"Oh, wreck it," said Isabelle. "It doesn't matter." And it didn't. Something had begun for Isabelle that morning as she lay on her bed with Amy, bright sunlight entering at the edges of the blinds, and that was a sense of giving in, giving up, letting go—what was it, exactly? But she had told Amy straight-out the situation with Dottie in a way she might not have otherwise, might otherwise have hedged—about "personal troubles"—but instead she told Amy about Wally Brown, Althea Tyson. (She ought to tell her now to go brush her teeth, Isabelle thought, glancing at the girl tucked into the corner of the couch; but she said nothing.) There had been, upon waking, some queer, mild flavor of freedom, beginning with the small realization that she would not make her bed today, nor would she go to church. Nor tomorrow would she go to work. She would call Avery Clark and tell him that Amy wasn't well, that she needed a week off. She had plenty of time coming to her, there would be no problem with that. And what if Avery didn't believe her, assumed she wasn't coming in because she was embarrassed to see him after he forgot to come to her house? Or what if he thought she was angry?

It didn't matter. It didn't matter what he thought.

And it didn't matter that her house was a mess, that a water stain right now was forming on the mahogany coffee table. No, it did not matter.

"I should go to Mass," Dottie was saying, directing the statement to Amy, who had no idea what to say and so only smiled back at the woman, shyly, from the other end of the couch.

"I s'pect God would rather see you eat a pancake," called out Fat Bev from the kitchen, and Isabelle had a sudden, intense desire to be Catholic.

If she were Catholic, she could kneel, kneel and bow her head inside a church with brilliant stained-glass windows and streaks of golden light falling over her. Yes, oh yes, she would kneel and stretch out her arms, holding to her Amy and Dottie and Bev. "Please, God," she would pray. (What *would* she pray?) She would pray, "Oh please, God. Help us to be merciful to ourselves."

"I like these skinny and burned, myself," said Fat Bev. "Need to whack them with the spatula."

With the smell of coffee and burned pancakes the morning drew itself together, limped along to begin another day, but there was the unspoken presence of death: the specter of a girl's body stuffed inside a car trunk, an empty house waiting for Dottie Brown to begin her sudden, unclean form of widowhood, and for Isabelle, too, most privately, for what would life look like now without Avery Clark at the center? And Amy, sitting on the end of the couch, unable to eat the pancake Bev had given her.

Isabelle watched the girl's baffled look, the incoherence on her shiny face, and wondered again what her daughter had been doing driving around the back roads with some boy, wondered again what the different facets were to the girl's grief, and knew it would take time to learn, that in fact she might never know.

One bite at a time.

Yes, it would take time, of course—all of it. She understood this, standing on the porch waving good-bye to Bev and Dottie as they backed out of the driveway. It would take time to arrange herself, her life, without Avery Clark at its core. Already she could feel the temptation from years of habit tugging at her—what would she wear tomorrow when she went back to work? But no. She would not go back to work, not for a while. No. He had forgotten to come to her house for dessert. She had meant little, or nothing, to him after all.

Except there were still these intermittent sensations of freedom, of clearheaded calmness. And there was Amy, the desire to keep Amy with her, to take care of her. For example, the girl could use a bath.

"How about a bath?" Isabelle said, and Amy shrugged, then shook her head. She was beyond a bath. "Okay," Isabelle said. "But in a little while. A bath will help." She opened the back door and the kitchen door to air the place out, then sat down by Amy on the couch. "We're not going to church," she said.

Amy nodded.

Birds could be heard singing in the trees out back.

OUTSIDE: A SOFT, almost-autumn day. The sun falling through the windows of the Congregational church was soft in the way it fell over the deep red carpet, over the backs of the white pews. The breeze was soft, too, as it moved the leaves lightly on the elm trees, so that inside the church was the slight flickering of light against the wall and the altar where the shadows from the leaves played. The congregation stood and sang slowly in a low, collective voice, *Praise God from Whom all blessings flow,* a background to the pipe organ, whose full notes pealed and tumbled from the choir balcony. *Praise Him all creatures here below.* The ushers in their gray suits and heavy shoes placed the collection plates on the table at the front of the church, and, touching their ties, serious and self-conscious (Avery Clark was one of them), returned quietly to their seats. *Praise Father, Son, and Holy Ghost. Ahh-men.* The congregation sat down, an occasional knee knocking into the back of a pew, a hymnal with a soft thump falling to the floor, a pocketbook clicked open, shut, the soft blowing of a nose. (Emma Clark, furious with her husband, was pretending to listen to the Scripture reading and wondering if Isabelle Goodrow was seated somewhere behind them, carrying her affront with righteous dignity.)

Pots of white and wine-colored chrysanthemums lined the steps of the altar. The black robe of the minister moved as he raised his arm over the pulpit, slowly turning a page of the large Bible spread there before him. *And Jesus stood up and said to them, Let him who is without sin . . .* From the back of the church came the faint sweet smell of grape juice, for it was communion Sunday and waiting up back, alongside the silver plates of tiny squares of bread, were the round trays that carried the minuscule separate glasses of grape juice. (Timmy Thompson's eyelids drooped until his wife's stomach growled loud enough to waken him.)

The organ played again, the minister backing away from the pulpit, bowing his head, while above him the choir director, Miriam Langley, stood, faced the congregation in her own black robe and holding before her the black folder of music, a certain pious agony overtaking her small, plain features while she swayed slightly, and then began her solo. (Peg Dunlap, seated next to her husband, pictured the face of Gerald Burrows between her legs, felt a corresponding warmth, fixed her eyes steadily on a pot of white chrysanthemums.)

Soft flickers of sunlight across the pulpit, muted sounds of traffic on Main Street, the drawn-out, swaying *amens* of Miriam Langley's solo, a persistent muffled cough from somewhere in the balcony, brief crinkling sounds of a piece of hard candy being unwrapped, and then a burst of joyful organ music, as though perhaps the organist was glad Miriam Langley's solo was finally done; the minister moving back to the pulpit, getting ready to give his sermon (titled in the program "To Peel a Sour Grape"), and the congregation arranging themselves in little ways, a quiet sigh here and there, settling in for the long haul now.

A crying baby was taken outside by a father who was not unhappy to sit in his car in the sunny parking lot and miss the sermon; Clara Wilcox, having gone as usual to the early service, was cleaning up in the activities room with Barbara Rawley from the earlier coffee hour and looking away with embarrassment at the number of times Barbara Rawley was putting a doughnut hole into her mouth. Sunlight came through the window and made the coffee urn twinkle before it was carried off and stored in the back room.

And back inside the church when the minister concluded his sermon (briefer than usual, because communion needed to be served), the ushers rose again, this time to pass out the communion trays; the minister turned again the large pages of the Bible on the pulpit before him, *Let all who eat of my body remember me . . .* There was one more hymn to sing, the congregation rising with some relief now the end was in sight, and then finally there was the benediction, the minister standing in the back of the church with his hand raised over his dearly loved congregation (is how it appeared to those who peeked, the man standing solemnly in his black robe, eyes closed, blessing all), *May the words of our mouths and the meditations of our hearts be always acceptable in thy sight, O Lord,* at the very same moment that Isabelle Goodrow, in her tiny living room still filled with the lingerings of cigarette smoke, was telling Amy quietly the ending of the tale of Jake and Evelyn Cunningham and the three children they had raised in California, saying finally and softly that she had been wrong not to tell Amy all of this a long time ago.

Amy had watched her mother's face intently, watched the couch intently, the window, the chair, and in the long silence that now followed, her eyes moved more and more quickly around the room before they landed once more on Isabelle. "Mom," the girl finally said, her eyes, her face, her mouth, widening with comprehension, "Mom, I'm *related* to people out there."

Chapter

25

THE TUESDAY AFTER Labor Day was chilly, almost downright cold. The women in the office room worked quietly and steadily, tugging at the edges of their cardigans. In the lunchroom they lingered over coffee or cups of tea, idly fingering the remains of their lunch-bag wrappings. Lenora Snibbens, looking pleasant and mature in her navy-blue turtleneck, asked Rosie Tanguay what spices she used in making beef stew.

"Salt and pepper," Rosie said. "Never anything but salt and pepper."

Lenora nodded, but really she was indifferent; her question had simply been to signify the ending to a feud. Everyone understood, and pretty much felt the same desire for peace in the office room now, for Dottie Brown had let it be known quietly the week before that her husband, after twenty-eight years of marriage, had left her for a younger woman, and that she would not be discussing it further. The women were respectful. Those who wished to talk this over did so in the evenings on their telephones; during the day they worked quietly. Dottie's misfortune made them glad for whatever blessings their own lives might hold.

Isabelle Goodrow's desk remained tidy and untouched, the chair tucked under. She had taken some vacation time, that was all anyone knew. Although when someone mentioned how the body of that girl, Debby Kay Dorne, up there in Hennecock, had been discovered in the trunk of some car in a field by a couple of teenagers, Dottie Brown and Fat Bev were careful not to glance at each other.

"I wish they'd find the guy who did it, and arrest him," said Rosie Tanguay, shaking her head.

"String him up by his toenails," Arlene Tucker said.

"Can't they get the fingerprints?" Rosie asked, tugging on the tea-bag string in the mug she held. "Or trace the license plate?"

"Fingerprints don't last for months," Fat Bev said. "Not outside, like that. And the car belonged to the old farmer who's owned those fields for years. Elvin Merrick. He's always got some old car lying around out there. They say one part of his land's practically a dump."

"He got a ticket for that. Did you see that in the paper?"

Bev nodded. "But they'll find whoever did it," she said. "These days they can track down fiber and match it to some carpet in a whole nother state."

"It's amazing what they can do these days," Dottie Brown agreed.

(Although in fact this case would never be solved; no one in the years to come would ever find out who killed Debby Kay Dorne.)

" 'Member when Timmy Thompson found a body in his barn?" Arlene Tucker asked. "Must've been twenty years ago at least." Some remembered, most did not. But everyone remembered when the bank had been robbed seven, no eight, years ago November. Patty Valentine had been tied up and gagged and stuffed in the vault; it was hours before she got out. After that Patty taught Sunday school. Every year she told the class of seven-year-olds how she had been tied up with a gun pointed straight in her face, how she had prayed inside the vault, and how it was the praying that got her out. The class would be told to draw a picture of praying hands. One year a little girl went home and had nightmares and her father complained to Reverend Barnes and the Reverend spoke to Patty, and somewhere in the course of this, Patty became upset and told Reverend Barnes to "ƒ himself," and then she didn't teach Sunday school anymore.

"That part of the story is hard to believe," said Rosie Tanguay. "Nobody speaks that way to a minister."

"Oh, but Patty's crazy," said Arlene, whose firsthand knowledge of all this was supposed to stem from the fact she was friends with the mother of the little girl.

"Reverend Barnes's wife is a little nutty herself," someone said, and others nodded at this. "Annual clothes drive every year, all the rich ladies from Oyster Point donate their clothes to the Episcopal church, and a few days later you see Mrs. Barnes walking around wearing the best things."

Lenora Snibbens nodded. "Whatever fits her, I guess."

This was common knowledge and not of much interest; the goings-on of the Episcopal church seemed fairly removed from the office room, from Shirley Falls in general—it was the Catholic church and the Congregational church that dominated the town. (Although in twenty years' time, the daughter of Reverend Barnes would accuse him of doing to her, in childhood, unspeakable things, and then there would be a great deal of gossip, Reverend Barnes subsequently losing a number of congregants, and retiring a bit early.) Anyway, no one much minded today when the buzzer rang and it was time to return to their desks.

In the far corner Fat Bev and Dottie worked quietly, Bev keeping a cautious eye on her friend, ready to murmur a word of support when she saw tears brim up in Dottie's eyes. "Hang in there, Dot," she said now. "It'll get better. Time helps. Time always helps."

Dottie smiled. "The way to eat an elephant," she said. "But I got some indigestion with this one, I can tell you."

"Sure you do." Bev shook her head in sympathy. "Let's call Isabelle. See what she's up to today."

But Isabelle wasn't home. She had taken Amy to get her hair trimmed. "Shaped," Isabelle was telling the woman at Ansonia's Hair Salon, "just see if it can't be shaped a bit." The woman nodded silently and steered Amy toward the back to get shampooed, while Isabelle sat up front flipping through magazines she found there. In two days Amy would start school again; they were going shopping for clothes after her hair was done. Meanwhile Isabelle held an open magazine on her lap and stared out the window at the people walking by. It always seemed to her odd to be out in the world on a workday; it surprised her each time to see how much life went on outside the office room: people walking into the bank, holding closed their sweaters or jackets on this chilly day; two mothers pushing strollers down the sidewalk; a man stopping to check in his pocket for a slip of paper that he glanced at before starting to walk again. Where were these people headed? What were their different lives like?

Amy, draped in a plastic cape, was staring straight ahead in the mirror while the woman clipped away. Still wet, her hair looked dark and short, but when the blow-dryer whirred Isabelle could see Amy's hair begin to fluff out in a curved shape below her ears, the different shades of blond and gold appearing again. She was gratified to notice the momentary pleasure in the girl's face. The new hairstyle made her look grown-up; startling to see the girlishness gone. The hairdresser, pleased with the outcome, said, "Let's just put a touch of makeup on."

"Oh, go ahead," Isabelle called out from her chair, seeing Amy's reticence and knowing that it of course stemmed from the imagined disapproval of her mother. Isabelle smiled and nodded again, then looked out the window once more. Awful to think she was a disapproving mother. Awful to wonder—had she always frightened Amy? Is that why the girl had grown up so fearful, always ducking her head? It was bewildering to Isabelle. Bewildering that you could harm a child without even knowing, thinking all the while you were being careful, conscientious. But it was a terrible feeling. More terrible than having Avery Clark forget to come to her house. Knowing that her child had grown up frightened. Except it was cockeyed, all backwards, because, thought Isabelle, glancing back at her daughter, *I've been frightened of you.*

Oh, it was sad. It wasn't right. Her own mother had been frightened too. (Isabelle's foot was bobbing quickly, in tiny little jerks.) All the love in the world couldn't prevent the awful truth: You passed on who you were.

Isabelle put the magazine back in the rack. *Dear Evelyn,* she composed in her head. *Many years have passed, and I hope this letter finds you in good health. May I apologize for once again intruding in your life . . .*

She looked up, startled at the young woman standing before her, tall and unfamiliar, eyes blinking slowly once, twice. "Okay, Mom," Amy said. "I'm done."

They were shy with each other, uncertain, as they moved down the sidewalk. A nippy wind from the river lifted Isabelle's skirt for a moment as they stood gazing in the window of a shoe store. "They're kind of expensive," Amy said, as her mother indicated a pair in front of them.

"It's all right," Isabelle answered. "Try them on at least."

The store was carpeted and empty, quiet as a church. The salesman bowed slightly and disappeared into the back to find a pair in Amy's size.

"But do you think she would have told them about me?" Amy blurted out in a whisper, sitting down next to Isabelle. "I know you don't know, but do you *think* she did?"

So it was this that had been on her mind, these busy thoughts about Jake Cunningham's kids. "Honey, I don't know." Isabelle felt she had to whisper too. "I was a child the last time I saw that woman. I don't know enough about her to know what she would do. I don't know anything about her at all, really."

"But you'll write?"

"Yes, soon." And then as the salesman returned, "Tonight."

The man kneeled before Amy as he slipped the shoes on her feet; and then later, when he took them in their box up front to the register, Amy said, "The girl's name was Callie?"

"Yes, short for Catherine, I believe."

"Callie Cunningham," said Amy, running her fingers through her newly shaped hair. "Boy, that's just so cute."

Isabelle REWROTE THE letter many times that night, and mailed it the next day. After that there was nothing to do but wait. A terrible thing to wait for a letter; each day formed around the morning of hopefulness and the evening's fog of disappointment. It was a wound, the disappointment, inflicted every afternoon at the same time. The scant containings of a mailbox pulled open by Amy on her way up the driveway from school provided only a bill or two, a reminder from the dentist that Isabelle needed a cleaning. How dreary the world was when all that greeted one was the promise of a new set of luggage if you filled out a certain sweepstake form. How oddly silent this kind of rejection, a simple emptiness of space, a persistent arrival of quiet, a disk of "nothingness" surrounded by vapors of speculation. Perhaps Evelyn Cunningham didn't live there anymore. (But the letter would be returned—Isabelle's return address was there on the envelope.) Perhaps the letter got lost in a post office or on the street, or was collecting dust right now beneath some Californian stairwell.

They stopped mentioning it after a while.

It rained a lot that fall. The rains were harsh and strong and steady, as though in a hurry to make up for the long pause of the stultifying summer. Now the river seemed immense, churning, roiling, thundering over the slabs of granite, its muddy darkness rushing beneath the bridge. It was tempting to stand and watch, and sometimes on the morning after a heavy rain a pedestrian or two could be seen leaning over the railing on the sidewalk of the bridge, staring down, as though mesmerized by the power of this river.

Isabelle, driving over the bridge on her way to work, would wonder fleetingly if the person was thinking of jumping. Even knowing that such a thing was unlikely (only once while she had been living in Shirley Falls had a person jumped off the bridge, a poor drunken man, late one night), she would watch for a moment in her rearview mirror, for Isabelle's habit of expecting disaster had not left her—nor would it ever, entirely. No, Isabelle was still Isabelle.

And yet she was different, of course. She had to be: there were people in Shirley Falls now—Bev, Dottie, Amy—who knew that she had never been married, that she had become pregnant at the age of seventeen by her father's best friend. It was like removing some dark undergarment that had been pressed to her middle for years; she felt exposed, but cleaner. Both Dottie and Bev, and Amy as well, had said they wouldn't tell anyone, but Isabelle had only responded, "That's up to you." She didn't want them bearing the burden of secretiveness—although she could not help wondering who, if anyone, they had told. Still, it was amazing after years of sitting tightly on this shame, how little she cared now if other people knew. Partly because Dottie and Bev, and even Amy, had not seemed to judge her the way she thought they would, but mostly Isabelle had other things on her mind.

Like Amy. She hurt for Amy. It was searing, at times terrible, when she saw the quiet anxiety in Amy's eyes. Having spent the long hot summer reeling from Amy's betrayal, Isabelle entered the shortened days of autumn with a sickening sense sometimes that Amy had only narrowly missed some very grave danger, and that far from Amy's having "betrayed" Isabelle, it was closer to the truth the other way around. The memory of the evening she had cut off Amy's hair rose in her mind at times now with an increased sense of dismay; that she had done it was irrevocable, and it was the starkness of that fact which bothered her the most. *What we do matters* is a thought Isabelle had again and again, as though just now, well into adult years, she was figuring this out.

But there were times, too, when Amy's face was clear, her eyes steady in their gaze, the new hair shaped around her chin, and Isabelle caught a glimpse of who Amy might become, who she might already be, and it was reassuring, comforting.

And then of course there was Avery Clark, and of course that was weird. He had not mentioned again the forgotten invitation, and she had no idea if he thought of it. But when he returned to work after being laid up with a bad cold toward the end of September, Isabelle brought him a basket of oranges.

"Look at that," Avery said, when she put the basket down on his desk. "Isn't that nice." His nose was flaky, and very red.

"Well," said Isabelle. "I thought you could use the vitamin C."

"I certainly can," he agreed.

She could not tell if this gift made him uncomfortable or not. But it seemed to her a necessary thing to do. For her, the gesture signified, somehow, a tidying-up of messy things, as though being able to give him these oranges had now swept something clean.

"And I liked their color," she added, because this was true—the vivid, tightly packed skin of these small globes.

"Oh, yes," Avery said. "Very nice. Thank you, Isabelle."

So who was this man, anyhow? A tall figure, shuffling through papers as he stood at his desk. His eyes, when she glanced into them, seemed only watery, small, and old. When she tried now to imagine what food he ate for dinner, what sort of underwear he wore . . . well, she could not.

But at night, sometimes, in the dark, she still yearned for him, remembering him as he had been to her: important, kind, someone to love.

She had wanted someone to love, so there was this sensation of something central missing from her life, and she knew that if he should suddenly encourage her, lean forward and whisper a long suppressed endearment in her ear, fix his watery eyes on her with longing, she would respond immediately. But of course Avery Clark did not encourage her, and the air between them in the office room (or church) remained stale, dull, uncharged.

Once or twice, oddly, she had even sat behind her typewriter and simply felt free—there was no simpler way to put it. It was like after a thunderstorm when the air seemed suddenly relieved of a headache. Such a feeling, such clarity, took her by surprise. How different not to have life oppressive! To not be frightened by the sight of Barbara Rawley in the hardware store. ("Hello, Barbara," moving past her easily.) To not feel that every little thing was a burden. The begonia on her desk at work, for example. Instead of something that would dry up and die without her care, she saw it now as a pretty thing, a little plant with blossoms. And her love for Dottie and Bev, along with a tender enough affection for the rest of the women, made the office room thick with human detail, not a barren place at all.

Isabelle would leave. She saw this in these moments of clarity, recognized how her warmth for those around her stemmed partly from a growing distance.

But she didn't know yet what she would do, or when it was she would leave this office room where she had been sitting for fifteen years. She knew she would have to leave before the routine of these days caused her desk, her work, the lunchroom, Avery Clark, to take on significance once more. There was going to come a day when she would have to hoist herself up and out, she was aware of that, but right now as she stood up and moved to Avery's fishbowl with a letter for him to sign, she felt her legs in their pantyhose, the comfortable slight tilt of her black pumps as they stepped against the wooden floor, the simple, unexalted feeling of coherence.

And then it would disappear, and she would worry about Amy again and wonder why Evelyn Cunningham had never answered her letter, and she would long, again, for Avery Clark. And sometimes then she would think about praying, because she had not prayed for a very long time, not since earlier in the hot summer when she would come home from work and lie on her bed and pray for God's love and guidance. She could not do that now. It had seemed phony even back then, but she hadn't known what else to do. So now she did nothing. It was not that she had given up on God (no, no) or that she thought God had given up on her (no . . .), it was more that she was aware of some large and fundamental ignorance deep within her, a bafflement that lived, not uncomfortably, with whatever else she might be feeling; and she accepted this.

At school Amy's new hairstyle and a certain edge to her face, a quiet defiance as she moved through the hallways, brought attention that surprised her. She was invited to a party and Isabelle let her go. ("Parties suck," Stacy warned her, puffing on a cigarette in their spot in the woods. "I don't think I'll go. Josh and I will probably just hang out at his house that night."

And what did that mean, Amy wondered, remembering the book on sex that Josh had bought Stacy last summer. What did you do when you hung out at your boyfriend's house?)

The party, held at the home of a boy whose parents had gone to Boston for the weekend, appalled her. People lay sprawled on couches, beds, floors, drinking bottles of beer, their expressions ironic, almost bored. Cigarette smoke filled the rooms as Amy, holding a beer someone handed her, moved cautiously through the house pretending to look for a bathroom. What surprised her most were the people making out, how many of them were not the couples seen walking together in the hallways at school but appeared instead to be a random matching-up of this person with that. Stepping out the back door she saw Sally Pringle, the deacon's daughter, French-kissing the pimply-faced Alan Stewart, a bottle of liquor protruding from the pocket of Sally's leather jacket. And further away from the house, on the edge of the lawn, she saw other couples, some lying down, boys moving on top of girls the way Mr. Robertson in the woods had moved on top of her. But she loved him! Did these people love each other? Alan Stewart now was pressing Sally Pringle against the side of the house, her leg lifted around his waist—no, they couldn't love each other, groping madly right there for anyone to see.

Passing back through the kitchen, Amy saw Karen Keane, hair mussed, cheeks bright, buttoning her blouse and saying with a deep giggle, "Guess who just had oral sex three times."

Amy called Paul Bellows and he came right away and drove her home.

OH, SHIRLEY FALLS—the darkness coming sooner, one more season passing, one more summer gone; nothing was forever, nothing. Poor Peg Dunlap, rushing down the sidewalk to meet her lover, rushing, rushing, thinking of her big-boned ten-year-old daughter, who had quit Girl Scouts because she had no friends, thinking of her nine-year-old son, who had friends but failing scores on every single math test, and her husband, who said there was no problem, they were normal kids, just let them be. Rushing, rushing, as though to press her nakedness against another's flesh were the only comfort left. But why, thought Peg Dunlap, rushing down the street, should love be so hard?

And love was hard. Barbara Rawley believed her husband when he said he didn't care about the scar running from beneath her arm across the flattened breastbone; but then why wasn't it comforting to lie next to him at night? Life is what mattered, and love. But she felt angry, and she was ashamed of feeling angry. Still, she was privately sickened by herself every time she undressed; she was not what she used to be.

And why did it have to be agony for Puddy Mandel to love Linda Lanier? Because he loved his mother, too, and she did not love Linda. (But dear Linda would bear this patiently—taking him for the next thirty years into her heart, her bed, she would forgo the children she had always dreamed of, to live out her old age with this man, would mother him when, old himself, he was finally motherless.)

Most of them did the best they could. Is that fair to say? Most of them did the best they could, the people of Shirley Falls. *I have no regrets*, you could sometimes hear a person say at one of those ritual gatherings—a birthday celebration, a retirement party at the mill—but who was it that had no regrets? Certainly not Dottie Brown, lying in bed at night, remembering times when her husband had needed love, and she had not given love to him. Certainly not Wally himself, who lay next to Althea Tyson in their white trailer, afraid to fall asleep sometimes because of the dreams that came to him.

And not Isabelle Goodrow either, who, in spite of moments of coherence and hope, watched her daughter's anxious face in the evenings and knew that she had failed the girl in numerous ways; who, in driving to a small cemetery in Hennecock and hunting out a small girl's grave, knew that she was placing flowers there not only for the murdered child, but somehow for her own child, too, and for the mother of Debby Kay Dorne, who Isabelle imagined was living her own lifetime of private, ravaging regrets.

AND THEN NEAR the end of October, a letter came. It was a Saturday and Isabelle, having just returned from the A&P, stood in the kitchen with her coat on and read the letter immediately. Amy sat with her eyes closed, until her mother said, "Amy, your sister wants to meet you."

Evelyn Cunningham apologized for not having answered Isabelle's letter sooner. She had been in the hospital with pleurisy and only received the letter recently. She hoped Isabelle hadn't felt "snubbed" as a result of the delay. Isabelle, reading this again over Amy's shoulder, felt tears come to her eyes at this (she felt) undeserved openheartedness. The three Cunningham children, now grown, of course, had been told a few years ago of the existence of "the baby." They were eager, particularly Catherine, the oldest, to meet their half-sister. Catherine was married and lived back in New England, in Stockbridge, Massachusetts, and she'd just had a new baby. The boys were still in California. ("They don't call her Callie anymore?" Amy asked. "I guess not," Isabelle said, and together they kept reading.) On the last weekend in October the whole family would be meeting in Stockbridge for the baptism of Catherine's baby, and would Isabelle care to bring Amy down for a visit one day on that weekend? She knew it was short notice, and Evelyn ended the letter with an apology: She had often thought of Isabelle and "the baby girl" over the years, but her feelings had been "raw" for some time. For this she apologized. Time changes things, she wrote. Water over the dam. She and her children wanted to extend warm greetings to Isabelle and "Jake's daughter." She hoped Isabelle would agree to visit Catherine on that Saturday, and that they would all meet each other soon. She enclosed Catherine's telephone number.

. . .

"Cool," said Stacy. "But it might be boring. Relatives are usually boring."

Amy smoked her cigarette. She hadn't told Stacy that these were more than relatives, these were brothers and sisters. She didn't know why she hadn't told Stacy that, but she hadn't, and she didn't know how she could do it now. She had only said they were going that weekend to visit some long lost relatives of her father. She added, "I think my mother's afraid they won't like her."

"Why wouldn't they like her?" Stacy was not really interested, but who could blame her.

Amy shrugged. "My mother's kind of shy." Leaving it at that.

They smoked in silence; it was cold, overcast, autumnal. Most of the red leaves had fallen by now, scattered thickly on the ground, covering rocks and cold-looking ferns. Some trees were completely bare, brown twiggy outlines against the barren sky, though there were still a number of trees that had yellow leaves clinging to their branches, leaves that rattled crisply in the small bursts of autumn breeze.

The baby that Amy had glimpsed in the hospital's nursery that summer was never mentioned out here in the woods. Nor was Paul Bellows, or the body of Debby Kay Dorne. There remained a deep affection between the girls, a familiarity that allowed them long moments of silence, but the urgent unhappiness of Stacy seemed gone, and her thoughts often appeared to be elsewhere as they smoked in the woods. Amy's thoughts were elsewhere too. As though to compensate for this, they touched each other frequently, sometimes stroking for a moment the other's hand, huddling their shoulders against each other as they leaned against the log, and when the bell rang, they packed away their cigarettes, then paused to press their faces together in a brief kiss.

("Godfrey," Fat Bev was murmuring to Isabelle in the hallway at the mill, "I hope you have a good trip down there.")

It was the last day of daylight saving time. Here and there throughout the town different lights went on in different kitchens. Emma Clark had brought a cup of coffee back to bed, while Avery read the paper. Ned Rawley, having risen to urinate moments before, was now reaching for his wife, Barbara. Across the river Dottie Brown lay sleeping, relaxed by her thoughts in the middle of the night of how she would spend the day shopping with Bev; she would not have to be alone. Isabelle Goodrow sat at her kitchen table, listening to the sound of Amy in the shower upstairs, and watching the light arrive on the yellow ginkgo leaves outside the side window (seeing one, then another, then another of the leaves fall, knowing that when she returned the leaves would all be gone because ginkgoes did that—lost all their leaves almost at once).

For the rest of her life she would remember this day the way one remembers the last moments spent with a loved one, for in Isabelle's memory, somehow, it seemed to her to be privately and profoundly the last day she "had" Amy. Always in her memory the leaves would be golden, the turnpike lined with golden-leaved trees, showered in the sunlight of morning, stiff with autumn.

Stepping out of the car to use a rest-stop bathroom, the sharp unrelenting air of autumn packed around them as they moved side by side without speaking; taking turns in the filthy toilet, one standing guard outside the blue door. Walking across the parking lot, Isabelle said, "Are you hungry, Amy? Would you like something to eat?" And Amy simply shook her head, not able to speak because of some swift, unarticulated compassion for her mother. But Isabelle in her memory, for the rest of her life, saw Amy's indifferent shake of her head as proof that already the girl had been lost to her; already Isabelle's basic attempts to mother (for what was more basic than feeding?) were being dismissed; already the girl felt herself handed over, already the girl was eager to go.

Although later, as they drew closer to the place they were going, Amy said she felt sick, and maybe they should stop to get some food. So it was in Howard Johnson's that a man, paying at the cash register, glanced at Amy and continued to watch her as he was handed his change. Amy noticed, and watched as the man left the restaurant, watched as he turned his head at the door to glance at her again. She met his eye through the restaurant window, and in that fraction of a second Amy Goodrow's life changed once more, for she had recognized her attractiveness to men, to older men, for this particular stranger had the faint beginnings of gray at his hairline. It was here, in a Howard Johnson's on

Route 93, that desire rose in her again, desire, and the power of her own desirability, and the half-formed knowledge that Mr. Robertson might be (in fact was) ultimately replaceable. Beneath her turtleneck Amy was conscious of her breasts tucked into their Sears bra, breasts that had been offered and would be offered again to men whose eyes became unfocused with longing. This power sent a thrill straight down her middle as she sat across from Isabelle, who was squinting at the menu and saying, "Honey, maybe you need a scrambled egg."

Back in the car Amy and Isabelle looked at each other. Amy raised both eyebrows and drew her breath in sharply as she smiled, as though to say, "Okay, let's go," and for a moment they were united, as if they had both agreed to blast off in a rocket and it was countdown time. For years Isabelle would remember that moment and wish she had spoken, had told the girl she loved her and always would, because for Isabelle, as she pulled out onto the highway, it began to feel more and more that it was Amy who was blasting off, Amy who was leaving forever, that Isabelle was only there now to pilot the ship, deliver the girl into the lap of her family, of siblings, of relatives who were hers, not Isabelle's.

They did not speak, but drove staring straight ahead.

Yes, Isabelle would remember this drive, the yellow leaves, the autumn goldenness. Long after Avery Clark had died of a heart attack sitting behind his desk in the fishbowl, long after Barbara Rawley had been arrested for shoplifting fourteen dollars' worth of cosmetics from a local drugstore, years after Wally Brown had moved back in with Dottie, when Isabelle herself had been married to the kindly pharmacist for some time, she would remember this drive with Amy. It marked to her the endless days of Amy's solitary childhood, and those endless hot days of that terrible summer. All that had once been endless would by then have ended, and Isabelle, at different places and moments in the years to come, would sometimes be surrounded by silence and find in herself only the repeated word "Amy." "Amy, *Amy*"—for this was it, her heart's call, her prayer. "Amy," she would think, "Amy," remembering this day's chilly, golden air.

About the Author

ELIZABETH STROUT was born in Portland, Maine. She now lives in New York City with her husband and daughter. She has taught at Manhattan Community College and at the New School. Her fiction has appeared in many magazines, including *The New Yorker*.

About the Type

This book was set in Garamond, a typeface originally designed by the Parisian type cutter Claude Garamond (1480–1561). This version of Garamond was modeled on a 1592 specimen sheet from the Egenolff-Berner foundry, which was produced from types assumed to have been brought to Frankfurt by the punch cutter Jacques Sabon (d. 1580).

Claude Garamond's distinguished romans and italics first appeared in *Opera Ciceronis* in 1543–44.